Girl at the Edge of Sky

Lilian Nattel

Girl

at the

Edge

of

Sky

Random House Canada

PUBLISHED BY RANDOM HOUSE CANADA

Copyright © 2019 Moonlily Manuscripts Inc.

www.penguinrandomhouse.ca

Random House Canada and colophon are registered trademarks.

Library and Archives Canada Cataloguing in Publication

Nattel, Lilian, 1956–, author
Girl at the edge of sky / Lilian Nattel.

Issued in print and electronic formats.
ISBN 978-0-7352-7704-5
eBook ISBN 978-0-7352-7705-2

I. Title.

PS8577.A757G57 2019   C813'.54   C2018-906689-X
                                               C2018-906690-3

Book design and illustration on pg i by Andrew Roberts

Cover images: (girl in field) © Mark Owen / Trevillion Images;
(plane) © rancho_runner / iStock / Getty Images Plus

Printed and bound in Canada

2 4 6 8 9 7 5 3 1

Penguin
Random House
RANDOM HOUSE CANADA

In memory of Julia Greenbaum, a mighty mite who was always up for a new scene and another chic scarf.

The idea was astonishingly graceful and beautiful.
It seemed to have given birth to itself—like a water-lily
appearing out of the calm darkness of a lake.

—from *Life and Fate* by Vasily Grossman,
translated by Robert Chandler

Prisoner

UKRAINE

August 1943

Her Fall

She bursts through the clouds and opens her eyes. The sound of engines is receding, the sky around her empty. There's no one to see that her eyes are grey, that she wears a scarf made from parachute silk tucked inside her collar to keep it from chafing her neck, that her boots aren't regulation, or that she is several kilometres above the earth on which human beings have evolved.

In this war, people are always falling from the sky. They're flung bouquets picked up by the wind, which carries them over fields and forests and towns. The wind fans pretty flames, it blows ash and smudges the sky. It spits the smell of mud, moss, rot, and the forge. It skims creeks and rustles leaves, it gropes in the gaps between wood and skin and blackening metal. The skin of a plane, the skin of a man, anything loose, anything fluid—blood, water— are all of a piece to the wind, which is neither friend nor enemy, though if you're the one in mid-air, you might feel otherwise.

Where is the wind taking her?

She has no other thought; the roar of air fills her ear. It presses her skin, and in its touch there's no protest from wounds, only the pleasure of wingless flight. She has as much substance as a god reclining on a bed of air. Above her, threads of cloud separate, and sun turns the heavens blue, more blue than colour can be. Everything she surveys is exquisite. The sky is her secret retreat, her private sin. She doesn't need a plane or time. She has no past. She floats without fear.

Her hand pulls the rip cord, knowing what needs to be done now. She feels the yank of straps as her parachute opens, capturing air, halting flight and sound. Her weight dangles from the harness. She comes back to what passes for reality.

———

Her name is Lily—Litvak or Litvyak. Something like that anyway. She's blond by peroxide. She's small by nature. Her age depends on the papers you look at. Nineteen is a possibility. This day, August 1 and about midday, she blacked out as she slipped into the clouds, regaining consciousness when warmer air struck her face. The wind is pushing her westward.

Smoke hasn't left her nostrils, nor the smell of tarry residue, though she sees no trace of the aircraft that were chasing her. Looking down, she finds her bearings by water: the meandering tendrils of green to the left are the Don River and its tributaries; the vast blue pool to the south is the Sea of Azov. She's over the Donetsk region in the eastern Ukraine, close to the border with Russia but behind enemy lines. Like anyone who still survives, she's had narrow escapes, and she plans on another as she descends, thinking the wind might drop her in the long grass of a field where she could hide until night.

The Don River leaves her field of vision. Mottled earth surges into shapes, the map below reconfiguring as she descends, more detailed than the one in her flight jacket and yet the same, made by an uneasy alliance of hands, nature's and men's: undulating rivers, lumpy hills, tracts of green and gold in squares and parallelograms. Men like geometry. Nature throws herself at her materials with abandon, which is how Lily flew her plane and drove her commanding officer crazy. She wears men's underpants because the army can't seem to get the hang of making any for the million women in it. As the harness pulls on her, the underpants get into the crack of her bottom, and the tugging bothers her more than her injured shoulder and the burn on her hand.

A squiggle in the landscape expands to a twisting line closer than the Don. This is the Krynka River, marked on her aviator's map. It's small, narrow, a peasant of a river invisible from any higher altitude. The golden fields could be wheat or rye, the green must be corn. It's been ages since she's smelled an unburnt field. Her world has been a desert of grey and black and red, its odour of crushed tanks and half-buried corpses reaching a kilometre high.

The river snakes through and around the fields, stopping short of the ruler-straight grey line that is a road. She closes her eyes for a moment, hoping to God, if there is one, that she won't go to a POW camp. Any other fate she'll accept. And though she doesn't pray, she recites a rhyme her grandmother taught her: *Don't give a fuck what people say, make your luck and make them pay.*

As the wind dies, she stops moving in a westerly direction and drops straight down toward shades of green along the peasant river. Colour takes on dimension. Trees spring up: a stand of woods near a stream, and she's rushing into their humble leafiness, these steppe trees that hug the water, a refuge of sorts. A branch catches her parachute, the harness yanks her shoulders. Still damp from the clouds, she pushes up her goggles and takes stock.

She's wounded, but not mortally. She has a knife and her pistol. The war is two years old. She doesn't think she'll live long enough to have children.

Nesting birds call and bring food to their fledglings as if she's just a fruit or an oversized flower or even a large fungus growing out of the tree trunk. From here she can see the other bank of the Krynka River, steeper, rockier. Pasture without sheep, a ramshackle cottage and beside it a small garden. Beyond her sight, farther west, her grandmother is living under German occupation.

This side of the riverbank is dense with low vegetation where she can hide if she detaches herself from the tree, but she can't move. Her muscles are flaccid, her brain rambling; all this peaceful greenery is sapping her will. Where the sun falls on her between the leaves, she feels patches of warmth. Shell fragments are embedded in the flesh of her right shoulder. She can bend her arm a bit, but lifting it is agony. Blood seeps into the sleeve, a slow leak, and as long as she stays still, nothing will hurt more. The harness holds her like a child's swing, like the ones in the Moscow park where she climbed her first tree. She tore her dress and knew she'd get spanked for it, but she pushed herself to the high branches, where she stood as still as if bark grew out of her bare soles, eye to eye with a yellow-chested bird. It was only later, after the spanking and after the rip was sewn up, that she felt remorse over the scarring of her favourite dress.

In the fields beyond the woods, distant figures like cloth dolls bend and stand. If they come any closer, they'll show themselves as human, and of all the varieties she knows, there are few she wishes to encounter while strapped to a tree. Unthinkingly, Lily moves her left hand, brushing its blistered back against some leaves. She can't stop the odd sound that issues from the base of her throat, half gulp, half moan, and she clamps the uninjured palm over her mouth. She isn't entirely alone; she hears voices, they've followed her from the plane.

You silly girl, what did you do to yourself? Don't tell me you can't get down. Am I talking to a wall? You need a smack to clear your ears? Pull the left strap high up. Like that. See how easy the hand goes through? It's fine. Don't make a noise. You want the neighbours to hear? If you're so feeble, you have no business shooting down planes. How many today—two? My God, what am I going to do with you?

The left strap is off. Panting, head hanging, sweat pooling under her leather cap, Lily holds on to the branch with her burned hand, all the weight of the harness on her shot shoulder as she tries to slide out of its strap. Her grandmother can scold, but Lily is done. She's going to fall.

What a face you're making. It isn't time for a vacation, lazy girl. Forget the shoulder. Just pull the strap down. Get the arm out. So the parachute is stuck on a little branch. Pull. Again. Don't sit with it in your arms like a wedding dress. Roll it up. Hurry. Stuff it into the pack.

Her grandmother's approval was never easy to come by. Lily has to stand, relying on her left arm to support her, clinging to the trunk as she seeks a foothold on a lower branch.

Good girl. My beautiful Lil'ka.

The next thing she knows, she's on the ground.

When she opens her eyes, she's on her back and dizzy, long grass striping her view. An accelerating aircraft exerts on its pilot a force several times that of gravity, but a good pilot won't faint under the pressure. Yet she toppled like a toddler. It's embarrassing. A fly walks on her cheek, an ant on her neck, everything that's earthbound creeping and scratching like capitalists. She hopes there aren't any snakes.

As she rolls over, the sheathed knife in her belt knocks against her hip. She wants to put her hands on the ground and hoist herself up, but her hands have no class loyalty, the left rising to escape the biting grass, the right hanging at the end of a wet string of an arm that refuses to take any weight. Fine, then. She'll manage without them. Leaning on her left elbow, she humps herself to her knees like a cripple sent home from the war. She slides the elbow up her thigh, moving her centre of gravity as she sits on her knees. Her right arm still dangles uselessly, but her flight jacket and uniform have soaked up its blood. Nothing's dripped on the grass to mark her presence. Not yet. Softly cupping the underside of her left knee, she inclines right and pushes up from her buttocks and out with her left foot. Uninjured, dependable foot, a shock worker that meets and exceeds quotas. It deserves a medal, the Red Star at least. Shifting her weight onto it, she stands, triumphant at the exertion of her will, recklessly exposed.

From her magnificent ground-level vantage point, she sees tree trunks. Thin-leafed and thick-leafed bush. A small bird flying up. She turns her head. The steep and rocky left bank looms, a miniature version of great river embankments like the Don's and the Volga's. And, in her peripheral vision, a flash of brown that's off-hue, a tint that doesn't match the woods, like a glint in the sky that is the enemy coming in from the sun. Overhead, crows are chasing a hawk, their loud caws covering the sound of her belated dive into the closest cover.

Like Other Men

Dr. Gerhard Fischer is a staff veterinarian in the German army, and he's come into the woods for a break after the morning's surgery. He has one man with him, a young assistant, who's seated behind him on the horse, their lunch in a saddlebag. Fritz Vogel, the assistant, takes his camera everywhere he goes. He's a volunteer not a soldier, and so technically not under Gerhard's command but under his wing just the same. The horse is a chestnut mare whom Gerhard has named Helga, though soldiers shouldn't name army horses any more than a farmhand should a pig.

Leaving the mare to drink and graze, Gerhard and Fritz walk up the riverbank and into the woods, Gerhard using his sabre to cut a path through the underbrush. The odour of his sweat mingling with the smell of water and trees reminds him of his camping days, though his memory seems implausibly rosy. (Not one of his scouting friends lost body parts or crossed over to the enemy or went up in smoke.)

Gerhard would be a handsome man if he took more care of his appearance. As it is, he looks like nobody in particular: a lowish-ranking officer with a respectable medal on his chest for nothing better than surviving a battle most others didn't. He's more interesting undressed: in the shower other officers notice the abdominal scar offset by an Aryan endowment, which evokes the occasional whistle. The scar, reminiscent of a half swastika, was the result of an untimely encounter in a public washroom. A young labourer took Gerhard's teenage glance for interest and decided to ward him off with a knife. Gerhard is fond of the scar, for not only does it give him an otherwise absent mystique, it reminds him to blend in and lie through his teeth. He's in his late twenties, doesn't much care if he dies, but would rather avoid torture or starvation. (He hates the

POW camp on the western edge of town. The smell of it is the smell of the front in winter: pus and unrelenting hunger.)

Gerhard would like to be fastidious, but he's learned to imitate normal men. His hair is receding, though not too obviously yet. It's sandy, his eyes blue, his nose straight, his chin relatively if not markedly square, his arches high, his ass equally so, his ancestral tree Germanic enough for him to obtain permission to marry if he chooses. The war has given him a reprieve on that score, but he'll no doubt marry someday, and he'll have children, and his children will have children, and thus the Aryan race will persevere. He was at Stalingrad—hence the medal—and the current offensive along the Ukrainian border was looking to be a similar meat grinder when he was reassigned to accompany horses in need of recuperation back from the front line. He's smarter than most of his superiors, though he values duty as much as they do. The question is only whether he can stomach it.

In a small clearing, Gerhard stamps down the grass, and Fritz imitates him with exaggerated steps that make Gerhard laugh. He takes a cloth from the saddlebag and lays it on the grass. They sit on the cloth, eat their lunch, pass a bottle back and forth. The boy is free with his movements and eats with unrestrained pleasure, his lips—full lips—shining with grease. He's just old enough to be drafted, barely shaving, his long limbs charmingly awkward. His hands are broad, confident, as if they know more than the rest of him; a nervous horse, feeling his hands on its flank, is soon calmed. His eyes are green as a river, his lashes a rich border, and he gazes with concentrated intensity when Gerhard speaks, as if gauging the state of a man's soul. It's illusion—the result of lip-reading. Even so, to Gerhard it's better than schnapps, making everything worm-eaten and vile and commonplace recede into forgetfulness. As far as the army is concerned, the boy's deafness has been caused by the war, and Gerhard doesn't inquire into the story any more closely than he asks the provenance of the roasted meat they have for lunch. When they're done, Fritz licks his lips, reaches into a pocket, and triumphantly produces an orange.

An orange! Gerhard hasn't seen one since the Christmas before the war began. "Can I believe what I'm seeing? No mirage?"

Fritz nods and grins. His teeth are still good. He eats at his uncle's table, and his uncle commands the Gestapo in town. As a favour, the kind of favour that can have no good end to it, the boy's uncle—Sturmbannführer Vogel—has asked Gerhard to keep an eye on Fritz. On the palm of his hand, the orange is a sun at the opening of a day isolated from battle and so new that it takes Gerhard's breath away. Fritz peels it and hands half to Gerhard. His own half he lifts to his nose and inhales the fragrance. Then he uses his teeth to separate a segment, his curled tongue to flip it into his mouth. He's a noisy eater, sucking and chewing, making every bite sound delicious though he can't hear it.

Gerhard cradles his half, making himself wait while Fritz lays his camera aside and removes his jacket and shirt to lie bare chested in the grass. The hair on Fritz's chest curls, coppered by the sun, his arms spread to welcome it as if nothing ever burns. His torso is hard from ordinary work, not marching, its smoothness—unmarred by knife or gun—belted into trousers, and Gerhard glances away as if his eyes could damage the skin. Maybe he'll touch the boy's foot. Then Fritz will sit up to listen, and Gerhard could reminisce about camping or his antics at veterinary school. The orange will lie in the future. Fritz will appear to listen until Gerhard's face falls still. Then he might write a question in his notebook and extend it to Gerhard, who will spout off again. It won't matter how much of the story Fritz catches. What matters to Gerhard is remembering, as if the detail and quality of his memory could restore the broken world.

When the saliva in Gerhard's mouth accuses him of throwing away riches, he can wait no longer, his need as urgent as if a mortar shell is on its way to take him out and the last thing he'll experience is this Christmas sweetness. He stuffs the whole half in his mouth at once. It fills him, his cheeks puff to accommodate the ecstasy. And then it's gone. All that's left is the remnant of flavour, a scent on his sticky fingers. His surroundings come into focus again: wind rustling the massed levels of greenery, Fritz's soft breathing, a corner of the cloth flapping against the empty bottle, a crow's caw, and then something else.

In a trench, you rely on your ears for warning. Sound is your alphabet: the buzz of planes before they're seen, the rumble of approaching tanks, the click of a rifle nearby. At a distance, in the direction of the rye fields east of the woods, there's a new background noise, louder and quieter as it recedes and advances, with changes of angle to left and right. A meandering natural sound, nothing alarming, Gerhard decides.

Fritz's remarkable eyes flutter open. He hasn't seen the front. He wouldn't find it funny to pick up a stick and bat at a hung partisan. He smiles at Gerhard now, easily and naturally, like a hen laying an egg, something delicious housed inside the thin membrane, and even if there's a spot of shit on the outer shell, it can easily be washed off. Gerhard doesn't know how to smile like that anymore, so instead he talks.

"My dog's name was Adolf," Gerhard says. "When I was eighteen, we had to change his name, of course—it wasn't respectful. He was a schnauzer, not very big, but he always took my side. We were all sitting in the parlour as it was a formal occasion, a family meeting to decide his new name. The dog was tied up outside so he wouldn't leave hair on the furniture. It was my grandmother's, heavy, dark, and uncomfortable but elegant. She wanted to call him Kaiser. A good woman, my grandmother, but not very political. The conversation went on for a very long time, and I was bored as well as angry that here I was, an adult really, and everyone else's views had to be taken into account regarding my dog, who wasn't even there for the discussion. My youngest brother, Fredi, was Father's favourite, and I was afraid that he'd give in to Fredi's ideas, even though he was being silly, and I would end up having to call my dog Fart or Jew. Mother, who was always the peacemaker, finally suggested Pepper because he was white and grey, and so we all agreed. But the poor dog never adjusted to the new name. I always wondered, if I'd called out 'Adolf,' whether he would have turned and avoided the streetcar that hit him. That's when I decided to become a veterinarian."

Fritz writes in his notebook: *Sorry about Adolf.* After a beat, his expression unreadable, he scratches out the name and writes, *Pepper.*

The boy is either dangerously naive or savagely witty—Gerhard can never decide which—and there's also the possibility that Fritz is his uncle's informant attempting to provoke a reaction, and so Gerhard takes the prudent course, one that has served him well, of proceeding as if it all goes over his head. "My dog died a good death. Quick. I wouldn't mind one like that."

He abruptly stops talking, causing Fritz to look around questioningly while Gerhard attends to the woods and the sounds emanating from it, now more distinctive, unidirectional, heading closer. *Urrr Urrr.* A pack of growling dogs. "Shit! Quick!" He stands up with a jerk. "Get your shirt on. Pack up."

The dogs mean Russian quarry. Just when you think you've got the enemy under control, one pops out of a hole with a rifle aimed at your balls, another falls on you from the air, a group of them plants explosives and dives away. But dogs are on the trail. If anyone is hiding nearby, Sturmbannführer Vogel will order his men to tear down every tree in the woods and mow the bush so that nobody can use it again, and then Gerhard will have no refuge. Already the clearing seems the kind of place that teases you into lowering your guard until you step on a ripe body or an unexploded shell or find yourself invited to a pleasant engagement with the Gestapo, having recklessly revealed yourself. Alders lean over the river like keening old women, bushes mass like their imprisoned sons. Beyond the woods are fields, and behind them the road to town. Men will come from there with chainsaws, and the timber will heat the stove in the headquarters the police share with the Gestapo across from the railway station. Unless Gerhard locates the problem and deals with it himself.

As he runs into the bush, all he can see are shades of green— round, fat, tall, endless as the Russian reserves; no matter how many you cut down, there are more behind. The rise of the embankment makes his breath quicken, vines trap his boots, roots trip him. His right foot, damaged from frostbite in the last winter campaign, throbs. His nostrils widen, taking in the leafy scent as he claws with the sabre, stepping over, bending below. Vegetation and men both smell of their guts when separated from life. It's the smell that makes him hate the war and everyone in it. The smell stays in your nostrils, it follows you in retreat, and even the burning of everything left behind, so that the enemy crawls over blackened earth, can't cauterize the memory.

The smell is coming for him now, a fleeing scarecrow, a bundle of stink that wafts on the wind, a corpse-bride carried to her honeymoon suite, the woods, his haven, rotten with it, and his rage at the defilement drives away fear and crushes hope as if it were remorse. Fuck the woods. Fuck everything and especially the enemy at the end of it.

He hacks left and right, not caring what he tears down. All that matters is movement. Up. Down. Forward. Thrust. The habits of the front take over as sweat sticks his hair to his scalp, his shirt to his back, his pants to his groin. A space opens up before him. The underbush is thinner here, sunlight hogged by a copse of trees.

Breathing hard, he sheaths his sabre. The barking is loud. The dogs aren't far now. Gerhard runs as if they're pulling him, as if he has no injured foot, as if he has no feet at all, no body now, only need. Dead leaves crumple, birds fly up from the trees in alarm, and he breaks out between trees at the same time as a figure coming from the right.

Does the tatterdemalion look around and see a German uniform? Does it glance over its shoulder to gauge the distance of the dogs, or the chance of re-entering the bush? Does it wonder what to do next, or think of anything at all? Gerhard doesn't ask, not then; he has no existence, no dimension. He is direction, the figure is pure movement. An endgame that repeats with endless variations of weather and topography but always the same. Gerhard is blind, he's deaf, he runs toward the smell, forcing himself into the muddy bog of it, the fly-fed swamp of odour.

When he's in deep, he shouts, "Halt!" in Russian.

Momentum carries the enemy forward, legs bowed under the weight of organs swinging in a sack of skin, the shoulders hunched, head huddled between them as if to protect itself from hanging. A few steps and the enemy stops. Fifty metres behind is a field of rye, in it the yapping dogs and men following them, bobbing heads visible against the sky. Shouts: *Dog Food, we got you. No point in running.*

The Russian rotates slowly like a windsock.

"Here," Gerhard says, exhausting the extent of his Russian. He stands still, pistol raised, held steadily with both hands. "*Schnell*," he adds. Everyone understands *schnell*.

The prisoner obediently totters a few more steps, hands raised. A reply, which Gerhard doesn't understand, but it gives him time to aim. He shoots well and does not have to spend a second bullet. His enemy falls among the wildflowers, a prisoner of war in the customary striped rags, who must have somehow got away from the cement factory or the railroad repair detail. As he falls, the rags pull up on one side. His leg is hairless and white. The knee is grey.

Gerhard feels the familiar relief that he's proven himself the same as any other man, a son of the Fatherland, a good soldier. Then bile rises in his throat, and he vomits, knowing that he's not like other men who can refrain from retching on Death's shiny new shoes.

Pre-revolutionary Vegetables

When Lily wakes, the sun is low and she's relieved that the shot she heard was only a dream. She backs out of the bush, bottom first, face down, a breech birth. Free of the smacking leaves, she sits on her heels, taking stock. To the east are unknown roads; she can't be more than three days from friendly territory. It's been twelve hours since she's eaten, but thirst has driven away hunger, dehydration making her dizzy. She'll have to drink and fill her canteen before leaving the river behind. She rises to her feet and stumbles toward the water.

At the edge of the embankment, she looks down. Twilight plays with a person's sight, making distances shorter or longer, hiding angles, merging air and rock, so she'll have to feel her way. Crouching, back to the water and face to the earth, she lowers one foot, finds a crevice to lock her toes into, and lowers the other. Her feet find purchase, her good arm hugs the embankment as if it is a kind but ugly man she's learned to love. She bends, extends a leg, her foot meets air and smooth rock. She retreats and tries again, the other way. There's nothing to hold on to. She can slide or jump, scar her face or break her neck. Never much of a question. She throws herself away from the earth, but the drop is unexpectedly brief, flinging her onto her bottom, bruising her tailbone. When her head clears, as much as it can, she realizes she's at the river's edge. Forgetting her injuries, the dryness of her tongue absorbing all attention now that relief is near, she bends over the surface, scooping water, lapping it up. She scoops and slurps again, making her throat work though it's sore. Then she fills her canteen, drinks, and refills. Her thirst slaked, she sits, her pack bumping against her hips as she studies the cottage across the river and the smoke rising from its chimney like an offering to the end of day.

Once the sun has set, she could easily lose her bearings in the dark and end up walking in circles. She needs more than crops to hide her: a roof, water, food, bandages. Her eyelids are burning, a slight shiver between her shoulder blades, signs of fever. *Look twice, shoot once*, her commander used to say. In the west, the red sun has drawn a line on the water. Over there is a cottage and in her holster a pistol. She only has to get from here to there. An owl hoots, waking up early to hunt before mice and hares get down into their nests.

She puts one foot into the water, then the other, using her left hand as eyes below the surface, feeling for rocks, wondering how much damage the river will do to her nice box calf boots. The cold water stings her burn. One foot then the other pulling out of the sludgy river bottom. Five metres, ten metres. She follows the pink trail in a zigzag, now veering to the right of it, now left, easing herself over a high, flat stone and then bringing herself back to the rosy arrow. When she skids on something vegetative and slimy, she tries to regain her footing, but her pack overbalances her, and she goes under.

She pushes with both arms, numb now to pain. She pushes up again, thinking her first effort must have been feebler than it felt. Yet she still can't rise, something holding her face down in this ridiculous half metre of water. She struggles. Her lungs burn, urging her mouth to open. A mouth will open for anything eventually, giving her to the underworld, drowning her in a puddle. The ghosts of pilots she shot down must be laughing. And then, somehow, with one movement, she squeezes her shoulder blades back and lifts her chest, shrugging out of her pack. Gasping, she rises from the water. She can't see what her pack is caught on. She pulls, but the pack holds fast. She'll have to leave it. She's almost at the embankment. Just a few more steps.

She climbs out of the water, heavy with the weight of it, still breathing hard as she approaches the cottage. She stops for a moment to rest and think. In the sky everything is clear. Your friends are marked by the stars on their tails, your enemies by their swastikas. Who will she find inside the peasant's hut? Every village she's liberated has had collaborators. They look like anyone else, a mother in a kerchief, an old man in felt boots. You don't see a sign in anyone's face that here is someone who lies in bed with the enemy, who gives up their countrymen for a sausage. What a prize—a Soviet officer! That must be worth something good. She removes her pistol from her holster.

Pushing open the door, she enters the unheated entranceway of a typical village hut: dark, cold, the shadow of a barrel in the corner, a bucket and a tin cup, enough room for a couple of hens or a goat, but no sound or smell of either. She shuts the outer door quietly and feels her way to the latch of the inner door, which she pushes open a crack, her pistol ready. She smells a wood fire and herbs. Through the crack, she sees mushrooms and drying plants hanging from the rafters. Pushing the door fully ajar, she steps through the opening. There's no one inside but an old woman sitting at the table. A whitewashed clay stove with a large hearth and a sleeping platform on top takes up most of the room. Under the window is an iron bed, beside it the table. The floor is wood, not dirt. There are books on a shelf. Not quite an ordinary peasant's hut.

"You aren't here for female troubles, I'm guessing. You're soaked," the old woman says by way of greeting. She has as many teeth as could be expected of someone her age. Her hair is loose and wispy, cut short as if she's come through an illness, but no one this old could survive a wartime sickness. She closes the book she was reading. "Put down the gun. You're shaking, and I wouldn't want it to go off in my direction."

"I'm afraid you'll have to take your chances, Citizen. I'm wounded, but I'll be on my way as soon as I can."

"Maybe you should lie down before you faint." She gestures to the bed. "You're not very big, but I'm very old, and I don't think I could lift you."

Lily obeys, her pistol still pointing toward the old woman. The bed is covered by a quilt made with intricate needlework. She's only seen one like it in a display of old-regime artifacts at the museum, as an example of worker abuse. "Where did this come from?"

"My mother made it. I'm Vera Semenovna Sarbash. That's a Greek name. We gave you the alphabet. And you are?"

"A soldier of the Red Army. Your liberator."

"Well, Comrade Liberator. Will you let me check your wounds?"

Lily nods and, as the old woman helps her out of her flight jacket, can't help but groan.

"I see it's not the first time you've been shot," the woman says. "We'll need to clean that up. Lucky for you, I hauled water up from the river this morning."

The old woman's heading for the door, maybe for the Germans. Lily swings her legs down, keeping her grip on the gun despite her dizziness. It's her friend, her reliable comrade, and she won't abandon it. "Where do you think you're going?"

"The entrance." The old woman waves the tin cup at Lily. "Or fill the bucket yourself, then."

"Go on. Do it." She hears the slosh of water scooped into the bucket. Vera returns, puts it on the table and a pot on a stove ring, then pours water into the pot. Puttering here and there, she picks leaves and dried blooms from the hanging bunches and throws them into the pot.

"These days my remedies don't smell so bad. But when I was at the collective farm, I cooked up a good stink. Especially when I made the tincture for a man's problem. You know what I mean.

Men have only one problem that matters. The Party Secretary was a regular customer and entirely satisfied. My grandmother used to get boiling water from the samovar before putting in the leaves. But I like a slow cook because as a general rule, not always, but generally, if you put the plants into cold water, they release more of the juices. Now me, I learned the cure for a man's problem from a Jewish midwife in Poland. My first husband, who was an officer in the Tsar's army, was stationed in a small town there."

"I'm not surprised you're a former," Lily says with an attempt at bitterness. But her voice comes out in shallow exhalations, no air in her lungs to spare for commentary.

"Everyone's a former something when you get to be my age, darling."

"And do you get payment from the Germans for your remedies?"

"Why else is an old woman awake after dark?" She dips a cup in the pot.

"You're an opportunist."

"A pragmatist. Moscow took our grain, then Berlin took our grain. Famine is famine. Better a morsel to eat." Vera picks a few more leaves and crushes them into the cup, then tops it up with hot water from the samovar. "This doesn't taste good, so if you have to hold your nose, do it. It's important to drink every drop." She carries the cup to Lily. Steam rises from it, and despite Citizen Sarbash's caution, the odour isn't unpleasant, just strong, like a peasant mash that would quench hunger and thirst at the same time.

What else could the potion do but make her sleep so that the old woman can alert the Gestapo? "I'm not going to drink anything. Do what you want with my shoulder."

"So you want me to dig out the shell fragments, just like that."

"That's right," Lily says.

"Suit yourself." The old woman's knees creak as she leans over a chest at the foot of the bed and lifts the lid. From inside, she extracts a knife, rags, and a small jar. The rags and the jar she puts on the table. She takes the knife to the fire, heats it until the blade turns red, and lays it on the rag to cool. From time to time it seems as if she'll speak again, but she just glances at Lily and shakes her head.

"At least have some vodka," the old woman says. "I can vouch for it. I make it myself."

"Just get on with it."

The old woman grabs the jug on her way to the bed, uncorking it with a practised movement. "For sterilizing."

"I said I'm not . . ."

But Lily doesn't complete her sentence. The old woman is pouring the alcohol onto her shoulder, and, like a novice pilot overcome by the multiple G-force of a steep dive, Lily faints.

The bed in the old woman's cottage is hot from the sun coming through the window, the four-square pane of dirt-stained glass pleated with light, the shirred curtain pushed aside. So quiet. No engines, no gunfire. Lily doesn't stink and her arm feels like an arm again. The bandage around her burned hand must have been changed several times because it isn't glued to her skin. The hand sticks out of a sleeve she doesn't recognize: a nightgown, old and worn, the broken fibres of its life softening it. Lily reaches for her pistol, but it's not where she dropped it and not in sight.

The old woman bends over her, peering at her with flat, unreadable eyes. "Get up," Vera orders, shaking Lily. "Don't think I left you in my bed out of sympathy. I prefer to sleep over the stove. I get cold at night."

In the light of day Lily sees a photograph of seaside bathers and a coloured circus poster. There's a calendar. A stub of candle and a small religious icon of the sort people used to hide. She shakes her wrist, wondering if the drenching killed her father's watch. It's stopped, but by the angle of the sun she thinks it's before midday. The old woman wears a shabby dress, her shawl draped over a chair. She's as thin as anyone in the Ukraine, but she doesn't have the breath of someone who is starving.

"Is it morning?" Lily asks.

"You should ask what day."

"What?"

"It's been days since you arrived."

"That can't be." Lily pushes aside the covers and swings her feet over the side of the bed. Her soles skim the smooth floor, and she looks down at her feet like they're someone else's, these naked feet with narrow toes and delicate bones; unwrapped, unbooted, they can't stamp their imprint in the earthen floor of a dugout or run to a scramble. And as she tries to stand, one of her ankles wobbles, objecting to her weight. She must have twisted it when she jumped down to the river.

"It's Friday. Stand up slowly. You'll be all right. The fever broke last night."

"Give me my uniform and my gun, and you can forget me," Lily says as she takes the two steps needed to reach the table, then lowers herself into a chair, which graciously keeps her from sliding to the floor. "And if you give me what's on the stove, I'll forget you."

"That's what I'll say down at the police station," Vera grumbles. "And if I tell the Gestapo with a handful of the Tsar's gold rubles, they'll just give me six months' hard labour. You want to dig under my outhouse? Maybe you'll find a pot under the shit." She scoops soup from a steaming iron pot and places the bowl on the table. Then another for herself. "Not just potato peelings. Potatoes, onions, and fat. Even . . ." she whispers, "a piece of sausage." The old woman sits. She works the soup through her thin, wrinkled lips and her gravestone teeth. It's only in Western fairy tales that there are fairy godmothers. Russians make do with their witches.

"And what's this?" Lily picks out a suspicious yellow bit.

"Rutabaga."

"Never heard of it. And this?"

"*Pasternak.*"

"The only 'Parsnip' I know is Boris Parsnip the writer."

"Pre-revolutionary vegetables," the old woman says. "If it's too reactionary for you, give it to me."

Lily puts a protective arm around the bowl and digs in, pausing only for a swallow of tea to lubricate her throat. Too soon, she's done. "Any bread?"

"Do I look like an officer's mistress?"

Lily laughs. She's warm, fed, slick as an oiled river. The old woman could have given her up to the enemy and didn't. She'll stay until nightfall and then head east. When she gets back to base, she'll be questioned by the NKVD. The special agents aren't known for their friendliness, and it won't be pleasant, but she hasn't been captured. That's what matters. No one should accuse her of giving up or being a spy. She has nothing to worry about. She just needs to keep her mind on her unit, her comrades, the aircraft pining for her. "Thank you for the hospitality, Auntie. Just give me my uniform so I can dress, and soon I'll be off."

Vera shakes her head. "I burnt it and your papers."

Lily stares at her in shock.

"What? I decided to save you."

Without her uniform and papers, Lily's a deserter. The special agents won't believe her story. They won't care. Stalin's Order 270: Prisoners of war are traitors. "You don't mean it."

"I'm also not eager to be shot for sheltering you."

"You don't know what you've done. I'll be court-martialled."

"If you were a soldier. Now you're someone else. I have good papers for you. Real ones." The old woman crosses to the foot of the bed. From the chest, she removes a slip and a dress, stockings, a garter belt. "This will cover you." She holds it all out to Lily, who takes it numbly. A clean slip. Soft stockings from before the war. A city dress. Blue with small white flowers. "I kept this for you too." She hands over the scarf that Lily dyed with cornflowers last summer.

How can she go home now? A flick of a match and she's not a pilot anymore. On the whim of an old woman, in the hearth of a peasant's stove, a small bundle burned, and she's been turned into a criminal. Like father, like daughter. "My boots?"

"Hidden."

"Get them." She'll have to walk the earth in bare skin, plucked, beak and wings cut away.

"The boots don't look right. You need shoes. Ones that a girl around here could wear." Vera reaches into the chest again, takes out a pair of shoes and smacks them on the table. "Take off the nightgown."

"Turn around, then." Lily will cut a stick and walk to the nearest town. Connect with a partisan cell. Will they trust her with no papers? But she has a pistol. They'll take her for that. The heat in her cheeks has moved into her hands, and the only relief would be in using them. She looks at the old woman's spine, beginning to curve between her shoulder blades, her jutting neck unconcealed by hair. Lily wonders if her grandmother's broad back has also become so thin, her neck as bony as a chicken's.

"The dress was my youngest granddaughter's," Vera says. "She brought it from Mariupol. She was small like you."

Lily's arm is still sore and stiff, her hand tender as she unbuttons the nightgown and lets it drop to the floor. Sitting on the chair, she pulls her feet away from the pool of cloth. Garter belt. Stockings. She rolls them on evenly, she still has the knack, with or without papers. She steps into the slip. The old woman waits patiently, unmoving. Lily winces as she pulls the dress on over her head. It matches the scarf, which could be an omen or not. "You can turn around now."

The old woman does, nodding with grim satisfaction. "I'll button the back for you."

"What happened to your granddaughter?" Lily asks to distract herself.

"Sofia died. Does it matter how?"

"I'd like to know," Lily says.

"She was just a girl. A nursing student. I thought she'd be safer in the country. Before I had a chance to register her, she got sick with pneumonia. I buried her at night."

They look each other in the eyes, the old woman's hooded with loose skin, framed by wrinkles, and the young one's set in a permanent state of indignant grief.

"You served a soldier of the Red Army. And you attended to my injuries. You fulfilled a Citizen's obligation," Lily says quietly as she sits down again. What's she to do with this old broom of a grandmother? "But you destroyed my papers. You destroyed me. I can't cross back over."

"That's what you're worried about? The Germans will shoot you once for being a Red Army officer and again for being a Jew." Vera laughs, then coughs like a stuck pig as she places a cup of hot water on the table. Into it she throws a few leaves plucked from a bundle that hangs from the rafters. She seats herself across from Lily, her arthritic hands cradling the cup. "They love Jews so much, they're even willing to spend bullets on them. Well, maybe their property is compensation. The baker had nothing worth anything, but Chelpanov, our chief of police, now lives in the doctor's house. He's a thug they let out of jail. His nickname was the Artist because of how he used his knife. I'm sure he'd be very welcoming to a Litvak."

"Litvyak."

"However you want to spell it, that's a Jewish name, and if you lived in Moscow another thousand years, you would still be a Jew."

"Lieutenant in the Red Army."

"Jew. My family came to the Crimea two thousand years ago. Look at my papers. You'll see what they say. Greek. Still Greek."

"My passport is stamped Russian. But you burnt it."

"Ow. Let go of me. What's wrong with you? I'm just telling you how it is here."

Lily is surprised to find the fingers of her bandaged hand on her host's bony shoulder. How interesting the rubbery dip between tendons, how fragile the clavicle. Lily opens her fingers. She lowers her hand to the table.

"The police and the Gestapo are out looking for the owner of a parachute," Vera says. On her neck a thumbprint blooms. "They'll go to every door and uproot the bushes. Wait until they come here. You'll be my granddaughter."

Lily might get away with it. She speaks Ukrainian, and everyone around here is fluent in Russian, too—schools are taught in it, and many residents are ethnically Russian. "What then?" she asks.

"After that, you can leave and go where you want," Vera says.

Lily needs to search the cottage, find her pistol, feel the embossed star under her thumb, the flat barrel against her belly as she tucks it into the waistband of her underpants. She can still make her life count. "Why are you doing this?" she asks.

"Seven of my grandchildren were soldiers. Six boys and a girl. I have one left. He's a pilot too. By the grace of our Lord, he hasn't been captured. If he's shot down, someone will help him because I helped you."

Vera stands up, shoving her chair back. From the shelf of books she selects one and places it on the table. It's a children's book with a moral lesson. The cover has the ice cream truck and the greedy capitalist with the gold watch that Lily remembers from her childhood.

Vera withdraws identification documents hidden between pages that illustrate the glutton getting colder and colder until he turns into a mountain of snow for children to slide down. But it was the vividly coloured ice cream scoops that had fascinated Lily.

"I hope you're right, Auntie. Just give me my pistol and I'll go."

"What for? As soon as you're searched, you'll give yourself away. Anyway, it's no use. I had to trade it for the papers. See how nice they did it? Look at your picture. No one can tell it came from the passport. You're Sofia. That's all."

Finding a forger, negotiating with him, transporting the documents back and forth. It's dangerous. It takes courage. That's not what Lily expects from an old woman who deals with the Germans, taking their money. On the ground, nothing makes sense.

At the sound of approaching motorcycles, Vera's eyes flick to right and left. When the engines stop, her hands tremble like mice. The knock on the door needs no translation: a fist on wood will shortly be followed by a shoulder separating the door from its hinges, and any pain this causes will be visited tenfold on the reluctant inhabitants.

Vera hurries to unlatch it, muttering, "Dear Saint Niphon protect me now, don't go wandering like a man. Saint Anne, grandmother of our dear Jesus, hear my prayer, protect my soldier."

Lily hobbles to the stove. She puts her hand on the iron poker.

Four men crowd into the small cottage. A civilian, an army officer, and two SS officers. One of the SS men wears a captain's insignia. The other, a junior officer, gets down on his knees to search under the old woman's bed. The civilian—a large, blocky man—identifies himself as Chelpanov, Chief of Police, then speaks to the SS captain in broken German. A leaner man, the one in regular military uniform, stands at the table, flipping through the picture book as if he's in a library.

"I should be lecturing to a classroom of intelligent students or dictating notes," the SS captain says. He walks as if he has an egg in his pants, legs splayed to avoid breaking it. His cap is stiff, the piping unsoiled from combat. He's weak-chinned and slope-shouldered. "Check the hearth, Chelpanov. These big clay ovens are built to hide people. You, girl, give him the poker."

There's nothing for Lily to do but hand it over. The chief of police thrusts it into the hearth.

"I'm a Doctor of Law," the SS captain says. "And I'm stuck with an army horse doctor. Are you here with us, Dr. Fischer?"

The man with the book looks up. "Yes, Hauptsturmführer Hoffmann."

"If we find someone, I expect you to fix him up so we can interrogate him before he dies. And if it's the owner of the parachute that was floating in the river, you can be sure that I'll mention your assistance in my report," Hoffmann says, as if it's a generous offer. "There could be a commendation in it for you."

"I'm not a physician. I'm a veterinarian."

"We've had this conversation before. Animals are a step above these Russians. They should be grateful to have the care of a veterinarian. Girl—your name."

"Sofia," Lily says. If she still had her gun, she could die respectably.

"You speak German. I noticed you listening."

"Yes," she says. "It was a compulsory course in high school."

"Nothing gets by me. I know what you are." Hoffmann taps his nose. "I can smell it. You're not Russian, are you?"

"Greek."

"As I suspected—classical features. Those limpid eyes. Something of the ancient Greeks who inseminated the Aryan race remains in them. The shape of the head—it has the perfection of a Hellenic bust. Sergeant Sauer, do you observe?" The junior officer, a boy

really, his face sunburned, glances at Lily's breasts. "Lift your eyes,
Sauer, the head! If there's nothing under the bed, you can empty the
trunk." Hoffmann stares at Lily. He taps his nose again. "I detect
something else. That's not school German. The grammar is poor,
but that accent . . . it doesn't hurt my ears. You hear, Chelpanov?
This is how German can be spoken. Who taught you, girl?"

"My grandmother." She ignores the old woman's shake of the
head. What does anything matter now?

"Aha! I knew it. A German grandparent. Pity there's not two."

"Do you want to see my papers, sir?" How did *sir* come out of
her mouth? The politeness nauseates her.

"Give them here." She complies, he looks them over. "Nursing
student?"

"Yes. Before the war. It was my dream," she says, playing the
part because she must—for the old woman who fed her, for her own
survival.

"I had a dream before the war," Hoffmann says with a glance
that could be sympathy. "I studied animal protection: an end to
the torture and suffering of animals used in experiments, the pres-
ervation of natural environments. But now I'm looking for a Soviet
pilot. Have you seen anything?"

"Nothing at all. I've been sick with a fever."

"My granddaughter works," Vera says in terrible German, her
face worried. The sick are disposable.

"You seem healthy enough to me, Sofia. Your German is pass-
able. I have use for you," Hoffmann says. He redirects his attention
to the job at hand: examining the spilled contents of the trunk.
Shoes, clothes, nothing wet, nothing stained from water, no papers,
no weapons. He checks it all, glancing from time to time at the veterinarian standing in comfortable idleness. "Dr. Fischer, can't you
think of something useful to do?"

"Not really."

"Not *weally*," Hoffmann mimics the veterinarian's accent. "You east Germans, practically in Poland. Are you too lazy to pronounce every letter? Imagine the sign above the entrance to a concentration camp: *Wok Makes Fee*."

"What do you wish me to do?" Dr. Fischer asks. He's a strange man with his inattention and his nonchalance. "I'm at your disposal."

"Search outside. Check the outhouse. Beat the bushes. Am I the only one in the world with a brain?"

As Dr. Fischer turns to go, Vera stops him with a word in Russian and a gesture. Apparently he understands one or the other because he pauses and raises his eyebrows. The old woman pokes an index finger through the circle of her other hand. From a small cupboard, she takes a bottle filled with liquid.

"It's for the clap, Hauptsturmführer Hoffmann," Chelpanov says. "A village girl came to her for treatment, and she's offering it for a good price. She claims it works before symptoms appear."

"Ask the old woman for the name of the sick whore," Hoffmann orders.

Vera says that she doesn't know. Nobody gives her their names. The girl didn't wear a kerchief, she was medium height, smelled fishy.

Chelpanov repeats what she says in German.

"Like them all," Hoffmann says. "Ask her for the name of a clean one. This is for your benefit, Sergeant Sauer." The young SS officer is listening attentively.

"Olga," the old woman says, and adds, "the hunchback."

Chelpanov translates.

"No wonder," Sauer says.

The men laugh, Dr. Fischer unconvincingly, Chelpanov greedily, his eyes raking Lily as if he expects to have her when his betters are done with her, like hand-me-down trousers, the sort a bourgeois mother would pass along to her gardener's son when her own son outgrows them, the bottoms stretched and baggy.

Vera speaks rapidly, urgently.

"The old woman says her granddaughter is a good worker," Chelpanov says in heavily accented German. "Since she knows something about nursing, she could help Dr. Fischer with the animals."

"I'll have her with me in the Gestapo office. For filing," Hoffmann says. "And translation."

"You've got Chelpanov." For the first time, Dr. Fischer seems alert, his voice animated. "I have to deal with locals too. And she could help me when I have to treat your patients."

"*Stabsveterinär*, we may both be captains. Technically. But I'm an SS officer, and you're army support." Hoffmann smiles genially and snaps, "Check the outhouse. Make sure to get your arm right down in there. Shit hides in shit."

"No problem. I've put my arm up many a rear," Dr. Fischer says. "I'll want soap and water after." He mimes washing his hands. Vera shakes her head. "No? None? Well, I can make do with vodka, either to disinfect or make me not care. Not any of that either? Pity. Heil Hitler!" He whistles as he leaves.

"Chelpanov, check the floor and walls," the SS captain says. "Sauer, strip the bed. Throw the mattress on the floor and cut into it. You, girl, come with me."

Lily precedes him into the entranceway as he indicates, refusing to give him the pleasure of seeing her repugnance. Light comes through the cracks in door and walls. Hoffmann's pasty forehead sweats milky drops. "Check the water level," he says. When she bends over the barrel, he presses against her, and she straightens sharply.

"Water?" she asks.

He shakes his head and takes a flask from his hip pocket. After a swig, he says, "You'll work for Dr. Fischer. There's a smell on him—it reminds me of cologne. You'll keep me informed. Regarding him and his assistant, a boy named Fritz Vogel. For example, their exact relationship. Yes?"

"Yes," she says.

He throws open the door, taking his need and his irritation outside into the fresh air. The wind is blowing eastward from his homeland, carrying on it the scent of orchards and wisps of a tarry malodour like pus, like ulceration, like gangrene. Every soldier has a moral duty to overcome his scruples and clear out the sickness. War will end, the burned earth will be fertilized, the slaughtered forests reseeded. He'll smell the pine trees and cup his hands in pure water. Frogs will sing on the lily pads.

Loitering near the peasant hut, the freckled boy who brought them the parachute is awaiting his reward. In the hierarchy of nature, he ranks below frogs. According to the law, which Hoffmann helped draft, the thighs of a frog shall not be ripped out while it's living. He strides toward the urchin, and when the boy looks up, an avaricious slobber at the corners of his mouth, the *Hauptsturmführer* lifts a foot and smashes first one knee, then the other.

The mattress sack hangs empty on the bed frame, its viscera exploded, straw on the floor, on the cupboard, on the door latch, clinging to a remnant of the icon still on the shelf. In a slash of dirt, specks of glass and china catch the light as the policeman tosses a broken floorboard. It falls on the injured trunk, its wood bowed and splintered. A shred of paper clings to the junior officer's sleeve, the rest of the book stuffed into the hearth. Downy feathers flutter around his boots.

"What's next?" Sauer asks.

Lily can still feel the imprint of the *Hauptsturmführer*'s buckle in the small of her back, the swastika and eagle branded where he pressed against her. Outside, someone is screaming. It sets her teeth on edge.

"Give me the watch," the policeman says. He leans against the stove, elbow on the sleeping platform as he slips a whetstone from his pocket, then swipes his knife back and forth on it. He's left-handed. What would he carve in her face?

"It doesn't work," she says, lifting her wrist. "See for yourself."

The policeman comes close and unbuckles the strap so as not to damage it. He winds the watch, shakes it, listens to it. Then he throws it into the hearth. "Shoes and stockings," he says.

The room is too small, the air sucked out of it by the straw, the stove, the men. Her path to the window is blocked, so is her path to the door. She would have to leap over the chair and the iron bed frame. She would have to fly. She bends to lift the hem of her dress. The SS boy watches her, his eyes glistening.

Chelpanov wags a finger at him. "You need a feel? Go ahead. I won't say anything."

The boy's collar swims around his neck, the lightning bolts on the collar wobbling as he swallows hard. A step, two. His sweaty hands squeeze her breasts. He presses his chapped lips on the rise of her chest, on her bare skin. She should rip them off. She could, she would, what's wrong with her that she submits like a kulak's cow? Shame rises between her legs, hotter than desire, shooting up her back, spreading along her shoulders, flushing her throat. She turns her head. She looks through the window but can see nothing, only the flat land, not the source of the screams that took up residence in her head, evicting the soldier, leaving the girl. Someone should deal with the girl. Finish her off. She puts her hands on the boy's chest and pushes. He holds on to her, hands gripping her arms, crab lips scuttling up her neck, and she shoves harder, with the heels of her hands and a knee. He stumbles back. He reaches for his gun. Chelpanov is laughing, the old woman pale.

"That's enough," Chelpanov says, his hand on the boy's shoulder.

"But she!"

"Save some for the boss." He points his knife at Vera. "You didn't do much of a job with your granddaughter. Teach her respect." He studies their faces, comparing them. "Was your daughter-in-law a whore? The girl doesn't look like you." A spot of red, like blood, rises on Vera's cheek, but she doesn't speak. "Show me those papers."

He holds the documents to the light that comes through the window. He brings them close to his eyes then farther away. He touches the seal. He studies the photograph, which was affixed to her army documents. The edge of the stamp that covered the left corner of it is gone. Outside, the screaming stops.

"Where were you born?" he asks Lily.

"Mariupol," the old woman answers for her.

"Shut up. You, answer. Where did you study nursing?"

"The Mariupol Institute for Nursing," Lily says without hesitation.

"That's not a southern accent."

"Because I grew up in the north."

"What's your grandfather's name?"

"Basil Konstaninovich Sarbash," she replies, again without pause. Truth or lies aren't easily distinguishable. Only conviction.

The boy waves his gun uncertainly. "Should I shoot her or her?" he asks.

"Put your thing back in your pants." Chelpanov moves closer, standing over Lily. He says to the boy, "You have to think about later and what you can get. Shoot when there's nothing." He motions to her legs, her feet. "Those. For my wife. Take them off."

She doesn't want them anyway. It's too hot. Beads of sweat are trickling down her neck. Bending, she lifts her skirt, fingers finding the garter tab beneath. Before she releases it, Vera puts a hand on her arm, arresting her movement.

"She needs them," Vera says.

"No. It's fine." Lily shakes her off, but the old woman draws herself up as if she swore an oath, as if Lily was the last child of Mother Russia.

"The *Hauptsturmführer* said she's to work for him and the doctor. She can't walk around barefoot. It's not field work. You can't take anything till the *Hauptsturmführer* comes back."

"What did she say?" the boy asked.

"Nothing important," Chelpanov growled.

"What will the Germans do if you steal from them?" the old woman asks insistently. "They'll put you back in jail where they found you. Tell the Herr Gestapo that when he returns, Granddaughter."

Chelpanov smacks Vera across the mouth, and she falls like a dead fly with translucent wings and bulbous eyes, smacking the floor. At the sight of the old woman prone, skirt hiked above leg wrappings, wrinkled knees bared, Lily feels a rush of anguish. But before she can lift the old grandmother, Chelpanov puts the point of his knife on Lily's cheek. His other hand slides up her stockinged leg to bare thigh.

"You for me. Later. I'll fuck you in the mother tongue."

"Only if I cut it off," Lily says.

"What? What?" the boy asks.

"She likes you," Chelpanov says. Baring his teeth, more cracked jaw than smile, he releases her. "After the captain has his fill, I'll share her with you and your friends. There's enough to go around, right?"

The outer door creaks, the inner door is pushed open. Chelpanov and the boy turn toward it.

"Heil Hitler!" They both salute, the boy vigorously, the man with dispassion.

Coming up behind Hauptsturmführer Hoffmann, the veterinarian carries his jacket with his left thumb hooked over his shoulder, holding his other arm away from his body. Brown drops fall into the straw. Hoffmann's eyes flick over the old woman lying in the wreckage.

"Find anything?" he asks.

"No, *Hauptsturmführer*," the young officer says. He pinches his nose. "The veterinarian stinks."

"Unbearably. Use the barrel of water, Dr. Fischer," Hoffmann orders.

"I'll go down to the river."

"The barrel. I don't want to waste any more time here."

"*Hauptsturmführer*." Dr. Fischer pauses in the doorway, speaking over his shoulder. "Don't forget, I want the girl to help me."

"Tomorrow, she'll be at the Gestapo office at 0800 for her papers. Chelpanov will have them ready. Correct?"

The policeman mutters his affirmative, and she nods.

"You'll meet us there, Dr. Fischer. Before you take her to the stables, I have a special prisoner in the basement cell. He's a bit . . . under the weather, and I still have questions for him. You and your new nurse will treat him first thing in the morning."

Through the open door, she sees Dr. Fischer drop his jacket and strip off his shirt. With his square jaw and his blue eyes and the scar striking downward, he looks more the SS officer than the *Hauptsturmführer*, except for the obvious limp. The veterinarian rubs his arm with straw, then he scoops water with the bucket and pours it over his arm. More straw, more water, taking the extra time as if he cares that plunging his arm directly into the barrel would taint the water.

———

After the policeman and German officers depart, Vera hands Lily her father's watch and sweeps up the mess. Now and then she stops to pick up shards of china, piling them near the stove. There's straw and feathers in her hair, on her arm, in hills and valleys on the floor. As she sweeps off the sleeping platform, another hill forms while Lily sits at the table, repairing the mattress cover with small, even stitches.

"I'm finished," she says. "Let me stuff it for you, Auntie."

"All right." Vera shakes off her bast shoes and puts on a pair of men's boots. "I'll be back soon," she says.

"Where are you going?"

"To the still. There might be a few potatoes for us there. Maybe something else."

When Vera returns with a sack, the mattress is back on the bed, the embroidered quilt over it; Lily has cleaned off the mud as best she can. Vera drops Lily's boots on the floor and a small, thin knife on the table. "My grandmother was a nurse," she says. "It was hers. Now it's yours. Remember you're Sofia Sarbash, that's all. Don't throw away her life."

When the light is failing and the chill wind reminds them of fall coming, they sit down with their bowls. Vera has magicked a soup out of something grey and something brown she plucked from the rafters, with mushrooms, onions, a morsel of meat, a potato, a few pre-revolutionary vegetables. As Lily spoons it down, the warmth and thickness of it settles in her stomach, making her blink with fatigue, as if war and the readiness for war have passed, as if paradise has finally been built, as if she sits across from her grandmother.

Pilot

RUSSIA

Two Years before Her Fall

June 1941 to March 1942

She Held On to a Fragment

When the war began, Lily was in Moscow. The weather was mild that first day of summer in '41. Her sleeves were rolled up as she listened to the announcement that came through the loudspeakers of the flying club. At four a.m., the German Fascists had crossed the border into the Soviet Union. The truth could only be understood in the spaces between words. Tanks were rolling across the flat plains of the Ukraine as if Soviet weapons were no more than tinsel that caught on their treads and turrets. The western half of the Soviet Union was falling under occupation. Its slaughtered children were the gravel over which tanks moved east.

By mid-October, the German army was within sight of Moscow, and the formation of the women's air regiments was announced with a call for volunteers. Interviews were taking place in the Palace of Red Aviation on the outskirts of the capital. Here, in the only imperial palace that remained, Napoleon had watched Moscow burn rather than give in to him. Now it housed Zhukovsky Academy, an elite school for military aviation set in a park with a rosy brick tower on each side.

In what had once been a ballroom in the palace, hundreds of young women milled about. These girls who lived for a perfect future, who carried steel girders and installed marble in the subways, these girls whose faces were sooted in mine shafts, who were polar explorers, who'd owned the skies until their skies were stolen from them, were expecting war. They were not expecting humiliation.

Two and a half million of their soldiers had been encircled, captured, and starved. Aircraft had been bombed before they could get off the ground. These girls wanted guns, they wanted revenge.

Behind a closed door off the ballroom was Marina Raskova, pilot and navigator, wearing the Gold Star of a Hero of the Soviet Union. The young women had cut her picture out of newspapers. They'd listened to her broadcasts and watched her on newsreels. Among themselves, they called her Marina; she belonged to them. And soon, they hoped, she'd be their commander.

Those closest to the door waited anxiously for each candidate to emerge and then peppered her with questions. *What was she like? As beautiful as in the pictures? What did she ask? What did she tell you?* Information floated under the vaulted ceiling of the ballroom. Rumours, all rumours, but these girls were used to sifting innuendo and gossip for a hint of the truth.

Before the war, official news was always the same: reports of exceeded quotas and happy peasants on collective farms. Everyone was always cheerful. Everyone sang songs. Everyone was hardy. When people travelled to Moscow, they had to use the published maps of what Moscow would look like when the socialist dream was fully achieved, not as it actually was. If they got lost looking for roads that hadn't yet been built, or fell into the pit of a building that hadn't yet been erected, they were supposed to sing happily and march on without missing a beat.

Male teachers and students watched with bemusement as high-pitched excitement bounced off the walls. Necks were craned, grand staircases ogled. Nerves made girls bite their nails and then clutch their hands behind their backs, hoping their anxiety would go unnoticed. They wore leather flight jackets, blue coveralls. One of the girls had come in an alpine climbing suit to demonstrate her ability to breathe in the thin air of high altitudes. Lily wore the coveralls she'd taken in at the waist and, around her neck, a silk scarf with polka dots.

"Ninety-six!" the student on sentry duty called. The door opened and closed.

Girls studied their application forms. Three hundred flying hours became six hundred, five hundred became eight hundred. Lily considered the possibilities. Her grandmother always said, *Never change anything by more than a letter.* By replacing a 4 with a 5, she'd added an extra hundred flying hours. In her hand she held a fragment of newspaper with a number chalked on it. Her papers were in her satchel: her passport, her reference letters, including one from the secretary of the local Komsomol, the Young Communist League. On the application form, under Relatives with a Criminal Record, she'd put, *None.*

"Ninety-seven!"

"That's me!" Lily shoved her way through the throng. "I'm ninety-seven," she said, and passed over the paper proving it. The sentry ushered her through a doorway and into a small room. As the door closed, the hubbub outside was reduced to the hum of a furnace.

Formerly a powder room, the office was windowless, a whisper of its former decadence in swirls of decorative plaster on the ceiling. In the corner was a flag, on the wall a small portrait of Stalin with a red ribbon around it. Below that was a desk and on the desk a reading lamp. Lily placed her application package there in the pool of light, beside Marina Raskova's illuminated hand. The fingernails were pink and trim.

Lily's eyes moved to the Gold Star on the famous pilot's jacket. She'd got it for navigating the airplane *Rodina*—Motherland—from Moscow to the Pacific: six thousand kilometres non-stop. On the way home the plane had run out of fuel, and before it had crash-landed, destroying the navigator's pod, Marina had had to bail out. For ten days she'd wandered on the taiga, a lone woman without even a compass to guide her, making her way through swamps and woods until she found the rescue team.

She was in uniform, as were two other women seated in chairs to the left and right of the desk. One of them was curvy in her military jacket and leather pants, but downplayed her looks as well as she could with hair severely pulled back and fingertips yellowed from nicotine. The other one was old, maybe even thirty-five, naturally homely and sour-mouthed, and yet with a touch of vanity in her angled beret and expensive boots.

Opposite the desk was a table where an elderly clerk, promoted from groundskeeper, was managing forms and files, officiously opening and closing the drawers of a filing cabinet, which squeaked and slammed. There was a samovar in the corner. On the desk, next to the lamp, was a tea glass in a silver holder. Steam rose as Marina Raskova lifted the glass to take a sip. The office was cold.

"Sit there," said the officer in the beret. She pointed to a three-legged stool in front of the desk. "I am Major Kazarinova." On her chest she wore the Order of Lenin. Rumour had it that such medals had been given out in the years of the Great Purge for denouncing enemies of the people. "This is my sister, Captain Kazarinova, chief of staff for the 122nd Air Group. And Major Marina Mikhailovna Raskova, the commander."

Lily sat on the stool. The legs were almost even. If she didn't fidget and remained calm, it wouldn't rock. "I'm so honoured to meet you, Comrade Raskova," she said.

"Comrade Major!" the older Kazarinova snapped.

"I'm sorry. Comrade Major," Lily corrected.

"All of the female career officers in the air force have been generously allocated to me," Marina said. "I'm so glad that they're here to guide me and turn our volunteers into soldiers." She looked down at the form. "Lydia Vladimirovna Litvyak. In your reference letter, Lily. Which do you prefer?"

"Everyone calls me Lily."

"Good. Then let's just have a bit of a talk, Lily. The recommendation from the Komsomol secretary is all in order. You understand that the 122nd is a training group?"

Lily nodded.

"We're going to start with general assignments. Every volunteer who's accepted will be designated as a pilot, navigator, gunner, mechanic, armourer, or staff. Your aptitude during training will determine your final placement in one of the three women's regiments: fighter, dive-bomber, or night bomber."

"I've got perfect peripheral vision. I should be a fighter pilot." Lily could hear that she sounded too young, too pleading. She'd just turned eighteen, though her papers made her two years older.

"I'll judge how you can best serve your country," Marina said. "And whatever I decide, you'll give your whole heart to it and work hard. Correct?"

"Yes, Comrade Major," she said with as much obedience as she could muster.

"I know you will." Marina's smile could cure frostbite; even the elderly clerk cracked a half smile, suddenly careful to file his papers more quietly. "You're a flight instructor graduated from Kherson, I see. Good aviation school."

"The male pilots I taught are already at the front with less than a quarter of my flight time. It's not fair. I want to go too."

"I understand," Marina said. "But that will soon change. So let's talk about your flying experience. You have over five hundred hours."

"She's young, she's barely got the minimum requirement, and everyone out there wants to be a fighter pilot," Major Kazarinova said, her face made uglier as she frowned. "I didn't leave a unit of accomplished pilots to put up with mediocrity." She turned to pull her jacket off the chair and slip it on. She had the most wonderful box calf boots, and she belted the leather jacket in a stylish way. The scent of lavender powder wafted from her. None of it endeared her to Lily.

"I was born to be a pilot," Lily said.

"Speaking of which, is it possible you made a mistake on your form?" Captain Kazarinova asked, tapping the paper with a yellow finger. "You've written here you were born in 1921. And how propitious, on Aviation Day."

"My passport is right there," Lily said.

Marina slid the passport over to Captain Kazarinova's side of the desk, but she didn't give it a glance. "No father?" she asked.

Lily blushed and shrugged. "My mother is as good as mother and father."

The captain butted out her cigarette and lit another, not shifting her gaze from Lily's burning face.

"My parents are divorced. I don't know where he is," Lily said. As long as she wore his watch, his heart must still beat somewhere.

"What are you thinking, Miley?" Major Kazarinova asked her younger sister.

"The candidate's name." Captain Kazarinova cleared her throat, but her voice was still hoarse, a rusted nail poking its way through the shredded sole of an old boot. "I recognize it."

Lily didn't move. She didn't blink. She didn't cough. Only her thoughts raced, her neck pulsing under the silk scarf. They knew she was a liar. She'd be disgraced. Her family would lose everything, and she'd be sent to a forced labour camp in the far north to dig in ice with her bare hands. Somehow they'd found out—her origins were tainted, her biography stained.

Soviet children were raised by their grandmothers because parents worked and studied, improving themselves while they built a socialist utopia, and Lily's family was the perfect example of the new equality. Her Russian Orthodox grandmother kept religious icons, which were forbidden, hidden in a cupboard. She had perfect grammar, recited Pushkin, and taught Lily to read. After she died,

Lily's Jewish grandmother—her father's mother—came to Moscow from the Ukraine, hid her Sabbath candlesticks in the same place, and taught Lily everything else. Grandma Rose had bright button eyes, she wore a blue kerchief, and she could speak many languages, all of them with gusto and an intimate knowledge of the vulgarities.

Lily's mother managed a shop, and her father was an engineer designing railway parts. Nothing was more important than Stalin's trains! After a while they were able to move out of the communal apartment they shared with other families because they were assigned their very own flat with three rooms and a kitchen. The janitor of their new building liked to hook his finger in little girls' blouses and lift their skirts with the handle of a mop. He had warty fingers, and he smelled like bleach. Lily couldn't avoid him altogether, and one night after an encounter she was unable to get warm, not even with tea, not even though Grandma Rose stroked Lily's forehead and said she'd take care of everything.

Go to sleep, Grandma Rose said.

Can you tell me a story? Lily asked. *Grandma, tell me about the Russian girl who fought Napoleon.* Grandma Rose made a sound for which there was no Russian word, crankier than a sigh, softer than a groan. *I'll read you something from* The Literary Gazette. *How about the story by Vasily Grossman? It has one of your relatives in it, Litvak the Grocer.*

Lily didn't want to hear about pathetic Jewish relatives. The world hated the Russians too, but they had the Red Army, which protected all Soviets, even the minorities in their native costumes. *A Russian story*, she said.

When her grandmother replied, her voice was whispery. *That you can learn in school. I'll tell you a secret I never told anyone because I swore I'd say nothing. Just between you and me, I met a Vila. Do you know what that is? Shh, keep your voice down. A Vila is a spirit of the air. When she sings, the wind blows. If she dances with a man, he dies. That's her vengeance, because the Vila was once a woman who fell for any pretty thing a man gave her.* . . .

The janitor was fired—her country protected the innocent—and in time Lily nearly forgot him. When she was fourteen, her father was given a holiday spot for his family in a resort for employees who made significant contributions to the Department of Railroads and Transportation. Under the August sun, they swam in clear water. Her little brother, Yuri, caught a fish and fell out of a boat. Lily returned home with a tan and a bottle of peroxide. She was an ordinary teenager, going to movies with her friends, complaining about teachers, free with her opinions. She bleached her hair, read fashion articles, sewed her own clothes, filled notebooks with poems and pictures of aviators cut from the newspapers, hated the word *no*.

There were flying clubs everywhere—Stalin loved aviators. He kissed them on the cheek and gave them gold medals. Pilots were heroes and aircraft the future. Students flocked to the clubs. Lily was too young to enrol, but she persuaded the instructor to take her up anyway, though he wouldn't let her try a solo until she brought proof of age, minimum sixteen. She had to fly, she'd die if she didn't, or she'd run away, and she cried bitter tears until Grandma Rose agreed to help. It was only later that Lily realized her grandmother had had her own reasons.

They went to a records office. Over the entrance, a tattered banner flapped: *Life has become better; life has become merrier.* The man in charge had a grandmother too, and it just so happened they were old acquaintances. Some rubles changed hands. Letters vanished and reappeared, transformed. Lily Litvak was officially Lidya Litvyak, age sixteen, with her own passport, which was the required proof of identification for every adult citizen. Lily's grandmother wouldn't say why her name had been changed, only, *A good lie is ninety percent true. Changing a letter here and there can mean everything.*

Lily flew solo for the first time. She felt no separation between herself and her aircraft. She was winged, and the sky was endless.

It was 1937.

There had been purges before, the removal of bad elements. But this was different. First there was ethnic cleansing. Poles, Germans, Finns, Estonians, Latvians, Chinese, Kurds, Koreans, and Iranians were exiled to Siberia. There were other enemies of the people too. An especially large number of them were found among railroad employees, also statisticians, writers, actors, artists, astronomers (sunspot development wasn't Marxist), composers, weather fore-casters, Buddhist lamas in Mongolia, Old Bolsheviks, and officers of the Red Army—particularly those in the air force. (Since show-ing initiative had become a cause for arrest, the remaining officers tended to be indecisive. However, their prospects for promotion were excellent.)

Those arrested were tortured for more names. Passports had to be carried at all times since having no proof of identification was sufficient grounds for arrest. Anyone with a grudge could denounce a workmate or neighbour. Conversations were reported. Jokes were dangerous. The misuse of Stalin's name or image was a terrible crime. Anyone could be listening. They were all listening.

In the night, Lily woke up to pounding on the door of a nearby apartment, and the next day there was tape on it, sealing it off. Arrests were like a contagious illness. Everyone in a factory or everyone in a family came down with it. First an uncle, then a cousin, then a brother, then you discovered that in the night you'd caught it yourself. Some were executed, others sentenced to hard labour. Children were taken away when parents were arrested: teenagers went to forced labour camps for delinquents, and younger siblings were sent to orphanages, where they were beaten to teach them what they deserved. Anyone with a convicted relative was relegated to the dirtiest work, the worst living conditions. Lily tore pages out of her notebooks, poems she'd copied from the books of poets who were now banned, and she felt guilty that she couldn't erase the memorized words from her mind.

One day she arrived home from the flying club to find her father packing. He was being transferred to Leningrad, away from the capital, the centre of life where only the most trusted men could remain.

You have a good job at the shop, he was saying to Mama. *You have the apartment. You'll manage.*

The apartment isn't important, she said, though it meant everything to her.

Nobody noticed Lily standing near the door, her school satchel in her hand.

Her father said, *We've discussed this already. You've got to divorce me. The last man who had my job disappeared.*

Mother said, *Not now. Not yet. I'll wait to hear from you. See how you settle in.*

He was insistent, her mild father, slamming shut the suitcase. *No. Apply for the divorce,* he said. *If nothing happens to me, then you'll come. It'll be as good as having an affair. We'll marry again.*

He turned and saw Lily huddled against the wall. He took his watch off his wrist and put it on hers, still warm from his skin.

Grandma Rose arranged everything for the divorce. So there wouldn't be any doubt of its validity, because she was Papa's mother, as soon as the divorce was final, she abandoned them too, going back to Zhytomyr, her hometown in the Ukraine. She kissed Lily on the cheek. She left behind her candlesticks, her advice, a knack for picking up languages, a few stories, some naughty songs, the memory of her voice.

NKVD men (secret police at least as adept at extracting information as the Gestapo, having had twenty more years of experience at it) arrived in the customary dark car. When they came for Lily and her mother, they said that Vladimir Litvak had been charged under article 58 (specifically sections 6, 7, 9, and 11: espionage, sabotage of transport—the usual). He'd been convicted and sentenced to ten years of corrective labour camps without the right of correspondence. There would be no communication. Not a letter from him, none permitted to him.

It wasn't night. That's what kept Lily's mother sane as they held hands in the back of the car making tracks in the snow. They weren't being arrested. Her brother wasn't being removed from school to be sent to an orphanage. There was no tape on their door. Not yet. And even though her grandmother had drilled her on what to say in the event, Lily was confident that the authorities would soon realize the impossibility of the charges against her father. There were enemies of the people, the number was unfathomable, but her father wasn't one of them.

They were questioned by the NKVD for hours, held in separate interrogation rooms. Under the bright light that made her eyes overflow, Lily answered every question the way she'd practised it:

My parents are divorced. I couldn't stand their fighting. No, not because of politics. Because my mother didn't get along with my grandmother. When he went to Leningrad, that was the end of it. The trials are scary. So many traitors! I don't know any of my father's friends. He was always working. I don't understand politics, I like poetry. I want to be an aviator like Marina Raskova.

After they were released, her mother never spoke of it. What good would it do?

Lily waited for her father to return. Unlike America, where Black men were lynched, her country was fair and free. It was run by a single party, the Communist Party, which loved the people. As soon as the authorities realized that her father was innocent of any wrongdoing, they'd send him home. She imagined it would be at night, just like the arrests, and she stayed awake, waiting for the click of the door and the sound of his voice, his slight accent, the seriousness, the quiet affection. Sometimes she thought she heard him and jumped out of bed, startling her mother. Once she stubbed her toe, outraged at the small injury, as if her toe or the edge of the bed was keeping her father away. Eventually she realized he wasn't coming back. The day she was certain of it, her mother went to work as usual, her brother to school, and Lily got dressed, surprised that her face looked no different. She'd become two people: the inner part of her shocked with grief, the outer part mechanically carrying her to the flying club.

There was no interrogation in the air, no demand to name names. The sky didn't care about her family tree or the stain on her social origins. It was a poem of wind and gravity, and in it, she belonged to the universe.

A few months later, Lily applied for membership in the Young Communist League, which was mandatory for admission to aviation school. She was accepted first into one, then the other. If anyone found out about her father's conviction, she'd be expelled and exiled to the cold places treacherous people were sent. She kept to herself and didn't make friends, wearing her loneliness like a fashionable coat. What other choice did she have? She loved her country, but it didn't love her.

"Do you know her, Miley?" Major Kazarinova asked her sister.

"I know something, Tamara. It's just on the tip of my tongue."

"You couldn't," Lily protested. "I'm not anybody."

The three officers assessed her with their gazes, a troika of judges with special powers to sentence. It was an old story.

"Don't be so modest," Captain Kazarinova said. Her tone wasn't unfriendly. But that was how someone got to you, lulling you into lowering your guard in the hope that if you gave something, anything, they'd go away. They never went away. Not without you.

The clerk unrolled brown paper, which crackled as he flattened it beneath the sausage that was concealed within. He began slicing it with a small knife. The smell of spiced meat made Lily's stomach grumble. It'd been a while since she'd had meat as anything more than a flavouring for potato soup.

"The name is familiar to me too," Marina said. "And I think I know why. That article on flight instructors in *Airplane Magazine*. Aren't you the girl who broke the record for longest continuous flight instruction?"

Lily nodded, her mouth dry.

"How long?" Marina asked, with what seemed to be genuine interest.

"I flew with students for eight hours and forty minutes," she said. "Each flight was twenty minutes. I had no breaks between them. I didn't need any, because I love being in the air."

"Well, Lily . . . I think we can make you a pilot." There was no mistaking the warmth of Marina's voice now. It made the sisters roll their eyes: so much fame; so little discipline.

"As an instructor pilot in a biplane, she's useful enough," Major Kazarinova said. "But she's too small for combat. Would her feet even reach the pedals of more advanced aircraft? And Miley has a point about the birthdate in Litvyak's papers. She seems very young. This isn't a kindergarten, it's war."

"The girls are as patriotic as their brothers. Nobody asks *them* too many questions about their age," Marina said. "But even so, you must tell me the truth, Lily." She was looking straight at her, pilot to pilot, as if to plead, *Help me out here.*

"I may be young and I may be small, but I'm Russian," Lily said. The words she needed came easily. Hadn't she heard the speeches, seen the posters, cut out newspaper reports, written everything down in her notebook? "The Fascist enslavers have no idea what's in store for them. Look at my hands." She held out callused palms. "When the Germans were bombing Moscow, I stood on the roof to throw off any incendiary sticks that landed there. I dug anti-tank trenches. That's what a bunch of girls did. And I dug as much dirt as anyone for the Great Patriotic War. But I'm a much better pilot than I am a ditchdigger. It would be a shame to waste my talent."

Marina laughed. "All right. Let's find out what you've got." *Pilot*, she wrote on Lily's application. "Take this paper to the second floor. Get your uniform and train ticket. We're leaving from the Belorussia railway station tomorrow. Don't be late."

Major Kazarinova slurped her tea. She glanced at her sister, who was making notes. In picture books, a virtuous child might be rewarded in summertime with a miraculous hill of snow and a sled to slide down it. The army, however, ran on other principles.

Lily had a final meal at home. There was meat in the stew, and she ate quickly. Her little brother, Yuri, nervously scratched the back of his neck. The *Moonlight Sonata* was playing on the gramophone. On the cabinet was a postcard: *My darlings, no news worth telling. Don't keep the candlesticks for my benefit. Lily be brave. Yuri listen to your mother. Remember that I love you all.* The postcard was stamped, *Zhytomyr Ghetto, Ukraine.*

Her mother helped her pack. Lily put two silk scarves in the bag. Her mother added wool socks. Lily added Pushkin's *Collected Poems* and *The Language of Flowers* and a notebook. Her mother tucked in gloves and a sewing kit. When they were done, Lily put on the oversized uniform. Her mother knelt at her feet, pinning the hem, then stood to mark shoulders and sleeve length. She stroked Lily's cheek as if to memorize her skin, then pulled away, embarrassed by the display. All night they sewed, straining their eyes in the light from the one lamp allowed during the semi-blackout.

Overnight, winter arrived, unexpectedly and early, with air so cold it pinched Lily's nostrils as she left the apartment, swinging her bag, and walked to the train station. There she waited, and when evening came, she was still waiting.

In the darkening sky, barrage balloons floated like an aerial conference of whales. Every tree and every statue was grey, the train station's tower, its spire, the wings to the left and right of the grounds, the leaded windows bleeding with the falling sun. The temperature was still dropping and the newly recruited women of the 122nd Air Group shivered in their summer uniforms. The government had already been evacuated. Factories had been dismantled, machinery parts shipped east to be reassembled beyond reach of the enemy.

The Germans were coming, and in a panic, Moscow gagged, spilling its citizens all over the pavement and across the platforms of the train station. Handcarts, horse carts, wrapped bundles, babies, kerchiefed babushkas, women with mouths extended as they screamed for their children to stay close, shabby old men trembling with weakness, trolleys of equipment, pallets of bricks, a honking car with a frustrated chauffeur leaning out the window, a shipping container of left-foot galoshes. As ice formed on the tracks, a hundred trains carried away 150,000 civilians, who plied fists and lowered heads to push their way to the inside or outside of the train, latching on to every possible surface, including the roof. The women of the Air Group were leaves swept up by the skirling wind of sound: wheels on metal, tin on cement, split cardboard expelling worldly goods, the rise and fall of voices deep and shrill, words unintelligible, only the intention clear. Families shouted, cried, screamed, scrambled, pushed, tripped, squeezed, dragged. An old man, late to the fray, a vodka stink of fortification about him, cursed in gutter Russian. The darkness was lumpy with cowardice.

While the women of the 122nd took shelter inside the train station, Captain Kazarinova ordered Lily Litvyak and Katie Budanova to stand guard over the Air Group's mattresses and packing cases, which were stacked up at the far end of the platform. They trotted along together, led by the captain's kerosene lamp, and then she left them at their post. Even here, the racket was audible, and the wind was more biting. It carried the flak smell of bleach and nail polish and the sound of enemy fighters beyond the Moscow River. Searchlights criss-crossed the sky.

Katie slouched against the stack of mattresses while she lit a cigarette, cupping it against the wind. She was a tall woman in her mid-twenties, an experienced pilot who worked in Moscow and had flown in the annual air show. She wore a greatcoat, which she'd inherited from her father along with an aquiline nose, her long chin, and a liking for well-built women. This preference wasn't exactly a crime. Homosexuality—the male variety—was against the law. But Soviet women were supposed to be tough, weaned on the milk of glaciers, and nobody much cared what they did in their spare time as long as they were discreet and didn't wipe their rear ends with the part of the newspaper that had Stalin's picture in it.

"You want a smoke?" Katie asked. "American. Good cigarettes."

"So it's true that they're giving us supplies. Our enemies."

"Former enemies."

"Still, I don't know that I'd put my mouth on it," Lily said.

Katie laughed. She was warm in her greatcoat. "You'd be missing out. They're lending us aircraft too."

"Who'd have guessed?" Lily stamped her feet and rubbed her hands to keep from freezing. "Nice coat."

"My father left it to me. That and my nose. Would you say it's a Roman nose?"

"At least you got the coat."

Katie laughed again. Maybe the night wasn't going to be as long as she'd expected.

"I wish I could smoke," Lily said. "It would be something to do while guarding mattresses with my life. But my mother would kill me."

"If we talk, the time will go faster," Katie said.

"About what?"

"Anything you want."

"How about a story?"

"Is it about love? Tell me it's about love." Katie's voice was a cheerful wall. No one would know what she might be thinking behind it.

"I don't like love stories," Lily said.

"Why not?"

"If it's true, it's sad. And if it's happy, it's a lie."

"Ha! You've got that right. Old stories are the best."

"How old?"

"Ancient. Before the Revolution."

"I could tell you about my grandmother running away."

"What from?"

"Boredom," Lily said. "Being poor is so boring. She came from a nothing place."

"I know what that's like. I grew up in Smolensk."

"The city?"

"No, the countryside." It was a region known for resistance to government policy, its stubborn peasants none too keen on Communism. However, all that had been forgiven, at least for the time being, because the same peasants had held out against the Nazis longer than anyone had expected. "I moved to Moscow before you needed a residency permit, and I started working as a carpenter in an aircraft factory when I was fourteen. But we were talking about old stories."

"Actually, it's a little bit about love . . ."

"There you go!"

"My grandmother was a wild thing," Lily said. "Always running away with some boy. First an anarchist and then a socialist."

"Some grandmother. Mine was a virgin for five years after she got married."

"And she told you?"

"She was proud of it. Hoped I'd be the same. But she doesn't have to worry. I'm never getting married."

"Me neither," Lily said.

"Why not?" Katie wore her cap low over her forehead. It half-hid her eyes, and she bent her head to light another cigarette. "You're kind of small, but you're not ugly or anything."

Lily didn't take offence. "I told you, love is sad. People die, they disappear."

"Who said anything about love? I was talking about marriage. Anyway, you were telling me about your grandmother."

"She fell for someone who saved her from a riot, and he convinced her to get married."

"Your grandfather?"

"Yes."

"Finally!"

"They went to his home in the Ukraine, and he fought for Communism in 1905." That was the first revolution, a good one even though it was crushed. The grandfather's honour would be the family's.

"Did he go to prison?" Katie asked.

"He died before he was caught. Then the Tsar's soldiers came looking for his family, and my grandmother hid in the woods with my father. I don't know if you'll believe this . . ."

"At night, you can believe anything."

"A spirit protected them from the soldiers."

"What kind? A wood nymph?"

"No, a spirit of the air. A Vila."

"I never met one of those. But I saw Koschei the Deathless." In folk tales, the villainous Koschei couldn't be killed because his soul resided outside his body, hidden within layers in a buried chest.

"You're making that up."

"No more than you. I'll just tell you that Koschei didn't look anything like the pictures. But it was him all right. Come over here. It's making me cold looking at you." Sitting on a crate, Katie pulled her arms out of the coat and slung it over her shoulders, opening it for Lily to slip in beside her.

In the morning, Lily was stiff and tired, relieved when another pair of recruits arrived to take over guard duty. Wanting tea, Lily went into the train station, and while she was at the samovar, Captain Kazarinova pulled Katie aside. They were still speaking when Lily felt the rumble of the locomotive edging down the tracks. It stopped at the siding where the 122nd Air Group lined up: three hundred young women, sixty of them pilots, a third of those destined for the women's fighter regiment.

They boarded the train, which then made its slow way down, away from the front, following the Volga River. As they proceeded southward, the weather changed. Winter receded; snow turned to rain and fog. The women disembarked at Engels, a small port town upriver from Stalingrad, known for its beer and its German population, which had been exiled to Siberia when the war began. The first order of business was a severe haircut at the military school's barbershop, and then formal induction into the Workers' and Peasants' Red Army.

Along with the rest, Lily stood at attention in the parade ground. When it was her turn, she recited the Red Army oath, swearing to be brave, to obey, to keep the country's secrets, to sacrifice blood and life for victory. With as much earnestness as every other recruit and maybe a bit more, she swore, *If I break this, my sacred oath, let me suffer the harsh punishment of law, the total hatred and contempt of my people.*

Her Eyes Were the Plane's Eyes

Military Aviation School No. 14 consisted of an airfield and a collection of low wooden barracks, which housed the dorms, dining room, reading room, classrooms, and gym. The instructors lived with their wives in town, as did the school administrator. Directly across the river from Engels and connected by a bridge was the city of Saratov, an industrial centre that shipped machine parts to the tank factories in Stalingrad. Every plant that had manufactured machinery in peacetime had been converted to military purposes. In Stalingrad, tractor factories made tanks, and in Saratov, the old harvester factory was producing a newly designed fighter plane— the Yak-1. Marina Raskova had secured a promise that her girls would receive the first completed batch of planes.

Lily was relieved to learn that the older Kazarinova sister had duties that would take her away for some time. However, as chief of staff, the younger Kazarinova was everywhere, shadowing students and observing them. They had instructors from the aviation school, but Marina Raskova oversaw their progress. She taught some classes herself, reviewed the tests that the girls wrote in others, woke the recruits for surprise drills, admonished and encouraged them.

The girls slept in bunk beds erected for them in the gym. At the front of the gym was a piano, which Marina played at night, and sometimes Katie stood beside her, singing her comrades to sleep. Every few days Marina spent extra time with the most promising of them. Lily longed for her turn, but it never came. Classes filled twelve hours each day: navigation, aerial gunnery, aerodynamics, meteorology, combat tactics, instrumentation, engines, and history of the Communist Party. They had flight training in U-2s, First World War–style biplanes that were still used for supply drops and lifting out the injured. Instructors sat in the back of the open cockpit, shouting instructions into the headsets. In November, snow fell. Eyelashes were laced with ice.

Aerobatics

"Every move is intended either to put you in a better position to shoot down your opponent or to move you out of a position where you're vulnerable to him. Let's take the barrel roll. In combat, the purpose of the helical roll around the straight flight path is to slow forward motion. . . ."

They rose in the dark and marched to the dining room. They marched to morning classes still in darkness, and in the evening they returned in darkness to the barracks. If snow fell too thickly for flying, they were taken out for more marching drills in a darkness that was blistering white. In the reading room where they studied, the political officer tucked her large self into a chair now at one table, now at another. It was her job to make sure their thoughts didn't stray from Communist Party doctrine, but she also shared the sweets that the top brass got when there was an important visitor. The girls cut their treats into smaller pieces, and everyone had a bite of the future. They came from all over the Soviet Union: Ukrainians, Russians, Tatars, Turks, Armenians, aged eighteen to thirty. And while they practised the skills they'd need to defend their country, they mixed languages, they mixed customs, they shared stockings and cautions about sex, formed cliques, gossiped, and reluctantly acquired army discipline.

The standard-issue uniform included foot wrappings, rectangular pieces of cloth that were supposed to be wound around a soldier's feet and worn under boots. Girls caught wearing socks were reprimanded. As were those who kept perfume in the cockpit.

Or forgot to salute. Or danced in the reading room. Captain Kazarinova was on the alert for insufficiently patriotic behaviour, always making notes in her grey notebook.

But these young women were used to being watched, and soon they'd be in combat, where they could die for their country. So they danced, and when their favourite record, "Rio Rita," wore out, they got another. Katie made Lily learn the tango. They laughed because they were still alive.

Meteorology

"Cirrus are plumy, translucent ice clouds, as the name implies, elevation six to twelve thousand metres. Weather implications: Cirrus clouds don't in themselves bring rain; however, if you see them massed, it could indicate an approaching storm system and you need to be wary of lightning. . . ."

While Lily studied, she sewed. The small, even stitches affixed the facts to her brain as if her grandmother were still quizzing her on capitals of the world or German grammar while writing a letter for an illiterate neighbour or chopping onions for stew or singing cheeky songs in five languages. Five types of cirrus clouds: horse's tail, hooked, opaque, towers, woolly. Scientific names: *Cirrus fibratus, uncinus, spissatus, castellanus, floccus.*

Lily sewed for the other girls, taking on anything she could make more beautiful. A few of them were dating men in town or across the river in Saratov. They asked Lily to put in a surreptitious tuck to make a uniform more attractive, turn a wide skirt into a narrow one, add ribbon to shirt cuffs, make a handkerchief or a scarf with the fabric they brought her. A couple of them, Val and dark-haired Claudia, stood on either side of Lily for a snapshot, which she sent home in a letter. She wrote to her mother about her *comrades*, a good Communist word that implied no unnecessary closeness.

Lily's stitches were so tiny it was hard to believe that eyes could see them and hands make them. The more she sewed, the better marks she got. The other pilots caught on to this, and since they were all competing for places in the fighter regiment, they stopped bringing her any sewing jobs. Lily had nothing else to soothe the raw edges of herself.

When they were grounded because of a snowstorm, she cut the lambswool out of her boots and sewed it to the collar of her jacket. Fluffy, white, ringleted, it suited her well. All the girls said so until she got in trouble for it, and then they looked away as if she had a venereal sore on her face. For mutilating State property, Lily got a reprimand and a night in the guardhouse to reverse the damage with scissors and a dull sewing needle.

There was no chair in the cell, and so she sat on the hard floor, dutifully restoring her jacket to its original ugliness, her fingers cold and clumsy, hating herself. The best pilots in the Air Group had years of experience performing aerobatics in air parades. In her written work she did as well, but not in the air. Whenever an instructor spoke to her through the headset, she responded a speck too late, unnerved by him watching her from behind. Now her superiors would think her frivolous. She had lied to get here. Maybe she didn't deserve it. What if her father really had committed sabotage and she was no better?

When she heard a rap at the window, she stood on tiptoe to open it, surprised that anyone had thought of her alone in the night or cared. It made her divided self glad, and fearful of the gladness.

"You didn't get dinner," Katie said. Her nose was red from the cold.

"Part of the punishment."

"I saved you some potatoes."

"Thanks."

"I wrapped them in a handkerchief." Katie reached into the deep pocket of her greatcoat.

"I'll give it back."

"All right." Katie passed the bundle through the window but didn't turn away, not even though it would be a black mark on her record to be caught interfering with discipline. "You don't wear lipstick."

"It's greasy."

"And you don't suck up to Marina Raskova like the other girls."

"Not in my nature."

"So I don't get it. Are you happy now? Was this worth satisfying your vanity?"

"I'm not that vain."

"Then what?"

"Sometimes I . . . worry about my family. It's like a toothache and I have to pull out the tooth."

"With your bare hands?"

"In Siberia, people go insane from toothache."

"Next time come to me. I'll pull it for you."

"And report me?"

"Only afterward." Katie wiped her drippy nose with the back of her sleeve.

"Then I will."

"I'm holding you to it." Katie passed a small lump over the windowsill. A rock of sugar. "I snuck this for you too."

"You should go," Lily said. "Someone might see you talking to me."

Katie moved away from the guardhouse, into the shadows cast by the moon on the flat field of snow.

Combat Tactics

"You haven't been in combat yet, so all you want to hear about are flying tricks. But when you're in the air and the enemy is all around, you mean more to each other than your own family. Shooting down an enemy aircraft isn't as important as watching out for your comrades. . . ."

Another snowstorm turned into days of blizzards. The inactivity drove Lily crazy. In the reading room, she was cutting up an old dress just to have something she could put back together when she heard the news: a pilot trying to reach Engels was lost in the steppe, downed by a broken propeller. Whoever it was would freeze to death, because nobody could bring a replacement under the no-fly order. The girls wondered who the lost pilot was, if he had a wife or a son. They shook their heads. It was tragic. Lily nodded and said little. But as she plied her scissors, she was thinking that an enemy of the people wouldn't risk his life and his rank to save someone. If she went, didn't that mean something? About herself, about her father?

No one except Katie noticed her slip out, and she followed Lily as she fetched her winter flying gear.

"What do you think you're doing?" Katie asked.

Lily said, "We're fellow pilots. He's looking up at the sky, waiting for someone to come."

"You won't make it."

"What if it was one of us? You or me. Falling asleep in the snow. Turning to ice under the wing of the plane."

They were raised on self-sacrifice. It was expected, even taken for granted; the question was only whether it had been authorized. So Katie said, "But there's a fly ban. I'll have to report you."

"Then keep your promise," Lily said. "Do it after I take off."

The airfield was a ghost of itself in a cemetery of white burial mounds. Katie held Lily's shoulders and asked if she was sure. Lily nodded. She didn't speak—it was too cold, the wind too harsh. They exhumed the last U-2 in the front row, which was farthest from the barracks, and when it was cleared of snow, Katie stood at the nose and Lily took her seat in the cockpit.

Katie shouted the old hunter's formula for luck, "Ни пуха, ни пера!" *Neither fur nor feathers.*

"To the devil!" Lily yelled back.

"Throttle closed! Brakes set! Mag off!" Katie called, and Lily raised her hand at each check. Katie pulled the propeller through a rotation to lubricate the cylinder walls and draw fuel. Lily still had time to jump out of the plane. Go to her next class. Avoid trouble. Act like everyone else. "Contact!"

Turn the mixture to rich. Throttle open. Feet on the rudder pedals, hand on the stick. Magneto switch on. She saluted, and Katie rotated the propeller with enthusiasm. The engine caught, she heard the familiar *trrrr trrrr.* Katie kicked away the chocks and moved away. Lily taxied into position, the airplane's skis skimming the white crust layered with fresh powder. The spare propeller blade was in the front seat, the weight balancing hers. There was no air-to-ground radio in the plane; as soon as she was airborne, no one could order her back. Katie raised her arms and waved. *Go!*

Lily watched the airspeed indicator. Ten knots, twenty knots, fifty knots, wings spread to split the air, pressure building below, decreasing above, ready to lift, needing to lift. She pulled back on the stick and the nose rose easily, naturally. Luck was with her—the wind had dropped—and as the plane gently climbed, the receding ground turned into ribbons and squares as if that was its true nature, not road, river, and barracks. She waggled her wings to say goodbye. Katie was a toy, then a dot, then nobody, and Lily was alone with the sky, unchaperoned as she crossed the Volga.

Her wings were fluttering. Her hands and feet moved without thought, adjusting the trim and shifting the stick to compensate until there was an equal amount of sky between the upper wing and the horizon, left and right. These were her elevators, her ailerons, her rudders. Her eyes were the plane's eyes, and her heart made the engine thrum. It had no life without her. The trail of smoke was the breath of a winged woman who lived in the sky and moved by force of thought. She had no word for this feeling. Only the need to come back to it whatever the cost.

Visibility was negligible. Cloud cover was low, uniform. She needed to get below the cloud, but she descended into a strong wind that bounced her up and down, wrenching the stick. She held on, keeping level while marking the featureless ground, and then climbed, trying to get above the turbulence, eight hundred metres, a thousand, twelve hundred, sliding on the ramp of the cloud. It could be two thousand metres thick, and her ceiling was three. It had a horizontal structure. Nimbostratus. No sub-varieties. The wind was less erratic here. She'd need to descend again in order to resume visual inspection, but first she wanted to get into the general vicinity of where the plane went down. Eighteen minutes out, she moved lower again to search for the black splinter in the snowy steppe. Pressure on the right rudder as she banked, release rudder and shift the stick right. She began her first circuit. The horizon tipped right, tipped left as she wiped her goggles with her scarf. On the second circuit, tightening the circle, she saw what she was looking for, a dot on the horizon, and now that she knew where she was headed, she pulled back on her stick to get above the volatile air currents.

Then she heard it: wires between her double wings were humming with the urgency of a telegraph. Airspeed was dropping. She yawed left, overbalanced, rolling. Her right wing was up, her nose was down, and she was flipping around like a top. All she could see was a twister of snow, and she had seconds to decide. In an unplanned spin, the pilot should immediately bail. If she split herself from the plane, relieved of the falling weight, the nose might come up, her other half might descend and live, or it could shatter its bones against the ground. If she dismembered herself like that, what outcome? Two lost pilots, a pair of splinters in the snowy waste. Another way? There was something her aerobatics instructor had mentioned.

She let go of the controls, the engine idled as she dropped. If it was a mistake, it was too late, she couldn't bail out now. The ground was rushing toward her. She tried to maintain her consciousness against the heavy pressure of gravitational forces multiplied by acceleration. Her head rattled. She was sorry that she wore her father's watch. She should have left it behind for Yuri. And then the nose lifted. Full opposite rudder against the yaw. Elevator control forward. She adjusted, shifted, accelerated, combusted fuel.

She descended to five hundred metres, scanning the unmarked wilderness. There it was, the black dot that shouldn't be there. As she approached, it became an oblong shape with something moving out from under the wing. She made a three-point landing, and she became, again, a woman, in a plane, on skis.

The downed pilot was slighter than Lily expected, the face behind the scarf visibly female, and her identity became apparent as soon as she pulled down her scarf to speak. Major Kazarinova. She looked as irritable as ever.

"About time," she said.

"Comrade Major!" Lily saluted. This was not the tragic figure she'd imagined, but a strict army officer—and how would Major Kazarinova react to a subordinate breaking rules?

"What took so long?" she asked.

"Poor weather conditions," Lily said nervously.

"Let's get the propeller out of your U-2. Hurry up! There isn't much time before it gets dark."

Not owing a lowly private thanks or an explanation of her predicament, Major Kazarinova offered neither. But through her complaints, while they worked together on replacing the U-2's damaged propeller, Lily gleaned that her superior officer had been involved in testing new aircraft, had been injured in a raid, and was none too pleased at being recalled to the Women's Air Group where, as she put it, "every stupid girl who's read *War and Peace* thinks she knows how to face combat."

They worked in tandem, Major Kazarinova barking instructions. As the temperature dropped, they wrapped their scarves around their faces, leaving only slits for their eyes. Lily's scarf was stiff; with every breath she melted it a little, the wet wool chafing her chin as the new propeller was attached. She took off a glove only for a moment to grip small pieces in her fingers, holding the wrench tightly so she wouldn't lose it in the snow. The final bolts were tightened. Major Kazarinova checked Lily's work.

"Adequate. I see you've learned something at that school," she said.

"I hope so," Lily said with relief.

"The instructors must be very patient."

Major Kazarinova climbed into the cockpit. Lily stood at the aircraft's nose and rotated the propeller, priming the engine. She raised her arm to indicate contact. Major Kazarinova taxied away and flew up into the wind. Only then did Lily realize she was stranded.

Unless her U-2's wheels were blocked by chocks and the tail tied down, if she primed her engine by herself, the plane would start moving before she got back into the cockpit. Lily hadn't thought to bring chocks. There was nothing onto which she could hook the tail. She tried running to the cockpit, setting switches, and returning to the propeller to rotate it. The engine caught and the machine rolled away, the tail rising up and shaking as she trotted along behind, head bent into the wind. When she caught up to her plane, it was half on its side, nose down in a slight gully. She stood and squinted against the blowing snow. Night was coming, bringing with it a cold that would freeze her in moments.

The steppe stretched to the horizon, marked only by a scattering of bushes and the parallel furrows of the plane's skis. Beyond the horizon, the steppe continued for thousands of kilometres to the mountains. Before the war, she'd thought nothing was worse than a nighttime knock at the door. After the Germans invaded, she'd believed nothing could be worse than to be captured by them. But there in the twilight of a white, indifferent earth with no sound but the wind whipping snow to create tunnels and drifts, she knew— for a brief time—the value of any companionship, however feeble, however untrustworthy.

She had to keep moving or she'd freeze. So she walked with no destination in mind. She walked so that, if death came for her, she'd fall into it, exhausted, and not hand herself over a piece at a time, a frostbitten nose, a blackening hand, a mind falling in and out of unconsciousness. Her feet didn't feel cold anymore, they burned. To keep herself awake, she recited Pushkin, her cracked lips moving against her scarf: *The sky concealed by stormy mist, a snowy maelstrom spins* . . .

The earth wasn't as flat as it seemed. There were small rises and dips like the one that had tipped her plane. By the demand on her lungs, she thought she was climbing a low-angled but extended ridge of land, the incline so gentle that she wondered if the rapid beating of her heart was just a signal that she'd had it. But then the muscles in her legs shifted, and she was walking downward, and at the edge of her vision she saw something in the snow, a dark spot moving like a friend. She closed her eyes, made herself count to sixty, then opened them. The black dot was still there, maybe bigger, it was hard to say. She closed her eyes and counted to two hundred. When she looked again, the dot was an unidentifiable shape. She counted to three hundred, and this time she opened her eyes and shouted to the dark shape that was growing larger, and she kept shouting and shouting until she could only whimper hoarsely, "Comrade, Comrade," afraid it wouldn't find her if she stopped calling.

Coming out of the snow was a sleigh pulled by a camel, a golden lusciousness, and she was overcome by covetousness for a camel hair coat, a blanket, its shaggy throat to lean against. Its feet were wider than a horse's. The harness was buckled around its front hump, both humps diminished by winter. It bent its head to sniff her as she approached, and its dry breath stank. The driver, a burly man in a fur hat and blue coat, motioned for her to get in. The sleigh was serviceable, a wooden raft on rockers. The driver threw a blanket around her shoulders and offered her a drink from his bottle. She made do with that and his body warmth, not caring how close they had to sit. The blanket smelled like a barn. The camel's odour was worse, and she pinched her nose.

The man nodded sympathetically. "The smell of a camel scares horses," he said. "It's hard to get used to. What are you doing out here?"

"My plane is over there. Somewhere," she said.

"No worries, Citizen."

He had a shaggy, camel-coloured beard, and just before she fell asleep, she wondered if he sheared his camel for it. That was all she knew until he woke her up. He'd stopped in the middle of nowhere. The plane was behind the sleigh, attached to it with long reins. Her rescuer walked away and began digging in the snow with a wooden shovel.

"You're awake," he said. "There's another shovel at your feet. My grandfather's house is under here."

———

There were two rooms. The first was filled with bundles of hay to feed the camel, who contributed in Communist fashion (from each according to his abilities, to each according to his work) by supplying his dung for *kiziak*, which fed the stove in the second room. Lily huddled near the stove with an old man, a middle-aged woman, and the driver of the sleigh. She'd never seen anything like this: a peasant dwelling dug out of the earth. The driver told her that there used to be a hole in the roof for a chimney, but he'd recently installed a pipe—a remarkable improvement, the old man said. The wind rattled the pipe, and, curled up on the platform of the stove, their goat bleated, its legs twitching in disturbed sleep.

The driver's name was Oleg. He was the old man's grandson, the woman's nephew. He had two brothers who were serving in the infantry, or perhaps had served. There'd been no death notice, but they hadn't had a letter from either in months. Oleg would serve too, when he was drafted. His mother had died of one disease, his wife and child of another. These were Lily's people, the peasants for whom she'd sworn an oath.

"Thank you, Uncle, for letting me stay with you," Lily said, and the old man beamed. He was nearly blind with cataracts that clouded his eyes like a dirty sea. He had no teeth, but it was fine because there was nothing worth eating.

The grandfather's saggy chin was lit by the small oil lamp on a barrel next to him. His beard looked like an old woman's, spiky spare hairs springing out here and there. "It's not like the old days. I don't read or write, but they made my Oleg a teacher," he said.

"Is the soup all right?" Oleg asked her.

"Good and hot," Lily said, sipping the carrot broth. In it were a few dried vegetables. "What do you teach?"

"Nothing now. We're at war. So I'm a camel driver."

The grandfather busied himself with repairing a harness, his hands knowing what to do without eyes to assist, educated by long, dark winters in the dugout. The woman carefully cut the buns Lily offered them into equal pieces. No one minded that they came from her coveralls pocket. The old man tore off a bite, rolled it between his fingers, and popped it into his mouth, chewing noisily with his gums.

"You have a good fire," Lily observed, doing her best to keep up the conversation.

"I prepare the *kiziak*," the woman said modestly. She was as wrinkled as her father, only the quantity of her teeth differentiating them in age. "The trick is to make sure it dries completely after you mix the dung with straw. If there's any moisture, it smokes and smells. But dry, it burns beautifully. Your flying school makes good bread. No sawdust in it."

"Oleg taught in the German school," the grandfather said. "No students there now, all exiled to Siberia, or is it Kazakhstan?"

"Shut it, old man," his daughter said.

Sleepily and thoughtless, not considering the implications of what she asked, Lily turned to Oleg. "If I recited a poem in German, could you translate the words that I don't understand?"

He shook his head vigorously, his beard flapping away any notion of connection to exiled enemies. "I only know Russian poems. Classics. From authorized school books, though I don't have any, because they were State property and returned to the central district authority."

"Maybe you want to sleep. I'll make a bed for you on the straw," the woman said, at once pushy and timorous, picking nervously at her skin. "Oleg, go get a bundle and bring it in here."

She began sorting through a pile of rags to find something to cover the straw. Oleg told her to use his greatcoat. Grandfather went on about his wife who made cheese from goat's milk when he was young and they'd had a dozen.

They were all afraid, Lily realized. No one had ever been afraid of her. They glanced at her and away, as though she could scoop up the dugout and squeeze them out between her fingers, dropping them in an Arctic labour camp. There was nothing here she wanted, but if there were, she could have it. And it was tempting to ask for something just to see them give it to her, as if she had the power of an NKVD agent or at least a trusted informant. The worst of it was that the feeling was a pleasant one.

"The government doesn't need my goat," the grandfather said. "What would they do with one little goat?"

His daughter cuffed him on the back of the head. He picked up a hammer, its head wrapped in leather. His hand shook with the weight as he attempted to swing it. There was a scuffle, a curse, no perceptible damage. The old man ordered his daughter to help him outside so he could relieve himself. She offered him a can. The sound of tinkling, the sound of spitting. Soon they all retired for the night on beds of straw. They lay head to head. Someone scratched noisily. They shared breath, they shared the odour of breath. Theirs had the pungent smell of insufficient protein. Lily couldn't identify the sounds of the steppe that whistled through the pipe. Was it wind, was it wolves? What did these people have to do with her?

In the morning, the storm had cleared. When Lily stepped outside, she had to shade her eyes with her hand. Oleg brought out hay for the camel. They shovelled snow into buckets, which they placed on the stove. Then the whole family, even Grandfather, worked together, clearing off her aircraft. The woman's kerchief was embroidered with white snowflakes. Over the kerchief, she threw a shawl. She taught Lily a bridal song while she swept the wing with a besom broom:

I am a green reed,
I'm an unripe berry
I am so young, so young,
A dove, little dove
How hard it is in the far-off land
I must learn to live in the strange land.

They refused payment. When the aircraft was ready, Lily poured hot water into the cylinders to warm the engine. The camel plucked hay with its lips and lifted its head to chew, golden strands hanging from its mouth. Lily showed Oleg how to rotate the propeller. Then she climbed into the cockpit, and soon she was in the air. The family watched her take off, looking fat in their layers of cloth and fur, like the pictures she saw in school, no sign of the gauntness beneath, the murderousness and the hospitality. As the plane climbed up, the dugout disappeared into the steppe. All this land that had once been the Mongols' was now her country. It glittered like sapphires and diamonds that had been crushed and embedded in folds of white velvet.

After Lily landed at the aviation school's airfield, it was Katie who had the responsibility of escorting her to their superiors for judgment. Katie looked as if she hadn't slept and lit one cigarette from the butt of the other as they walked, while Lily explained what had delayed her overnight. Snow melted off her helmet, her shoulders, her boots, a dripping trail in the corridor outside the classrooms where other pilots were taking notes. The sound of chalk on a blackboard. The smell of oil from the gunnery workshop. Katie said, "I shouldn't have let you fuck yourself up. You're just a kid."

Lily's feet were heavy; she was unsure of everything that had seemed so clear yesterday. "I did this to myself. I always do," she said. Her lips were wobbling. She was afraid she'd cry when she saluted her superiors, humiliating herself before they humiliated her.

At the door to Marina Raskova's office, Katie said, "I'll wait for you. I'll be right outside."

Lily knocked. A voice said, "Come in." She opened the door.

The commander was at her desk, and Major Kazarinova, having recovered from her recent ordeal, sat to her right as she had during Lily's interview. There was another chair on Marina's left, waiting for the chief of staff.

Standing in the corridor, Katie didn't outwardly react when Captain Kazarinova stopped to pat her on the shoulder, but in her mind she swore as if she'd been stung by a wasp. Captain Kazarinova smiled and left her, then entered the commander's office. There was the sound of a chair pulled out, a squeak as the captain settled in it. Katie could do nothing more, now, but lurk in the corridor and eavesdrop while pretending to rearrange articles in the wall newspaper, wishing she wasn't the captain's informant.

Every regiment had informants. In that respect, the air force was no different from any other workplace. Everyone was watched to make sure that spies and saboteurs weren't hiding among them. Katie had been recruited during her interview at the Palace of Red Aviation. There was nothing incriminating in her own record, and she hadn't thought there was anything in her sister's either. But, as Captain Kazarinova had explained, Katie's sister had forgotten her passport at home when she went out one evening. Citizens were supposed to have their internal passport with them at all times to show that they were permitted to be where they were. The policeman who'd stopped her had let it go, but that was his mistake. In Captain Kazarinova's opinion, it was possible that Katie's sister might be brought in for interrogation. No one had to say that, in the

socialist paradise, there was only one outcome of an interrogation—
a verdict of guilt. However, there would be no need to pursue the
matter if Katie was inspired to serve her country with patriotic
zeal. As long as she complied and told no one else about her sister's
predicament, neither of them would be prosecuted. It came as no
surprise that this service consisted of reporting on her comrades.
And at the train station, the captain had pulled Katie aside to
express a particular interest in her keeping an eye on "that little
minx, Lily Litvyak."

"Before your improvised adventure, Lily, I was thinking of where
to put you," Marina Raskova was saying. "Now I have to reconsider.
We're at war." She paused, letting that sink in.

"With spies everywhere," Captain Kazarinova added.

Katie moved one of the wall articles and slammed the thumb-
tack back in with the heel of her hand.

"Private Litvyak's rash behaviour was to my advantage," the
older Kazarinova said, "but the army is for the people, not any one
person. Away without leave. Stealing a plane!"

"Actually, there's no stolen aircraft," Marina said. "It's right
where it was left. Lily risked her life for a fellow pilot, and she
successfully flew in difficult conditions."

"But can she be trusted?" the captain asked. "What does the
oath say? *I solemnly swear to unquestioningly obey military orders.* And if
not? Harshest punishment of the law. Do you remember your oath,
Private Litvyak?"

"Yes, Comrade Captain." Lily's voice was thin, as if choked for
air.

"She did violate orders," Major Kazarinova said.

"A weather warning, not a military order. That's the way I see
it," Marina said. "Would you concede that?"

"Technically, yes," Major Kazarinova said.

"And the outcome was a valued officer's life saved. Our pilots have to show as much initiative as the Germans' if we're to succeed. And more than any others, our *fighter* pilots need to make quick decisions in the air. If I give you a chance, Lily, will I regret it?"

"No, Comrade Major. I swear it!"

"Major Kazarinova is taking over the command of the women's fighter regiment. It seems to me, Lily, that you and she have a special bond . . . since you rescued her from the steppe."

"She was ill-prepared. She should have had chocks," Major Kazarinova said.

"Quite so," Marina agreed. "You have much to teach her, if she's willing to learn."

"I am!" Lily said.

"Good. It's settled. Private Litvyak will join the 586th Fighter Air Regiment and serve her new commander as wholeheartedly as she has me. Can I rely on your rigorous tutelage, Tamara?"

"Extremely rigorous," Major Kazarinova said.

There was some further conversation regarding documents and paperwork. When the four emerged, Katie waited for the officers to pass as if she was completely engrossed in the articles that formed the wall newspaper, with its stories of record flights and fictional good news from the front.

Lily stopped beside her and said, "Did you hear? Initiative! The war is changing everything."

"Not as much as you might think." It was as close to a warning as Katie could give. "We'll be together. I've been assigned to the same regiment."

She slung an arm around Lily's shoulders. They walked back toward the afternoon class in combat tactics. The younger pilot's eyes were teary, her face ecstatic. Lily said, "Did you know that the smell of camels terrifies horses?"

———

Early in the new year, Factory 292 in Saratov delivered the first batch of Yak-1 fighters, as promised, to the military aviation school. Alone in the single-seater aircraft, Lily regained her self-confidence when flying, and Major Kazarinova also kept her promise. Anything less than perfection from Lily in training exercises resulted in corrective duty: shovelling out the latrine or cleaning the grease pit. Major Kazarinova had flown speed bombers alongside men and had led them, serving in the real army, where soldiers didn't ogle the mirror. If Lily's hair grew a millimetre, the major combed through it for lice, lecturing her on the history of army epidemics. *Know the difference between head and body lice. On your head, it's just offensive. In your clothes or on your blanket, you could spread typhus.* Major Kazarinova always knew exactly where Lily was. *Come*, she'd say, and Lily had to do extra target practice. *Not good enough for combat*, the major always said. *One more time.*

In March, news came of a great air victory, the first triumph against the seemingly invincible Luftwaffe. *The Red Star* featured the story in giant headlines: SEVEN AGAINST TWENTY-FIVE! A small squadron of Soviet fighters flying Yak-1s had driven away the much larger force of escorted bombers. There were photographs of the pilots in the newspaper, letters from their mothers and neighbours, interviews by the writer whose stories Lily's grandmother used to read to her. And while Lily carried a bucket to the latrine, she imagined herself with the heroic squadron, shooting down an enemy pilot, who looked remarkably like her commander.

Prisoner

UKRAINE

August to September 1943

A Letter on the Wall

As the railway clock in Amvrosiivka strikes eight, Lily presents herself at the front desk of the police station. Through the window she sees the train station built of limestone, the soldiers guarding it, a flock of pigeons wheeling in the morning sky. Viewed from above, their wings are black, from below they're white, translucent, as if light shines up from the earth. Under her dress she wears the knife she received from the old woman; it's sheathed and the loop tied to her garter belt, which holds up the granddaughter's stockings.

"Hello, sweetheart." The man behind the desk wears a policeman's uniform and a swastika pin on his collar. He has a thorn bush of hair, a nose twisted from multiple breaks. "What you got in that bag?"

"Just my boots." She hands him the sack for inspection. The walk into town was harder than she expected, and she shifts her weight to give her ankle a rest.

"What are you here for?" the policeman asks. He puts the sack under his desk, and that's the end of the beautiful boots her mother sent her.

"My work papers," she says. "From . . . Mr. Chelpanov?"

"Chief's not in yet."

A youngish woman, seated at a metal table behind the policeman's desk, is typing. There are posters on the wall: ads depicting a girl in a green dress drinking German soda, and a blond family picnicking near their new Volkswagen; a health warning—the man with his head inside a fanged cigarette, below it a caption, *He doesn't consume the cigarette, it consumes him.* Lily catches a glimpse of holding cells along the corridor. A portrait of Hitler hangs in place of Stalin's. A red flag in the corner patiently bears the swastika.

"Need the latrine," someone calls out from the cells in the corridor.

"Shut your face!" the policeman yells back. "Piss in the bucket and be glad you're not in the basement for questioning."

"It's not piss."

"Hold it till my break or I'll have your face in it. We're not having any pollution in the police station. So, sweetheart, name?"

"Sofia Sarbash."

"Never heard of you."

"I've got the papers here, Grisha," the secretary says. "Hauptsturmführer Hoffmann's instructions. He said she's assisting Dr. Fischer. Can you take her downstairs?"

"I'm not going into that stink-hole. You take her."

"Well, I'm too busy. Can't you see the pile of transcripts I'm working on?"

"I'll go myself," Lily says. "Just give me the papers."

The secretary hands the papers to the policeman, who gives them to Lily. When she heads for the stairs, they're both lighting up cigarettes under the No Smoking sign.

In the basement, Lily gags and covers her nose with her hand. The stench is like nothing she's ever smelled, not something burning, not oil or corpses, not cabbage rotting in a field. If the dead grew cabbage from their orifices, if they fertilized it with their shit and leaked feasting maggots while watching it all with open eyes, that would be something like the smell. The basement is walled with high-quality cement and lit by a single bulb. Flies buzz around it.

The cells down here are reserved for prisoners under investigation by the Gestapo. There are two of these cells side by side. Near the stairwell is the guard's alcove with a desk, chair, and cupboard.

At the opposite end of the corridor is a door that leads to an interrogation room. From within it come the cries of a bird.

Hauptsturmführer Hoffmann is standing in the corridor with several men around him. Lily recognizes the veterinarian and the young sergeant, but not the man in a guard's uniform. "You got your papers?" Hoffmann asks Lily. She nods, and he turns to the guard. "Everyone's still alive?"

"Yes, *Hauptsturmführer*," the guard says.

In each cell door there's a small window, barred with wooden slats. Hoffmann peers intently through one then another, while Dr. Fischer and Sergeant Sauer wait. The guard, an older and more rumpled soldier with thin brows and thin nostrils, returns to his chair at the guard station.

"Get your fingers off your nose, Sauer. This is the smell of . . ."

Lily doesn't know the word.

"You want to become a *Kriminalkommissar* someday? Get used to it. Even our Dr. Fischer isn't hiding behind a handkerchief."

The young sergeant clicks his heels and replies, but she can't make sense of what he says. She knows enough of the words individually, but strung together, the idiom eludes her.

"I don't understand," Lily says, remembering the sergeant's breath, his lips, as he stares at her. His face is pink, moist, like a slice of ham. *If you're going to eat pig, let it drip from your chin.* Grandma Rose enjoyed her sausage. She would fry these specimens in a hot fire, but Lily has to swallow her hatred like spit, appear bland and pliant as boiled potatoes.

"Dr. Fischer will teach you more German," Hoffmann says. "You'll talk all day. Like a child learning. A smart child learns fast, remembers well, reports her lessons."

Lily blinks. Her eyes sting from the smell. "I have a good memory," she says.

Hoffmann looks her up and down. "That's not the attire for this job. Dr. Fischer, after you're done here, get whatever she needs. Sauer, come with me. Sergeant Müller," he says to the guard, "you'll fetch anything Dr. Fischer requires. Your priority is the pilot in that cell. He has to be revived."

He knocks on the door of the interrogation room. It opens, a rectangle of bright light streaming into the dim tunnel of the basement corridor. The bird cries she hears are the high-pitched noise of something mannish hanging by the wrists. "I can't talk to him like that. Take him down," Hoffmann says. The door closes behind him.

"Bucket and soap," Dr. Fischer says to the guard while he removes his jacket and rolls up his shirt sleeves. "Is it possible to get a hose?"

"Thanks to me. They didn't have running water down here, but I was a plumber's apprentice. Before." Sergeant Müller rummages in the cupboard, removes the items requested, then finds a length of hose. He fills the bucket at the tap before attaching the hose to it.

"The door, if you please."

The key turns in the lock. Müller opens the door and stands back as Dr. Fischer enters, Lily hovering behind him. She avoids looking at the lump in the corner. He's a traitor. All POWs are traitors. No exceptions, Stalin had declared, not even his own son, a pilot who'd been shot down and captured by the enemy too.

Scratched on the walls are names and messages no one will ever read.

Here sat E.L. Ziza.

Girls why do we do this? I'm pregnant and going to die.

Peter lived twenty years and four months.

Greetings, dear wife, your husband writes from far away. I see your picture in the cracks in the wall. . . .

"Sergeant, hose down the floor."

Now that he's alone with Lily and the veterinarian, the guard is talkative. While he hoses the cell, he tells them about the partisans who occupy the other cell, three men and a woman. Hauptsturm-führer Hoffmann will get everything out of them. The problem is the prisoner in here. He ate some papers before he was caught. They'd never have known except that they found a few shreds he missed. Hauptsturmführer Hoffmann said this was so important that if they got the information, everyone in the office would be promoted. So far they've learned nothing from the son of a whore. What luck he fell into their hands and what rotten luck he'll have to be transferred to the aviators' camp.

"His name?" Dr. Fischer asks.

"Victor Karyukin."

The thing in the corner, pulpy, studded with congealed blood, whistles as if through holes in his bones as the veterinarian rolls him over, first one way then the other, while the floor is rinsed. Then Müller brings in a bench and puts on it the bucket, soap, a towel, a cup, the veterinarian's leather bag. He stands at the door, hand on his pistol as if the prisoner's skeleton might suddenly gain flesh, like Koschei the Deathless, and attack him with the strength of a hundred.

"What can you do for him?" Lily asks Dr. Fischer. "He's more dead than alive."

"A man is like a horse. Muck out his stable, groom him." He makes brushing motions. "That alone is an improvement. Then you give him a *Spritze*." Again he mimes, repeating the last word, carefully enunciating the *r*.

"What should I do now?"

"Speak to him. Use his name. Tell him that he'll drink and get cleaned up."

Lily translates, and Dr. Fischer fills the cup. He lifts the man's head, using his knee to support his back, and puts the cup to his lips, which part. Dr. Fischer tips the cup, slowly dribbling water into the man's mouth. The man's throat moves, his head falls back. The veterinarian lifts the bucket and soap from the bench and places them on the ground beside her. "Now wash him *sanft*, like you must *üben* at school."

"I need a rag," she says.

"Too rough." He shows her his palms, then lovingly makes circular motions on his arm. "Like that. Skin"—he touches the surface of his arm with a finger—"is softer."

"Excuse me, Victor," she says in Russian. She pulls back the man's shirt, then turns her head away from the smell. It could have been her lying here.

With great effort, the prisoner raises an arm and drops it across his chest. "Go away," he croaks.

She forces herself to face him. "My brothers are pilots too. Let me wash you." She soaps her hands and places them on his chest, breathing through her nose lightly, steadily.

"I wish them better," the soldier says. "What units are they with?"

She touches his skin gently. Even so, he winces. "You heard of the Seven Against Twenty-Five?"

"The first air battle we won. It gave me hope." He wheezes and waits until he can croak some more, as if this is his last conversation, a letter on the wall he has no strength to print.

"That's the regiment I mean." As she washes, his skin is turning from blooded dirt, the ground of battle, into something living.

"Are there many brothers?"

"Were. They're gone." Her eyes are welling up, and she hasn't enough willpower to stop it. She tries to block out the wailing and banging in the other cell.

"What's he saying?" Dr. Fischer asks.

"We're just talking. If he's distracted, he'll let me do everything. Is that okay?"

"Yes, good."

"What did you tell him?" Victor asks.

"Something smokier than goat shit burning on the steppe. Don't laugh!" she says, as if the injured man could. She bends over him, supporting his back while removing his shirt. He groans, but relaxes against her arm. He's so light, there's so little left of him. She lays him down gently.

"They're coming soon," he says. "Our people. Liberation."

"Then you can take me to a movie." She dips her hands in the bucket, rinses them, and soaps them again.

"You're beautiful," he says.

"Every nurse is a beauty." She washes his face, wiping away the grime, the blood, the ooze that seeps from his eyes. She dips her hands in the bucket and rinses the soap from his face with grey water.

"Don't get caught, little bird." His finger bends to admonish her. "Fly away. The wind is behind you."

Dr. Fischer squats on his haunches, studying the prisoner. "He's had water, he's talking. Tell him that I want to give him an injection. You understand the word *injection*? Good. Say that it won't kill him, just make him stronger."

"The doctor wants to give you a shot that will make you feel better, Victor."

Dr. Fischer stands up and opens the leather bag. From its wide mouth he withdraws a bottle and a large syringe.

After the shot is given, Victor tries to lift his head. "Are my hands clean?" he asks.

"Yes," she says.

"Come closer."

She glances at the veterinarian, who's looking on curiously, making no movement to intervene.

"Closer, please."

She leans forward.

"You're truly beautiful." Victor puts his hands on her cheeks. He breathes shallowly to keep his sour breath from her. His eyes lock with hers. "Kill me," he says.

"How can I?"

"Find a way."

"Is it that unbearable?"

"I might talk. I don't know if I can help it."

"Shh." She doesn't see the face of a traitor. Only pain and fatigue and a terrible loss that's familiar to her.

"Please."

The horse hospital is at the edge of town, a few blocks south of the POW camp and the cement factory. It's in a converted building, previously High School No. 1. On one side are town streets, on the other a hill of manure, a corral, fields. Gerhard Fischer breathes deeply so that the smell of hay and horse and muck can dispel the miasma of the Gestapo prison cell.

He's understaffed, relying on local boys to make up the short-fall, and now this student nurse, Sofia, whom he'll have to train. Gerhard cracks a sunflower seed between his teeth and pockets the shell. His classmates used to tease him for this, his reluctance to spit even in a stable.

"What did you give the pilot?" she asks.

"Strychnine."

She says a word in Russian. *Poison*, he guesses.

"It's a stimulant. Athletes used to take a shot to improve their performance. In veterinary medicine it has several applications, including heart function." He hands her a clipboard. "Today's list. I examine horses who are post-surgery daily. Others on rotation. The horses are listed by induction number, and this indicates the stage of recovery."

Fritz is grooming the chestnut mare while one of the Ukrainian boys scoops manure and dumps it on a pallet, the shovel as tall and wide as he is.

"How's Helga?" he asks the boy.

Fritz takes his pencil and notebook from his pocket and writes, *Needs new shoe. Right foreleg.* He glances curiously at the girl as if she's a new variety of horse.

"Hold her steady."

Helga has a bit of a temper, but Fritz knows how to handle her—nothing quick, nothing forceful, just calm, persistent direction.

A horse is the only one who won't betray you, not until she gives out. Gerhard runs his hand down the mare's front leg and picks up the hoof. "Come here, Sofia," he says. "You see these bumps? Rat droppings have got under the horseshoe."

"She has this . . ." Sofia runs her finger along the flank.

"The word is *scar*," he says.

"What's it from?"

"Shrapnel."

"Like Russian," she says. "Also strychnine." She pronounces it with an *s* instead of *sh*, and a rolling *r*. "And the word for this place, *Lazarettstaffel*, is almost like ours."

"Russian is Slavic. It's nothing like German." Gerhard takes a thermometer from his pocket, spits on his fingers, and rubs it. Then he lifts Helga's tail and deposits the thermometer in her bottom. He checks her temperature, digs the drum of his stethoscope into Helga's armpit, puts his fingers under her jaw to time her pulse, counts her breaths. "Temperature normal. Heart forty-two beats per minute. Breath normal. Pulse normal. Write that down." He listens to the horse's abdomen, walks around and presses his ear against the other side. "Digestion, normal." He flips the mare's lip to look at the underside. "Nice and pink. Good moisture."

Fritz nods proudly, pointing to himself, and grins at the girl. In his notebook he writes, *Should I tell my uncle about the nurse?*

Gerhard shrugs and nods. Does it make any difference how he replies? In the next stall is a horse with a broken leg. Its torso is nestled in harness straps attached to a pulley that hang from the ceiling. Before the war, he'd have been shot. Now he's indispensable. The horse whinnies and nuzzles Gerhard.

He says, "We're going to the other side of the hospital, Sofia. The cold-blood horses are big, but they're more delicate, so they're kept separately."

"Size isn't everything," she says. "Sometimes it's nothing."

The sound he makes might be a laugh. While they walk to the other side of the hospital, he tells her about the uses of arsenic: for heart palpitations, for fatty heart, as an antispasmodic, as a sheep dip.

Dr. Fischer eats his dinner outside in the August sunshine, still in his white medical coat. The meal is embarrassingly plentiful. A middle-aged Ukrainian woman with a hint of dark fuzz on her upper lip lays out the table: butter, potatoes, boiled eggs, sauerkraut, apples, and chicken. Defying her rumbling stomach and watering mouth, Lily takes a single potato from the table, estimating it to be her official ration. Dr. Fischer pays no attention as he sits between Mr. Bender, who runs the dispensary, and Mr. Schultz, the farrier. The stable hands perch in a line on the fence, hunched over their dry rations as if protecting them from bandits and birds, while Lily finds a grassy spot beneath a tree.

After dinner, they continue. Dr. Fischer drags his right foot when no one but she can see. He doesn't ogle her or leer, which makes her more jumpy than the lecherous stares of the Gestapo men. At least their intentions are clear. One minute he's voluble, explaining German words and technical terms; the next he clams up, pursing his mouth like he's found a worm in his soup. He listens to horses' bellies, checks their pulse, their gums, their temperature. She washes the thermometer. She lifts tails. There are more horses than she's ever seen, standing wearily in their stalls like encircled prisoners of war, heads down, waiting for the next disaster, or outside in the corral, nipping at grass as if it might explode under them. German horses, she reminds herself. No longer pulling artillery carts or anti-tank guns. When they arrive at the surgery, he tests the straps and scowls at the platform that serves as a surgery table. Lily offers to clean it, and he accedes. It's a first step, getting him accustomed to her moving about on her own.

At the end of the day, the boys bed down in the stables, and she needs to make one for herself. She might even find a spare apple; stealing food isn't collaboration.

"May I leave?" she asks when Dr. Fischer removes his white coat and drops it in a basket.

"Take that box. You're coming home with me."

"Why?" There's no need for him to reply, and he doesn't. She forces herself to breathe, to feign ignorance. Her skin tightens around her throat, her backside, her thighs, constricting every entry point.

He takes out a bundle of keys and locks up while she thinks about finding a place to hide before he returns. Hay. A dispensary cupboard. The gas chamber that isn't being used for mange because there's a shortage of gas. She rises to her feet. She leaves the office, its faint light guiding her. She can hear the boys' voices murmuring in the darkness, and she turns away, unsure now of her direction. She hears his uneven footsteps, sees the flashlight.

"Let's go," Dr. Fischer says.

They leave the hospital on foot, hobbling under the moon, and in its light she can see the bulge of a pistol in his pocket, reminding her that he's an enemy officer and she's still a soldier with a knife. They don't have to go far. In a house near the hospital, Dr. Fischer has two rooms and a bath to himself. These were the quarters of the previous head of the hospital, an *Oberstabsveterinär* who's been transferred, leaving behind furniture and books. It's more elegant than she'd have suspected from the outside of the house, and when he throws himself into an ornate chair, he squares the lace doily on the low table before dropping his medical bag on it.

"Our work is dirty," he says. "If you work with animals, it's impossible to avoid the splatter of shit. You wash so as not to communicate diseases to other animals or yourself. If you get ill, you're of no use to me, and if you make me ill, I'm of no use to my country. So go and bathe. Leave the dirty clothes in the basket next to the tub. I have a woman who washes them."

The door has a latch, and when no contradictory order comes from the front room, she clicks it shut. There's running water and, under the tub, a coal burner to heat it. She lights the kindling with matches she finds on a stand that also has soap and a brush, and adds coal from the bucket in the corner. Then she waits, occasionally dipping her hand into the water. When it's warm, she undresses and steps in. It's been so long since she had a bath, and the soap isn't harsh lye but softly sudsing and fragrant. Lavender or lilac. The fragrance reminds her of Major Kazarinova, the interview in a palace. Her mind shivers, running from one thought to another while she mechanically washes. Her grandmother's busy hands. A horse dangling in mid-air. What could she write in a letter now? *Dear Mama and Yuri, I've been captured. A fellow pilot asked me to murder him. . . .* He's braver than she is. Lily picks up her knife. She touches it to the inside of her elbow, and her hand, shocked, pulls away and drops the knife beside the tub. She drifts. For a few seconds she dreams she's in a dugout, her best friend breathing beside her. She blinks. Until the war, she didn't know what a friend could be. She steps out of the bath, dries herself on a towel. The knife goes back in its sheath. Her stockings are in the basket, the rest of her clothes on the floor. She puts them on again and attaches the sheath to the garter. For courage, she straps on her father's watch.

Dr. Fischer looks up from his book as the door opens. "I told you to leave your dirty clothes in the basket," he says.

"What am I supposed to wear?" She doesn't know what she'll do if he says, *Nothing*.

"Get one of my shirts from the wardrobe. You sleep in my bed."

"I sleep on the floor," she says. Under her dress, she feels the weight of the knife against her hip.

"In my bed." He uncrosses his legs, his booted foot hits the floor, and she flinches.

"Floor."

"Bed." With a fluid motion, his pistol is in his hand and pointing at her.

She holds up her hands. "Bed," she says. "At least give me privacy to get undressed."

"All right." He motions with the gun. "Go in there."

In the bedroom is a wrought iron bedstead with a featherbed, a wardrobe, a bookcase, a stand with a pitcher and bowl, a candle, which he lights while she turns toward the small window. She might be able to climb out, but the drop on her already injured ankle could cripple her. Still, it's worth a try.

"Don't even think of the window," he says. "There are . . ." A word she doesn't understand. "They'll kill you."

Dr. Fischer goes out and shuts the door. She hears a key turn in the lock. The room dims, lit by the moon and the candle. First she checks the keyhole, but no light comes through it, no eye visible, the key still in the lock. Then she removes the knife and hides it under the pillow. From the wardrobe, she takes out a shirt. It looks long enough to cover her thighs. She undresses and changes into the shirt, her clothes left in a puddle on the floor. She gets into bed and brings the covers to her chin. "Finished," she calls.

She lies there, planning for the moment. She'll have to slip the knife out from under the pillow after he's on top of her and so absorbed in his pleasure that he won't notice her hand or care if she has one. She might miss his heart, merely wound him, but if she succeeds, she'll climb out the window and drop and take her chances.

Minutes pass, then an hour. The candle melts. The flame sputters, giving off an odour of sulphur, and goes out. When the moon is gone from the window, she watches the black of night until a flicker of lamplight and the sound of a key make her lower her lids.

From under her lashes, she sees Dr. Fischer enter and put the lamp on the table. As if she's awake and he's shy, he turns away to undress. He crawls into bed, still wearing his underwear. Lies on his back. She stays awake, curled on her side at the edge of the bed, one hand under the pillow, touching the knife, waiting for him to roll toward her, to push up the shirt, to move into position. She can't freeze; she needs hatred to guide her.

His breathing slows. He begins to snore, at first lightly, and she wonders if he's feigning—but to what end? She waits, and he doesn't move, lying as still as a corpse except for a jerk when his snoring is interrupted by a horselike snort. She puts her hand on the knife, pulls it down to her side. But his breathing deepens, his snores accompanied by the uncontrollable rumbling of her intestines. It's so easy after all. She can just walk out, find a place to hide, run. She reaches down with one hand to get her clothes, and the snoring stops. She lifts her hand back to her side. She lies still, on her back, forcing herself to breathe evenly, slowly. He falls asleep again.

In the morning, Dr. Fischer gets up at first light and dresses. Through half-closed eyes she notices that one of his feet is yellowish, missing toes, and she wonders where he left them. He picks her clothes up from the floor. When he glances at her, she rolls over on her side, away from him, listening to his footsteps. Through the open door she sees an old Ukrainian woman carrying the basket of washing and eyeing her balefully. On top of the pile of clothes are the dress and stockings she wore yesterday, spattered with blood. The old woman leaves, so does Dr. Fischer, but if Lily runs away now, wearing just a shirt in full daylight, she'll be caught as soon as she's on the street. Before she can come up with a better plan, Dr. Fischer returns to the room with a package. "Women's underwear," he says. "There's coveralls in the box." She's to get dressed and accompany him to the *Lazarettstaffel*.

That day eleven horses arrive at the hospital. Their coats are dry and dull, eyes sunken, ribs visible against skin, and one of them requires immediate surgery to remove bullets embedded too deeply to manage at the dressing station. Lily learns how a horse is lifted and strapped onto the surgical table, translating for Dr. Fischer while the boys' malnourished arms shake with effort. She learns how to administer chloroform. She learns the names of his medical instruments. For dinner, she chooses a large potato and retreats under the tree. The second night is nearly the same as the first. She bathes, she protests, Dr. Fischer waves his pistol, she clings to her knife, hidden under the pillow, and he snores.

On her third day at the *Lazarettstaffel*, she sits with the veterinary staff and eats everything, having decided that if she pretends to be getting used to this, the staff will grow careless around her. That evening Dr. Fischer reads aloud the first pages of *Old Surehand* by Karl May, explains the words she doesn't understand, then makes her read it back to him. *Chapter One. Old Wabble. On my many journeys and wanderings, especially among so-called savages and the semi-civilized, I very often found men who became my dear friends. . . .*

The doctor has found another pair of coveralls for her and
while he reads, she's shortening them. To relax him, she asks
about veterinary school, which he describes fondly. She mentions
that she has a brother, and he volunteers that he's the oldest of
three brothers. The one closer to him in age grew up as a member
of Hitler Youth and is currently a captain in France, drinking
wine. His youngest brother, Friedrich, died of meningitis. Fredi,
they called him. He was the family favourite, and at the funeral
their father had turned to Gerhard and said, *It should have been you.*
For a heartbeat he isn't her captor, and then Lily wonders which of
them is disarming the other. Still, that night, he doesn't wave his
pistol to force her to bed. In the morning, the old Ukrainian
woman collects dirty laundry as usual, brings in clean laundry,
and glares at Lily.

By the fourth day, she has her own shirts, a nightgown, and
hairpins, which Dr. Fischer acquired from the laundrywoman.
Mr. Bender, the pharmacist, is calling her Kitten, taking her
presence for granted, and leaving the dispensary door open,
though the cupboard with arsenic and strychnine is still locked.
With her help, Dr. Fischer lectures the boys on how to properly
dunk a mangy horse in sulphur dip. Fritz takes her picture as
she sits on the back of a Panje horse, then leads her around the
field. On the fifth day, Dr. Fischer lets her replenish the bottles in
his leather bag. He has a pair of boy's boots for her, and she's
relieved at the prospect of wearing something more suitable for
tramping around a barn until she finds out they were confiscated
from a deportee.

"I don't want them," she says.

"Someone else will," he says.

That's the day he discharges all the horses stabled in Room 1,
those that have fully recovered. His face is expressionless as he
watches the transport soldiers take them away. By this time she's

stopped waiting for Hauptsturmführer Hoffmann to send for her, thinking that he's lost interest, and when the guard arrives that afternoon, she's furious with herself for becoming complacent. Dr. Fischer dismisses her with as much emotion as he displayed for the horses.

The guard doesn't speak on the drive to the police station. She walks up the stairs with his rifle at her back.

The Gestapo office is busier than the police station below it. Despite the sunshine outside, electric lights blaze. Men sit crowded together at desks, talking, examining files and folders of pictures. Phones ring. Someone removes a name from what appears to be a duty roster and adds another. Two women are typing, a third going in and out of an office with an open door. She hears a name repeated: *Sturmbannführer Vogel requires it; Those are Sturmbannführer Vogel's orders; Yes, Sturmbannführer Vogel convinced him to talk.* At the filing cabinets that fill one side of the room, a young officer is riffling through a drawer. The portrait of Hitler is large, the flag slightly pushed to the side by a table. On it is a platter of fruit—large grapes, pink peaches, canned cherries—and an unopened bottle of wine, as if everyone has already had as much as they want. They glance at her curiously: prisoners usually go down, not up, the stairs. The guard pushes her into a short corridor then marches her to the end, where they stop in front of a closed door.

The guard knocks. He's given permission to enter an office with two desks, one of which is empty, Hoffmann sitting at the other, a small, carved mahogany desk with a matching pen stand on it. The portrait of Hitler is on the left, an oil painting on the wall opposite his desk. It's not of Russian origin. The landscape is too placid, the colours smeared like a dream after wine. Maybe French, she guesses. A door to an adjoining, larger office is partially open.

She can see a single square desk, a wall covered with photographs and a map, and a tired-looking man standing with his hands behind his back, studying the wall.

Hoffmann dismisses the guard and enters the other office, confers with his superior and returns, closing the door behind him. "Sit," he says, pointing to a wooden chair at the side of his desk. She sits, and he draws his own chair closer. He speaks quietly, and she smells cigars and toothache on his breath. "So, Miss Sarbash, what have you learned about our Dr. Fischer?"

"He works long hours."

The Gestapo captain clasps his hands, index fingers joined, supporting his chin as his eyes burrow into her. "Is that what you consider a report?"

"No, Hauptsturmführer Hoffmann."

"Where did you sleep?"

"In his bed."

Hoffmann considers this. "What did he do exactly?"

She flushes. "What do you mean?"

"Step by step." Every woman alive would know the meaning of that smile.

"He pointed his pistol at me and told me to undress." Hoffmann's eyes are fixed on her, his left leg slightly trembling. "He took off his clothes. He has an injured foot. Toes are missing," she adds for authenticity. "He got into bed. He went to sleep."

"Did he touch you?"

She isn't sure how to answer this, whether truthfully or a lie, and if a lie, how much, so she bites her lip, furrows her brow, stutters while she watches Hoffmann's leg. "I . . . He . . ." Hoffmann's leg trembles harder. "He kissed me," she says.

"That's all?" His leg steadies, and he leans back.

"Yes. All for now. That was what he said." Her voice is innocent, young, she's always sounded young. Who could guess how many planes she's shot down? On her right, the window faces north. The curtains are white.

"Hmm." Hauptsturmführer Hoffmann doesn't say more, and she wonders if she's gone too far or not far enough.

"He keeps the medications locked up," she says. The curtains are parted, and through the window she sees a train, a ramp, horses walking into the cars. "I'm not sure what I'm supposed to be looking out for."

"You'll catch on," he says. "Does he read poetry?"

"He did read to me. . . ."

"Yes, yes, that's what I mean."

"It was a book by Karl . . ."

"Marx?"

"May. *Old Surehand.*"

Hoffmann's mouth purses, and she wonders how much trouble the veterinarian is in, not that it's any concern of hers. "That is the Führer's favourite author. It's no good, I tell you. There must be more. You have to remember every detail: who he spoke with, what he said, and especially what he did."

"He spoke with the deaf boy, Fritz, about the rat problem—"

Hoffmann interrupts her. "I don't want to hear about the veterinary treatment."

"All right," she says.

He drags his chair closer. He puts an arm around her neck, lays a finger on her pulse. His breath is wet. She feels his sweat on her skin. "And what can you tell me about Fritz Vogel?"

"I don't know. He likes horses. Is he related to the *Sturmbann-führer*?" she asks.

"His nephew." Hoffmann's lips are dry, cracked, swallowing her ear.

"If you'd explain, maybe there's something I've seen that I didn't realize is important."

"Very well." He withdraws his arm, the chair screeching as he pushes away. "Let me put it simply. The Jews invented ethics. *The meek shall inherit the earth.* It upsets the natural order, putting the weak in the place of the strong. Then you have the Communists, driven by ideals. Theirs is a class struggle, but what is this class or that class? Nothing. An idea. A confusing idea. What is real is nature and the struggles of nature. The Aryan race, being the strongest, naturally took from the weaker race, the Russian, all the land required to feed itself. Yet we are retreating. We've been ordered to pull back from Amvrosiivka, to move the Gestapo office and the hospitals. This is unnatural! Therefore, I ask why."

"Long supply lines?"

"Are you stupid, my dear?"

She shakes her head.

"There are still polluting elements hiding among us. Moral defectives. Genetic defectives. That's why my work is so important. The future of the world depends on it. Some don't understand this." He looks toward the closed door of his superior's office. "Old policemen cling to old principles." He moves his chair a little, tilts it back, rests his feet on his desk. His black boots bulge around fat ankles. "You'll tell me and only me what you see. Do everything they ask of you. Everything. We understand each other?"

"Yes," she says, rising to her feet.

"Heil Hitler." The sun is turning red in the northwest. It paints his glistening chin with blood. He stares at her, demanding a response.

"Heil Hitler." Her outstretched arm is straight, hard as a sword pointing at his throat.

When she returns, Dr. Fischer informs her that he's just received his order for evacuation. The medical dispensary has to be packed up, as well as all the surgical tools and supplies, and the horses readied for travel. He'll be at it all night, so he wants her to go back to the house and pack up his things. There's a suitcase under the bed. She's to return as quickly as she can; every hand is needed. Their destination is four hundred kilometres west, deeper into the Ukraine, and a train has been made available for the morning.

It's the first chance she's had to be on her own outside, and as soon as she's through the door, she's figuring out how to escape. She starts walking in the direction of Dr. Fischer's house, thinking that she just needs to get out of sight. Since the horse hospital is already on the outskirts of town, all she has to do, then, is cross a couple of streets and she'll be in the fields.

Haggard civilians are returning from work in the evening gloom, others making their way toward factories for the night shift. A group of soldiers jogs along the street, urged forward by their sergeant. In the light from a passing military truck, a pair of SS men emerges from a house. One of them is tall, the other stout. An old man shuffles between them, his mouth bloodied. As they reach the curb, Lily steps aside.

"Stop! Papers!" the taller SS man says to her.

"Right here, sir." She never goes anywhere without her papers. She reaches into her coveralls pocket and presents them. The stout SS man looks impatient, the other studies the papers with a flashlight.

"Not authorized for free movement," he says.

"I work for the horse hospital. I'm the veterinarian's assistant. His nurse."

"Then where's his signature? He's supposed to sign it. These work papers are out of order. What are you doing out here?"

She starts to explain, but the heavier SS officer interrupts. "My shift was over an hour ago," he says to his colleague. "If you think there's a problem, let's just take her to the station."

"We'd save more time by bringing her along with the old man and putting them both in the warehouse with the deportees," the other SS man says.

"Good idea. Let the next shift sort them out."

While the taller SS man cups a match to light a cigarette, swearing as it flares out, and the stout one offers a lighter, she glances up and down the road, but there's nothing she can do, guarded by these Nazis.

She says, "The stables are just up there. Not more than a block away."

The tall SS man slaps her, and her cheek stings. "Did someone ask you a question?"

Lily knows what the enemy does to people locked in buildings. They're set on fire. In a panic, she says, "I'm a nurse. I swear it."

"March!" The other SS officer shoves her between the shoulder blades. They're moving toward the black automobile that's parked by the side of the road, and despite the summer heat, she shivers, remembering the heat and smoke of her aircraft on fire.

She hears the horse before she sees it, the clip-clop of cantering hooves and a snort as reins are pulled back. The SS men keep pushing Lily and the old man forward. Afraid to speak, she lifts a hand in greeting. She's never been gladder to see anyone.

"Whoa! This worker is under *my* supervision," Dr. Fischer shouts.

"Workers under supervision don't have the right to be out on their own," the taller SS man says.

"As soon as I sent her out, I realized that. But I'm a busy man. It's the express wish of Hauptsturmführer Hoffmann that I have an assistant."

The SS men look at each other. The heavier one shrugs. The old man between them is silently weeping. "If she's yours, then take her," the tall SS man says. "Just make sure to sign her papers."

Dr. Fischer dismounts. He loops an arm through hers and leads the horse by the reins as they walk. The horse is sweating from her canter, and when they're back at the stables, she whinnies with pleasure as one of the staff rubs her down. Everyone else is preparing for departure while they listen to the sound of distant explosions coming closer. In the morning they board the train, pulling out before the battle reaches the city.

The Sound of War

When the guns fall silent in a small pocket of fighting southeast of Amvrosiivka, close to the border between Russia and the Ukraine, one horse remains on his feet. He's found some grass, his head is bent while he grazes.

The war can't move without horses. They trudge in mud and snow, leaving excrement and sweat in their wake alongside the men, who were drafted too. They're hungry together, exhausted together, fight lice and mites with fingers or tails, ribs heaving when they stop for a rest. Horses pull carts loaded with ammunition, supplies, food, and the wounded, both human and equine. They pull artillery guns, they pull the field kitchens, they carry officers. There's a horse for every four infantrymen, and for the horses there are handlers, veterinary officers, assistants. The sound of war is the sound of horses whinnying, nickering, neighing with heads held high for their fellow horses and their fellow men.

There are as many horses in the war as there are people in Austria, more than in Switzerland or Denmark, twice as many as in Norway, almost exactly as many as there are Jews being shot or gassed, though only two-thirds of the horses die. They have their minorities to deal with too—mules and oxen, in the north reindeer, in the south camels. Engines stall, animals don't. Tires sink and skid to a stop in snow or mud while hooves pick their way. Oil requires tankers, oil is scarce. Oats and hay can travel in ordinary train cars, along with men, along with horses going west with Soviets and east with Axis soldiers, toward the marshes and the forests where horses quietly move between trees, ridden by men on reconnaissance missions. They journey with men, are wounded with men, and when they are exhausted, they recuperate from men. If wounds are light, they're treated at a dressing station and put back into service. Otherwise they're sent to a division hospital, and if more complex treatment is required, they'll be sent, like men, to larger facilities far from the front. Horses scream too, when shells are falling. They remember the fields they once knew, the grass and the wildflowers. But there is no returning home for them, no spouse who needs to adjust to a permanent injury. There's only the front and carrying their load. When they can carry it no more, they become rations for the men who keep on fighting.

In a burnt-out village near the border, the two men who survived the attack are watching a horse peacefully graze. One of the horse's legs dangles, bleeding, the foreleg blasted away. The horse stumbles on his three legs, but at least he's had the pleasure of the field before the men lift their rifles. They shoot him together so that neither of them will know who's done it, and then they weep for their company's last horse.

The Unskinning of Him

From the horse hospital's new location on the banks of the Dnieper River in the central Ukraine, Lily can see German aircraft flying out of a base on the other side of the river. The base is on the edge of the city that she knows as Dneprodzerzhinsk but has been renamed Kamenskoje by the Germans. The city is important for its steel mills, and the Gestapo is stationed there, its operations expanded by staff transferred from areas retaken by the Russian army. No bridge spans the river at this point, and an unmilitary atmosphere permeates the isolated village.

The horse hospital has been set up here because there are existing facilities that house uninjured but exhausted horses recovering from combat. Beyond the cluster of huts that forms the village, there is a cornfield. On the other side of the field is the village school, then the convalescent facilities: stables, corrals, a staff dorm, pastures, and a large outdoor vat dug into the ground for dip treatments. One of the stables has been allocated to the horse hospital, and the village school has been expropriated for the surgery and a medical dispensary. The staff of the convalescent facility, already resentful at being squeezed for space, refuses to share personal quarters with the new arrivals. Instead, beds are given to them in peasant huts.

Lily is billeted with Gerhard—as she thinks of him now. She's become familiar with the shapes his body makes in sleep. He forms letters of the alphabet: curled away from her in the "З" of запад, *zapad*, west, the old word for sunset; or rolling onto his back with his arm over his head in a "Г" as in герой, *geroy*, the hero—which he isn't at all, just a man who beds down with her as though she was a cow, a goat, a fellow soldier, for warmth and the reassurance that something still lives. She knows his smell, horsey with a hint of chemicals, his dungheap farts and their popping sound, the grumble of his dreams, the long pitch of his scream. She sleeps with Gerhard in the cold storage room of the peasant hut because he believes that the cooking fire in the main room attracts more fleas to the straw that covers the dirt floor. He inhales and exhales in creaky sleep while she lies beside him, sleepless.

Gerhard draws up his legs, scrunching into the "с" of слова, *slova*, words. He's dreaming again. Shallow, rapid breaths, then the *brrr* sound low in his throat, his muscles twitching. Before he starts screaming, she puts her hand on his shoulder and shakes him.

"Wake up."

He gasps, elbow hitting her in the chest. "Help me."

"It's just a dream," she says.

"My throat." He pulls at the neck of his undershirt, gurgling as he speaks. "I'm dying."

"You're fine." She turns on the flashlight and he squints, flings his arm over his eyes. "Not a scratch." She runs her hand roughly up and down his throat. "Not a drop of blood. Look at me. Look around."

He takes her hand, examines it, holds on to it as he scans the storage room. Low window. Chest of drawers. Seed bags. Hoe lying across them and throwing an axe shadow.

"We're in the village."

"Yes."

"Across the river from Kamenskoje City. No roads. No running water. They made room for the horse hospital."

"That's right."

"And we're surrounded." For a moment she thinks he's sunk back into the fantasy of his dream, but he props himself up and sighs. "The veterinary convalescent facility is here, their staff has never seen combat. They have a pig." It's hidden whenever there are rumours of requisitioning. Soldiers in the rear siphon supplies before trucks get to the front lines. At the front, hungry soldiers also steal whenever they have the opportunity.

"I'd like an egg," she says.

"Who wouldn't? Don't waste the batteries."

She depresses the button; colours flicker in the afterglow of her eyes. Now he'll talk. He always tells her about his dreams, forcing on her words, if not his body, because he's her captor, still. And she takes them readily, not because she's his captive, but for the unskinning of him, his fright as naked under his authority as she is under her clothes.

"I was riding a stallion," he says. There aren't any stallions in combat. That much she's learned. They're kept at stud farms because a whiff of a mare could set them off, and even a gelding could be attacked. "You know that a stallion can kill another horse or a man by biting out his throat?"

"Is that what happened to you? In the dream?"

"We made it to the edge of the forest. He turned on me just as we left the trees and faced the sun. He threw me off his back. I felt his teeth ripping through the skin, the tendons, the jugular. I can still taste the blood." He speaks in the neutral tone of reporting operations, military or medical. "Before the stallion, everything was normal. Real. The dressing station was supposed to be a few kilometres from the front line. But the line shifted and our radio man was misinformed. I saw Ivan coming, they were all in white, on skis. Someone told me to pick up a rifle, and then I was standing guard, thigh deep in snow." His voice rises in pitch, he speaks in a rush of words. "We heard their howl, 'hurrreee.' That sound, it makes you crap your pants, and I knew I was going to die, but I didn't. Instead I was somewhere else, and I couldn't remember how I got there with a few men and a few horses, all that was left standing. I was the highest-ranking officer among them even though I knew less about soldiering than the corporal. We got orders over the wireless: go into the forest to flush out partisans. We did, and we all came out alive."

"That should have let you know you were dreaming," she says.

"And I thought so too, but then I remembered Stalingrad, when the veterinarians were evacuated—that wasn't a dream. I saw the light. We were at the forest's edge."

"There's no forest there. Just steppe."

"The mosquitoes . . . Your country is unbearable."

"Nobody asked you to come." They lie side by side in the black night, invisible to each other, the straw mattress warmed by their bodies, every movement passing through it, words tracing a trajectory.

"We were encircled. The world was against us."

"The world was against *us*," she says. "You broke the pact."

"Do you think any soldier wants to leave home? The Jews made us."

"Jews?"

"And the English."

"What about the Russians?"

"Like animals. They never get tired."

"You should know that isn't true. Horses have to recuperate."

"And you can tell that a horse isn't a pig. You don't have to wonder."

"If you look up—you see the markings on aircraft that tell you who's who."

"On the ground, you can't tell who's going to knife you in the back," he finishes her thought. "Or shoot off your balls."

"It could be your own people."

"Just as likely. Give me the flashlight. We're getting up to check the dispensary."

"Now?"

"I don't want to sleep anymore. Might as well get something done." He pulls his trousers off a hook in the wall. The bed rocks as he struggles into them and reaches down to retrieve his boots. When his feet are safely barriered against any fleas in the straw-strewn dirt floor, he swings his legs to the ground. He crosses the half metre to the chest of drawers and lights the kerosene lamp. In the pool of its diesel odour, he pulls on his shirt and draws up suspenders, then puts on the uniform jacket with its carmine collar and shoulder patches.

From his pants pocket, he takes a brown pill bottle. *Pervitin* is printed in big letters along its length. He tosses a pill into his mouth, holds out the bottle as if to offer her one. It's a methamphetamine that used to come in every soldier's kit, in either chocolate or pill form, but it isn't as easy to obtain now. She shakes her head, and he returns the bottle to his pocket.

"Get dressed," he says, turning his back.

"Who gave you those?" she asks, pulling the nightgown over her head.

"Hauptsturmführer Hoffmann. Before we were evacuated, he was kind enough to offer them to me, but now, alas, the river is between us."

"I like the river."

"Do you?"

"It's more peaceful, here, than in Amvrosiivka." Straw pricks her feet as she stands up and reaches for her shirt and coveralls.

"As you say." He blows out the lamp, opens the door, and shines his flashlight across the warm stove. The old peasant woman in whose hut they're billeted lies on its sleeping platform. A line of drying laundry hangs above her. Fritz sleeps with his arm dangling over the edge of a straw mattress placed on wooden trunks.

They exit through the back door. The night is clear, and she can smell animal dung in its many varieties. It could be any autumn, any year on a farm. The pig lies on its side in a sty, the goat sleeps in a pen. Hens huddle in the coop, but not for long—soon they'll be wintering in the attic. Corn is ripe in the field and getting low in the corncrib, raised on stilts to protect it from mice and damp. Straw and hay is stacked against a stone wall near diminishing mounds of dried sunflower stems and corn stalks. They walk on night-brittled grass, past the well and the makeshift shower stall for washing at the end of the day. Passing the cornfield, they come to the village school. Below a sky overwhelmed with stars circling the crescent moon, she can imagine the headmaster still asleep in his quarters at the back, waiting for dawn, the ringing of his bell, the arrival of students who'll soon disappear into the harvest.

The school is a wood-frame building with a tin roof and an iron stove that doesn't provide half the warmth of the old-fashioned oven in the peasant hut. Gerhard removes the key from its hiding place inside the bell that hangs over the door and unlocks it. The surgery smells of blood and horse sweat and the exertions of men. Ropes and harness dangle from pulleys, shifting in the draft as she shuts the door. A kerosene lamp provides light; Gerhard carries it to the back room and places it on the desk.

"Read the inventory to me," he says, handing her the clipboard.

The kerosene lamp flickers in the reflection of the window where the curtains don't meet. The desk is kitty-corner to an old cot with the teacher's impression still in the mattress, pushed against the long wall between the window and the back door, which is latched by a bar from the inside. Small tools and hardware supplies are stored in the cabinet against the wall opposite the desk.

"Where should I start?" she asks.

"With these." Gerhard stands facing the shelves of bottles and powders that line the long wall on her right, adjoining the surgery. "Alphabetically." She reads out the list. He lifts bottles, rattles them, counts, mutters that they're low on this and that, opens lids and sniffs while she follows him, clipboard in hand, wondering what she can do to thwart the enemy's war effort. A partisan cell of one. Hungry for an egg.

———

Showing no signs of sleep deprivation except for wide eyes and a tendency to repeat himself, in the morning Gerhard goes off to the quartermaster's depot, confident that he can replenish their supplies by pretending to be from the General Staff, whose collar patches are the same carmine colour as the veterinarian's. By mid-afternoon Lily is glazed with exhaustion. Her hands are raw from washing and blistered from carrying buckets. Her head swims, she craves sleep like an addict, she yearns for the rough bed in the peasant hut beyond the corrals and the stables, past the village school and the cornfield.

"More?" she asks Mr. Bender as she pours diluted arsenic into the trough.

"No, that's enough." He stirs the vat with a pole. Wooden boards form the gate, the ramp, the trough. The sun is breaking through puffballs of stratocumulus cloud, and under it the horses will dry quickly in the far pasture. "Did you tell the Ukrainian shits to make sure they take the horses well away from the vat after they're dipped?" Mr. Bender asks, dropping the pole and grabbing the dipping fork.

"Yes." She can see the stableboys shuffling barefoot, the treated horses with tails curled between their legs as they move toward the meadow south of the dipping vat.

"And they understood you?"

"I told them a few times."

"All right, then."

Fritz leads the last of the Panje horses to be deloused and deticked. The little horse is agreeable and walks calmly through the gate, but as soon as a front hoof touches the galvanized iron on the slide, he balks, his rump goes down, ears forward, head up, snorting his jeopardy. Mr. Bender smacks him hard. He buckles and slides, protesting, into the dip. Mr. Bender pushes him under with the dipping fork. The horse comes up, snorting, scared, and is dunked again. As soon as he's let go, he scrambles out the other end, and Fritz grabs his lead, not letting go until the horse is far from the vat, the sun calming his shivers.

"Look, arsenic dip splashed all over my coveralls," she says. "I have to get out of them." Her eyes are gritty, her voice faint, as if she's already asleep and listening to herself.

"Go to the surgery, Kitten. There's an extra pair hanging on a hook." Mr. Bender has a bald spot like a medallion. He has a daughter her age.

Horses are grazing on the grassland, flicking ears and tails. A stable hand whistles as she makes her way past the stables, and she doesn't smile at him, but her hips sway in their own dream.

When she gets to the school door, she fumbles with the key, her fingers skittering ineptly around the inside of the bell and the surface of the lock. Once inside the surgery, she divests herself of the wet coveralls. She washes her hands, using water from the barrel and the soap that's in the dish beside it, and puts on the coveralls she finds on the hook. She rolls up sleeves and legs, transfers the contents of her old pockets into the new, washes her hands again, leans her forehead on the barrel. She could stand here forever bent like the "б" of бабушка, *Babushka*, her grandmother. The barrel sits in a square of sunlight coming through the unshielded window, and she remembers lying in the park with her head on her grandmother's lap, watching the colours on the insides of her eyelids dance with the sun on her face.

There's an empty burlap sack on the ground beside the barrel. She'll just take it with her, sneak into the back room, and, if nobody's there, find a spot to curl up. "Hello!" she calls as she pushes open the door.

The dispensary is empty and as orderly as when she last saw it except for Fritz's camera, which he must have left on the desk after he came in for a new bulb. The bed is neatly made with a blanket. Though it's inviting, she doesn't want to be caught resting, and so she crawls under the desk. Sheltered by the wall at her back and the modesty panel at the front, she drops into sleep on the plank floor, covered by the sack, lulled by the sound of ground squirrels as they build winter nests in the walls.

When she wakes up, she thinks she still hears the squirrels squeaking and chewing. She eases herself out from under the desk, moving with the groggy caution of someone whose instincts have been honed by purges and informants. The filtered sun offers little light except for the narrow beam that shoots through the gap between the curtains, and her eyes are still blurred by sleep. She can make out shapes and a strawberry stripe. Moving lumps. The cot shifting. She barely knows what she's seeing or why she picks up Fritz's camera to take a picture, as if she's enamoured of the novel device with its synchronized flash and just wants to try it, or as if, somewhere in her half-sleeping brain, a conniving survivor perceives an opportunity.

The flash turns bare skin marble. A back arches, a head shoots up. She doesn't see his face as he pulls up his pants, flings the latch, and scoots out the back door, and since he doesn't turn around, he hasn't seen her, only the burst of hot light. But she recognizes the stable hand from the convalescing horses' facility by the crimson birthmark on his neck, and then she sees Gerhard's stony expression as he pulls the blanket over his nakedness with one hand and reaches for his pistol with the other, and before she can draw another breath, the gun is pointing at her.

"Wait," she says.

Gerhard glances at his gun, surprised that it's still cool. There's no smell of burnt powder, only the comforting pharmaceutical odour that can be found in any dispensary, yet here he is, awkwardly perched on a schoolmaster's cot, with a snub-nosed Mauser in his hand.

"Listen," she says, lowering the camera to the desk.

"Seems that I am." He can hear horses whinnying in the distance as they return to their stalls.

"It isn't news."

A shaft of sunlight parts the curtains, lighting the girl's hair. He knows that she gets boys to sneak peroxide from the dispensary, and he admires the frivolity of it. The flower that cracks concrete.

"We've slept together for weeks," she says. "Just slept. If I wanted to tell someone you're a birdie, I could have done it any time."

"Is that what you call Uranians?" He likes the old term. It was coined by a lawyer who was one himself and makes him think of Karl May, who might not have been one but wrote about cowboys and their beloved Indian blood brothers.

"My grandmother did." Sofia's eyes dart from the back door to the door to the surgery, looking for somewhere to run, but there's nowhere she can go, this girl who shares his bed, who some hours ago assuaged his terror. He had offered her his last pill in gratitude. "Hoffmann suspects. He wants dirt, and I lied for you."

He likes her, worse, needs her like a smelly old blanket, like a yappy schnauzer who doesn't run into streetcars. "Then why take a picture?"

"I didn't think about it. The camera was there."

"To blackmail me."

"Only if I had to."

Soldiers have no right to keep pets. They're not SS men, who can have anything they want, not just a little Ukrainian nurse like Sofia—they'll even take a pretty Jewess to screw before shooting her. Gerhard isn't keen on shooting a girl, less in screwing one. At the thought, his dick shrinks into the nest of his balls, which would be cut like a gelding's if he went to prison. Not that prison is his concern anymore. Men like him are sent to Auschwitz.

"Give me the camera," he says.

"If you take out the film, it'll look suspicious."

"I'll replace it."

"How? There isn't a shop in the village."

"So what do you suggest?"

"In the bottom of the camera, there's a slot for a blade that comes with it. You can pull the film out, just one frame, and slice it with the blade. The rest of the film stays inside. Fritz won't notice." She pushes the camera toward him, across the desk.

"You do it."

Carefully, she upends the camera, shows him the blade, and then with exaggerated motions cuts out the piece of film and brings it to him. With his free hand he holds the negative up to the fading light.

"Now burn it."

She takes an ashtray from the desk, and a box of matches, and sits down on the cot beside him, his pistol following her. The tide of methamphetamine is rolling out, and all the little crustaceans, the crabs of anxiety, are scuttling over his body like lice. A scratch, a flutter and burst of flame. She drops the film into the ashtray, then sets it on the floor.

"Are we finished?" she asks.

"There's still you. It's embarrassing that I've waited this long."

"This isn't your duty as a soldier."

"That doesn't stop a soldier. If I wasn't . . ." Something is biting him under his skin. He needs to wash his hands.

"Don't give me that. I know a boxer. He's a champion. And a gomosexualist."

"Homosexual. So you're saying there's something else wrong with me?" He would laugh if he didn't want to flay his skin from his bone.

"Of course there is. You keep me up all night. If I wasn't so tired, we wouldn't be in this mess. Those pills are bad for you. Would you give them to a horse?"

"Their physiology is different." Amphetamine increases the heart rate of a resting horse but has no discernible effect on a horse in movement. At veterinary school he used to study on his bed so he had more room to spread his textbooks. His handwriting was tiny to save paper. He ordered his notes alphabetically: *Amphetamine*; *Argenti Nitras*; *Arnica*; *Arsenic, uses of*. A good list. Thinking of it makes him itch less.

"I understand why you want the pills," she says. "I was at Stalingrad too."

"You? How?"

"I went east, running away from the German advance, and I ended up in Stalingrad. I was there during the bombing. I saw the river burn. The smoke made a cross you could see all the way to Saratov."

"The smell," he says.

"The smell." She agrees because she knows. Who else around here does?

"War takes you to lands you never knew and wish you didn't," he says. "And when it brings you home, you don't recognize it anymore. How did you come back to the Ukraine?"

"I don't know . . . It's all a blur. There was fighting. People were scared . . . Some of them crossed over to your side . . . I think it was a group of students—they must have taken me with them. All I remember are fields of rye and wheat, and missing the friends who'd died."

"I used to have friends," he says. "My unit was closer than my family. When they died, other men took their place. They died too. It wasn't worth learning their names."

She nods as if she's remembering. "Then war's the only thing left. Everything else has become strange."

"And when you get to the rear, you're supposed to act like being a soldier is some kind of holy thing."

"Maybe it's better to be enemies," she says. "You don't have to pretend."

He lowers the pistol to his side, his hand sick with sweat, and he thinks about taking the last pill, wondering how much longer he can hold out. A noise is coming from the surgery. Footsteps, something shoved aside. Sofia turns her head, he lets the blanket drop away.

Fritz flings the door open and stops abruptly, gazing from Gerhard lying naked on the cot, hands behind his head, to Sofia, hair dishevelled, flushed. And all Gerhard can think is how beautiful the boy is in his anger as he throws a note on the cot.

Boatman here. Orders. Dr. Fischer and nurse to the transit camp.

"Hoffmann wants us," he says to Sofia. "Pack my bag."

Pilot

RUSSIA

One Year before Her Fall

April to December 1942

Smoke Plumed over the Wall

The Women's Air Group split up as each of the three air regiments—fighter, night bomber, and dive-bomber—was mobilized in turn. Lily and the other fighter pilots were based up the road from the school. Assigned to Air Defence, they guarded the factories of Saratov, which were crucial to the work in Stalingrad, as well as the new railroad that would ensure undisrupted transport between the sister cities. The railroad was under construction on the east side of the Volga River, farther from the German line, and it had to be completed quickly, before the next enemy advance.

Hitler believed that the war would be won by wrecking the Soviet economy and removing its wealth to the Reich. He'd already absorbed the rich soil of the Ukraine and the coal of the Donetsk region on the border with Russia. His next target was Stalingrad and the industrial area around it on the banks of the Volga River. By taking control of the river—the longest and deepest in Europe—he would cut the umbilical cord through which supplies flowed into central Russia. The fact that the largest city of the region was named after their country's supreme leader added to the pleasure of conquering it.

To build the railroad, seven million cubic metres of dirt had to be excavated; thirty thousand metres of surface paved; three thousand wooden bridges erected. It was all done by hand. The men—shoeless, hungry convicts living in tents—came from the Saratov labour camp, which was built for the purpose. The convicts carried boulders in wheelbarrows. With rusty shovels and bare hands, they dug the earth. They worked like machines, rapidly, unceasingly, legs and arms pumping with muscles thinned by malnutrition and lubricated by the will to live. On their backs were numbers: E-358,

E-500. Lily flew overhead, back and forth, wondering what number her father wore and if he ever fell in the mud like the convicts sometimes did, and was beaten until he got back on his feet. A line of camels carried supplies, and horses pulled carts up steep riverbanks. After a week's work the horses—more delicate than camels—were sent away to recuperate. They had value, unlike enemies of the people.

The night that Saratov was bombed, there were no fighter planes in the air because the aircraft, unequipped with radar, were night blind. On the ground, anti-aircraft guns were manned by unskilled volunteers. It was late June, warm, a beautiful night. Lily and some of the other pilots were in town for an evening out. They'd seen a movie. They'd had a drink. They'd gone dancing. They'd just left the dance hall when the first bomb fell, and they scattered, seeking shelter.

Behind the brick wall of a schoolyard, Lily crouched as she counted the explosions: two, three, four, five, six, seven, eight. The dark sky was blasted by pillars of light, dotted lines, a knobby pyramid that shattered into arrowheads, orbs, cones, shapes for which there were no names. The steady beams of searchlights swept back and forth. Gold pierced by red and green tracers. Debris crashed against the wall, dislodging a brick that barely missed Katie at her back. Metal flew over the wall, hitting the windows of a warehouse; glass shattered; shards scattered and fell; smoke plumed black, brown, purple; a column of concrete rose into the sky like rubbled fireworks and showered onto the street. Even with her fingers to her ears, Lily's head was ringing. She estimated the size of the bombs by the pressure behind her eyes. Fifty kilograms, she guessed. Then two hundred kilograms. Then half a ton.

When the all-clear sounded, she was covered in dust. She pulled up the scarf from inside the collar of her coveralls so that it covered her mouth and nose. She could feel the heat, and as she got to her feet, she clutched her chest, trying to cough out the fumes from the molten metal, the coolant on fire, the combusted chemicals. Someone was shouting, running past her: "It's the ball-bearing plant. We have to put out the fire." And she ran too, in the direction of the factory.

Searchlights and signal flares turned it white, green, red. The factory had been sliced and diced, the outside wall gone on one side, the staircases visible, desks and cabinets that had crashed through one floor in a heap on another. Broken pipes were pouring water, the metal hissing. Live wires hung, swayed, sparked. Dismembered pieces of machinery had been flung in a jumble around the factory. The wire fence around the yard was three metres high. Someone dangled from it. Survivors huddled or scrabbled through rubble or stood alone and screamed along with the sirens. A night worker, clothes aflame, tried to drag his mate through the ruin of the factory wall. Someone pushed him to the ground and rolled him, putting out the flames. Fire burst from spilled oil; it clambered over every wooden structure, gobbled it down, raged for more, rearing from doorways, flaring from blasted windows.

Lily found herself next to Katie among a group of men passing along buckets of water. Her hands were slippery and the bucket sloshed as she struggled with the weight, handing it up the line. She wiped her hands on her coveralls, grabbed the next bucket. There was a trick to this, a rhythm to find, allowing you to lose yourself in the collective effort so that you didn't get tired. Bucket and bucket, water and water. At the head of the line, men threw the water on the fire, which sizzled and rose higher, their effort no more than a drizzle of rain on a conflagration. But they didn't give up; that was what it meant to be a social being, a Soviet, an atom that was part of the greater whole. Always keep going, keep up the pace. A tin can came into her hand. They'd run out of buckets. Then pass along the tin can, and if the edge cut your thumb, that was more liquid for the crackling flames. When the fire truck came, men leaped from the back, and Lily moved aside for the unrolling hose. The line broke down into its component parts, and she disappeared into the crowd, pushing deeper into the devastation with Katie following her.

Bodies had been laid beside the tumble of bricks, concrete, twisted metal. Over them bent mourners and searchers looking for a known face. Lily ran past them, heedless of Katie, who was trying to speak to her. In the wreckage of what might have been a metal workshop, rescuers had given up on a space too tight for anyone to get into. Lily crouched by the gap in the rubble to get a better sense of what was inside. Maybe she heard something, maybe not. Who could tell in this noise? As she moved a chunk of cement to enlarge the opening, Katie tried to pull her away. *Don't be an idiot! You'll be trapped.* Lily shook her off and crawled in, the gap widening enough for her head and shoulders. Turning sideways, she slid forward another half metre, and there—in a pocket of space below a broken beam—she found someone. *Can you hear me?* No answer. Unconscious or dead. She dug her hands into the person's coveralls, held tight as she wiggled backward. Katie's arms reached past hers, grabbing on to the boots, and together they hauled out a kid who'd been working on a lathe or a cutter when the air raid sounded. He still held a scrap of metal in his hand. Lily put her ear to his mouth. It tickled. He breathed. Women in white took the boy, lifted him into the back of an ambulance. At a streetside aid station the wounded were bandaged by volunteers with trembling hands and clenched teeth. The night was lit by flames.

Katie wanted to find the girls from their squadron and nobody was stopping her, but Lily wasn't done. Preserving a single young life wasn't enough to prove to herself she was a good Communist.

There were other bombed buildings where survivors must be trapped. Lily moved away from the factory, and again Katie followed as she clambered up on broken concrete, poking into every small space. She was one of the rescuers, a part of the whole, saving, saving, saving the nation. For a long hour she found nothing, and then, on a side street, climbing on a pile of rubble, she spied something red, a shoe in a gap too small for a child to wriggle into. Not even a doll would fit through it. But Lily squatted and pushed away debris until she could stretch her arm through the hole. She grasped the shoe and strained as she leaned back, but there was no resistance and she fell against Katie. In Lily's hand was the shoe and in the shoe was a foot. Lily tucked it back into the crevice. She took the scarf from her neck and laid it over the foot.

Katie helped her climb down. They sat on a stoop, leaning against the door of a one-eyed shop, its double window only half broken. Searchers pushed past them. Someone stopped to ask if they needed help and, when they said no, hurried on. There was a distant *pop-pop-pop* as something belatedly ruptured.

"A foot," Lily said.

"Evidently."

They remembered they were soldiers. Neither of them looked over to see if the other was shaking.

"In a shoe."

"With laces."

"You could have gone to look for the rest of our squadron," Lily said.

"I have to look after you."

"I can take care of myself."

"You? The pilot that's famous for spending the night in the guardhouse over her fashion tastes? I should call you Boots."

"Not Shoe."

"No."

Lily laughed. She couldn't help it. She knew that Katie would think she'd gone mad, and she put both hands over her mouth, trying to keep anyone from hearing as her chest heaved, squeaks and hiccups escaping the sharp corners of her mouth. Then Katie's shoulders were shuddering. Strangled sounds from her throat, ripping through pressed lips. Their shoulders rattled against each other, ball and socket joints bumped as they rocked, shaking with laughter, leaning against each other, faces flooded with tears.

"You're bleeding," Katie said, pointing to Lily's forehead.

"Am I?" Lily felt a trickle, and when she touched it, her fingers came away red. "Is it bad?"

"You're not dying. Let me." Katie tore a strip from her shirt and wiped the cut.

"If I die, it'll just be my mother and little brother."

"Same. Except older sister. I'm the only man of the house."

"You could pass as one."

"Really?"

"A young one, not shaving. If your hair was cut like theirs," Lily said, studying her seriously. "I think you could."

"Thanks."

"You'd need a name. How about Vladimir?" A common name. Her father's.

"Like Vladimir the Great?"

"Not so great."

"You could call me Volodya." A pet name for Vladimir . . . like Katie for Katherine.

"That's for other people. I'll dance with you in the barracks, but I'll still call you Katie."

An emergency response truck turned the corner. Volunteers with shovels and brooms stood in the back of it. The truck stopped. Volunteers jumped out.

"We should probably go and help," Katie said.

"Soon."

"Tell me, Lily. Are you afraid of dying?"

"Sometimes. Mostly at night. You?"

"Not the death, but the pain part. Another thing," Katie said. "I can't stand it when my sister is hurt. I'd do anything to stop it."

"I'm also afraid of snakes," Lily said. "Not big ones, but little ones you might step on and squish, and then there would be flat snake on my boot. I think of it when I'm in a field. And little fish. When I swim underwater, I'm scared that one will get in my mouth. Also lightning. I saw a man get hit. And of letting my family down, all the time. Can you tell?"

"Not at all."

"Good. You're a man, and I'm fearless."

"Not to mention that we live in a socialist utopia."

Lily chuckled, she hiccuped one last time, and a feeling came over her, not unfamiliar but childish, disconcerting, discarded years ago. The feeling that it was safe to trust someone because they were friends. Before she could be misled by it, she said, "Come on, let's go help with the cleanup."

At dawn, after the last of the fires was doused, excavators and diggers were brought in to collect the rubble and move it away so that the morning shift could get in to work. Electricity was restored. News came through the public address system stationed at every major intersection. The enemy had targeted the ball-bearing plant because it produced eighty percent of the nation's ball bearings, which were necessary to every kind of military equipment. There were thirty fatalities and two hundred serious injuries. The plant would reopen for work at 0900 hours.

Wind carried smoke to the river, where it hovered like a memory.

The Germans were practising.

Stalingrad Settled

On a dishevelled airstrip thirty kilometres from Stalingrad, a pair of Yak-1s and a bomber landed in a swirl of reddish dust and ash blown by the wind. Lily and Katie opened canopies that were steaming as the cold of the sky met late summer heat. Because no transport planes had been available, the bomber had carried their mechanics in an emptied bay. Pilots and mechanics disembarked, looking for someone to greet them and take them in, and when no one appeared, they came together instinctively, like steppe antelope with gas-mask snouts. As they walked, they kicked up dust, which soon lined the creases of their clothes and the creases of their eyes. Tumbleweeds rolled in the wind, a defensive circle of brambles, a prickled net, a crown of thorns. There were scattered carcasses on the field—crisped hulks of planes, wings broken, tails smashed or ripped away—and craters where the brick dust of Stalingrad, carried east on the wind, had settled in dry red pools.

The attack on Stalingrad had begun when August fruits had ripened. In the fields and orchards outside the target area, German troops had picked melons, tomatoes, and pears while they'd watched 1,200 aircraft from the Luftwaffe's Fourth Air Fleet drop a thousand tons of bombs on the city. Oil tankers had exploded. Pavement had flowed like water. Water had burned. Fire had risen from the river, its black smoke forming a giant cross that was visible all the way to Saratov. German officers had taken photographs. When the film was developed, they'd written on the backs of photos, *For the Death of Stalingrad*. After the city had been reduced to rubble, German troops had moved in, and they soon held most of the ruined streets. Against the Fourth Air Fleet, the Soviet air force had the 8th Air Army. It was poorly equipped, short of aircraft, its pilots young and hastily trained, the officers who might have guided them having been exiled or shot in the purge that had taken Lily's father. The mortality rate at Stalingrad was high, and every regiment in Air Defence had been ordered to transfer pilots as replacements.

Lily heard rumbling from afar and, close by, the warbled caw of alarmed buzzards, but not a human voice anywhere. No cook was cursing and smacking an assistant, no groomer was cleaning the airstrip, no horse driver was whipping the supply wagon forward, no camel driver was bringing water, no quartermaster was grumbling over supplies, no radio operator was twisting the antenna, no mechanic was finding a make-do for missing parts, no pilot was studying maps.

As they approached HQ, the telephone rang ten times and stopped. It rang again twenty-two times and stopped. HQ had no door. The canteen was caved in, the roof gaping, keeling to the side. From somewhere behind it, as if he had come from a rolling tumbleweed, a man stepped out, stared at them, ran with his hands up to push them back, yelling, "Are you crazy?"

"We're here to reinforce the 437th Fighter Air Regiment," Katie said.

"Can't be." His pants were blackened and torn. "We were bombed, and more German fighters are on the way. My regiment was based here, and everyone's pulled out."

"What about you?" Lily asked.

"Waiting for a ride. My machine's one of those." He jutted his chin toward the graveyard of planes. "Hurry up and go!"

"Where to?" Katie took out her map and he jabbed a finger at it.

"Central Akhtuba. Get out while you can."

"You'd better come with us," Katie said. "You can squeeze in with the mechanics in the bomber bay."

They ran back to their aircraft, Lily smallest and last, behind
Katie, the bomber pilot, their mechanics, and the man in the ragged
pants. The bomb bay opened; he climbed in with the ground crew
while Lily caught up, gasping. She clambered up on the wing of her
plane, jumped into her cockpit. Radiators off. Throttle forward.
Engine on. They taxied out the way they came in. Katie first, the
bomber in the middle, Lily at the end. Pull back on the stick. Climb,
raise landing gear. Below and behind, she could see columns of dust
from strafing fighters, and she wondered how many seconds until
the enemy realized the base was deserted. To her right, the Akhtuba
River, a small tributary of the Volga, beyond that the flood plain. To
her left, cracked earth. Katie wagged her wings: prepare to descend.

Lily pushed up her goggles, looked back. Her grandmother
used to say, *Never look back or you'll turn into salt,* but her grandmother
had gone back to Zhytomyr, she was under German occupation,
and Lily could see the Messerschmitt aircraft behind her. If you see
Messers, they can shoot you. The new base was close, there was the
village made of mud bricks and the airfield beyond it. Katie was
down and so was the bomber, but Lily was coming in too fast. She
overshot and turned, landing as the bomber bay opened, the crew
tumbling out. Lily slid back the canopy. A skim of dark air, engine
heat, shadow, machine-gun fire blasting grit in her eyes. She was
out, she was crawling on her wing, rolling under it to shelter herself,
hands over ears, and all she could see were boots stirring dust.
Someone pushed her flat, she smelled his sweat as he covered her
with his body.

Noise diminished. The pressure on her lungs lifted. The pilot
who'd hitched a ride was helping her to her feet. He had a stocky
build, a bulldog head. His fingers were roughened. He might have
dug trenches too. Other men were lifting themselves off the women
they'd rushed to protect. Was this all they had left—no cannon, no
aircraft, just arms, legs, bellies? Smoke stung her eyes.

"How can the Germans do this—where are our fighters?"

"Wish I knew. They've got five, maybe ten machines for every one of ours."

"What happened to your pants?"

He shrugged. He grinned. "My Yakki," he said ruefully, referring to his Yak-1 fighter. "It was on fire, but I landed it. Unfortunately, my pants got scorched in the process, and the quartermaster says I haven't finished out the time allotted for this pair. Good luck up there—don't die too soon. See you around." And he trotted off to find his own regiment.

Katie and Lily reported to HQ, were assigned quarters and told to attend the briefing session at 1100 hours. They were already on the roster.

The sky above Stalingrad was a hot, dark soup boiling with enemy planes, and in her Yak-1, Lily was a tiny flying morsel, a bit of kasha, a dot of potato, maybe a shred of cabbage soon to be dissolved. She focused on the regimental commander's tail, her duty as wingman to guard him. Below and to the left were the divisional commander and Katie. They were covering ground troops, providing air protection from German bombers. Flying in groups of two or four, they'd been ordered to spread out, appear more than they were. Lily didn't think the Germans were fooled. It took a thousand bullets to hit an enemy aircraft and ten times that to kill one. Sweat trickled down her back.

She'd thought she knew what she was getting into, but she knew nothing.

Her head ached with the shrieking whistles, exploding bombs, and cannon blasts, the smell of dying men, the screams of thousands. Stalingrad was cooking. German tanks rolled toward it from the south, German horses pulled artillery from the west and north.

In the cauldron of the sky, she looked for enemy aircraft painted yellow on wing tips, tail, nose, the double-engined bombers flanked by long-nosed Messers plunging through smoke, Stukas with their wailing sirens, Focke-Wulfs hunting meat.

It was their second sortie since the assault had begun. Colonel Danilov, the divisional commander, had a working radio and was supposed to be getting intelligence from command, but the newly installed radar couldn't read a crowded sky. Pilots had to rely on their own eyes and instruments.

They were climbing, trying to reach clear sky. Four thousand metres, she pulled on her oxygen mask, five thousand metres, she was breathing oxygen, seven thousand, her cockpit was cooling down. Colonel Danilov signalled: to the right, below. A large group of bombers with stragglers, three Ju 88s to the side. At this height the guarding Messers were faster; he needed to make the most of their position and the Yakkis' agility. Danilov rocked quickly from wing to wing and slid to let them know that he was drawing off the Messers. He dived, Katie with him, while Lily's leader slipped into a wisp of cloud, moving toward the bombers. She stayed on his tail for long seconds, keeping watch above, behind, to left and right.

As soon as they broke out of the cirrus clouds, he went for the bomber on the right, and she nosed up. Left stick, she banked, then came straight on the horizontal, aiming full speed at the middle of the group. They didn't believe she meant it, they thought she'd climb before she slammed into them. When she got too close, the bombers scattered as a Messer lunged between them, shooting as it came. Her wing shuddered as it was hit. She flipped, the clouds her carpet, the sky's blue walls spiralling away. She forced her nose down, hoping she wouldn't vomit from the pain cleaving her temples as she came into the horizontal. Above and port side, momentarily alone, a turgid bomber was still carrying its load. Tight turn, accelerate. She was gaining on it, getting in close and closer, coming from below, a crazy manoeuvre. Wings were spread over her, white belly, black crosses; the bomber occupied her field of vision like a lover returned from away. Her heart lifted, the noise of twin engines roared into her ears as she fired. A gorgeous bloom of fire exploded from the belly. She fired again, and the bomber's left wing folded up; it dropped, expired. She was mantled in smoke, the sky smelled of oil and melting steel. Everything below her wavered in a heat shimmer.

Bombers were crashing down in fireballs, and her leader was wagging his wings. Climb! Climb! Get out of the way! But below and starboard, she saw a Messer gunning at Katie, who wasn't firing back. She must be out of ammunition. Lily's friend was hit, a sister bleeding smoke, and the enemy had her in his sights, so absorbed he didn't notice Lily above. Adrenalin was her friend, killing fear and opening eyes, lungs, shoving blood, sugar, everything she needed into muscles so she could push her stick with both hands, pressing it with her knees as she pointed her nose down in a dive so steep and abrupt she blacked out for a second, blood trickling from her nose as she pulled up in his blind spot at six o'clock. She was at thirty metres before he noticed her and rolled too late. She fired. He was hit, aflame. He shot wide. She turned and shot again. The fuselage streamed oil, and flames licked the skull painted on the side of his machine. She could see the pilot pull off his helmet, radio, oxygen mask. He hesitated, punched the canopy; it must be stuck. Everything was clear to her, now. This Fascist was to blame for the ruined city below her, for the spies in her country who had made its leaders suspect her father, for every misery she'd known. All she had to do was shoot him down. He punched the canopy again, desperately. Before she was able to turn to fire again, it opened, and the wind hauled him out.

———

The base was camel-coloured, camel-scented, dull and motionless. As soon as Lily jumped out of her Yakki, she longed to be back in the living sky. Katie kissed her on the cheek and without any envy proclaimed Lily's achievements. Two kills! Her first day! Pilots were debriefed, losses assessed, and they paid tribute to the fallen with shots of vodka: *To Stalin, to victory, to our comrades!*

Lily drank, her fuzzy head making her feel more girl and more soldier, as if there was no contradiction, and she didn't object when Katie pulled her along with the other pilots toward the community hall. An idea was blooming out of the rich waters of Lily's inebriation: she would become a hero—a Hero of the Soviet Union with a Gold Star. When Stalin pinned the medal on her with his own hands, she would explain that the NKVD had made a mistake, and her father would be released because the almighty father of her country would rectify every wrong.

The gramophone was cranked and cranked again for "Rio Rita," "Champagne," "Your Fingers Smell of Incense," "In This Sleepy Town," "The Blue Kerchief," "Ah Yes the Guy," "Wearied Sun." Watermelon was on the table, seeds on the floor, white and black in the red dust that blew through the window. A pilot with a crooked grin and a dimpled chin introduced himself as Vladimir Lavrinenkov and asked Lily to dance. Her hips were rolling, his hips were rolling, her hand was in his as he twirled her around him. Circle, circle and don't land, not yet. As long as they danced, this Vladimir was hers and she was his, only the song would change. Now it was slow, his arm was bent, his hand gripped hers, hip bones touched. Now it was fast, she was laughing, he was laughing, their eyes met, who needed more, she was holding on to his shoulders, he was holding on to her waist, lifting her toward the sky, her secret dacha. The timbers shook with stamping and the roof with singing, and they'd go on drinking and dancing until they couldn't pronounce the name of anyone who'd died. Rain didn't fall. The ground was dry and cracked. Lightning flashed, and she had no fear of it; the holes in the roof were dazzling.

Flying from dawn to dusk without let-up, Lily fought the enemy in the sky above the rubble of Stalingrad, once a city of bubbling fountains and wide white avenues. Every time she survived the blast and stink of battle, she was elated and fell into bed at night with a tiredness that banished thought. For the first time since her father's arrest, she was a part of something great. The enemy pressed with all its strength while defenders held on to slivers: ruined factories; a grain silo where Soviet soldiers were breathing chaff and slowly suffocating; houses defended room by room, German soldiers on one floor, the Soviets holed up in the basement with the rats. A rickety boat trying to ferry wounded across the river was blown apart. The Volga frothed with blood. And still, they held on. Russian soldiers hugged a fragment of riverbank and told their stories to the newspaperman who sat with them and their hunger. They said, *If you bury your clothes and leave just an inch of cloth above ground, the lice will climb up for air, and you can hold a match to them.* Autumn rain turned to icy sleet.

A fuzzy picture on page two of the newspaper, *The Red Star*, October 30, 1942, Issue No. 256, right below the large-print banner that read: *Soldiers of the Red Army! Strict order and iron discipline, the pledge of our victory!* A pilot in heavy flight gear, gender indeterminate, stood on the wing of a fighter, leaning an elbow on the cockpit. The misspelled caption read: *SERVING THE ARMY. Fighter pilot Sergeant L. Lyatvyak takes down a Ju 88 in single battle and Messerschmitt 109 in a group. Photo by B. Zeitlin.*

———

Some regiments were so depleted of pilots who'd died in combat, they existed in name only. The commander of the 8th Air Army reorganized them and created an elite regiment by transferring top pilots from across his service to the 9th Guards, which had been all but demolished. Among them were Vladimir Lavrinenkov, Katie Budanova, and Lily Litvyak, who couldn't believe her luck. To be recognized this way! Maybe her drunken daydream wasn't far-fetched. She imagined it again—standing on the podium, Comrade Stalin bending as he pinned the medal, listening earnestly to her.

Their air base was in the wreckage of a collective farm outside Stalingrad. Last summer there had been sheep, horses, cows, herders, horsemen here. There were none now. The stream was frozen. Caponiers disguised under mounds of earth and sod served as airplane hangars. The fields around were pocked with craters, and snow-humped broken tanks dotted the landscape with their spoor of abandoned ammunition. All that remained of the farm were a couple of peasant cottages with clay roofs and walls made of mud and dung: HQ and a canteen, the female pilots allocated cots in its storage room. Dugouts were built, hay found to burn for fuel. Engineers constructed stoves and roofs with metal pieces scavenged from the debris that was scattered across the fields, and soon the dugouts were spewing homey black smoke.

The elite male pilots were square-jawed, cleft-chinned, each one more beguiling than the next, their chests glittering with medals, adored by photographers. When they all assembled for a portrait, the girls were placed at either end to make perfect bookends. This was Soviet womanhood: the Amazon and the flower. Unfortunately, the flower was unpicked as the men refused to fly with Lily in combat, and they were supported in their resolve by the regimental commander. Katie was all right, she was practically a man. They called her Volodya, and why not? She looked like a man, she played like one, she was just as willing to take a village girl from the dance to a dark spot, and none of them complained when they came back. It was the best prank ever. The only thing she couldn't do was piss standing, and she took their ribbing with good cheer. Vladimir Lavrinenkov, who came from the same region as Katie, was happy to have her as his wingman.

Lily was grounded, a fish out of water, her thoughts like worms eating the fishy brain. She worried that someone was investigating her, she worried that her father was dying in the cold of a labour camp or her grandmother in the Ukraine, while in the daylight hours between a winter's dawn and its dusk and its storms, her comrades were hacking at the enemy. Sometimes German pilots parachuted and lived. One of them had red hair and a quiet voice; he carried a picture of his family. Vladimir offered him a cigarette, and the fallen pilot had a smoke before being taken for interrogation. When a transport plane fell without exploding, they harvested its goods, and supper was full of surprises: truffles, bottles of champagne. Katie was promoted to lieutenant.

Every night, Amet-Khan Sultan, a darkly handsome pilot—his mother a Tatar and his father a Dagestani mountain man—pointed his pistol at the snowy sky and shouted, *That's for the living.* Every day, Lily begged the boys to give her a chance. They put up their hands and asked for mercy from darling Litvyak, their sweetheart, their pet, the light of the regiment. Would she sing for them? Give a little kiss? Fix the rips in trousers so holey their balls were frosty enough to be ornaments for the New Year's tree? A million Soviet men and a thousand tanks were hiding by day in emptied villages, advancing only at night, inching toward Stalingrad from all directions. The battle was turning, and Lily wasn't a part of it. She pleaded with Colonel Shestakov, the commander: "Put me on duty, Comrade Colonel, give me something to do, anything."

"You can guard the snow for us," he said, and laughed at his wit.

———

Holding a rifle against her shoulder, Lily stood at the edge of the airfield. She'd been standing there since dawn like a scarecrow in the voracious wind. A scarf was wrapped around her neck and chin, but her cheeks were raw, and like a big brother, Vladimir came over to wise her up.

"It's warmer in the dugout," he said.

"Nobody told you to leave it," she replied.

"Look, I understand. It'll be three days until my plane is repaired." He felt legless, armless, it was driving him crazy, and he wanted to throttle something, but he'd left his mechanic's side just to come out here and freeze his ass for this girl's benefit.

"Ha! Just three days. Try it as long as me," she said.

"So why stand here? It doesn't help. Come inside. You want to play cards?"

"No. I'm on duty."

"Come on. You're being silly. The commander was joking." He put a hand on her arm and she ignored it, keeping watch of nothing, her eyes narrowed against the wind.

"I'll stand here until I'm given another assignment," she said.

"It's not going to happen."

"Keeping me grounded is cruel."

She was missing the point, and Vladimir didn't know how to tell her. If you found a man with his head blown off, or a child who was skin over bones and a swollen belly, or a pile of them, the words for it were *enemy, victory, strength*. He also knew a lot of words for sexual body parts, their uses and their misuses. But how could he say that his only shred of decency—their only shred—was protecting this girl, right here? Not from danger, because the whole country was in danger. And not by preventing her from seeing the unbearable, for they were raised on it. But just in this: keeping her off the front line.

All other terrors he was helpless to guard her from, or his sisters, or his mother, or his one-legged uncle, but if he and his comrades could stand like a wall in front of this one terror (he had nightmares of it—his skin catching fire, melting like his wing), he could hold on to a moral self. He was a defender of his country. Of a pure girl upright in the pure snow.

"Coward! You just don't want to cry over a girl," Lily said.

"Be as stubborn as you want. It's your frostbite." Vladimir shrugged and left her standing there. Let the wind spit its icy grit in her face. He was going back to the hay-fuelled stove.

He was nearly there when he heard the hysterical roar of a low-flying bomber. By the time he returned to the airfield, she was already aloft.

The German bomber had no fighter escort. Behind it, the rest of Lily's regiment was coming in from a mission. They were dots against the clouds, tips of fingers pressing the sky, and the bomber paid no heed to them. Under its belly there was a payload, dozens of small bombs to carpet the air base and destroy it.

Lily recognized the aircraft's shape, its flat-headed, broad canopy, the gondola under the nose: a Dornier 217. Muscled with guns above, below, through the nose. Their ammunition would take a sixth of a second to make contact with her aircraft. Ten rounds a second. They had a crew of four. Swivelling turret. Twinned BMW engine. The bomber was a brute. As fast as her Yak-1. What was her advantage? Manoeuvrability. Mischief. Their unguarded rear.

She reached the bomber's altitude at the edge of its shooting range. The gunners shouldn't bother wasting ammunition on her. But they did—they couldn't resist another notch in their belt even though they were supposed to focus on moving toward their target. Their tracers were way off the mark, and she kept climbing. Five hundred metres above, she pulled flat, they nicked her wing, and she overshot at speed as if she didn't know the sky and where she was in it. Let them think she was an easy lay, those eager boys. Put their eyes on her sweet and creamy ass.

In her headset, she heard the commander's baritone ordering her to desist, move off, but no one could land with the bomber in the way.

"Can't copy. Radio malfunction," she said as she looked back through the glass canopy at the streaky sky and the Dornier continuing on its southeast heading.

Nobody knew what she had in mind; she was a girl, and what boy understood how she thought? Nor did they care as long as they could get her under them, which they would, only on her terms. She slammed the throttle forward, hauled back the stick, her stomach fell as she pulled into vertical, airspeed dropping. A near stall. Hard rudder input. Guts, heart still flying up as the plane flipped, trying to fit through her throat while her wing swung over the top of the turn, following her nose, preserving the energy of movement as she rushed back down her path, facing the other way. Facing them. Above and behind that vulnerable tail and in position for an up-and-under manoeuvre.

The baritone in her headset asked, *What the fuck do you think you're doing?* and commanded, *Fall back immediately.*

She dived through the Dornier's blind spot, coming up below, hoping that she was too high for their ventral gun. She lined up the port engine in her gunsight and fired a five-second burst. In mock battles, the enemy dropped as soon as it was hit, but they were still in flight.

Those boys wanted her now, their gang of dicks aimed at her metal skin. The ventral gun hit her first, the dorsal gun as she passed above. Fuel pressure dropped. Her tank was pierced. She shuddered and fired at their fuel tanks.

Jump, she heard in her headset. A low voice, female despite its huskiness, pitched higher than usual. *Jump, Lily! Don't be stupid.*

The bomber wobbled, twisted, the port engine smoking, pieces dropping off. She had seconds or none to split herself in two, desert the soaring half of herself, consign it to oblivion. Her cockpit stank of oil, her instrument panel was sparking, but she thought she could bring her Yakki in. Five hundred metres, three hundred metres, she was too low to bail. No time to lower gear. The airstrip rushed at her. She bumped along it, the floor of her aircraft hot. An emergency vehicle was roaring across the airfield. She flung open the canopy, jumped from the aircraft and landed on smoking boots, ran and rolled as flames engulfed the wings and tail.

In HQ she stood at attention while the regimental commander, Colonel Shestakov, sat in judgment between his chief of staff and his political officer. They were both silent, though the Party man was taking notes. The commander was smoking rough Russian tobacco like an ordinary grunt. Stubbed out one cigarette, rolled another. He was in a bad mood; his field wife—as officers called the women they bedded—wanted to get married.

"I could have you court-martialled and sent to a place so cold you'd think Siberia is a spa," he said. "Or shot. Bam, through the guts, right here behind HQ. And I would do it, too, except that you'd stink up the base as soon as there was a thaw. What the hell got into you?"

"I was on guard duty." She'd thought there would be some acknowledgement that she'd proven herself.

"That was a joke! Is there a woman alive who has a sense of humour?"

"I thought you gave me an order, Comrade Colonel." The soles of her boots had melted away. Her feet were cold, her eyes hot with unshed tears. "And I got a kill."

"So you want to claim that? You're fucking kidding me. She's kidding me, right?"

"No, Comrade Colonel. There were two observers. You and Sergeant Lavrinenkov," Lily said.

"Your aircraft burnt to shit. Nothing's recoverable. Not a damn screw. You think you deserve a bonus for that fuck-up?"

"No, not for that, but . . ." A rat ambled across the floor. The telegraph operator reached for his signal book and smashed down. The rat scurried. "The bomber would have destroyed our base and every plane in the airfield, Comrade Colonel."

"Maybe you forgot we have anti-aircraft guns. You know? The things that point up at enemy planes and go *rat-a-tat-tat.*"

There was only one working anti-aircraft gun on the base. It was old, it had a tendency to jam, and the gunners were short of ammunition, though officially they were oversupplied, counting the abandoned ammunition of unsuitable calibre rusting all over the base. She said, "They're not strategically placed."

"A piss-ass little girl does not get to make that decision! I ordered you to pull back. Where in that teeny-weeny brain did it even occur to disobey a direct order?"

"My radio wasn't working."

"Convenient."

"There's also the matter of her uniform," the political officer said. He looked pointedly at her stockinged feet. "Insubordination and destruction of State property. After everything we've done to make you girls welcome. I'm disappointed, Litvyak."

"I'm sorry, Comrade Verkhovets." She imagined her father in a labour camp, a convict, a *zek* with a number on his back, emaciated, pushing a heavy wheelbarrow and looking at her with disappointment.

The chief of staff wrote something on a form, then spoke in an undertone to the commander. Shestakov leaned toward him, a muscle twitching in his grim jaw. He nodded.

"No kill, no court martial," he said. "A week confined to quarters. I don't want to waste any manpower keeping you in the guardhouse. Dismissed."

In the December twilight, the sun was a ball of red syrup melting into the white crust of earth.

Since Lily couldn't leave their quarters in the canteen's storage room, Katie brought her a bowl of stew for supper. Lily was sitting on her cot, adjacent to the sacks of flour and jugs of cooking oil, writing a letter home by candlelight. On the other side of the thin door, boys were noisy with their food and their evening hijinks. They never tired of offering each other tobacco rolled in exploding flash paper.

"Thanks," Lily said, putting down her letter and taking the warm bowl.

"You saved the base." Katie sat on her own cot. "You want more? Let me know and I'll bring it."

"So you're allowed to talk to me."

"Confined to quarters—I didn't hear anything about not talking. Don't look so sad. It's only a week."

"And then what?" Lily asked. "No one in this unit will fly with me."

"You could go back to the women's fighter regiment. Major Kazarinova's gone to Moscow, so no more lice checks. The new commander is supposed to be all right."

"Not Air Defence! I have to be at the front."

"You've got nothing to prove."

Lily dug her spoon into the stew. Only a child longs to offer up her heart in whispers, not realizing that heart is cheap meat, full of good protein. So why did she feel so lost, so lonely? "Everything was different in Stalingrad at first."

"Yeah, no sleep, eating dust, Germans all around, shitting your pants. You've got to love it."

"Because I belonged. I was just like everyone else. But now . . ."

"You think I don't get that? Me, of all people?"

"What I mean . . ." It was hard to find words. Not the slogans, so practised, so easily said. But her own words, both true and safe. "I was in the thick of it. And then at night I was too tired to worry about anyone. Too tired to think."

"Like I don't have family to worry about too," Katie said.

"Do you?" Lily asked quietly. They looked at each other and were silent. No more could be said without endangering themselves or the other.

Katie nudged Lily's knee. "Remember the mice in the gym at Engels?"

"You mean the time you jumped on the bed?"

"I wasn't the only one," Katie said.

"I wonder if they still listen to 'Rio Rita.' Remember how everyone danced to it?"

"Of course! I like dancing with girls."

"I know."

"Then why don't you call me Volodya?"

"Because."

"That's not an answer."

"Why do I have to?"

"It suits me."

"The whole squadron calls you Volodya."

"But not you. Who gave me the name."

"Katie's a nice name."

"It's not who I am. I thought we were friends."

"We are."

"There must be a reason. Come on, tell me."

"Look. If either of us gets captured . . . you . . . me . . ." Lily's cot squeaked as she shifted to gaze at Katie's face in the shadowy flicker of candlelight. "The Germans will find the same thing under your pants as mine. They'll do the same to you as me."

"We've got pistols," Katie said.

Someone banged on the door to the storage room. "Hey, Volodya. What are you doing in there? Sultan's piss drunk and we've got to catch up."

"I'm busy," Katie said.

"With what?"

"Puking. Go on without me."

"You're giving up an evening with them?" Lily asked.

"They'll manage without me." Katie pulled a pack of cards from her pocket, shuffled, and dealt them each a hand. "Besides, you smell better."

Until the candle burnt out, they played cards, reminisced, teased each other, laughed. In darkness, they shuffled out of uniforms and lay down under their blankets in long underwear. They lay side by side wakefully in their cots.

Katie spoke to the night. "Tell me something about your wild grandmother."

"She's in the Ukraine. I'm going to rescue her from the Fascists."

"Of course. I'll be there. What else?"

"She had a pair of beautiful boots. Every time I heard the boots in the hallway, I felt like everything was going to be all right. She knew a lot of languages. She spoke Polish with our neighbour. Their son was cute, but they went away."

"In 1937?"

"Yes."

"Better tell me an older story."

"My grandmother had an axe. She took it into the woods with my father."

"What woods?"

"When the soldiers were looking for them. He didn't want to fall asleep and let her stand guard alone, but he was only ten."

"An axe is heavy."

"And she's small like me. My father's tall like the other side of the family." Lily thought about her last name. It was just a tiny fiction, altered by a single letter. A vowel, an extra exhalation. How could that make her father not her father? A man who smelled of machine oil, worked late, shaved before bed, kissed her forehead and whispered, *Good dreams.* She wore his watch, listened to it ticking time. *My father is an enemy of the people.* She could think the words in darkness. If there was light, someone might read the words on her face, and her only friend would look at her with disgust.

Katie yawned, her breathing slowed into sleep.

Dear Mama and Yuri,

You would laugh if you saw me shuffling to the latrine in the boots I made from rags, cardboard, and twine! Mine got wrecked, and I'm not due for another pair yet. The Fascists' Fourth Air Fleet loves us, they fly over every day, but it's just a lot of racket. Don't worry about me! I'm an expert at jumping into a trench. What I'm really dying for is a pair of box calf boots. That would be a dream come true, but any boots at all would be wonderful if you can get your hands on them, Mama. Also, my notebook is full. Could you send me another?

I miss you terribly. I am sending a million kisses.

Your Lil'ka.

Despite Hitler's belief that Russians lacked the brainpower to mount a pincer attack, it was accomplished at Stalingrad. Soon after Lily's confinement to quarters was over, the Germans were encircled, and their surrender was imminent. On the last Friday in December, her boots arrived. She took them out of their newspaper wrapping and bent to smell the soft new leather, which made her forget how long it had been since she'd bathed. In the canteen, she showed them off, and, like the other boys, Vladimir smiled indulgently. Katie said, *All you need now is an axe.* The female mechanics expressed satisfactory envy and sat in a huddle, day-dreaming about the dresses they'd sew after the war when all their sacrifices would be rewarded. Silk. Taffeta. Layers, swirls, ruffles, with no thought of scrimping.

At Auschwitz-Birkenau, four crematoria were under construction, but the work there was halted so that civilian workers could spend Christmas at home with their families. Bureaucrats were filing reports on the liquidation of a million Jews, giving the impression of a miracle operation: water to wine; unsavoury elements to vapour. In a concentration camp barrack, an inmate drew pictures on the wall to entertain children in their last hungry hours.

Inside the Stalingrad pocket, gaunt and lethargic German soldiers were rousing themselves, harnessing their ebbing strength. Supply drops had been insufficient and then stopped altogether. It had been a long time since they'd eaten their last horse, but they'd made tiny Advent crowns out of steppe grass, carved Christmas trees from wood scraps, saved candle stubs. A lieutenant gave his men the last of his cigarettes, his paper, his bread. They worshipped at the shrine of a picture drawn by their doctor in charcoal: the barefoot mother of God cradling her baby and herself in the womb of her shawl. Around her image were words. *Stalingrad Fortress. Christmas in the Cauldron. Light. Life. Love.*

Prisoner

UKRAINE

September to October 1943

The Wearied Sun

The Kamenskoje Transit Camp for Aviators sits in the corner of the German Fourth Air Fleet's main air base. It's a two-storey building, a former workers' hostel surrounded by three rows of barbed wire. The interrogation room, where Lily and Gerhard have been summoned by Hauptsturmführer Hoffmann, is large and sparsely furnished with a table, lamp, the requisite flag and portrait of Hitler, a few chairs. On a wall map the Soviet 8th Air Army's forward bases, rear bases, and HQ location are marked on an overlay. Lily recognizes the locations, which means they're a month out of date. Hoffmann sits at the table beside a military man, Major Petersen, who wears the Luftwaffe insignia.

The table is bare except for a telephone, black and shiny as a raven or a judge. There are no oil paintings, no platters of fruit, no wine, only a pitcher of water and a glass from which Hoffmann sips in front of the thirsty prisoner, who is precariously seated on a rickety chair. Someone has just been in with a mop; the smell of ammonia lingers.

Gerhard is washing his hands in the basin, muttering under his breath the way he does when he's stressed. "Cherry trees. Cyanide in leaves and bark, especially wilted leaves. Lethal. Horse exhibits bright-red mucous membranes, respiratory distress, convulsion. Antidote: 660 milligrams per kilogram sodium thiosulphate by mouth hourly. . . ."

Lily hands him a towel, keeping her back to the men in the room as long as she can, not wanting to see the prisoner's eyes as he looks at her. Before they brought him in, she recognized his voice. The regional accent so much like Katie's, the smooth tenor of this man, who asked her to dance in the community hall where pilots waltzed and tangoed and ate watermelon. She liked his voice and his crooked grin. A month after they danced together, they were serving in the same regiment. The prisoner's name is Vladimir Lavrinenkov. As soon as she turns around, he'll recognize her, and then what?

"How is it you've been able to persist? What drugs are you given?" Hoffmann is asking. "Pervitin?"

The Luftwaffe officer translates.

"Never heard of it," Vladimir says.

"I need technical information," Major Petersen says in German. "Let me speak with him."

"You Luftwaffe have no political understanding. All you think about are planes and engines," Hoffmann complains.

In the window she sees a flicker of movement. Chairs scrape as she turns around. Even Dr. Fischer salutes.

"Heil Hitler! Sturmbannführer Vogel!"

The prisoner looks up. His eyes fix on Lily's. She nods, agreeing to something, maybe his estimation of her: a slut working for Germans. The lamp casts featureless shadows, generic officers, prisoners.

"At ease, comrades." The Gestapo chief is tall, ruddy-faced. He carries a black binder. "Good afternoon," he says. "How is it going?"

"I can't work like this. You might as well send him straight to a POW camp," Hoffmann says. The cleaner has missed a spot of blood, a light smear camouflaged by speckled tile. "Stripping a workmen's dormitory does not make it an interrogation room. I need my men, my apparatus."

"Of course, and I've put in a request. You've been at this all day, *Hauptsturmführer*. You should have a drink, some food."

"Maybe." He seems to consider his options. "I won't be gone long. Come, Sofia," he says to Lily. She can smell the particular ripeness of Hoffmann's sweat. They've been separated by a wide river, by the lack of a bridge, by his focus on establishing himself in a larger city where his immediate superior only heads a department, not the entire Gestapo office. He's due for amusement. The prisoner would be pleased by that, he'd think it her just reward.

"I'm not needed here?" she asks. "Dr. Fischer?"

But it's Sturmbannführer Vogel who speaks up, his voice courteous. His eyes are as green as his nephew's, as thick-lashed, more calculating. "Didn't we send a boat we couldn't spare to bring Dr. Fischer and his nurse across the river? I assume that this was unavoidable?"

"To assist with Victor Karyukin, the prisoner I worked with in Amvrosiivka. He was supposed to be brought in first."

"Then we'll make the most of them now. Dismissed!"

"Yes, Herr *Sturmbannführer*!" The salute is impeccable, and Hoffmann leaves with just a single enraged glance as he pauses to adjust his trousers.

"My nephew has mentioned you," Vogel says to Lily. "He's teaching you to ride?"

"Yes, sir."

"Good. Keep him out of trouble." He doesn't immediately take his chair, but stands in front of the map and opens the thick binder in his hands. Studying one of its pages, he frowns, gazes at the map and down again, wrests an oil pen from an inner pocket, rolls it between his fingers. Then he crosses out several points on the transparent overlay, replacing them with others. "Intelligence reports," he says in German, adding in mangled Russian, "Latest information."

The prisoner leans forward, looking from the corrected map to the Gestapo officer seating himself at the table. His eyes meet Lily's. He opens his mouth to speak. She dreads it, she is eager for it. The strain of hiding finished. Her identity revealed. No more decisions. Whatever the cost—it's over as soon as he says, *Hello, Lily*. "Water?" he asks.

Major Petersen pours a glass while Vogel leans on an elbow, flipping through the binder until he finds the page he seems to be looking for. "Lieutenant Lavrinenkov, I'm glad to meet you at last. Yours is a famous regiment." He flips to the back of the binder, pulls out a sheet of paper. "Don't be surprised that we know about your unit. Intelligence has to make itself useful with something. So this is just a formality—whatever information you have is no longer of any use. You've been our guest for several days, and your regiment will have moved on to other missions. Still, procedures have to be followed." He shows Vladimir a document, official-looking, adorned with a red cross, though Lily can see that the German is some kind of pseudo-Gothic nonsense. Vogel bends to it, applying his pen as if nothing is more satisfying than a lengthy form.

"A regiment of aces," Major Petersen says in much better Russian than Vogel's. Petersen is about thirty-five, his cap pulled low over springy hair. "I'd like to fly against them, but I'm stuck here at HQ. You wouldn't ever want a desk job, would you, Lieutenant? Cigarette?"

Vladimir takes it, and the major flips open a simple trench lighter, glancing over at the Gestapo officer. "You don't mind, do you, sir? Officially nobody smokes. But a soldier's life isn't a bureaucrat's, is it? How about you, Dr. Fischer? You're a man who knows the trenches."

Gerhard accepts a cigarette, takes a drag, and cups it toward his palm, hiding its light like a soldier in a ditch. Major Petersen sits on a corner of the table, tapping a cigarette for himself from the pack.

"You've got a fine commander," he says. "And your friend Amet-Khan Sultan is one of the best pilots of any nation. Is he everything people say?"

He used to joke, Lily remembers, about being both the Khan and the Sultan. How do they know his name? Do they know Katie's? Hers?

"He's a good hand at his trade," Vladimir says. The cigarette trembles between his fingers. His eyes are bloodshot, the cloth around his neck bloodstained, his uniform wafting the urine smell of homelessness. Exhaustion is taking him, he slumps in the chair.

"Pilots are better with engines than politics, aren't we?" Petersen says.

"I met one of yours. Quiet. Showed me family pictures." He coughs, hand on his throat as blood seeps again through the cloth. "I had a letter."

"Didn't you get it back? You should have. I'll look into it. Who put that rag on your neck?"

"A soldier. Yours."

Sturmbannführer Vogel glances up. "See to him, Nurse."

From the veterinarian's bag she removes disinfectant and a bandage. The cloth around Vladimir's neck is glued by dried blood, and he winces as she pulls it away. "I'm sorry," she whispers. He grips her fingers in his. He twists, wrenching her wrist, but she doesn't cry out. When he lets go, she drops the dirty cloth in a wastebasket and applies disinfectant.

"Do you like your new aircraft?" Major Petersen asks. "I hear those Cobras are foul with an inexperienced pilot but do well in the hands of an ace. Tricky planes. Like our Focke-Wulfs. Not that they're equivalent—the Fw 190s have superior specs in every way, but they stall. Put me in a Messer, I say."

"There's flying and there's shooting," Vladimir says. He's aged since she last saw him. His skin is mottled, his neck extends like a turtle's as she wraps it in a fresh bandage. "You can't beat the 37-millimetre cannon. A single hit and your enemy's done for."

"Yes, but you have to be smart. You've only got thirty rounds," Major Petersen says. He removes a hip flask from his pocket, takes a drink from it, and offers it to Vladimir, who tips back the flask, drinks, wipes his lips.

Lily stands beside the prisoner, hands in her pockets, awaiting further instructions. She imagines herself in his chair, flattered and frightened, too tired to think. She fingers the contents of her pockets—a shoeing nail, a couple of hairpins.

The conversation continues while Vladimir crushes the cigarette butt in the ashtray, accepts another, drinks from the flask again: cannon, fuel tanks and the best time to dump them, air-cooled engines versus liquid-cooled, the use of tracers and the purpose of their colours. The German and Russian pilots' voices rise and fall. Intermittently, Sturmbannführer Vogel murmurs as he fills out the form—birthplace, unit, air base. The flask changes hands, and Lily watches the major's eyes light up with enthusiasm. Vladimir's voice trails off. He was prepared for torture, not this—fellow pilots chatting. He stares blearily at the Luftwaffe officer, who's taken no notes but seems content. Their discussion has provided all that he'd have wished. As easy as skimming cream.

"You can't be too careful with paperwork," Vogel says. "Just one more minute, here."

"Finish this off." Major Petersen shakes the flask at Vladimir. "Still a drop in here."

Vladimir drains the flask. Then he puts his hand on Lily's, lightly this time, his eyes watering from sleeplessness, from the high alcohol content in the flask, from confusion. "What's your name?" he asks, as if he doesn't realize it's a false one.

"Sofia," she says.

"Sonya." The Russian pet name. He crooks his finger and she bends closer. "We'll get home. It'll be all right," he says.

It isn't all right; it can't ever be. But she sighs as if his forgiveness is enough.

"Neither fur nor feathers," he says.

"To the devil," she replies, slipping an iron nail into his hand.

Major Petersen gives Vladimir a few cigarettes to take with him.

Maybe he'll exchange them for food. Maybe he'll smoke them. Maybe he'll be killed for them. As the guard arrives to return him to his cell, another prisoner, unsteady on his feet, is pushed through the doorway, Hauptsturmführer Hoffmann right behind him as he falls.

A person's zeal can be amply restored by food and drink and a bespoke pill that provides an extra dash of energy and sharpens the edge of appetite. In the kitchen, Berti Hoffmann had picked out the biggest, hairiest woman for a digestif and pumped her over potato peels. Now he can affably salute his (for the moment) superior officer, who tells him to proceed and departs with hardly a glance at the bare-chested prisoner collapsed on the floor.

The veterinarian is at the water basin. His skin will come off if he washes his hands again, and he's wasting time. Fortunately, Hoffmann is prepared as always. He hands Dr. Fischer a full bottle of Pervitin. "Take one," he says, and the veterinarian obliges.

Hoffmann paces around the room, listening to the smack-smack of his good shoe leather on cold tiles, a German drumbeat to the march of his thoughts. The blond girl speaks, Dr. Fischer applies himself with stethoscope, Major Petersen refills his flask from a bottle. Hoffmann listens and paces, his thoughts moving more rapidly than humanly possible, tumbling cogs in an adding machine, rotating discs in a coder, every configuration new, each one tripping an electrical circuit.

Hoffmann's superior, who stands in the way of his advancement, should have been put out to pasture years ago. But all things play out in time. Hoffmann keeps a dossier on everyone. Every dossier has its conclusion. In Sturmbannführer Vogel's there's a recently obtained medical report. Vogel's brother is sterile. Therefore, the brother can have no son. Hoffmann had suspected that Fritz Vogel, the supposed nephew, is actually the Sturmbannführer's son; their physical resemblance is evident. Now he has proof. An affair is no crime, even with your brother's wife, as long as you're both German. But concealing your son's medical or moral defect certainly is. All that remains is for Hoffmann to determine which of his suspicions about the "nephew" is correct: is Fritz Vogel deaf due to heredity or is he a degenerate homosexual? Hoffmann was sure that the fondness between Dr. Fischer and Fritz was unnatural, but then the good doctor took the girl to bed. One must not move too soon. Patience is key.

He pauses in his pacing, picturing himself as others must see him, outlined by the window, the power of the Fourth Air Fleet visible through the glass behind him. Even the colour of the sky is pleasing—a stern backdrop, a martial grey. His face is a mysterious shadow, his eyes a penetrating eagle's.

Victor Karyukin groans. All his chest hair has fallen out and there's no tone in his arms, but he's awake and aware, his gaze taking in the Gestapo officer's boots and baton, shifting to the veterinarian, then focusing on Lily's face.

"I remember you," Victor says. "The little nurse from Amvrosiivka."

"You're looking better." She has something to ask him, but Major Petersen speaks Russian, and if he overhears, they'll both be lost. "You don't smell like a corpse."

"They take care of me. The other prisoners."

"His heart is still erratic," Dr. Fischer says. "At least, so I think. It's hard to tell when you're used to horses. Anyway, I'll give him another shot when we're done. Also, his ribs are broken. Should we fix him up with bandages or not?"

"Do everything you can." Hoffmann waves his hand magnanimously.

Dr. Fischer gives Lily his stethoscope and asks for bandages, which she removes from his bag. "Get him to sit up," he says.

She put her arms around the prisoner and heaves him into position, as close to sitting as is feasible. The telephone rings, and Major Petersen picks up the receiver. It's her chance. "I remember your last request," she says quietly. "I've prepared two vials. One of them has a horse's dose. It would kill a man. Be careful. Major Petersen speaks Russian."

"What are you talking about?" Hoffmann asks. He's looming over them, sniffing like he wants something up his nose.

"Music. I asked if he likes 'The Wearied Sun.'"

"You mean the suicide tango?" Dr. Fischer asks as he finishes wrapping the bandage. "Get me the syringe and vial."

"You make it sound bad!" Lily glances over her shoulder with the hint of a smile as she rustles in the medical bag. "That song was very popular among the girls when I was in high school. We all thought it was so romantic." In Russian she adds, "Do you still like it, Victor? The suicide tango?"

"Not really." With an effort, he turns his head. "To be honest, it doesn't appeal to me anymore."

"You're sure?" she asks.

"My friends prefer other songs. Don't you think it's better to sing together?"

"Of course." She's not surprised by her relief, but she is by the joy that surges through her at the prospect of this man going on, this pilot she barely knows, whose future contains only condemnation. "Stay alive, my brother."

Retrieving the smaller dose of strychnine, she brings it and the syringe to Dr. Fischer. After the shot is administered, he washes his hands and repacks his bag, removing this and that and reorganizing it in his finicky manner. Major Petersen takes off his cap and runs a hand through his hair while he chatters on the telephone.

Lily starts to roll down her sleeves, but Hoffmann is beside her, his fingertips pressing the flesh of her pale arm. He stares into her eyes as if he can watch her brain work like the inside of a clock, as if he can pull out a spring and replace it with one that's tighter, not realizing the clock is in pieces and she doesn't know how to put it back together.

"Encourage the nephew," he says quietly, so only she can hear him. "Find out what he's hiding."

The sky is dark, bereft of the moon. The Dnieper River is black where it's not cut by reflected stalagmites of brightness. Above the cliffs, night shifts work the steel mills; flames shoot up through open valves; hot air blasts through iron; chimneys spew while the ferryman rows. Oars swoosh, he grunts with effort. His passengers sit across from him, holding on to the sides of the boat, a medical bag at their feet. Gerhard doesn't speak, neither does Lily. Wearily, they breathe in tandem, resting in the flame-lit night.

The Sweetness of Coca-Cola

When Fritz exercises the horses, sometimes he takes them through the band of woods along the water, and he'd been happy that this time the girl agreed to accompany him. Now she's lying in a crumple on the ground. It's his fault she fell. It's no excuse to say that Sofia asked to ride the mare, that when he mounted the small Panje horse for a joke, she laughed and smiled at him like a girl in a Coca-Cola ad, her eyes crinkling into almond edges, her mouth a half-moon cake. He should have been on the mare.

Her stillness shocks him into speaking, his lips issuing breath, his tongue touching teeth, throat vibrating as he says, "Sofia, Sofia," before giving any thought to what he discloses with his open mouth. If only he could have heard the roar of the plane taking off from the air base in Kamenskoje. It used to happen sometimes, one ear or the other opening to sound, but not anymore, and the horse reared before he could grab the reins.

He bends over her, kneeling on a mat of last year's leaves, his face close to hers. "Are you alive?" he asks. "Are you awake?"

She's a broken doll, white-faced, her parted lips forming no shapes, but her breath softly puffs against his with the potato scent of breakfast. Fritz puts a hand on either side of her cheeks, gently turning her so that he can see her lips. The skin is gritty on the side where she fell. He brushes the dirt away.

"Where does it hurt? Talk slowly."

"My head. Back. Ouch." As she tries to sit up, his arm goes around her, and she leans into him, as light and helpless as a misspoken word, her cheek shivering against his throat.

"I can't understand if you're not facing me." She pulls away, and he wishes he'd kept his mouth shut.

She moves her arms and legs, rolls her feet. "Nothing broken, nothing sprained. Just my head."

He runs his hands over her head, feeling the shape of her skull, the overlay of soft hair. She smells like a schoolmate, not a foreign worker. "You're getting a goose egg."

She winces as he touches the spot. "I didn't know you can talk."

"I can, I just don't." Lip-reading, he can get about half of what she says and fills in the rest with a guess, the same as with anyone else. If she has an accent, he can't see it.

"I never heard you."

"I talk to the horses when I'm alone, so I won't forget how." She wears coveralls but has done something to them so that they hug her body. Her ears are creamy labyrinths with hair tucked behind them.

"You sound good."

"My uncle doesn't think so." He knows that she shares a bed with Dr. Fischer. He wants to touch his finger to the cleft above her lip. He wants to feel the ticklish thrum of her lips on his palm. "I'm not supposed to talk because I sound stupid, and stupid people are useless eaters."

"Not to me. How did it happen, your going deaf?"

"It started with one ear."

His father had smacked his head, and for a few days until the ringing and dizziness stopped (he was eleven years old, he milked it as long as he could) he was exempted from chores. Several weeks later his ear felt heavy, and he dug his finger and then a twig into it, trying to excavate whatever was stuck there, but nothing came out, and he went to his mother, who candled it. He lay on his bed, he could feel the pointy end of beeswax in his ear, but he couldn't hear the crackle and pop of the flame. His mother served his father burnt stew for dinner.

Uncle Frederik, who lived in town and was a policeman, always came to the rescue, though he was Father's little brother (tall as he was) and not the head of the family. Fritz was named after Uncle Frederik—his godfather—and called by the diminutive Fritz to distinguish them. As soon as his uncle got the news about Fritz's ear, he came in a car, and the three of them drove to the doctor's— Fritz, his uncle, and his mother. In the waiting room Uncle Frederik held Mother's hand between both of his. He spoke, she lifted her wet eyes, and Fritz strained to hear them, but there was no further conversation.

After examining Fritz, the doctor diagnosed sudden hearing loss. The cause, he said, was unknown, and the smack had nothing to do with it. Fritz's hearing might return or he might lose it in the other ear too. As with any condition that had an unknown cause, the doctor blamed it on the boy putting his hands where they didn't belong, which was why his father had cuffed him in the first place. To promote recovery, the doctor prescribed exercise and cold baths.

Fritz became the strongest, cleanest boy at school and developed a habit of tilting his head to one side. His hearing fluctuated; his other ear was affected. Some days he could hear more, and on others his teacher gave him the strap for inattentiveness. His father didn't hit him again, not until he lost all hearing in his other ear. And then, despite anything the doctor had said, his father hoped, if he smacked Fritz on both sides, it might reverse the damage. He hit and hit until he himself was sobbing. There was no other son, there was not even a daughter who could give him a son-in-law to inherit his land.

After the schoolmaster came to visit, his mother pressed her lips together and filled a trunk with new shirts and short pants. His father didn't look at him. *Where are you sending me? Why?* He knew he screamed, he felt it in his throat and his mother covered her ears. Then she sat him at the table and wrote on the back of feed receipts with a pencil stub. The schoolmaster had to report on the racial hygiene of every class, and though he, personally, had always liked Fritz and his family, what was he to do for the boy? How could he be trained in a village school? How could he learn to read lips? Hadn't his parents already seen the problem? There were near misses, a vehicle he didn't hear coming up behind him, and what about the bull? It was all very well to be good at handling horses, but the Fatherland would become mechanized, and he wouldn't be able to cope with a tractor. And what about sick animals—could a boy like this hear their pathetic groans? If his parents cared for him, if they cared for the National Community, they would let him go to a place for children like him. The boy needed to harden his resolve; they mustn't write letters and weaken a character already enfeebled by disability.

Fritz loved the farm. He loved the horses, the cows, the smell of hay, everything about it, even slaughtering the chickens, and he was nearly as good at it as his father, better than the itinerant farm-hands who worked for drink. He'd already had as much school as his father had had. He begged them to let him stay. He hid in the hayloft, and his father dragged him out. This was as the school-master had predicted: deformation of the senses made him weak, girlish, a burden to the Fatherland. And anyway, it was too late. His parents had signed the papers, his mother because the school could give him what she couldn't, his father because an education was all that was left for someone who couldn't be useful.

The Institution for the Deaf was in Heidelberg, some thirty kilometres from home. Fritz hated the soot and snobbery of the cramped city, he hated the pinch-nosed teachers, the headmaster's pince-nez, the postman who never brought him a letter from home. Only his uncle wrote him and in his letters said that his mother missed him and thought of him every day, but he never saw her large and laboured script. At first he was snubbed by the other boys because he spoke well and understood nothing, but he learned to sign, he made friends. They spoke with their hands at night in the beam of their flashlights or when the staff wasn't looking. If they were caught, teachers hit them for gesturing like apes. When visitors came, Fritz was one of the boys allowed to shout, "Heil Hitler."

Parents were required to fill out questionnaires; students were examined by a medical officer, and a list of names was posted with their hereditary biology rated on it. Children disappeared from his class. Some of them returned subdued, the boys snipped, the girls scooped. Others never came back at all. There was an exam on the Law for the Prevention of Hereditarily Diseased Offspring. *Question seven: Name five types of life unworthy of life.* His best friend got the highest mark in the class, but he was a homely boy with a Jewish nose, and one morning his bed was empty. Fritz examined his own nose in the mirror, measured it with a ruler (on the sly he also measured his penis—it was starting to grow), and wrote a fearful letter to his parents. It was returned to him by the headmaster after a caning for worrying his parents with lies.

Uncle Frederik came to visit and took him to a café, and while they ate trifle with whipped cream, they talked about football. After the trifle they drank Coca-Cola. Uncle Frederik kept asking him to repeat himself because he'd become harder to understand, and Fritz wondered if he'd be allowed to shout "Heil Hitler" at the next school inspection by important people.

When they got back in the car, Uncle Frederik drove out of Heidelberg to the small town where he'd been promoted to Chief of the Gestapo. He brought Fritz to his apartment and made up a bed on the sofa. Nothing was said, no reason given, and Fritz was afraid to ask if he could go home in case that reminded Uncle Frederik to return him to school. Days passed, clothes were acquired for him, and he stayed in the apartment and read while his uncle went to work. He wasn't allowed to speak or sign. Even the widow who lived across the hall and brought a plate of strudel covered with an embroidered cloth was an informant. Who would know that better than the Chief of the Gestapo?

An accident, his uncle told neighbours, a hit on the head when the boy rescued a toddler from being run over by a horse. Still had all his wits about him. Only his hearing was affected. The war began, they moved to another town, where Fritz was apprenticed to a photographer, and the story became that he'd rescued a toddler from the rubble of a house and a beam fell on him. The shock of it made him mute. Someday he might speak again if Germany won the glory that she deserved. His uncle provided Fritz with an endless supply of pencils and notebooks, and gave him a Kine Exakta camera for his birthday. With it, Fritz took pictures of brides and grooms and babies for the Fatherland.

When Uncle Frederik drove him to the farm for a week's visit, his mother wept and his father looked up because Fritz was now as tall as his uncle. There were civilian workers on their farm, girls from Poland who wore a "P" on their chest. For a day or two, because fraternizing with foreign workers was against the law and he didn't want to put his uncle on the spot, he just watched a girl who seemed to be about his age. Then he realized that his uncle, a policeman and a Gestapo officer, was already a criminal, having aided and abetted, even worse, instigated, a runaway from the government school, and he brought the starving girl food. He watched her mouth carefully, and she didn't scream, not ever, when he did as he pleased. But it seemed to him that although the sensation was warmer and wetter than touching himself (which he'd never ceased, having decided that, since he'd already gone deaf from it, he might as well continue to reap its benefits), something more ought to happen than a lifted skirt and an absent countenance. But before he could figure it out, Germany had invaded Russia. Young men were dying; young men out of uniform were regarded with contempt. Useless eaters were denounced; there was wild euthanasia. His uncle was transferred to the eastern front and arranged for Fritz to go with him. He sometimes wondered why his uncle was so fond of him as to do any of it.

If Fritz had stayed home, he'd have been a farmer and a patriot. Instead, he came to believe that speech was mostly just noise that people made while protecting their own interests. The previous veterinarian, for instance, didn't let Fritz go near the horses but set him to record-keeping with his neat deaf-school script, assuming he wouldn't understand the implications of what he recorded. There were six causes of equine death that didn't require an inquest. These happened to be epidemic among attractive thoroughbreds. If they had a second life somewhere, Fritz didn't begrudge it, nor did he resent the doctor's nice car and the women who hiked their skirts as they slid onto the seat. By contrast, Dr. Fischer was morose and made no use of his position, and still got the girl. Yet for all that, he didn't underestimate Fritz.

In his silent world, he isn't distracted. He observes and draws his own conclusions.

"It just happened," he says to Sofia. "Gradually, I stopped hearing."

"Your voice is a bit different, but if you got more practice, it would improve. You could try me instead of a horse."

"Do you like Dr. Fischer?"

"Lower your voice a little and try again."

"Why do you like Dr. Fischer?"

"Better. He cares about the horses," she says.

"What else do you like?"

"Flowers. Most girls do."

The woods are full of flowers in spring, but not now, not approaching fall here among the cities of steel mills and dry scrubland. "Is there anything else?"

"Do deaf Germans know sign language?"

"No, I don't like to." It's a sign of defectiveness and degeneracy, words of many syllables he learned at school and wouldn't attempt to speak aloud. Lately, though, he's been thinking of how much he could say with his hands, more beautifully than the awkward shapes of an open mouth.

"Show me just a little."

"Why?"

"It's a secret language. Didn't you ever have a code with your friends?"

"Maybe."

"One word. What's *no* or *help*?" She flutters her hand and he takes it, gestures for the other so he can show her the signs, his hands engulfing hers, shaping them. Fingers together and palm forward for *no*, a swoop of two thumbs out from the chest for *help*.

"When you take the horses' temperature, write down that Helga's isn't normal," he signs, then writes it for her on his notepad because speaking aloud is hard and he's tired of it.

"Why should I do that?"

So Dr. Fischer keeps getting up in the morning, he writes. When the doctor is angry, his face takes on an uncanny calmness, as if his features have been arranged by an embalmer, but it's worse to see him lie in a tangled lump of blankets, depending on Fritz to coax his boneless feet into boots. *His favourite horse.* Fritz underlines *Helga*, and for further emphasis signs the name.

"Are those letters? What about the alphabet?" She holds out her hands to him. "Show me, please."

Before they get on the horses to return, she's able to sign, "Helga is naughty."

———

As they emerge from the woods, Lily is chastened and cautious, still sore from her fall, and she holds her horse to a walk behind Fritz, who's riding Helga now. He's the only one who doesn't treat her like a captive. He has no demands, not for protection or information, and he's never threatened her. He's just a boy who likes her the way any boy might like a girl who's already taken. In the calm solitude of the woods, she can pretend to be just that. The leaves are changing. They're the colour of sunset, almost ready to drop. On the first windy day, the branches will be swept bare.

They reach the village, where an old woman is dumping a pot of night soil. They ride past the huts and the school. Several men are hauling bales of hay. The blond stable hand who's as muscled as an uncut horse has stripped to his undershirt. He's heavily tattooed, drawing attention from the port-wine stain on his neck and lower jaw. His mouth puckers in a whistle, and Lily waves as if she believes it's meant for her. At the far stable allocated to the hospital, Fritz dismounts from Helga. She slides off the smaller horse without assistance. He's sturdy and sweet-tempered and reminds her of a poem she memorized before it was banned and the poet sent to the Gulag.

> *I'm that poor, like nature*
> *And that simple, like the sky*
> *And my freedom is ghostly*
> *Like a bird's midnight cry.*

"Why doesn't this little fellow have a name?" she asks.

Most of them don't, Fritz writes in his notebook. The boy's green eyes are nearly black, sucking light from the gloom blown across the river by the wind. If it turns, they'll smell the steppe.

"Well, he should. And a Russian horse should have a Russian name." Slowly, correcting herself by shaking her hand to erase a malformed letter, she signs, "V-o-l-o-d-y-a."

Fritz glances at a spot on the small horse's neck, then moves in to examine it more closely, his hand on the horse's flank, calming him. He flips the ear open.

Lily taps him on the shoulder. "What's wrong?"

Quarantine, he writes. She looks at him in alarm, wishing she understood signing so he could quickly explain. *Ticks. Not too serious*, he writes. *Keep him away from Helga.*

Fritz chooses two brushes from a bushel basket, and they begin to groom the horses. She says, "Don't you like this, Volodya?"

Katie's nickname. The pet name for Vladimir. Which also reminds her of Vladimir Lavrinenkov, who, rumour has it, escaped with Victor Karyukin during transfer from the aviators' camp. If he makes it to a Soviet base, he'll be interrogated, and what will he say about her then?

A Higher Standard

The air base is empty. The Kamenskoje Transit Camp for Aviators has recently shut down, its prisoners shipped away in cattle cars. The cells are unoccupied, smelling of old piss and fermenting shit, doors ajar. The corridor is spattered with bits of debris, torn paper, ash-spotted broken glass, rat prints in dust, droppings.

Nobody stops Gerhard or the policeman at his back, nobody asks them for papers as they climb the stairs to the second floor and walk past interrogation rooms, empty and blooded. Through an open door he sees men packing files in boxes. Hauptsturmführer Hoffmann and his subordinates have already been evacuated.

Overhead, a light bulb flickers, clicks, goes dark. The mole-chinned policeman pokes Gerhard to keep him moving. His bad foot weakens as he progresses along the dim corridor to the end, where the window looks onto the waiting city. Glass trembles in its frame; from the steel mills above the riverbank comes the muffled sound of explosives destroying plant equipment so that it won't fall into the hands of the Red Army, who've broken through defences just up the river. To his right is the Gestapo chief's office. The policeman knocks on the door.

"Come in," Sturmbannführer Vogel says. On his desk is a pipe gone cold while he works. He appears calm in his reading glasses, reviewing papers as if, in the adjoining room, there remains a secretary to file them for him. The photo of the Führer hangs alone on an otherwise blank wall, pale squares where maps have been removed.

"Heil Hitler! Dr. Fischer is here," the policeman says.

"Thank you. Dismissed." Vogel waits until the door is shut. "Please sit, Gerhard. May I call you that?"

Gerhard seats himself in the wooden chair facing Vogel's desk. "Of course." He's been called here for no stated reason, therefore the reason must be ominous. If there are pleasantries before it's revealed, Gerhard might as well enjoy them.

"Let's have a chat, shall we?" Vogel opens a drawer and removes a bottle and two glasses. "*Prost!*"

They both drink.

Vogel fills his pipe, lights it. The smell reminds Gerhard of his great-uncle, a spectacled (unmarried) zoologist who surprised everyone by moving to Berlin. When his uncle came home to visit, he'd puff on his pipe while Gerhard unwrapped the present he'd brought back for him. Vogel has the same expression on his face—genial, anticipatory. His teeth make the same sound as he shifts and grips the pipe, and Gerhard relaxes despite every instinct warning him to put his hands over his balls. "So, you're being transferred to Hostau. Quite a distance. You can't get any closer to the Fatherland. Are you pleased?"

"Not really. I'd rather go to the front."

"In your place, so would I. In the first war I was a soldier too, and I remember what it was like for me in the rear. Boring, irritating, bewildering. Am I right?"

Gerhard nods. "If it weren't for my foot . . ."

"I know, Gerhard, and I wish I could say that all will be well." Vogel fills their glasses, the bottle empties. "But there's a problem we have to consider."

"Which is?" Gerhard wonders how long he'll be able to hold out before incriminating the young men he's slept with.

"Every non-infectious and mobile horse has been called into service, but you've kept at least two of yours back. Their charts show elevated temperature, though in truth they could have been discharged weeks ago. That isn't good, you must know it."

His sphincter opens with relief, and he has to clench it against the gaseous bubble. "There are no roads. I've got no gas for my motorcycle. We have to have some form of transportation."

"But to falsify documents. And there is a more serious issue I'm aware of. Your . . . living arrangements with the nurse." Vogel lowers his voice, forcing Gerhard to lean forward to hear what he says. "It's *Rassenschande*."

"You're not serious!" God must be having a good laugh at this one. "Everybody does it."

"Well, the military looks the other way. Men are men, and they have a lot of steam to blow off, especially after a battle. But I'm not the military. The Gestapo has a higher standard. We're the police, we have to uphold the law. A crime's allegedly been committed. Sexual relations between a German and a Ukrainian—it's racial pollution. What am I supposed to do?" He opens his hands as if helpless. "I'll have to bring in the nurse for questioning."

She reads to him when he wakes from a nightmare. They've finished *Old Surehand*, and she convinced him to pick up a book of poetry. It isn't bad, he's had to admit, better than the dull shit he had to memorize in school. He says, "It wasn't her fault. I forced her."

"What difference does that make? But you're a plain soldier, I'm a plain policeman. Why should we beat around the bush? The enemy advances, we retreat. It's all falling apart in slow motion, my friend, but many things can happen in that slow fall." He studies his pipe, removes his glasses, gazes through the window as if he can see the city cracking open. "Maybe we can help each other."

"How? You've already got your nephew as an informer. He knows everything I do."

"Ah, to the point like a good soldier." Vogel tamps his pipe. "Speaking of my nephew, it hasn't escaped my notice that you and your nurse have looked out for him. I appreciate that, Gerhard, I do. My nephew trusts her. He would listen to her, and she'd keep him out of harm's way, I believe she would. In the right circumstances, the right place. It would mean a great deal. He's a son to me, my only one."

"And the problem of Racial Disgrace?"

"Hoffmann reported that she has German grandparents." He puts on his reading glasses. "Yes, here it is. Even though it's only on one side, he says it's obvious, she speaks German very well. However, I checked into her papers myself. Greek on one side, Ukrainian on the other. So where's the German? Was my officer mistaken? Not at all. One can deduce that she must be adopted. These Russians, their records are terribly sloppy. Such blood has to be preserved, especially when one considers that most Volksdeutsche in the east have completely forgotten their heritage. It wouldn't be impossible, not even so difficult, to obtain the necessary identification papers."

He must have already done so, Gerhard thinks. He's just holding this out like a biscuit to make the little dog dance on his hind legs. "What would it take for her to obtain them?" he asks.

Vogel makes a steeple of his fingers and looks over his spectacles, earnestly. "Simply put, if you take her and my nephew with you. An out-of-the-way corner of the Reich. That's what I want for him. And for you—congratulations on your engagement. No soldier can be ashamed of that, especially to a nurse serving the National Community until she bears its children."

"And in this fine story of ours, what is Fritz's part?"

"Your youngest brother died, I believe."

"Yes, Friedrich died of meningitis when he was eleven. What of it?"

"It's hard to lose a brother, nearly as hard as a son. What a wonder to have yours restored to you. A true miracle of the Reich. As long as he's safe, so are you all . . ."

Gerhard has to grant the *Sturmbannführer* agility of mind, all contingencies covered. "And what should I do about the horses?"

"Just notify HQ that they're available for service. I'll have train tickets and papers delivered to you. Make sure the seal isn't broken when you receive them."

A week later the envelope comes, the seal intact until Gerhard breaks it and examines the contents. There are three train tickets for the following day. And two sets of identity papers. For Rose Allendorf, ethnic German. And for Friedrich Fischer, Reich German. Exempt from military service due to non-heritable hearing loss. Also a note:

Dear nephew, I want you to know firmly and without doubt that
Dr. Fischer has my complete confidence and you are to obey him
as you would me, knowing that this is my wish and my directive.
You are to be a brother to him and his fiancée. I know that they
hold you in their esteem as dearly as you are in mine.

Uncle "Fritz"

Soldiers arrive the next day. Rifles slung over their shoulders, they bang on the doors of the village, ragged children emerging from the field while Gerhard is shouting at their sergeant, "This is a total fuck-up! I notified HQ that we've got two healthy horses ready for service. Healthy!"

Sergeant Pfister recognizes the captain's stripes even in the veterinary colours, so he reaches into the truck and pulls out a sheaf of stamped papers. Everything specified, itemized, signed off. Nothing about animal transport, just military staff. The rest of it, see here. Horses. Stables. Granary. Fields. Houses. Village school. Listed for demolition.

Gerhard tries to make him understand. "Do you know how hard it is to kill a horse with a single shot? When it starts to panic? Let me do it. At least let me sedate them first."

Sergeant Pfister is patient—you have to be with a higher-ranking officer—explaining that his men have semi-automatic rifles, and they can fire enough shots to do the job as long as the horses are confined to their stalls. Then all they have to do is pour a bit of gasoline here and there in the stable, throw a match into the straw, and it'll catch as easily as a synagogue. The sergeant shields his eyes with his hand to look up at the sky. He doesn't like the look of it, but even with a bit of rain the corpses have to be burned so the enemy can't use them for food, the village set on fire so it provides no shelter. The old peasants understand and aren't wasting their strength screaming useless protests. They're putting pillows and dead men's boots onto carts and wheelbarrows, getting ready to join the tired line walking toward the nearest city with a bridge across the Dnieper River.

The obvious solution for Helga and Volodya is to be refugees too. Gerhard will take the chestnut mare and the Russian gelding to the bridge himself. It's only a two-day walk—nothing compared with the long marches on the eastern front. From there he'll find a way to get on a train west. In the chaos of retreat, nobody will think him AWOL for a few days' delay. He rides Helga to the far field past the dipping vat, leaves her safely behind the fence, and returns for Volodya.

The rest of the horses have to be rounded up, led from the pasture to the stables, shut into their stalls, allowed to munch on hay while their fellows are brought in. Some horses comply with just a whinny, head raised, making sure that a familiar person is in sight. Others are suspicious. The routine is unusual, they smell something on the men, and they balk until Fritz calms them and leads them inside. Nobody tells Fritz they're going to be shot. The last horse he brings in is nuzzling his shoulder, angling for an apple, when he feels the vibration.

The soldiers have located a still in the village and, before destroying it, are determined not to let its contents go to waste, nor does

Sergeant Pfister care if his men, who have to go hungry and thirsty when supply lines fail, avail themselves when they come across a windfall. Several soldiers pretend to be cowboys, swinging imaginary lassos and real whips, which they found in an unopened crate in the surgery. One of them whips the flanks of a lame horse until her mouth is frothing and blood drips from her tail, and Pfister punches the soldier in the side of the head for wasting time.

The horses scream. Like children squealing in panic. Until they don't.

In the noise and stink as he frantically injects a few of the horses with sedative, how could Gerhard notice a soldier slink off to the far field to drink himself unconscious? How could he know that the soldier (a myopic private who's just acquired crabs from the prostitute hired by his mates for his birthday) has shot a couple of horses in the field so he wouldn't have to bother taking them back to the stable?

Gerhard's hearing hasn't recovered from the close sound of gunfire, and he walks beneath a peaceful sky. The clouds have broken up, are cottony puffs, their upper surface lit by the sun, and there won't be any rain. When he gets to the meadow, he can see Fritz and Sofia (he'll have to start thinking of her as Rose) but not the horses. Puzzled, he wonders where they are, his wearied foot slowing him down as he limps.

She holds a thin blade. Gerhard recognizes the type, having seen ones like it in the hands of field doctors cutting off gangrenous digits. The boy is gesturing to himself and jabbing the air with finger leaps. His face is red, he's crying, his mouth stretched wide with it. He motions to Sofia, she shakes her head and kneels in the grass. Gerhard takes in the state of the bodies lying there, noting details to be re-examined later. The Russian horse is covered in blood and yet still alive, barely, mercilessly. His nostrils are wide and struggling for air. A hind leg twitches as if he's trying to run in the dry grass.

Sofia's lips form words: *Don't be afraid, Volodya.* She strokes the horse's nose, then puts her finger on his throat, making sure she has the correct spot. The knife slices and the twitching stops. She turns her dry-eyed and loathing gaze to the figure lying in vomit. As she moves her body in a half twist, hiding the knife from view, it's Fritz who lunges forward to grab her wrist.

She probably yelps when she drops the knife, but Gerhard still can't hear. He can smell blood, and he can smell vomit, and he can smell the fire started in the stable, but he can't hear the sound of his foot making contact with the ribs of the snoring lump of spattered uniform. The boy pulls Gerhard off; good old Fritz with the papers-conjuring uncle shoves him and doesn't stop shoving even when Gerhard smacks him in the face and his nose bleeds.

The other horse lies a few metres closer to the fence. On the autumnal feather grass and drooping sage, Gerhard squats beside Helga and speaks to her for a while, his hand on the scar on her flank, half-concealed by her chestnut coat. Drifting smoke makes him cough, it makes his eyes water. He barely sees Fritz bending over Sofia, lifting her and carrying her away from the carnage.

The sergeant apologizes for his man's mistake and, to make up for it, offers them a lift to the station. In the barn, a Kine Exakta camera is melting.

Pilot

RUSSIA

Seven Months before Her Fall

January to March 1943

It Scattered Musk

On the cover of the January 4, 1943 issue of *Time* magazine, Joseph Stalin was America's "Man of the Year." In three-quarter profile, he looked into the distance; his salt-and-peppered hair was windswept, his moustache touched with white. Below his neck, tiny rifle-bearing figures in winter camouflage bent into the gale of a snowy steppe. The caption read: *All that Hitler could give, he took—for a second time.*

In the five-month battle for Stalingrad, a million of his soldiers had died, but the Red Army had won against the invincible Germans, and their sacrifice had earned them a show of confidence from the government. Political officers, formerly called commissars, no longer had supreme authority. A new sense of freedom was in the air.

The magazine cover was pinned to the wall of the fighter pilots' canteen at a large air base not far from Stalingrad, recently abandoned by the Germans. The survivors of the 8th Air Army had come together to rest before the next phase of war. One of them sounded out the caption. The only word his comrades understood was the Führer's name. They booed. They shouted, *After Stalingrad . . . Berlin!* Another pilot, known for his imitations of Hitler and his resistance to gonorrhea, made an entrance with his trademark goose step. Senior officers hooted and applauded. The canteen blazed with testosterone. It glittered, it scattered pine and musk, it was muscled and boned in a sheath of urgency.

Lily made a circuit of the room. As soon as she'd arrived, she'd cornered the divisional commander and obtained permission to transfer . . . if someone would take her. Now she stopped beside Boris Eremin, who led an air reconnaissance regiment and had his own specially engraved Yak-1 for his part in the famous Seven Against Twenty-Five. She made her request. He shook his head and

told her that his unit flew deep behind enemy lines; if she was captured, he couldn't live with the guilt, thinking of what the Nazis
would do to her. He turned away, the matter settled.

"Wait," Lily said.

"You won't persuade him. These old guys born before the
Revolution, they're backward. He's stuck in his ways. You should
feel sorry for him." The man speaking was standing directly behind
her, the stocky pilot who'd got a ride from the empty base and then
shielded her from strafing enemy planes. "I should know, I used to
be his wingman."

"You flew with Boris?" she asked.

"Before he got his own command. I'm Alexei Solomatin."

"You're one of the Seven. I should have recognized you."

"Why would you? A newspaper photo can't do my beauty
justice."

"I'm Lily Litvyak." She smiled. She liked his plain looks, his
lack of arrogance. "You're still with your old regiment?"

"Wouldn't leave our commander. Just four of the Seven still
living. Boris there, who deserted us. Ivan—he's even older than old
Boris—me and Sasha. Come on, I'll introduce you."

Their commander was Nick Baranov, a major whom they called
Papa. Before the war he'd been a blacksmith, and now he was known
for organizing whatever his people needed. Food, boots, baths.
They had the lowest rate of lice. The second-highest kill rate when it
came to enemy planes. His deputy, Ivan Zapryagev, was a master on
the accordion. Lily inserted herself between the commander and
Ivan, while Alexei slid onto the bench opposite. He was just turning
twenty-two, but he'd been in air combat from the beginning of the
war. Next to him was Sasha Martynov, a head taller than Alexei,
with twice the nose and wearing the only Gold Star at the table.
They had superstitions to avert death: don't shave before a scramble, wear the undershirt with the cross sewn into it, never come to

the end of a stick notched with your kills. They slurped borscht like it was their last meal.

"The new pilots are afraid of steep dives. They can't take the Gs," Alexei said. "But I heard you did a perfect up-and-under, Lily." He licked the spoon, eyeing her over it, and in his gaze she wasn't the pest, the burden, the thorn in someone's flesh.

"Thanks," she said.

"The soup is thicker than yesterday's. A spoon could stand up in it. I'm going for seconds before it runs out."

"Wait. I've got something to ask," Lily said.

"For you, darling, anything. Even dry socks."

"Better," Lily said. "I'm not afraid of dives. Take me as your wingman."

Alexei tipped back his cap and grinned as if that had been his plan all along. "What do you say, Papa? She's peppery, but I like the flavour."

"That bomber she took down at her air base was nicely done," Nick Baranov said. Gossip travelled between regiments. Everyone must have heard about her begging to fly and her punishment for it. "We're short of pilots, and anyone with experience is hard to come by. It would be reckless to pass up a gift."

Alexei cheered and Sasha said a drink ought to seal the deal.

"Not so fast, comrades." Nick's hair refused to be slicked back, red curls sticking out around his ears. "Finding accommodation for women . . ."

"There's two of us. Isn't that worth it? Me and Katie—she's shot down five enemy aircraft. Katie Budanova, already a lieutenant," she said, offering up her friend.

"Now you're talking. Two hares with one shot." Nick shouted to Katie across the canteen, "What do you say, Lieutenant Budanova? Want to fight with us?"

"You can't have our Volodya!" Vladimir yelled back.

Katie shrugged. "I guess I'm staying where I am." She sat in the group of pilots with her cap tipped low and her knees wide. She had her own dream. What right did Lily have to shake her from it? And yet the rejection stung, it reddened Lily's cheeks like a slap.

"You're not going to refuse a pilot as good as Lily, are you, Comrade Papa?" Alexei asked. "She's a little thing. You can fit her cot somewhere."

"I'm sure I can," Nick said. "Welcome to the 296th Fighter Air Regiment, Lily."

"Thank you, Comrade Major."

That evening, Katie noticed Lily sitting next to Alexei in the dark canteen. Restlessness had made men irritable while they waited for orders. Battle tactics had been reviewed, kill rates boasted about, boots nailed, rips repaired, wood scrounged, fights started and broken up, letters written on army paper—triangular in shape, points folded into the centre, no envelope needed. Someone had proposed a pissing contest and was taking bets, but before the political officer got wind of it, Papa Nick had made an announcement. Somehow he'd acquired a projector and a movie. The label on the metal canister read *Communist Education on Sexual Cleanliness*, and everyone in the division had groaned as they were ordered to pull out benches and settle down. A sheet had been nailed to a wall of the canteen. The projector crackled, the silver statues of a man and woman, arms raised together, slowly rotated over the sheet. It became clear that Papa Nick had snuck in proper entertainment under the misleading label of the canister. The credits rolled, a cheery song belted from the speaker. This was *Volga-Volga*, their favourite comedy.

Did Alexei have his arm around Lily's waist?

"That's not Communist Education," someone yelled.

"They look clean to me!"

The sheet fluttered under the close-up of a dark-haired man and a blond woman locked in an ardent embrace, and soldiers shouted, *Get out of the way, Motherfucker,* as a crouching shadow covered the lower part of the sheet. The projector skidded to a stop, the divisional commander gave a brief lecture on the symptoms of gonorrhea while an engineer fixed the nails, and the movie resumed.

Squashed close in their rows of benches, the soldiers were warm oblongs of darkness comforted by familiar songs and the well-marinated smell of winter woollens. Flasks were shared, they laughed at the actors' antics. There were madcap chases, girls caught in scanty clothing, gloomy horn players, a venerable steamboat, ordinary people getting the better of a pencil-pushing bureaucrat, a trophy, attractive actors kissing under a table.

Lily laughed, so did Alexei, at all the same parts. He was shorter than average for a man, his shoulder at a comfortable height, and if Lily wanted, Katie thought, it would be easy for her to rest her head on that shoulder.

Men drank, they whistled, they called out, *Whoa, what a piece,* and joined in on the songs, loudly and off-key: *Our free life will never end.* Before the movie was over, they were leaning on each other, swaying. And after the finale, they stumbled to their dugouts.

Katie believed she was walking upright until she realized that she was listing to starboard like a damaged plane, her arm draped around Lily's shoulders.

"You found me," she said.

"Here you go." Alexei took the other arm and straightened her up, more or less.

"Friends," Katie said. "Did you hear that Stalin, Churchill, and Roosevelt were driving together?"

"Where?" Alexei asked.

"In the countryside. Maybe Smolensk. I'm from Smolensk."

"Shh . . ." Lily said.

"No, listen. A bull's in the way and the car stops. Churchill gets out and kicks the bull, but it won't move. Then Roosevelt gets out."

"I thought he couldn't walk," Alexei says.

"He uses a couple of canes. He hits the bull with one of them. It still won't move."

"Not a good idea to go hitting a bull," Alexei said.

"But our leader, our great leader . . . he just whispers in the bull's ear, and it runs away. Don't you want to know what he said?"

"Shut up," Lily said, as if Katie could get into trouble for telling a joke about Comrade Stalin. Poor Lily. She didn't realize that Katie was a trusted informant.

"She's just drunk and with us," Alexei said. "Soldiers are entitled to a joke before they die. Finish it, Volodya, and let's get you to your quarters."

"He says to the bull, he says, 'Go on or I'll put you on a collective farm,'" Katie told them. At least, she thought she had when she was done laughing. It was hard to tell whether words had emerged from her mouth or just her icy breath as snow dropped from her nose. She felt Lily's hand pressing down on her head so she wouldn't bump it on the door frame, then pushing her into the dugout. Inside, she dropped to the earthen floor, which was surprisingly comfortable, but Lily wouldn't let her lie there. In the candlelight she was as pale as her name, hefting Katie to a sitting position.

"Where's Alexei?"

"Gone to his quarters. Come on. You'll freeze on the ground." Lily put her hands under Katie's armpits and pulled up. "Help me here. I can't do this by myself."

"He likes you. And you like him, I can tell."

"I'd like anyone who took me as his wingman."

Katie threw an arm around Lily, put her other hand on the cot—such a masterful German cot, not like the planks and straw they were used to. With a couple of grunts, hers or Lily's, she was lying down. How had she become so attached to the girl? Not even her type. Too small and pensive. "Tell me something about that grandmother of yours."

"Why do you always want to talk about her?"

"She reminds me of you."

"That's a funny reason. You didn't even want to transfer with me."

"Can't leave my comrades," Katie mumbled. Her reports to Moscow hadn't earned her any praise; she was under pressure to report something better than new boots or headache powder received from home. In her pocket was a letter from Lily's little brother, which Katie had opened and read and would seal before returning it to the mailbag. The letter was short, ending with hugs and hope for victory. The envelope contained an old photograph of their father fishing. It was a slim torment in Katie's pocket, flat as a run-over toad.

"I'm your comrade too," Lily said.

"My friend."

Katie had been surprised by the transfer. Oh, that Lily, she was craftier than Katie had given her credit for, but good little Soviets served their country on the sly, didn't they? And Katie thought . . . What was she thinking? Another drink was in order. She was getting sober enough to know how much she'd miss Lily.

"I wanted you to come with me," Lily said.

"What for?" Being in separate regiments was perfect, really. Katie wouldn't see what Lily was doing or hear her talking. No one could expect Katie to know anything about her. It was freedom. Release. She waved an arm. "You got Alexei now. You're better off." A man with a dick and a membership card in the Communist Party. Everything needed by a natural girl.

"I'm only going so I can fly," Lily said. "I have to fly, but I understand why you won't transfer. The 9th is a great regiment, the best fighter group in the air force. Why would you ever leave them? It's just that we've been together since training, and I thought we'd always be together. I don't know what I'm going to do without you. What's wrong? You're crying."

Katie put her hand on her face, surprised it was wet. "I need a haircut."

"It must be bothering you a lot." She pulled off Katie's boots.

"I want it shaved on the sides and back and thick on top. Will you cut it for me?"

"An undercut like Alexei's?"

"And Sasha's. Popular hair. If I'm going to serve with them, may as well look like them."

"You mean it?" The cot squeaked. "You'll transfer with me?"

"As a soldier of the Workers' and Peasants' Army, I swear."

"Then I'll cut your hair tomorrow. Move over. You stink, but the fire went out in the oil drum. It's colder than death in here. Just don't throw up on me."

For this sweet agony, who wouldn't give in?

The 8th Air Army was moving into the Rostov district, which was about three hundred kilometres from Stalingrad. Farther south and close to the Ukraine, it marked the bottom end of the front line. Under German occupation since July, the region was important as the gateway to rich oil fields in western Asia, which Hitler's army had failed to take as yet and desperately needed to feed its tanks and other vehicles. They had to be stopped. It was crucial that the Red Army regain Rostov, repair their pipelines, and block a German advance toward the oil of the Caucasus. During the debriefing, pins were pulled out of wall maps and repositioned: the forces that had wrested Stalingrad from the enemy were going south.

While Lily was trying to pack up, she was distracted by Alexei, who sat on her cot amidst her belongings.

"So you like Pushkin," Alexei said as she took the book from his hands.

She placed it in her duffle bag. "Who doesn't?" But lately random lines from banned poets were popping into her head. *Your murmuring foam will kiss* and *A white frost tries my lips to freeze* and *A shell without a pearl's seed*. Lines from love poems, the books destroyed. She wondered how they could possibly be treasonous. "What's your favourite poem?" she asked.

"Ha, me. Anything we learned in school." He began to recite "Ode to a Tractor."

"Stop!"

"I thought you liked poems," he said, and she smiled.

"Not all of them."

"Do you like practical jokes?"

"Not much."

"You'd like this one. Volodya with an exploding cigarette."

She laughed. "I can't believe you got her with that old prank."

"I put regular cigarette paper around the flash paper. Very carefully." He picked up a small pile of underwear.

"Get your hands off those. My mother sent them to me. I hate army issue."

"If you give me a kiss."

She pecked him on the cheek.

"That's all?"

"That's all you deserve."

"What do I have to do for more?"

"You'll have to figure that out," Lily said.

"If I teach you my flying tricks? Oh, I can see you like that idea. Don't try to deny it."

"I don't even know how good they are."

"I'll start right now."

"I'm not getting into trouble for taking a plane without permission again."

"No need. First a diagram. Before you try it out." Eagerly, he searched around the dugout for a stick, and when he found one, he began drawing in the dirt floor. She fastened her duffle bag and squatted beside him. That was where they were, heads bent over arrows and circles, when Katie threw open the door. Her face was pale, and Lily jumped up, thinking that something had happened to Katie's mother or sister.

"Who?" Lily asked.

"Marina Raskova," Katie said. "She's dead."

"No. She can't . . . I don't . . . What?"

"She just crashed. Near our old school."

Needing to refuel and pressed low by bad weather, Marina hadn't realized how close to the ground she was, nor had the aircraft following her. A horseman discovered the wreckage and rode to the nearest base. The other pilots and crew were buried where they fell, but Marina's body went to Moscow for the first State funeral of the war.

Lily and Katie wrapped their arms around each other. Lily wept because it wasn't spring, and she couldn't put wildflowers in her cockpit in honour of the woman who'd made her a fighter pilot. To comfort her, Alexei went to his dugout and returned with a postcard. It had a picture of roses on it, yellow like the number forty-four on Lily's Yakki. Later there was vodka, and commanders made toasts: to Stalin, to the Motherland, to Marina Raskova.

In the January 17 edition of *Spark Magazine* there was a full-page tribute to Marina Raskova with pictures of her and the funeral, the pallbearers, the crush of mourners in the street. And in the bottom-right corner, a photograph of pilots with the caption:

Raskova's youngsters, girl fighters: Lieutenant Katherine Budanova and Sergeant Lily Litvyak bravely fighting at Stalingrad. In one battle they destroyed a Messerschmitt 109 and Sergeant Litvyak personally shot down a Junkers 87 bomber.

She Wasn't One of the Pitiable

The Rostov terrain was steppe, just like the land around Stalingrad: mounds, ravines, rivers. From the sky, the villages of southern Russia were all alike, a cluster of grey shapes against the snow, unnamed in any geography book. Only an airman would know their longitude and latitude. Proletarsk. Salsk. Mechetinskaya. Zernograd. Kagalnitskaya. Villages on the way to Rostov-on-Don, the main city of the region. Someone should remember the names.

Lily's regiment was billeted in these villages, and in them she'd seen hollow pits emptied of their burdens.

There was always an old woman or a blind man or a child who grabbed Lily's arm, wanting to tell the story as if, in the repetition, the words would lose their meaning and regain some sense.

In every village there was a story of ravines. In the ravines, pits were dug. In the pits were bodies. Hundreds, sometimes thousands. Men and women were shot, but not the children. Their lips were brushed with poison; they fell into the pit alive, and earth was tossed over them. The mounds heaved and then stopped. After the main event, SS and police searched door to door. There were roundups and trucks with gas for stray women and children, who were easily identifiable, their ethnicity—Jew—stamped on their Soviet passports. Anyone caught harbouring them was shot. *Jude Kaput*. Lily couldn't get used to the sight of collaborators hanging from the gallows where partisans had been executed.

As at Stalingrad, her unit faced the Luftwaffe's Fourth Air Fleet, intercepting bombers and attack planes, guarding the turtle movement of men on foot, horses, and tanks pushing toward the city. When fuel ran low, pilots descended to an airfield near a recently liberated village. They cleared mines, they listened to stories. Lily's mechanic carried an air compressor to the side of her Yak-1 and applied air to the pistons to rotate the engine. Fuel was injected, and she was rolling down the runway again.

After a few days of fighting they moved to an airfield near another village. The pilots were hungry and running on adrenalin because supply trucks caught up just in time for the regiment to move forward. If they were lucky, they located abandoned fuel. Sometimes they found the unexpected: on February 10, in a shed, the body of a Soviet sniper still wearing the top half of her uniform, cut open. She was hanging on a hook, a broken bottle between her legs, nipples bitten through, one side of her face bashed in.

"Don't look," Alexei said to Lily, trying to block her view, but she stood on her toes and craned her neck because she needed to see for herself. The storage shed was large, metal, airtight. On one of the containers was a clipboard. The shelves were empty, the wooden floor swept, immaculate.

At first she didn't register what hung in the gloom, not until the door creaked as it was flung wider and light bounced off the glass, dust motes floating in its beam. She glanced over her shoulder. Katie's eyes were pained, and Lily thought, *Now you see what I meant.* Sasha's usually agreeable face contorted. He said something, his lips moved, but Lily couldn't hear him at all. He left and quickly returned with old Ivan, who helped Sasha take down the body. Someone took her arm—Simon, another pilot, short and wiry. When his aircraft was damaged beyond repair, he'd shared hers because there was less pedal adjustment between them than anyone else. Lily shook him off and pressed her face in Alexei's shoulder. He held her tight.

They buried the body behind the airfield, near a frozen creek. The earth was hard to dig, and even with pickaxes and substantial sweat the grave was a shallow one. On the other side of the creek they could see a bustard with its hopping run, wings held close to the body for speed, too fast and clever to be caught.

At the funeral for the sniper, whose identification they were unable to find, the pilots stood with their arms entwined, Lily's linked with Alexei's and Katie's, their backs to the wind and their ground crews. Snow mixed with ice frosted their caps, fur collars, the mound.

"Our valorous pilots will repay the enemy threefold," Papa Nick began his speech, then stood silent, hands clasped behind his back. An index finger flicked as if he wanted to signal that it was time for vodka. "Never mind the slogans," he said. "Fuck the cannibals. Fuck them until their asses are ripped and their tongues pushed out of their heads."

The next day they were all in the sky, trying to work off the smell of the shed. Their commander, with Katie as his wingman, led the four-finger formation. Lily flew last, above and behind Alexei. On the instrument panel she had the postcard of yellow roses.

Five thousand metres and climbing. After she hooked the oxygen mask over her face, Lily unclipped her shoulder straps so that she could move around to look to the rear, one of the tricks she'd learned from Alexei. She turned her head incessantly back and forth, twisting to see the entire sphere of the sky, her silk scarf easing movement. When she looked forward, she saw Alexei looking back. Even with helmet, goggles, oxygen mask, no one could mistake that bulldog head. He'd been coaching her as he'd promised.

If you black out from Gs, ease up on the stick to regain your vision. The Germans still outnumber us, but they're not able to replace their aircraft, and that's making them more cautious. They'll move off to save their bombers. Make them drop their load too short. A hit can do as much good as a kill. When you've been in air combat as long as I have, you've seen too many deaths. The risk isn't worth it, Lily. Just do your job.

And what was that if not shooting down the enemy?

As they broke through a grey layer of cloud, she saw what they'd been looking for. Trails of white vapour feathered the sky, and she quickly counted the group of enemy planes below.

Seventeen bombers escorted by a fighter screen of twelve Focke-Wulfs.

Butcher birds, superior in every way.

She buckled her shoulder straps.

Papa Nick wagged his wing because he didn't trust his radio, and Alexei signalled a reply. The first pair dived straight at the bombers, passing between enemy fighters. The bombers scattered and regrouped in two sections.

Alexei turned over and Lily copied, hard left pressure to the stick bringing the starboard wing up at right angles to the horizon, hard on the port rudder pedal keeping her nose down. Wing over and she was upside down like Alexei, her sight set on a Ju 87, the howling Stuka on its way to blow up Soviet troops coming toward Rostov-on-Don from the south. Good luck, Fritz!

She pressed the trigger, and through the canopy she saw the tracers spiralling away. A miss! She was too close to the Stuka, the collision would crack her bones like a chick's, and she pushed the stick as far forward as it would go. Her machine moved past the vertical, negative gravity flung her up like a toy, the waist belt digging into her solar plexus, her lucky postcard flapping against the canopy as she dived below the bomber. She pulled up, turned her Yakki to the right on ailerons, and heaved the stick back. Gravity turned to the positive, Gs pulling down her blood, a black veil over her eyes. Sightless, she eased on the stick until she was level and could see again. Tight turn, accelerate. She aimed at the leader; her deflection was off, but her shot struck the number two Stuka. It lost altitude, smoking, and dropped its load, but that wasn't enough. Her head was hot, her hands were hot. She chased and shot again, hitting the engine, and it burst into flame.

She was not one of the pitiable Jews.

She looked around, sorting shapes, rigid black on shifting smoke, cloud, friend, enemy. The rest of the bombers were pulling back, dropping their loads for speed and leaving the Focke-Wulfs to take charge of the sky. Her fuel gauge showed she was running low, but Nick hadn't given the signal to head back, and there was Alexei's Yakki, red fourteen painted on the side.

He was moving to the flank of the fighter formation, taking a wide sweeping orbit to port, climbing fast. She threw her machine onto its left wingtip to pull it around, then fully over to the right. A steep turn and around again, blacking out at each rise. Their climb was slow, they were vulnerable, and she was sure that Alexei was trying to draw off a pair of the butcher birds with the temptation of an easy kill. As she came out of a turn, she saw a double line of red tracers arcing. She shouted in the radio, but Alexei was flipping into a dive. She followed, and the pair of Focke-Wulfs came along. A hit on the right wing, a hit on the left, but her wings could take a lot of holes before she was too hurt to fly. Three hundred metres down, Alexei was yelling over the radio, *Like me.*

As if they were in her dugout, she could see the drawing sketched onto earth. Always take on the lead fighter. Clinging to the inside of a revolving drum, she barrel-rolled, emerged from it upside down, and pushed her stick forward. The engine spluttered and coughed, the carburetor starved of fuel, propeller idling for seconds as Alexei came at the Fw 190 from starboard. He opened fire with a long deflection shot and had a hit, but her engine caught and she was closer, in perfect nine o'clock position, her fire hitting the unprotected fuel tanks right under the driver. Flames gorged on the Focke-Wulf's beautifully crafted engine. The machine blackened, it was dying, it was dead, dropping into an uncontrollable spin.

And diving on her—the enemy's wingman. She rolled again to make him overshoot, still in the trajectory of his fire, frantically pressing the trigger button. She was out of ammunition, the German wingman was turning, and out of the smoke, red fourteen came zipping through the flight path. Alexei threw his machine and ammunition across the tracers. A German voice crackled over their channel, *Achtung, achtung, tiger fourteen returning mark-six.*

She flipped over, righting herself, climbing stiffly out of the smoke. They were alone in a sky emptied of enemies.

All done. Zoom home, boys and girls, Papa Nick's voice came from the radio.

Their base was eighty kilometres from Rostov-on-Don, outside a town of eight thousand built between rural villages with a model farm and an agricultural college near Camel Railroad Station, the station's tower standing out against the flat landscape. Lily was the last to land, and her mechanic clucked over the holes in the wings. Adrenalin had seeped away, and it was an effort to rehearse excuses for leaving her leader's tail to take on the Stuka, for running out of ammunition, for putting herself in a position where her leader had to save her and her machine. Most likely she'd committed other, unknown crimes, but she was too drained to make her brain work anymore. All she could do was steel herself for the usual trouble as she headed to HQ for debriefing.

The rest of her group was already in the dugout along with the other group in their squadron, Sasha and Ivan, as well as their wingmen. They stood at attention, their expressions serious. The portrait of Stalin was propped up on the radio, in front of it an ashtray. The chief of staff was writing up a report, puffing on a cigarette between bites of sausage. The supply trucks must have finally arrived. Major Baranov lit a cigarette, looking stern. Alexei gazed straight ahead. Katie put a hand on Lily's shoulder, eyes sympathetic, then let her hand drop.

Lily saluted, Major Baranov asked for her logbook. Trying to get a read on him, she removed the logbook from her pocket and put it on the table. The dugout was warm, and he'd taken off his cap. He was smoking Balmorals. Was that better or worse than if he was smoking American cigarettes or rolled tobacco? The light bulb flickered and squeaked. He stubbed out his cigarette and put another between his lips, flicking the German lighter he'd found when they were clearing mines. He inhaled, blew a circle of mild-smelling smoke.

"All in order except for one thing," he said.

"What is that, Comrade Major?" she asked.

"You left out that we beat our previous record. Four against twenty-nine! And with Focke-Wulfs. Well done, Comrades! At ease." Nick grinned, and she was engulfed by the other pilots, hugging, kissing cheeks, punching shoulders, all talking at once, Alexei bragging as if she were his own creation. *A great explosion, you should have seen it. Got the motherfucker.*

Nick surveyed them proudly, running his hand through his red curls, and scratched his scalp. "A visit to the bathhouse is in order," he said. "But for now, go and fill up in the canteen. Food first, debriefing after."

She had another solo kill and a shared. For that, she'd receive thousands of rubles as a bonus, which she would send to her mother. If she were flying for the Americans, she'd already be considered an ace.

———

They dragged her into town, her friends. They got her drunk and she didn't protest, but walked with them, arm in arm, eight abreast, through the liberated streets. They sang love songs at a volume intended to scare the enemy. An old woman poked her head out the window of a ruined and seemingly empty house to scold them roundly.

"So sorry, Babushka," Katie said.

They turned a corner and sang again. There had never been such a starry night, such sympathetic companions. The next day they were grounded by the weight of falling snow, and the others nursed Lily through her hangover. The boys teased her because it was her first and she was already nineteen. After she threw up, she felt better, drank some tea, and dragged herself out of bed.

It was Alexei's birthday. She gave him a proper kiss for it, and they all went out into the snow. It was wet enough to build a regiment of snowmen and a fort to attack it. They threw snowballs, Alexei caught Lily by the waist, but she refused him anything more than the kiss. He was a simple Communist, she was a simple Russian patriot. *When we have victory*, she promised like the girl soldier in a play. The sky soon cleared, calling the fliers to it, and until there was another break in the fighting that occupied their waking hours, she wouldn't have to decide what he really meant to her. Until then, she could play her part.

On the Sunday after Alexei's birthday, Rostov-on-Don was liberated and their regiment moved to its air base. The city was less than 150 kilometres from the Ukraine, and while Lily stood with her comrades on the parade ground, she was thinking of her grandmother on the other side of the border. Sunlight brushed the Don River with a sigh; its blue ice crackled. Snow dotted the banks. They were being honoured, and during the ceremony they faced

the river. Finally, their regiment had been granted a Guards desig-
nation, newly numbered as the 73rd Guards. Alexei was promoted
to captain, Lily to junior lieutenant, and Katie to senior lieutenant.
Their commander pinned medals on the women's jackets: the
Order of the Red Star.

"Don't send all your bonuses home, Comrades. Save something
for a night out." Nick pulled off Lily's cap and ruffled her hair. "No
more aerobatics when you're coming in to land. I don't want to risk
one of my best pilots. Promise?"

The next time she descended from the sky, she couldn't help
showing off with a roll. When she left the cockpit, she hung her
head in mock humility. She said, "The wind pushed me over."

Her commander said, "If the wind does it again, I'll ground you
till spring." Then he showed her a souvenir he was sending to his
little son, a Luftwaffe belt buckle. They found other souvenirs: more
cigarette lighters, even a pistol left behind. The German Fourth Air
Fleet had pulled back to the city previously named Dneprodzerzhinsk
in honour of Dzerzhinsky, the founder of the Soviet secret police.
Under the Germans it was known as Kamenskoje, having reverted
to its old name, meaning "the stony place."

They Shared Their Life and Fate

The next break came in March. The officers' lounge was noisy except for the circle of concentration around the billiards table, which was propped up on bricks, its cracked end nailed together. Cues slid and clipped balls like the white moons of Jupiter.

"Come and join us," Alexei called out to Lily. "I'll teach you."

"Don't bother. He's losing." Katie had just returned from the barber, her head shaved except for a topknot, well pleased with it.

"Not interested," Lily said. They were all making the most of a lull in the fighting while generals conferred over maps. "Let me know when you're going to the movie theatre."

In armchairs confiscated from the residences of collaborators, other pilots were playing cards and cursing over them, a pair were hunched over a chess set, and Lily was reading a book of poetry she'd found intact in the air base's library. Every so often she put the book down, memorizing her favourite lines while she gazed through the window at blackened timber amid the rubble. The ceiling overhead had been patched with tin scraps, but she had hot tea and even a lump of sugar, which she hadn't tasted for ages.

"Do you like the book?" the waitress asked, picking up Lily's cup to wipe the table.

"Very much."

"I prefer Osip Mandelstam." The waitress said the poet's name as if he wasn't a convict who'd been executed in a labour camp, or as if she was beyond fear of reprisal. "*And my freedom is ghostly / Like a bird's midnight cry.* It's perfect."

"You should read this one," Lily said, tapping the book.

"I don't have to. It's mine."

"Yours?"

"Yes, in that I'm the author."

"You're Elena Grinberg the poet?"

"I was. I don't write anymore." Elena's hands were large, the arms thin. She wore a kerchief, which hid her hair loss, but she had no eyelashes, and her naked eyes bored into Lily's. "Can I ask you something?"

"Of course."

Elena pulled a chair close to Lily's and sat down. "How do you deal with the jokes?" She nodded in the direction of the pilots playing billiards.

"What jokes?"

"Like the one about the Jew's crooked rifle."

"Oh, that. You should ask Simon Gorhiver. He's a Jew."

"Aren't you?"

"No."

"Excuse me, I just thought . . . your name."

"Well, my father, but I'm Russian like my mother." At sixteen a child of mixed parents had to declare one of their ethnicities as officially hers.

"Yes, I see. A practical choice."

"We're fighting for the freedom of all peoples in the Soviet lands and workers everywhere." The words came automatically.

Elena lowered her voice. "Twenty thousand of Rostov's Jews are buried in Snake Canyon."

"Peaceful Soviet citizens," Lily said. It was what the newspaper had reported. "Killed by Fascists."

"For being Jews. Should the memory of who they were be obliterated too?"

"They went to their slaughter with suitcases." It slipped out; she hadn't meant to impugn the waitress, the poet.

"You think we had no courage?"

"I'm sorry. I didn't mean you."

"Of course, not me. Even Nazis have pet Jews. Maybe you meant my brother? He was a researcher at the agricultural institute. When the Germans ordered Jews to assemble, he opened up his veins so that his Russian wife wouldn't be harmed. But he lived, and my sister-in-law put him in a handcart. She was taking him to the hospital when a German patrol stopped them. They were shot right then and lay in the street for dogs to lick."

"But why kill themselves and do no damage? Why not at least blow something up?"

"Even our soldiers retreated with their rifles and tanks. Houses were searched. What would you do?"

"Use my teeth," Lily said.

"And let someone else suffer for you. My old auntie lived with two former nuns, who cared for her. When the Germans threatened to kill them in her place, she turned herself in. Even the partisans don't take unarmed Jews. When you're among the powerless, you don't choose the road. It chooses you."

"But you're here."

"Me . . . yes. I was selfish. I was thinking of my daughter. While my neighbours were arguing over who would get my chairs, I ran with her to the western outskirts of the city. Near Snake Canyon, there were only a few houses. A school friend of mine who worked for the railway lived there, and she was willing to let us stay in her room for a few days. How could I guess that I'd walked right to the execution site? Maybe, for all that, it was the safest place for a Jew. What do you think?"

"It's hard to say."

"That's what I'm trying to tell you. Right after I arrived, all the inhabitants were ordered away for two days, and I hid in a shed with Liza, my daughter. I told her to put her fingers in her ears and I covered her eyes with my hands. Prisoners of war dug the pits, then they were gassed in trucks and thrown into the ravine. I suppose there weren't enough trucks for thousands of Jews. Through a crack in the wood I saw naked women walking from the zoological gardens, coming across the green grass. One of them had hair hanging to her waist. She was holding the hands of two children with ribbons in their pigtails. She crawled halfway up the pit before she fell back. An old man hit one of the German guards in the face. The guard yelled, knocked him down, and kicked him to death. The next day the Voice of Rostov proclaimed, 'The air has been purified.'

"I knew there would be no place to hide anywhere in the city, so I ran all night with Liza. In the village of Olginskaya, I asked for shelter, but everyone said that the mayor had to give permission for strangers passing through to spend the night. An old woman gave me bread, and my daughter and I slept in the cemetery. And so we walked from village to village. Every time I opened my mouth, a lie came out of it. Peasants aren't stupid. They knew who had to wander from place to place. Eventually, a woman with four children took pity on us and gave us shelter. I worked on the collective farm, digging up potatoes. I thought we could stay the winter there, but an argument blew up between the woman's brother and another family. To get revenge, they started grumbling about the Jew-bitch, so we had to run again.

"Liza was so thin, her skin was translucent. One night we were lying in a field, and when I thought she was asleep, I wept into the dry autumn grass. As hungry as she was, her voice was as sweet as bells. She said, 'Don't cry, Mama. Our Red Army soldiers will be here very soon.'

"Near Tuzlukov, a man met us on the road. He asked who I was, and in that moment my wits left me. I simply said, 'I'm a Jew.' He said, 'Don't be scared. I'm a Jew too.' We sat together, he shared his potato, giving the largest portion to Liza, but we didn't tell each other our names. When we separated, I didn't have a good feeling about the area. Something was different in the sounds from the road, and I fled into the river with my daughter. From the other side, crouching in the bush, I saw a car stop. Police came out and shot the man we'd just eaten with.

"We wandered like this for months. One winter day I thought it was the end. Ice was warmer than my skin, and my breath stank from starvation. No one would take us in, but I found a bathhouse with stones that were still warm, and I covered Liza with my body. The problem was that when we left the bathhouse, we were damp, and the wind froze our rags. That night I begged with my body. For life, I wouldn't do it, but for my child . . . We slept in the *izba* of an old farmer. He told me that I could stay, and we did. I assume the old man knew that I was a Jew, but he never asked, except once he said, 'So you don't believe in our Lord?' I told him I did. I said I was a Baptist. That evening I went to the Baptist church. They were on their knees, praying for the Red Army to wipe out the Hitlerites. I liked that, and while I lived in his hut, I went to that church every day.

"I don't know why I survived. Every day I ask myself, what for? Me, alive, among the thousands. I don't deserve it, that's certain, and sometimes I think that those who perished are luckier. My husband went to the assembly place with his mother. He said to me that they'd share their life and fate with everyone else. *No screaming, no crying, we won't give the executioners the satisfaction. Let's die with dignity.* But instead I ran away with Liza. I was driven because of her, and that's all."

"Is your daughter in school now?" Lily asked. "Is she happy?"

For a moment, Elena didn't reply. She slipped her thumb and index finger under the kerchief and pulled out a hair, then another. "She's not hungry anymore, at least. She grew so weak, she got a fever and that was it. My daughter was nine. She died three weeks before the liberation." Elena plucked at her lashes, but there were none left to pull out. "Life continues. There's no reason for it, and even so, the habit of it won't leave me."

She moved to stand up, and Lily impulsively put a hand on hers, wanting to give her a token, a sign of their commonality, though she wasn't sure what that was.

"Take this. Please." She removed the scarf from around her neck. Elena paused; their eyes examined each other.

The older woman untied the kerchief made of rough cotton and slipped it from her head. Her curls were patchy, bare scalp visible. Lily reached into her soldier's bag and took out a hairbrush. She stood behind Elena, who remained as still as a child whose mother was going to untangle her. When the hair was brushed, Lily wrapped the blue scarf around Elena's head and gently knotted it at the nape of her bowed neck.

A few days later, in the only movie theatre left standing in the city, Alexei and Lily were watching a historical drama about medieval German knights who conquered a Russian city with the help of a traitor. After the citizens are massacred, a Russian hero repels the invaders. The movie was several years old, they'd both seen it many times, and Lily wasn't wearing her usual silk scarf, which Alexei took as an invitation. During the Battle of the Ice scene, he kissed her soft neck, and she seemed to like it. Her hand went to his leg. So his hand reciprocated, stroking her warm thigh. Why did she push him away?

"What?" he whispered. The traitor onscreen was being torn to pieces, but the violence was only implied.

"Not now," she said.

"But you feel so nice."

"Are you deaf?"

He pulled away, crossed his arms. She blew hot and cold, he didn't get it. But she was beautiful and he wasn't, so he asked, "What did I do?"

"Nothing. Shh . . . We'll talk after."

At the end of the movie they left with the throng of civilians and soldiers who'd packed the theatre, and they walked quickly to get away from their comrades, who teased and called out, *Lovebirds can't wait*. It was a long walk back, first through detours around streets impassable with rubble, then across snowy fields to their air base. The full moon cast their shadows. Her boots made small footprints beside his.

Alexei said, "You like me or you don't?"

"I do," she said.

"Good. I like you too."

"In theory," Lily said.

"What's that supposed to mean? Shit, don't tell me. You've never done it before? Don't worry, Lily. I'll go slow."

"That's not the problem."

"Then what?" Some of his friends' girls wanted to register their marriage first. Or soon after, especially if there was a bump in their midsection.

"You're a member of the Party. You go to meetings."

Everyone knew that membership in the Communist Party led to faster promotions. "That's why you like me? So I can get you in?" He was an idiot, thinking she was with him because . . . what? He was so great?

"No! Don't mention me at a meeting. Please."

He *was* pleased. Foolishly happy in the bright moonlight. "So then what?" He reached out for her hand. He wanted to kiss her small fingers; the thought of it warmed the centre of his being. Maybe they should register. How could he ask?

"All I know about you is your flying tactics. And you don't really know me, either."

"Lily, if we like each other, that's all that matters. Let's have our pleasure before we die."

"A Communist is a role model—he's under scrutiny," she said. "You should have an idea of what you're getting into."

He had a good idea. His hand had touched it, his lips had felt it. "No one's getting criticized for having a girl, if that's what you're thinking."

"I'm thinking about those bodies in the pits."

"If that's what you've got on your mind when I'm kissing you, then I'm doing something wrong."

"They're all Jews, Alexei."

"Soviet citizens."

"Why do the newspapers say that when it's only half true?" she asked.

"You have to take the big view. It's for the war effort. People get more fired up about atrocities against Russians."

"I can't stop thinking about it. For two years we had a non-aggression pact with Hitler."

"I was surprised by that too—Communists and Fascists are natural enemies. But then I understood Comrade Stalin's wisdom. It gave us two extra years to prepare for war."

"That's what everyone says. But Alexei, in all that time . . . not one word about the Germans rounding up Jews for massacre. Our intelligence sources must have known, and nobody was warned."

Sex and intelligence reports? He didn't see the connection. But she was a girl who liked poetry. The spring snow was wet. It would get into his boots, his socks would stink, and Sasha would complain about it again. "Why is this so important to you?"

She squeezed his hand as if he'd finally said the right thing. "I have family in the Ukraine," she said. "Jewish family. They could have come to Moscow."

So that was it. He could have guessed from her name, but she hadn't talked about her family, and why would she? They had so little time together, who'd waste it talking?

"I don't care," he said. "So you're a Jew."

"Part," she said. "On one side."

"Part—it doesn't bother me. Look at you. Beautiful, a killer pilot . . . and brave—you're Russian enough. One of us," he said. "And I'm crazy about you."

"It doesn't *bother* you. Many thanks, Comrade."

"You're welcome," he said, and called out, "Lily! What?" as she took off on her own across the field, her footprints darts in the snow.

In the women's dugout there was enough room between the cots for an oil drum. The fire in it had burned out, the dugout now warmed by glowing lumps of coal. Katie had organized a kerosene lamp, and she read *The Red Star*, rustling the pages while Lily contended with her thoughts. A simple Communist—that was what she liked about Alexei—the contrast with her own complications. If she was honest, she also liked the kisses and the hand on her thigh, and yet it wasn't enough.

"Did you enjoy the movie?" Katie asked.

"I've seen it too many times."

What was wrong with her? He was the genuine, card-carrying article.

"Didn't seem like you were watching much," Katie said.

"Don't tease me." Alexei was a good Russian soldier, and when he opened up, within him was the same soldier, an identical wooden nesting doll, and if she kept looking, all she'd find at the core of him was a rolled-up and tattered copy of the Party's newspaper, *Pravda. Truth.*

"What's wrong?"

"Everything." He was crazy about her. As if he had any concept of what she was.

"Did he hurt you? I'll shoot him if he hurt you."

"No. It's just . . . What if you couldn't be with someone you wanted?"

"But Alexei wants you."

"I know."

"Then you don't . . ." Katie turned the page of her newspaper, folded it back, ran her thumb along the crease, then looked up at her. "You really just like being his wingman?"

"Not anymore," Lily said. She wanted his touch, and it repulsed her, too, because she craved . . . something. To unwrap a surprise and discover more to unwrap, another surprise, and then again. Each one deeper, more revealing, and unwritten. As if love was like flight and everything else a mere walk on the earth, a crawl on the flat surface. But she could never ask that of anyone, because she could never offer it in return.

"You could have fooled me," Katie said.

She'd misunderstood, and Lily wanted to correct the impression, share her confusion. How long could Lily keep every feeling hidden? Someday she'd break and it would all spill out, maybe at the worst time, in a terrible place, unless she could relieve the pressure of it. If there was anyone she would trust, it was Katie.

"I can't stand it," Lily said. To be so solitary, forever loveless.

"If you can't stand to be his wingman, you can fly with someone else. Better yet, the other squadron," Katie said. "It would be kinder to him if you stayed away."

"You think so?"

"It's got to be you. He won't be able to, that's for sure."

"I don't know . . ."

"Trust me, I do. You want the newspaper? I'm done with it."

"No, I'm too tired." Tomorrow. Lily could talk more then. Right now, she wished only to dream.

She lay on her side and pretended to sleep, imagining a different present, an altered past. In the morning, avoiding Alexei, she asked her commander to let her fly with another squadron. Assuming that she'd had enough of being wingman, Nick agreed without argument and said that she was ready to lead a pair. When the alarm went up, she scrambled, worn out and uneasy, flying with pilots whose habits were unfamiliar to her. It was the second day of spring. Snow was on the ground, sap running in trees.

Someone was saying, *Are you conscious? Just open your eyes, Lil'ka.*

The Fourth Air Fleet had sent an armada to destroy the infrastructure of Rostov-on-Don through which Soviet oil had started flowing again: bridges, railroad junctions, pipelines. Seventy-two bombers had arrived in rows, long steps in a ladder climbing from front to back so that rear gunners could shoot without obstruction. Thirty-two Messers were widely staggered as escorts above them. It was the largest group Lily had ever faced in combat.

Red stars and swastikas zipped toward each other, approaching the speed of sound. One second, two, five, and they were within range. In the twist and turn of the sky she shot down a fighter and a bomber. Detonations blazed, below her a bridge ruptured. The squadron leader surprised her by unexpectedly dropping altitude, the rest of his group following. On earth, you had time to make up your mind, but in the orb of the sky, nothing stayed still, no more than the sun and its planets whirring with the galaxy. Before she could dive, she was engaged by the enemy. Isolated, chased, she sustained damage to her aircraft. Her fuselage was hit, a shard snapped into her shoulder. Her metal skin fractured, and her leg jerked. The engine smoked. The heater was gone. Coming into the air base, she'd fainted and had no idea how she landed. Maybe Death had flown the last hundred metres, maybe her grandmother had bullied him into it.

Alexei was pulling her from the cockpit, blood all over his flight jacket. Ruining State property—it was a capital offence. She should tell him not to bother, but he was gone, and she heard Katie's voice from a great distance above.

"Can you remove the shards?" she was asking.

"We'll see. The bones are intact, and meat will grow."

Lily opened her eyes. Above, a canvas ceiling. A fly walked across it. She turned her head. Another patient. A bucket. Sticking out of it, blackened legs. She hoped the smell wasn't hers. The doctor rubbed her injuries with alcohol and gave her some to drink as a general anaesthetic. Her neighbour in the next bed woke up and lifted his blanket. Whatever he saw under it made him scream.

Fragments dropped into a basin. *Ping.* That was one. *Ping,* that was two. She fainted, and when she came to again, she was in a transport plane. The same patient was lying next to her. A Ukrainian boy from a village on the Dnieper River. His eyelashes were blond. She told him about the fighter pilot in her division who returned after amputation to fly with a leg prosthesis. If she'd been flying with Alexei, she wouldn't have been injured. Not by the enemy. The plane smelled better than the field hospital.

Prisoner

UKRAINE &
THE CZECH LANDS

October 1943

Alive After All

Land moves backward and the Dnieper River flows upstream; the troop train is smoking and rattling past vehicles stuck in deep, glutinous mud. At every station throngs of fleeing civilians clamour to get on and are held back by the military police. If someone makes it onto the roof, he's chased and unceremoniously thrown onto the cement platform. The smell of smoke, oil, blood, and excrement oozes through the gaps between train cars, the cracks around windows, the doors that open to let soldiers on or off in the slapping rain. Sometimes there are unexplained stops or detours around bridgeheads. They transfer west, and at the first junction they see a train dead on the tracks.

Fritz taps the girl's hand, shows her his notebook. *What are they saying?*

Train was attacked by fighter planes. Boiler exploded. We're switching tracks. Going on a branch line.

Them? He points to uniformed men, heads tilted back in laughter.

A joke, she writes.

What? He feels the edge of her hand touching his, her cheek grazing his neck, their quick breath mingling until she moves, taking the notebook from him.

A soldier drops his helmet, she writes. *When he bends to pick it up, he's startled by a face in the mud. The face says, You'll be even more surprised when I tell you that I'm riding a horse.*

He signs, "Good one."

She shakes her head as if he's too young to realize it's reckless to reveal himself by signing, as if she's the sensible one. She and Gerhard, who could have got themselves shot for attacking the soldier in the grass. The pair of them. A couple of peas in a pod, clinging to their separate stems, always space between them. Is that how lovers behave? No, he thinks she was forced—not with blows, but like the Polish girl on the farm, who submitted to *him* because of her need for food and protection from the only ones who could give it. His people, the conquerors.

In his notebook there's a sketch: a man, a woman, looking away from each other, at their feet a baby, its arm raised in the Hitler salute. And another sketch: a boy standing between two men, a balloon over his head with a one-word question, *Father?*

Now she is Rose, and he is Friedrich Fischer.

What life is worthy of life?

He had asked her that. Before they left, when they were in the barn and the horses were still alive. He was speaking aloud, practising as he did when they were alone together. Each time, he taught her a few more signs, which she incorporated into their conversation, and the effort touched him.

"I met a newspaperman," she said. "He was visiting a friend of his, a poet I knew. He said that every soul is unique and irreplaceable."

"I don't believe in a soul," Fritz said. "There is no heaven or hell."

She touched his shoulder, then withdrew her hand to sign wherever she knew a word. "He meant what's inside a person, how they are when they're not worried about the way they look or sound."

"That's never. Except when you're alone."

"He said that's freedom."

Fritz nodded. No one is free, so it made a sort of inarguable sense.

"And when people recognize it in each other," she said, "it's the only power that no one can take away."

"You believe that?"

"I didn't when he said it." The colour of her eyes was changeable. Right then, the shade of the sky when the wind was breaking up rain clouds. "I don't know. How would someone try it?"

"We could," he said, because he didn't mind standing there quietly for a while instead of exercising his clumsy tongue. "Look at me."

He stared at her, and she stared back. People often told him to stop gawking when he was reading lips, and he realized that it was harder to bear an undistracted gaze than he expected, like being watched when you're taking a shit. He tried to look deeper—he wanted to see her, all of her, as she really was, to feel this supposed freedom and this power. But all he saw was a girl forced into being kind to him because he was German and his uncle a policeman.

He broke his gaze, looked at the ground. Then he brushed away his disappointment and spoke with his hands. "You be the military police and ask me questions. I'll practise answering," he said.

"What?" she signed.

He repeated it aloud, and she replied with her lips, "Do you have a medical certificate, young man?"

"Yes, sir. I have it right here."

"You're dropping the *r* in *sir*. Look at my tongue."

Life that's worthy of life stays alive.

The rest—the salutes, the banners—is window dressing to fancy it up.

Except that his uncle risked his career, his neck, to send a defective boy away from the action of war. Fritz can't see the self-interest in it. He's tried, but it eludes him. And he's left with the uncomfortable feeling that he's hanging in mid-air.

He has no camera, no viewfinder to peer through. His eyes are unclothed. He observes and he draws, blunting his pencil with lines that he shades into three dimensions.

Gerhard returns from the lavatory and settles onto the bench. His pupils are large from the Pervitin he downed with generous quantities of vodka. "Hungry?" he asks.

Fritz shakes his head.

"I'm thirsty," Rose says.

"Here." Gerhard hands over his canteen. "Don't worry, it's water."

"I still smell them burning," she says. "The horses."

"Outside Moscow," Gerhard says, "I cut off the frozen legs of a dead Russian soldier and thawed them by the fire to remove his boots. Same smell. Poor fellow saved me that winter. If I'd had his felt boots at Stalingrad, I wouldn't have got frostbite."

It's still 140 kilometres to Zhytomyr, where they'll disembark from the troop train. Only trains for soldiers on leave, which have a lower priority, continue west.

Fritz draws a horse swallowing the locomotive.

The conductor walks through the stripped-down passenger car. "Zhytomyr! End of the line! Everybody out."

The last time Lily was here, she picked wild strawberries in the park. Her grandmother spat on a handkerchief and scrubbed dirt off Lily's face. They walked to the train station together, her grandmother's steps short and quick.

Next leave train departs at five a.m. Do not obstruct boarding of troop trains. Soldiers will assemble in units at the eastern gate. Transfers west move to the right for processing. Have your papers ready! Clear the platform!

Commanders shout orders, trying to be heard above the public address system as soldiers surge through the rail yard. Boots stamp in military rhythm, units march away, while ragged lines scuffle toward the Feldgendarmerie personnel in a shifting horizon of caps, helmets, khaki backs, slung rifles, bread bags, and knapsacks. The loudspeaker drones and squeaks. Flanked by Gerhard and Fritz, she shuffles forward, drizzle tapping her cap's visor. Men speak little, grip their papers, shift bags to the other shoulder. Examining their papers are a half-dozen helmeted military police in breeches and high boots. Around each neck, hanging from a chain, is an aluminum crescent a hand's breadth wide. It's embossed with a German eagle and a dark-grey scroll on which *Feldgendarmerie* is painted the same fluorescent yellow as the bird, visible even in a blackout. The gendarmes sit at a long table under a tarp supported by four poles, which wobble in the mud like frightened soldiers.

"Next!" The infantryman standing in front of Lily salutes the gendarme, who stares at him for a half minute, watching the boy's reaction. "Who gave you permission to retreat?"

"My captain, Herr *Feldgendarm*."

"And where is your captain?"

"Dead."

"But not you. Let me see your papers." The gendarme studies the stamps under a magnifying glass and again stares at the soldier. "Equipment." The young man shrugs off his knapsack and unloads its contents on the table. "Gas mask. Belt and buckle," the gendarme recites. "Mess tin complete. Cartridge pouch. Spade. Shelter quarter. Weapons: pistol, knife. Where's your rifle, *Landser*?"

The boy puts his hands on the table, leans forward. A murmured reply.

"There's no excuse for carelessness with State equipment. None! It's a capital offence, pig-face! Count yourself lucky that there's a long lineup and I don't have time to shoot you." He turns, gestures toward the men standing guard. "Feldwebel Busch, escort this *Landser* to questioning. Let a headhunter deal with him."

"What's that?" Lily whispers to Gerhard.

"Worse than these chained dogs. Military police for the Waffen-SS, looking for enemies of the people," he says.

"What sort of enemies?"

"The usual. Deserters. Self-mutilators. Homosexuals, Gypsies, Jews. Anyone associating with them."

The boy sobs as he's taken away. A soldier who's been processed nearby clutches his pass and breaks down weeping as he leaves the line. "Next!"

"Volunteer veterinary nurse," she says, and hands over the papers. She recognizes the man reviewing them—not his upturned nose or his rubbery chin, but, even so, she's met him before in a different uniform and another season. "I should know better than to be out without an umbrella at this time of year. I hope that tarp of yours holds."

"Coming from the east, Fräulein Allendorf?"

"I assisted the veterinary service in Amvrosiivka and Kamenskoje." He'll smell no fear on her. Why should Rose Allendorf be any more suspect than Sofia Sarbash or Lily Litvyak? But she isn't so sure about Fritz. "I've never been to the Sudetenland. I hear it's very pretty."

The gendarme looks at her papers, then at her relaxed smile. "Yes, almost like the Fatherland," he says. "I'm from Bavaria myself. Not far from Hostau. Flossenbürg in fact. Perhaps you'll have an opportunity to visit. Next!"

She ought to get moving, but instead she just stands to the side, lingering near the table while the gendarme stares at Fritz. He returns the gaze with the intensity of a boy dependent on reading lips.

"Eighteen and not in uniform," the gendarme says. "You look healthy to me. Are you a coward?" Fritz shakes his head. "What's this non-heritable business?"

"His deafness isn't a genetic defect," Gerhard says. "He was wounded in a bombing."

"And you are?"

"Dr. Fischer. Captain, veterinary service. You've got the orders for his transfer. He's indispensable to the shoeing of remount horses. There's a terrible shortage of farriers now."

"You'll have your turn," the gendarme says. "Let the boy speak for himself."

"He can't, he—"

"Shut up, or I'll send you to the headhunter now. Where's the medical certificate?"

Fritz glances at Lily, and she smiles encouragingly. It's as much a goodbye as she intends.

"Yes, sir," Fritz says, searching through his bag. "I have it right here." In a quiet room, someone might detect a trace of shrillness to his tone, but not here, not in this din. The gendarme scrutinizes the certificate's stamps and ticks an item on his checklist.

She slips into the crowd. Farewell is for friends, not captors.

The last time Lily saw her grandmother was in the early summer of 1940. Right after she graduated from Kherson Aviation School, which was also in the Ukraine, she'd arranged to stop in Zhytomyr on her trip home. Grandma Rose was waiting on the platform of the train station as Lily leaned out the window of the slowing train, shouting, "I'm here! I'm here!" She disembarked with her duffle bag, and Grandma Rose, more wizened than Lily remembered, still managed to run over and wrap Lily in a tight hug.

The house where she lived smelled of hops from the brewery nearby. In the communal kitchen Lily helped her grandmother cook the midday meal. The knife in her hand moved just like her grandmother's, rising and falling with the same percussive rhythm while they chopped onions, cabbage, carrots, and potatoes. They sang in multiple languages, and when the meal was ready, they were joined by a neighbour named Citizen Perelman, who lived in the same house. A night watchman in the brewery, he contributed beer, and, despite missing teeth, he had a kindly smile. He called Lily *the dear granddaughter*, as if he had trouble remembering her name, and responded slowly when she asked him a question. From his wallet he proudly withdrew a yellowed newspaper clipping to show her. "That was me," he said. It must have been at least thirty years old, with a sketch of a boxing ring rather than a photograph to illustrate the headline: LOCAL BOY IS CHAMPION!

After the meal, he left to sleep before his shift, and Grandma Rose took Lily to the park, a patch of woods by the river. Zhytomyr was the greenest town Lily had ever seen, as if the forests around it, disgruntled with the disruption of men's wires and cement, had sprouted within its streets, throwing up trees in full leaf. Light and scent intermingled: the lattice of leaves, fallen pine needles, wild strawberries, which they picked and ate.

Lily asked, "What's wrong with Citizen Perelman?"

"You'd be a little slow too, if you got hit in the head as many times as he was in the ring."

"How did he get into boxing?"

"It's complicated."

"I won't tell anyone."

"Well, to tell you the truth, he's a birdie."

"What?"

"You know, he likes to be with men. That way." The day was warm. Grandma Rose took off her sweater, and Lily noticed the loose, freckled skin of her arms. "He should have gone to a big city where he could find the same kind of people. But he was a good son. His father died, and he wouldn't leave his mother on her own. So he became a boxer, and proved what? I don't know. Now his mother is senile, she lives in a Jewish rest home in Kiev, and she doesn't know who he is anymore." Grandma Rose spat on her handkerchief and wiped a spot of dirt from Lily's face.

"That's sad," Lily said. And after a pause, "I've missed you, and I miss Dad."

"I do, too. All of you. Even your mother, though she never really liked my cooking."

"Then come home with me. Isn't it all over now?" The head of the NKVD who'd orchestrated the purge had been arrested, executed, and replaced.

"You know better than that. I left the candlesticks for a reason. If the worst happens, your mother can sell them for food or a bribe."

"I just thought . . ." She was a teenager, she wanted friendship and love. "Maybe things could go back to the way they were."

Grandma Rose took Lily's hand, turned it over, and patted it. "If your father is released, I'll take the first train to Moscow. In the meantime, let's go for a walk. Help me up. I'm getting stiff."

They strolled among the trees, refreshed by the scent. Lily asked whether the story about the Vila was really true, and her grandmother said, "Of course," and, "But I forgot to tell you about the axe. Your grandfather used it to protect us during a pogrom."

In the evening they cooked another meal, their hands alike, and when it was time for sleep, Lily curled around her grandmother's back, their feet touching. Lily heard her grandmother ask if she was awake, and in her dozy state Lily didn't reply. But her grandmother spoke anyway, so her voice could enter Lily's dreams. She said, *This I promise—I will never desert you, whatever comes.*

In the morning they walked to the train station. Standing on the platform, Lily threw her arms around her grandmother, kissed the soft-muscled cheek, felt the bristled chin against her forever-youngness, said, "I'll come back soon." The train arrived in a swirl of hot dust. A year later, the Germans occupied Zhytomyr.

When she was last here, walking with her grandmother, it was a summery day, and Lily had taken off her flight jacket, carrying it in the fold of her arm. The town was theirs. Civilians went about their affairs, worked, saw movies, queued for whatever was available. Now trees are naked of their leaves, and between their bare branches nothing obstructs her view of German soldiers as she makes her way from the station to Soborna Square, straight along Kiev Street. Trolley wires overhead. Church spires marking the middle and far distance. White buildings. Marble columns. Blue domes topped with crosses. Helmeted soldiers direct traffic. Puddles reflect trees, wires, banners. Banners with the swastika, banners with the German eagle. *Welcome*, one says. Another, from a second-floor balcony: *Grand Commissioner.*

The Germans are getting battle ready. Military vehicles drive up and down the avenue. Commanders stride purposefully, ordinary *Landser* stand at attention, salute, then slouch wearily after an officer passes by. *Feldgendarmerie* prod the only civilians Lily sees in the street, forced labourers who lethargically break rocks, unload sand, nail boards to create barriers. A car with curtained windows roars along Kiev Street, and though she jumps away, her legs are splashed with watery mud. A boy on a bicycle stands on his pedals to gain speed, a messenger bag slapping his hip. She can see the cathedral at the end of Soborna Square and the arrow-shaped signs indicating directions: right to Kiev Street and the train station; ahead to North Highway; left to Main Street, parking forbidden. Soborna bustles with soldiers patronizing German shops and restaurants, and as she crosses the square, Lily catches sight of herself in a window: visored cap on her blond curls; padded jacket, an eagle and cross on the sleeve; white shirt and tie; shoulder bag; single-pleated skirt; stockings and boots. She hurries, running from her own reflection.

As she exits the square, a *gendarme* holds up his hand and she stops. "Pass, please." No lightning bolts on his collar—just an ordinary chained dog with a sergeant's insignia, who's controlling traffic. His face is rounded under his helmet, he has a gingery wisp of moustache, his big feet are planted well apart. "On your own, Fräulein?"

"My train doesn't leave until the morning, sir." She unlatches her bag, takes out her pass and other papers, and hands them over. "I want to get some food. And also, if I'm honest, to get away from the smell of soldiers." She waves her hand in front of her nose.

"I'm sure, a pretty thing like you." He smiles. "But you must be careful, Fräulein. Girls shouldn't be wandering through streets. Take my advice. If you were my sister, I'd be happier for you to get back to the train station, soon."

"Thank you, I'll do that, sir."

As he steps into the road, military trucks with canvas-covered beds slow to a stop. He blows on his whistle and waves for her to cross.

She turns onto a side street, empty of people except for a street cleaner. Within a few blocks the billboard on top of the brewery is visible; it depicts a white-haired man holding up a full schooner of frothy ale. Though the sign and the lettering have changed, the smell of hops is just as she remembers. Behind the brewery is an alley, and at the end of the alley she turns right onto a short street of ramshackle old houses dating from the last century, built for workers by the brewery's owners. At the third house, she knocks on the flimsy door. From behind it she hears quick steps like her grand-mother's, and her heart beats faster.

The door is opened by a sick boy, his face covered with red pus-tules. Behind him comes a middle-aged woman who scolds and sends him back to bed. She wears a kerchief and a cross; her dress is ineptly patched. She twists her wedding band. "I have a permit to stay home with the child," she says in a mix of German and Ukrainian, fear in her tone, the resentment in her eyes no different from the peasants' in a hut dug into the snow-blown steppe.

"I'm not here to order you out to work," Lily says.

"Then what, Fräulein *Helferin*?" The woman looks at her suspi-
ciously, hanging on to the door as if it'll shut of its own accord
unless she holds it back.

"May I come in?"

The woman reluctantly steps back, and Lily enters. The house
smells as cabbagey as she remembers, the walls are as cracked, the ceiling as flaked. Her grandmother's room was at the front of the house, a
small room on the left that nobody else wanted because it had been
a windowless pantry. The door is half-ajar. Through it, Lily sees her
grandmother's narrow iron bed of which she was so proud, having
held on to it through all the changes of regime: emperor, tsar, chairman, general secretary. In it the little boy sits up, hugging his knees.
Jammed up against the bed is her grandmother's dresser with the
square mirror in its swinging frame. The bottom drawer held her
books and letters, the second drawer her clothing, the top drawer,
which locked, treasures and secrets, or so she imagined.

"This is someone else's room," she says, pushing the door all the
way back as she walks toward the bed. The boy sinks under the covers. He turns his feverish face away. In Ukrainian, Lily says, "This
is an old woman's room. I'm looking for her."

"This is my little boy's room," the woman says, coming as close
as she dares. "It was no one else's before. Nobody's. It's ours."

"She was an acquaintance of my grandmother's."

"You must have got the wrong address, Fräulein. The German
area is near the Kamianka River."

"This is the place. She wasn't German. Her name was Rose
something. The night watchman at the brewery lived here too.
Where is he?"

"Gone, and I don't know any Rose."

"Are you sure? I could ask a *Feldgendarm* to help me. There was
a nice young man who stopped traffic for me. Should I go back and
get him?"

"No, don't. Let me think . . ." The woman sits on the bed beside the little boy, hiding him with her back. "Maybe I remember something, but I don't see how it can help you. Her name was Rose Litvak."

"Yes, that's right."

"A Jew is who you want?" She looks at Lily in confusion, then over her shoulder for someone with a gun. "But there are no Jews here. I have my baptismal certificate. Do you want to see it, Fräulein?"

"I want you to see this." She holds out her wrist. "The Jew broke my mother's watch and has to pay for it. That's all I'm interested in here. Just tell me where she is."

"How should I know?"

"Then I'll have to take something to pay for it." There are pale squares on the wall where family photos hung, a slight depression in the floor where her grandmother always stood when she got dressed.

The woman's voice trembles as she stands. "But this is my boy's room. These are my things. I bought them myself with my hard work."

Lily shoves the woman aside, the boy's eyes clench shut as Lily shouts in German, "Stay where you are!" She throws open the drawers, one, two, three, yanking the top one against the silly lock, but all that's in them are the little boy's clothes, some girdles, a few tarnished spoons, which must belong to some other absentee Jew. Her grandmother had only the silver candlesticks, which she left in Moscow.

"Where are the old woman's things?" she shouts.

"The Germans took everything," the woman cries out, spittle at the corner of her mouth. "I found the spoons in a ditch. Who will miss them? They took the Jews and left us nothing. *Jude kaput*! And what's for us?"

"What do you mean *kaput?*"

"You'll never get your money. She's in the ground with the rest of them."

No—the woman is conniving and scared, she'll say anything to get rid of Lily and her uniform. Under the bed there might be a suitcase with her grandmother's sweater or a recipe book in her handwriting, maybe a photo of them together and a note that will say where she's gone. Glancing down, Lily sees the edge of a boot just visible below the dangling blanket. The kerchiefed woman's cheeks redden, she touches her cross. There are four people breathing in her grandmother's room. The one under the bed is what? An escaped labourer. A would-be partisan. Someone old or stupid to hide so obviously. Grandma Rose might be old, but she's smart and strong, and the Reich is desperate for workers. The nation of trains that run on time would have to take her for labour, and after the war she'll go home and light candles, and when she waves her hands over them, Lily's spirit will glide in on the air current to feel her warmth.

"You're right. There's nothing for me here," she says.

Nimbostratus clouds make night of evening and evening of day, soaking her jacket and blouse with pelting rain. It drenches the partisans' woods, it muddies the graves of the fallen, it washes her thoughts clean as she walks back. There's always a way if you're brave enough. When attack from a forward position fails, then you come at it from behind enemy lines. Or with respect to finding a grandmother, go farther from the Motherland and into the west. She'll search every labour camp if that's what it takes, and some-how . . . She sneezes, her imagination overcome by rain. Her feet squelch in her boots as she arrives at the train station and sees the glow of a flashlight arcing across the rail yard.

The military police and railroad staff are sensible enough to huddle inside, but Gerhard is looking for her, his poncho stained black with rain. As he approaches, he calls out in relief, "There you are," and she feels oddly reassured at the sound, her enemy, her bedmate, as close as lice. He doesn't ask where she's been, but leads her to a side building, where passengers for the leave train are waiting overnight. Her wet hands slip on the door handle, and he pulls it open, ignoring the men who curse the blast of wet wind. Inside, he swings his flashlight around, finds the corner where Fritz has set up, and makes his way toward him. She follows. Gerhard drapes a blanket over her shoulders and Fritz hands her a thermos of hot tea, which she holds, trembling, as she sits on the floor. Soldiers have settled themselves where they can, using a knapsack for a pillow or propping their backs against a wall, a barrel, a stack of metal ties. Night is disrupted by the flare of matches as cigarettes and pipes are lit; conversation flows in the warmth of deloused bodies mashed together. They talk of near escapes, of home. Someone sings. Substitute a Russian name, substitute a blue scarf, it's the same song, and when it comes to its mournful end, there's the same longing silence. She shivers. As soon as the familiar press and odour of travelling companions stills her body's revulsion, it erupts again. The conversation has taken a different turn.

They're tough dogs, the Russians.

We're too humane. They take advantage of it.

I had an adjutant, a chemist from IG Farben, whom they called up and sent to me for God knows what reason. After an action, he was done for weeks. He sat in a corner and wept.

Taganrog, there's a sweet town. Fabulous cinemas and cafés on the beach. I was driving a truck there. Lovely girls, Russian, doing compulsory service making roads. We pulled them into the truck, screwed them, and threw them out. Did they curse!

If you sleep with a pretty girl and then you have to shoot her, it's hard on you. Some of those Jewesses, they're nicely dressed and attractive. You could almost say they're ladies.

You think the winters are cold, but the summers! The heat in Zhytomyr. And here I am, back again in time for mud. Now I've had the whole Russian menu.

That voice is somewhere on her right. "You were here before?" she asks.

"That's right. I arrived with the first wave of soldiers in '41."

"What was it like?"

"It's always the same in the army, Fräulein. March, march, march. Shoot and shit your pants. Then sit around bored until you move out. So, when they announced an action, the break was welcome."

Another soldier says, "You got to see an action that quick?"

As if he can feel her disturbance, though excluded from the invisible conversation, Fritz moves closer, his hip and shoulder bolstering hers.

"I sure did. I think it was—yes, it was late July. First an army truck drove down Kiev Street with a soldier standing in the back, announcing through a megaphone that at three p.m. in the marketplace there would be a shooting of Jews. Some soldiers got there early and had good seats on rooftops and balconies. My buddy saved me a spot, but there was a change of plan, and everyone had to follow this guy on a motorcycle to another place. You'd think we Germans would be better organized. So then me and my buddy had to scramble, because down on the ground you couldn't see over the heads of the civilians watching. He spotted a ladder, and up he went, me after him, and we had a good view from the roof of the brewery. There were, I'd say, fifty or sixty Jews. First they had to jump back and forth over a ditch filled with water, and it was pretty funny when they fell in, and the SS had a go at them. But then they got to business and shot them, a few at a time."

"But that's only fifty. What about the rest—where did they go?" she asks.

"Into the pits, like all the Jews in the Ukraine. It's not like Poland, where they can hide with false papers."

"But Germany needs workers," she says, barely breathing. Beside her, Gerhard shifts position and grips her arm.

"Shh," he whispers. "You don't want to know."

"You really needn't worry, Fräulein. You think that the Fatherland would be polluted like that just when we managed to rid ourselves of our own Jews? In August, they were shot at the embankment."

"That must have been a big pit." The voice comes from across the room, interested, curious.

"Not so very when you have layers. The pit was about seven or eight metres long and four wide. The main thing is, it was deep. It was such a hot day, me and my buddies were in our swimming trunks. Who'd ever guess what winter was going to be like? Anyway, so we're there watching, and some general comes up, really pissed off. He says—you know the way they talk—'I categorically forbid these actions where people can look on. If you want to do it in the woods, that's your business, but not another day out here in the open. We draw our water from the river. We're drinking corpse water!' So in September the rest of them were taken from the ghetto and done in the woods. I assure you, Fräulein, all of Ukraine is clean."

"Even big cities like Kiev?" she asks.

"Especially them. Why are you so concerned, Fräulein? When you did your labour service in the east, didn't you see how well things are done?"

"My fiancée is a veterinary nurse," Gerhard says. "All she's seen is horses, and mainly their back ends. Hey, is the guy with the accordion here?"

"Yes, I am."

"Rolf, is it?"

"That's what it'll say on my death certificate, all right."

"Can you play any Beethoven, Rolf? Maybe the *Appassionata*, in memory of Stalingrad."

"How about this?" The bellows contract, fingers move across keys and buttons, the bellows expand, and the *Moonlight Sonata* floats over axles, oil cans, tires, barrels, hard-winged insects, and skittering rats, who are morally superior to every person under this tin roof. Her shaking ceases.

What she had done was lie to herself. She wasn't ready to die, and so she devised a purpose for going on, an excuse for her every crime: assisting the enemy, travelling with the enemy, protecting him from persecution and prosecution by his own kind.

She's known. Ever since Rostov, she's known.

There is no one left to save.

In the morning they board the train west. She doesn't eat when they stop, she doesn't speak, can't sleep. The soldiers sharing their compartment tease Gerhard, asking him what he's done to deserve the silent treatment from such a pretty companion. She's tight-lipped as they pass through Tarnau and Brody, where her grandmother was born, Wadowitz and Lvov, which was renamed Lemberg. At Kattowitz they're diverted to another small line; it takes them through the towns of Tichau, Auschwitz, Bielitz-Biala. At each transfer she isn't able to do more than disembark and board until Teschen, where they cross the border into the Protectorate of Bohemia and Moravia. The train stops to refuel at a coal station. Nearby, a railway bridge spans the Olza River, and she runs off while her companions are relieving themselves in the bush behind the platform.

When they catch up to her, she's struggling to climb over the railing, her chest resting on it, flakes of rust on her cheek, arms hugging the cold metal, one leg over and balancing awkwardly on the other, standing on her toes. Fritz pulls on her arms, shouting, "Don't do it!" heedless of what he reveals in the slurred squeak of his voice. If he dislocates her shoulders, it will be impossible to hold on.

"Let me jump," she cries into the railing, "or I'll tell someone that my papers are false. They'll shoot me, and then they'll convict you both of treason."

Gerhard repeats what she said so that Fritz can read his lips, and the boy's hands move to her back, firm but not attempting to remove her. She feels Fritz's breath on her cheek as he leans over, sees his green eyes darken with misery. That his closeness isn't unpleasant just makes her more determined.

Fritz straightens up and says, "I don't believe her. She wouldn't."

"You heard him," Gerhard says to her. "The boy has faith in your honour. Unfortunately, I know better."

"Then let me go. Why do you care?"

"He'll be upset, then I'll have to deal with him." She hears the flick of a match, an inhalation, smells a whiff of smoke. "And because I've wanted to do this often enough myself."

"You don't understand," she says. The river crashes over rocks. Spray strikes her face, and the sun is warm on her back. "Rose was my grandmother's name. I can't stand to hear it. Not because I don't want to live. It's that I don't deserve it."

"Who does?"

"You know I'm serious. I'll tell."

"Hmm, yes, though I suspect you haven't thought it through. For instance, my dear Sofia-Rose, before we're executed, they'll interrogate us. You can't be sure you don't know anything of interest. You've observed enough interrogations to know I'm right. And punishing me—that makes sense. You've been my prisoner. It's retribution. But what has Fritz done to you?"

A civilian casualty, she thinks. But of what military operation? She would be no better than the Germans are, condemning a boy because of her own shame. "It would be your fault," she says to Gerhard, "not mine. All you have to do is take Fritz off the bridge and leave me alone to do what's right."

"What's right." He stubs his cigarette out on the railing, tosses the butt into the water. "Remember the boy who lost his rifle? Carelessness with State property, that's a capital offence. He was shot while you were walking around town. It was right and legal. He was an enemy of the people. A frightened boy who probably lied about his age to enlist. So, he's my enemy. And tiny children are my enemies. Also old ladies. Terrible enemies, the old ladies. I mean, the way they bake raisin buns. Capital offence! Oh, and abstract artists! Does the Soviet State tolerate them?"

"No," she says. It's the strain in her muscles that causes the tremors, the exhaustion that causes her tears.

"Well, I could go on and on, but why bother. Believe me, I'd join you. My comrades are gone. They're done with this horror we call life. But there's Fritz. If I leave the world to the SS, what happens to him and the horses and other innocents who can't speak for themselves?"

"Dogs," Fritz says.

"Yes, dogs too. Shit . . . he means the *Feldgendarmerie*. The coal depot is crawling with them. If they catch us on the bridge, they'll think we're partisan bandits. We've got to go," he says. "Commute your sentence. Give it three months. By then, if you haven't found a reason to live, hang yourself. I'll give you the rope."

"Promise?" she asks.

"You can trust me. I nearly shot you once, didn't I? Come on."

She lets them help her down from the railing and hold her up when her legs don't work as they should, all pins and needles and twitching. The wind smells of rain, her stomach growls, pine trees scratch the back of the sky. She walks along the tracks with Gerhard clinging to her on one side and Fritz on the other, like drunks trying to get home, like brothers who've found their sister, alive after all, beneath the rubble.

Pilot

RUSSIA

Five Months before Her Fall

March to May 1943

They Stitched Their Lives Together

Sour smells. Bitter. Fecal. Guttural groans. A soft hand stroked Lily's forehead.

The night ward of the military hospital in Moscow was dark except for a candlelit nurse leaning over the next bed. At the edge of the flame's radiance, a ghostly figure sat in a creaky wooden chair. Lily's mother would sit like that when she came home after work and night school, sighing with tiredness as her father poured tea. A pair of spectres seen through half-open lids, whispering like the wind among reeds.

"Mama."

"Shh. Sleep."

These hands were the softest thing about her mother, who didn't speak through the night but smoothed Lily's forehead, rubbed her feet, held her hand. Somehow she was there, somehow she'd found her daughter. Lily wanted to talk, she had things she needed to say, but she kept falling asleep, conquered by the sedative.

"Yuri?" she asked when she next woke up.

"Your little brother isn't so little anymore." The soft hand squeezed hers. Lily's mother still had a callus under her thumb from working in a factory when Lily was small, but that was all. A worker's palm should be callused, its hardness the physical manifestation of devotion to working for the people. Lily's devotion had wavered. She'd let personal feelings come between her and her comrades, and she was still asking questions.

Her father had been in love from the beginning; her mother had fallen in love with him later. The Russian grandmother, religious, reactionary, hadn't been happy about a Jew for a son-in-law. Lily wanted to know how it felt to fall in love, how her mother knew, and whether it had shocked her that she'd loved someone her mother would despise.

But all Lily could say was, "I'm thirsty."

Her mother walked into the darkness and returned with a glass.

Lily drank and fell asleep. When she came back to consciousness, day had arrived. Blackout curtains were pulled back to reveal the ward: two rows of beds separated by an aisle for hospital staff to pass through. In each long row, the beds weren't side by side. Instead, the foot of one pressed against the metal headboard of the next, eliminating needless conversation between patients who had a patriotic duty to get well and get back to war or die and vacate the bed for another soldier.

A weary doctor listened to Lily's heart and lungs, he tapped her knee, he looked at her leg and shoulder with a sombre face, the natural expression of all Russians. He told her that she had no infection, but she was anemic and needed rest. He gave her a shot, and she slept. At night, her mother came from her war work, took away Lily's bedpan, cleaned her bottom as if she were a baby with no grandmother to care for her, sat in the creaky chair, and fell asleep, bent from the waist, her arms resting on the bed.

It was Lily's turn to stroke her mother's head.

Dawn came, and when the blackout curtains were pulled back, her mother straightened up, embarrassed and stiff. She looked older than Lily remembered, less knowing, as she glanced around uncertainly and asked the nurse when the doctor was expected.

"Soon," the nurse said.

Lily's mother couldn't be late for work. It was a criminal offence. She walked back toward the bed, her head jutting forward as if she was short-sighted and trying to get closer to her object of vision. Relief rushed into her face when Lily told her to go.

They kissed, and her mother left.

There was only a single women's ward in the military hospital.

All the wounded were here: the shot and the dying, the crippled, the deranged, the burned. Bloody sheets were changed, but even here, in the nation's capital, there wasn't enough pain medication, and what there was had to be saved for more important people. Patients moaned, they vomited, they screamed like they were birthing children. The nurse slapped a soldier who wouldn't stop biting her own arm. *Aren't you ashamed of yourself, Comrade? If you don't stop, I'll have to report you for malingering, and what will become of your little son then?* A trolley bearing bowls of cabbage soup rattled over the uneven floor, pushed by a pale school-age volunteer with long braids. At the end of the ward a woman with a shaven head, bandage over one ear, was shouting, *I'm ready for discharge! Nurse!*

The doctor who came to examine Lily that day was ancient. His face was pleated with wrinkles, the skin obscured by liver spots, and his wattle neck vibrated as he worked his stethoscope under her hospital gown. (He must have trained under the tsars— how had he returned from the frozen places that formers went?) He was as antiquated as pre-revolutionary vegetables, asking Lily to touch her nose and follow his fingers with her eyes, scratching the soles of her feet with his pen. He declared her improved but still unfit for duty, muttering about girls and shell-shocked wombs. How did those porous old bones hold him up?

"I'll get well faster at home," she said, "and I need to get back to my unit. We're short of pilots."

"Don't be in such a rush. Death is my friend, not yours."

"It's better to live a short while in the sky than a long time on earth," she said in imitation of a true Soviet.

"You'd better take care of that leg." With a grunt, the doctor stood up, studied her chart through his reading glasses, and agreed to release her to home care.

An administrative adjutant eventually brought Lily's paperwork and a cane, which he hooked over the foot of her bed. He told her that she'd been granted up to six weeks' leave, and the medical clinic would monitor the progress of her recovery. She must not miss any appointments. As soon as she was fully ambulatory, she was to return the cane. "I saw your picture in *Spark Magazine*," he said shyly. A rabbity groove ran from his nose to his nervous upper lip. His pen was poised above the form on his clipboard.

"If it isn't Guards Junior Lieutenant Litvyak," she heard a familiar voice interrupt.

"You!" Lily winced as she turned onto her side, then sat up and, with an effort, swung her legs over the edge of the bed. "What are you doing here?"

"The German armada's been visiting us every day, and I was banged around a bit, so then . . ." Katie swept the air with a heavily bandaged hand. "Papa Nick ordered me to get this fixed up in Moscow. Field surgeon not good enough for him. You know how he fusses. The nerves aren't damaged, they say, and won't be if I leave my hand alone. So I can do double duty and keep you out of trouble."

"Thanks, I'll refrain from stealing any planes for the time being."

"You look like crap."

"Who wouldn't in here? Where are you staying?"

"A hostel."

"That's no good. Take me home and stay with us."

"I don't want to put your mother out. I won't have much time to help—they've got me busy making speeches."

"Come anyway. It's no work to fix up a couch. I can do it."

"If you'll let me throw in my ration cards."

"Done."

Lily had nothing to wear, so she spent her first days at home making over a woollen suit. One evening, while Katie was giving a speech at her old factory and Yuri was out with friends, Lily asked her mother to put on some music. As she'd done a thousand times, her mother pulled the record from its sleeve, laid it on the turntable, wound the crank, flipped the switch to On, lowered the needle. When she returned to the sofa, the *Moonlight Sonata* was pouring through the gramophone's horn of plenty.

"Have you heard from Grandma Rose?" Lily asked.

"Not for a long time, but the mail . . . Nothing is coming from occupied territory anymore. Is your leg hurting you much?"

"Not too much."

"I'll rub the scar with ointment before you go to bed."

"Mama . . ."

"What?" Her mother's thimble pushed the needle through the thick cloth of the jacket's lapel.

"There's a pilot."

"Is there?"

"It's complicated."

"Love is."

"I don't think I love him."

"Really? Is there any other reason to talk about a man?"

"Mama! That's so old-fashioned."

"I didn't think you wore lipstick." Her mother's euphemism for sex, like a nineteenth-century reference to painted women. Lily couldn't say any more on that subject, not to her mother.

"Never mind, you're right. It's about love. You and Dad . . . How did you know?"

"For me, getting married was a practical decision. He had a worker's stamp on his papers. I didn't."

"But you love him, don't you?"

Her mother nodded, her eyes filling with tears. "More than I ever expected."

"I wish we knew where he is. At least then we could send him a package."

"He had a thick coat. If he was wearing it when they came for him, it would keep him warm. And boots. I hope he was wearing boots and not his good shoes."

"Do you think he'll come back to us, Mama?"

"I wonder. Every day, Lil'ka. That's the problem with love. It takes away a piece of you."

Lily kissed her mother on the cheek. The skin was rough with sorrow and age.

"But love isn't a choice," her mother said. "That's how you know."

Sitting hip to hip, a jacket on her lap and a skirt on Lily's, they listened to the music, stitching their lives together and with scissors snipping it apart.

At night Lily slept beside her mother, who soon complained that she was black and blue from being kicked, Katie sprawled on the sofa, Yuri made do with bedding on a couple of chairs they pushed together. Lily could see in him the little brother she'd left—if he was anxious, he scratched his neck, and his eyes squeezed shut when he laughed, darker eyes than hers. But he was fifteen years old now and agitating to leave school like his friends, who wanted to meet his sister the fighter pilot. They didn't come empty-handed, but contributed vodka and ration coupons. Her mother cooked, she poured tea, she encouraged her youthful guests to stay, to come again. In one of their rooms, an old woman now lived with her two granddaughters. When the little girls peeked shyly from their doorway, they were invited to dance to Tommy Dorsey's "Marie" until the record's grooves wore down.

When the woollen suit was finished, Lily wore it with her Red Star pinned to the lapel, and left the apartment. Moscow burst upon her. The multi-hued and fluted domes. The tall buildings, triumphal arches, bronze statues. Pigeons, sparrows, crows cawing. The canal jammed with boats, the bridge with convoys of trucks. The noise and colour of several million people running machines, lining up for theatres and cinemas, packing streetcars and the metro.

The panic was over, and everything American was in vogue. Moscow danced to Benny Goodman, laughed at *The Three Musketeers*—a musical comedy—admired Deanna Durbin, gossiped about *Lady Hamilton*, which Lily and Katie saw three times or maybe four. (She sighed over Laurence Olivier—who could resist the conqueror of Napoleon, enemy of Mother Russia? Katie sighed over Vivien Leigh—who could resist the conqueror of the conqueror?) Lily went to the opera, she saw plays, she even received a gift of tickets to *Swan Lake*. During the intermission everyone paraded in the lobby, and Red Army generals in their new gold epaulettes glimmered under chandeliers as they walked alongside American and British diplomats. Through it all, Lily hobbled, at first with her cane, then leaning on Katie or Yuri as she limped along, proud of her city.

A reception for the girl fighter pilots was held at the Lenin Young Communist Theatre in Moscow, formerly the luxurious Merchants' Club. As soon as they arrived, Lily and Katie were led through a side corridor to a long, narrow room with high ceilings, a row of tall windows. A space at the front of the room had been cleared for the photographer. His camera stood on a tripod. Beyond it were racks of costumes, a treadle sewing machine from Poland, a cabinet with large spools of thread, a corner table with makeup on it, a pile of head props (wigs, helmets, hats, animal heads, a birdcage). At the back of the room was a lacquered screen.

Lily hadn't realized there would be pictures and reporters.

"How could you not?" Katie said. "Boris!" she greeted the photographer. Beside him stood a young woman with a measuring tape around her neck and pins sticking out of her cushioned wristband.

"Hello again, girls," he said. After completing his prison sentence (for corrupting teenage girls—a minor crime compared to the charges against Lily's father), Boris Zeitlin had been assigned to take photographs of military personnel, including the female pilots at Stalingrad. "I see that the little one is still reluctant to stand for the camera. Don't hang back, Comrade. Look what we have for you! New flight jackets, goggles, uniforms, and lipstick! Don't trip over the horse head. Just go behind the screen and change. This is Svetlana, our seamstress. She'll sew you right up so that everything fits!"

"What do you mean lipstick?" Katie asked.

"Well, you're girls, aren't you? Aviatrices! Come on, darling, just put it on. I'll help if you want."

He made Lily laugh, and between his teasing and Katie's awkwardness with the lipstick tube she was still laughing when he snapped the pictures that would appear in *Komsomolskaya Pravda* and on the cover of *Spark Magazine*. Job done, the photographer disappeared with his equipment, the seamstress vanished, and, in their new uniforms, Lily and Katie were left waiting, as soldiers often are, until they're told what's next.

Overhead they heard feet running back and forth and someone singing in rehearsal. Katie cracked sunflower seeds. Lily sat down to try the sewing machine. There was a test swatch already under the needle, and she pushed the treadle with her feet until it rocked, the needle pumping out impressively even stitches. Through the window she saw a bedraggled group of German POWs shuffle down the street under guard. Passersby spat and threw rocks at them.

Finally, the door opened to admit not just one but both Kazarinovas, who'd been promoted through the ranks, the younger sister a major, the older a lieutenant colonel. Other than their officers' insignia, they didn't look any different from when

Lily first saw them at her interview in the academy. Lieutenant Colonel Kazarinova was as stylishly attired and unattractive as ever. Major Kazarinova had the same nicotine-stained fingers and forehead strained from the severity of her pulled-back hair. She flipped open the inevitable grey notebook and gazed at Lily with the same sharp eyes as in training. She licked her pencil, checked something off on the page.

"Lieutenant Budanova, you'll come with me," she said. "The Press Department has to review your speech."

"You're giving a speech?" Lily asked.

"It's nothing much." Katie shrugged and took the cigarette offered to her by Major Kazarinova. "Just opening remarks."

They strolled to the door, where the major paused. She turned to another page in her notebook, crossed something out with her pencil, and looked over her shoulder at Lily. "Yes," she murmured to herself. "Quite so."

Major Kazarinova and Katie left together, smoke wafting behind them while Lily remained frozen, standing at attention.

"At ease. Come, have a seat." The elder Kazarinova settled herself in the chair and pointed to the stool at the sewing machine. "This is just an informal chat between an old commander and her pupil."

"Thank you, Comrade Lieutenant Colonel." Obediently, Lily sat, studying Kazarinova's face. It was less sour than she remembered. Maybe the air of Moscow agreed with her former commander.

"You've made a splash in the air force." The lieutenant colonel's tone might almost be pride. "Twelve solos between the pair of you, plus six kills in a group. But you should have come back to your regiment in Air Defence."

"I'm seconded to the 73rd Guards." They were sitting knee to knee. Lily could smell lavender powder.

"I preferred to serve with men too. You quite remind me of myself when I was younger."

"Me?" Lily laughed and Kazarinova smiled, her eyes crinkling as if it was sincere.

"But fame is a responsibility you can't shirk."

"Am I famous?"

"You're not serious."

"But how?" She wasn't a Hero of the Soviet Union.

"You get noticed. Then chosen. You really had no inkling?"

Lily thought of the adjutant recognizing her. The reception that was turning out to be much larger than she expected. If she was famous, then she must be worthy. And if she was worthy, so then was her family. Could it be as simple as that? Her father would be released. Already she could see their happy reunion. She'd have a songbird in their apartment. A yellow canary. "And famous people can arrange things?"

"Especially if you're pretty. Do you never wonder how your beloved Marina Raskova suddenly became an air force major in charge of three air regiments?"

"Because she set an international record for distance flight."

"As a navigator. Who got lost."

Why would Kazarinova try to confuse her? A test? Then what was the subject? "Visibility was poor," Lily said.

"Still—she wasn't a top pilot. She just had the ear of important people. And when you have an ear, you'd better talk into it."

"Talk?" So this.

"And have something to say. At least until they get tired of you, and then all that attention turns into scrutiny. Faults are found. The highest fall lowest. Not Marina, of course—she died. A tragic loss. But if someone lives long enough . . . You're on the verge of it. Today's just the beginning."

"I don't want to make speeches. I just want to fly."

"I was an eager pilot too. Sometimes overly eager. That's why I offered to brief you. I know what it's like to stop flying."

"I'll be going back up very soon," Lily said. This sympathy in close quarters was making her uneasy.

"Ah, well. You were lucky, this time. You'll be shot down again, that's certain. And you could die or be crippled or, worse, end up behind enemy lines."

"Then I'll make my way back."

"And become a guest of SMERSH."

"What's that?" Lily had an idea; there were whispers of a special branch of the NKVD, secret police dedicated to uncovering spies.

"Everyone will know soon enough. I can tell you now that a soldier returning from captivity will be considered highly suspicious and questioned at length. I think you can imagine what those interviews are like. Where people end up after them."

"I don't know anything about it," Lily said. Her throat was tight, her heart pounded.

"And I want to keep it that way. I admit that flying is glorious. But it will end in disaster, one way or another, unless you accept a position on the ground while you have the chance. My sister . . . has a different opinion of your merits than I do. She seems to think you've got away with something. But you were under *my* command. And if you come back to Air Defence, I'll make sure you're transferred to my section in Fighter Support, here in Moscow. I can be your friend, Lily, guiding you just as I did when I was your commander."

"Why would you do that?" Now it would come—first the blackmail, then the suggestion that Lily could atone for her father's sins against the people by snitching on them. This was what she'd forgotten about Moscow. Nothing was as it appeared. What else didn't she know about Katie's activities while they'd been on leave? Was her hand even injured? There were times when Lily had been ready to confide in Katie. The thought of it was horrifying.

"I'd appreciate your dedication and loyalty," the lieutenant colonel was saying. "There are rewards for serving your country without reservation." If you had a soldier serving under you who had a secret, that soldier was yours. Unless, of course, Lily was approached by the secret police. Even watchers are watched by someone.

"I'm honoured," Lily said. She felt sick.

Kazarinova brightened. "Good. You only need to contact the current commander of the 586th. Officially, you're still with Air Defence. A horizontal transfer is simple."

"But it's not necessary. I'm content to remain in the 73rd Guards."

Kazarinova frowned, removed her beret and smoothed it out, then placed it carefully on her head at the same angle as before. "Someday you'll realize what you passed up," she said.

"I'm sure you're correct, Comrade Lieutenant Colonel. But my unit is short-handed, and they need me."

"You're determined to go back?" Her tone was more sorrowful than angry.

"I'm really suited to be a pilot and nothing more."

"Then all that's left to discuss is what's going to happen this afternoon. I've prepared your answer to the reporter's question." Kazarinova stretched out her bad leg, leaning over to rub the underside. "You realize that there will be foreign journalists at the reception?"

"I didn't know." Lily's voice was croaky; she was unnerved by the pity in Kazarinova's eyes.

"There's nothing to worry about. That's why I'm here—to provide guidance. You'll be asked what you think about in battle. Keep it short . . ."

The podium was set up in a meeting room with a long table bearing cake and a bottle of vodka for every man. There were numerous Russian officials, censors, translators, and several invitees from the foreign press, who were easily identifiable by the quality and style of their clothing even if Katie hadn't pointed them out to Lily. The chief correspondent for the Associated Press was a pudgy man with a round, red face—Eddy Gilmore, who, Katie told her, was engaged to a sixteen-year-old Russian girl. To his left was an Englishman who wrote for Reuters, Harold King. On the other side was the United Press reporter, Meyer Handler, a muscular New Yorker made milder by his glasses.

They all stood as the anthem came through the speakers. The editor-in-chief of the youth edition of *Pravda*, who'd organized the event, walked to the podium. Behind him came Lieutenant Colonel Kazarinova, then a child carrying a bouquet of flowers, another child carrying the air force banner, and Lily and Katie, arms linked and marching in step. *Girl pilots! Young Red Stars! Let the show begin!*

Lily endured the introductions, the editor's tribute to the youth of the nation and her former commander's history of Russian women in the military, leading to the formation of the women's air regiments and the accomplishments of the pilots at the podium. Then Katie spoke for a solid ten minutes. She said that she came from a peasant family. She was proud to serve in the people's army. She hoped that she could live up to the example of heroic revolutionaries. There followed numerous examples of revolutionaries and their heroics.

Gazing straight ahead as if she were standing at attention in front of a tribunal, Lily thought that Katie's voice sounded nothing like the friend she knew in the dark of the dugout. Hers could be any female voice coming through the radio or a public loudspeaker, the prelude to an announcement of triumph, followed by an outbreak of patriotic singing. Was any of it believable? Lily glanced up at the ceiling embossed with geometric shapes and circles and wondered what connection this woman orator had to her friend, or whether the friend was an act like everything else.

When the speech was finished, everyone clapped and cheered. The floor was opened for questions. Each of the reporters was allowed one, which they'd submitted earlier for approval. "Meyer Handler here. All of us Western journalists were taken to Stalingrad in January," he said. "We were escorted on our flight by pilots from the women's fighter regiment. They were very brave." The translator repeated what he'd said. Applause and cheers. "So I'd like to ask Lieutenant Budanova how Soviet airmen feel about flying with girls?"

"At first they regarded us with distrust," Katie said. "But that was dispelled when they saw us flying. They came to realize that we're reliable, loyal, and tough."

The plump journalist rose to his feet. "I'm Eddy Gilmore. Glad to meet you girls. What do you think about during battle, Junior Lieutenant Litvyak?"

Lily's reply was so quiet that Katie had to repeat it for everyone to hear. "When she sees the enemy insignia on his plane, she feels determined to shoot him down."

Then it was the Englishman. "Harold King," he called out in his deep voice. "What would Lieutenant Budanova like to say to my readers?"

Katie spoke slowly, allowing time for the translator to catch up. "British and American women could fly fighter planes if they were allowed to, as we are here. To the daughters of freedom, our sisters abroad, I say that we have a common enemy. The sooner we join forces, the sooner the world will be liberated from the brownshirt plague, and we can return to the family hearth and peaceful, productive labour. Death to Fascism! Long live our great Motherland! Forward to victory under the banner of our glorious army under the leadership of our brilliant, wise, and beloved leader and commander, Marshal of the Soviet Union, Comrade Stalin!"

Deafening cheers. Clinking bottles. Glasses were filled and drained. The journalists threw back their vodka like everyone else. (The first thing they'd learned in Moscow was that when there was a toast, a partially drunk glass was considered a sign of insincerity, and there was always a lot of toasting.)

"To victory with Comrade Stalin! Drink to the bottom!"

"To the Motherland and her allies! Drink to the bottom!"

"To the Red Army! To airmen and airwomen! Bottoms up!" the Englishman boomed. No translation required.

As bottles emptied, the talk got louder. A major general discoursed on Hemingway, demonstrating that culture was a Soviet value. A colonel asked Harold King about jazz clubs in London. Lieutenant Colonel Kazarinova and Katie circulated among them. Katie's lipstick had faded, and she'd tugged at her hair until it was a comfortable mess. Lily stood against the wall until Katie pulled her away and brought her around to greet the jolly officials and foreigners.

Eddy Gilmore asked if he could have a longer interview with Lily, and she replied, through an interpreter, that it wasn't possible as she'd be leaving Moscow soon. The interpreter, who was perhaps an informant—maybe they were all informants except for Lily—stayed close by even when not needed by the foreigners, for example the New Yorker, who was fluent in seven languages, including Russian.

"Moscow is a great city," he said. "I love it. Culture is open to everyone. Workers go to the ballet."

"I know. I was born here," she said.

"Then you must be enjoying your furlough."

"Not really. I can't wait to get back to my unit."

Lily couldn't survive believing in nothing and no one. War was the truth she could count on. When she was flying, she knew her purpose. Her friends were guarding her back. The enemy was shooting at her. As long as Lily was in the air, she could love her country, and her country loved her back.

It was unfortunate that the force of gravity compelled her to land.

The Globe and Mail
Toronto, Canada, Thursday 1 April 1943, Front page
MEAT RATIONING DECREED AT TWO POUNDS A WEEK
Forecast: Light Showers. 3 cents per copy

PRETTY RUSSIAN PILOT BAGS THIRD PLANE
Moscow, March 31 (AP)—Lily Litviak, a pretty apple-cheeked blonde who is a junior lieutenant of the guard but looks more like a junior high school student, was credited tonight with the destruction of a German plane. . . . She was wounded early in the attack but continued to fight, finally sending a Messerschmitt spinning to the ground in flames. Another famous girl pilot is Katie Budanova. . . .

Newcastle Journal
Newcastle upon Tyne, England, Thursday 1 April 1943
15 PLANES DOWN
In one big air battle when 100 German bombers and fighters tried to break through to an important town at a river crossing in the rear, Soviet fighters, although out-numbered, shot down 15 planes. . . . A well-known Red Army woman pilot, Sub-Lt. Litvak. . . .

The Evening Independent
Massillon, Ohio, Thursday 1 April 1943, page 10
SOVIET GIRL BAGS NAZI PLANE

Amarillo Daily News
Amarillo, Texas, Thursday 1 April 1943, page 5
RED GIRL DOWNS No. 3

The Brooklyn Daily Eagle
Brooklyn, New York, Sun 18 April 1943, page 2
RUSSIAN GIRLS DOWNED SIX GERMAN PLANES

The San Bernardino County Sun
California, Monday 19 April 1943, page 5
**PRETTY LIEUTENANTS PARTICIPATE IN AIR
BATTLES, SEE NEW FIELD OPEN TO WOMEN**

Birmingham Mail
West Midlands, England, Monday 19 April 1943
SOVIET GIRL ACE

Spark Magazine
Moscow, No. 15–16, 20 April 1943
ON THE COVER: Fighter pilots Guard Lieutenant Lily Litvyak
(left) and Guard Lt. Katherine Budanova. In aerial combat, they
shot down 12 Nazi planes. Together they've flown 280 sorties. . . .

The Salt Lake Tribune
Salt Lake City, Utah, Tuesday 4 May 1943, page 10
RUSSIAN GIRL FLIER PLAGUES LUFTWAFFE
A girl who can "give and take" is Lily Litviak, a Russian lieutenant . . . credited with having shot down a Messerschmitt during a
recent engagement on the southern front in the Donets region,
despite wounds she had received soon after taking off. . . .

Prisoner

THE CZECH LANDS

January to July 1944

Here in Hostau

Muttering under his breath, the postmaster organizes mail into piles for the stud farm and remount depot, which cover four hundred hectares at the edge of the village. There are three stables, each with its own veterinarian, ranked according to the quality of horses: the pure white Lipizzaners highest, the Arabians and other thoroughbreds in the middle, and, farthest away, in a hamlet with a stream and a bridge over it, the workhorses and Polish ponies. (The postmaster refuses to think of them as Russian Panje horses. Not here, so close to the Fatherland.) These are assigned to Dr. Fischer, whom history will forget along with his charges.

To be so close to the Fatherland, but not of it, is a thorn in the postmaster's side, a crown of suffering around his temples.

Just fifty kilometres away, a proper concentration camp stands on a real Aryan hill. Over there, in the German province of Bavaria, the small town outside the camp has red roofs made of clay tiles. On this side of the border, formerly Czech, now German Sudetenland (but not Germany), there are the same tiles, the same kind of Catholic churches with rectangular towers and red steeples. Here, too, German is the mother tongue, doors are solid, and the Führer is adored.

But over there, in Flossenbürg concentration camp, twenty thousand inmates are quarrying granite for what's left of their lives. And here? A few hundred enemies of the Reich groom horses. American, British, and French soldiers. Polish, who anywhere else are declared civilians and stripped of rights. (The commander of the depot even has a Polish cook!) And Russian prisoners? Not enough to warrant counting. While in the German concentration camp there's an entire separate section for Soviet prisoners of war, an execution platform, a crematorium. Visible from the concentration camp, the sublime ruins of a medieval castle on a hill.

Here in Hostau, the *Schloss*—the so-called "castle of the count"—is just some nobleman's hunting lodge, a modern mansion occupied by the commander and staff of the stud farm and remount depot. They're more interested in breeding horses than they are in punishing prisoners with hard labour. What do their prisoners produce for the Fatherland? Horse shit from the twelve hundred equine butts housed in the stables. For that, the prisoners get Sundays off and a half day Saturday to clean up or go into the village to spend the pennies they earn.

"For Stable C, Fräulein Allendorf." The postmaster sweeps the envelopes into a mailbag and hands it to the volunteer who's come for it. That's the Reich for you—even prisoners get their postcards in good time.

He yearns for a chance to prove himself. Just a small medal. Then he'll surely deserve a position in a bigger post office. Maybe even in the Fatherland itself. Munich. Nuremberg. Regensburg. The names roll around in the mouth like balls of candy. Nobody is a greater patriot.

"Nothing for you today, Fräulein," he says, wondering why such a pleasant, pretty little thing never receives a letter. "Happy New Year! Take a peppermint from the jar. It'll protect your throat from the wind."

The Red Army is still fourteen hundred kilometres away. They've just liberated Zhytomyr.

Wide Awake

Lily no longer translates what she hears into Russian. The meaning is just there, her thoughts a jumble of words in languages that blend unnoticeably unless she makes herself think in her mother tongue, and then what can she think? There is no future that she can imagine. When she sews, altering clothes or mending them, she loses herself in a reverie of the past. In her satchel she carries a spool of thread with a needle stuck through it as if she could stitch herself to the people she's left behind.

She's in the blacksmith's workshop at the remount depot. The blacksmith is out, and she sits by the fire to warm up, talking to Fritz before her last delivery, her mailbag on the brick floor. He speaks aloud while signing and she pays close attention, the effort of it focusing her mind and blocking out regret.

"The Red Army is getting closer," he says.

"You don't have to worry, you're a worker," she replies in a mix of German and signing. "The war was imposed on the ordinary people by Hitler and his clique."

"That sounds like a speech." On the anvil, a horseshoe is cooling while they talk. "Who said it?"

"The People's Commissar for Foreign Affairs."

"So when the armies meet and kill each other, it's not workers and peasants?"

"They would work and farm if they had a choice," she says.

"German workers and farmers were happy about the war until we started losing. People are greedy." They both have fake papers now; it makes them equals.

"And they take pleasure in another's misfortune . . . How do you say *i-d-e-o-l-o-g-y*?" She spells the word with her fingers.

"Ideology." He touches his temple with his index finger. Since they arrived in this valley near the ridge of the Bohemian Forest, he's been making up signs for words he didn't previously know because he learned to sign from children. This is becoming their private language, and in it she may say things she wouldn't think in any of the other languages she knows.

"Ideology can restrain someone if he's pliable. But it can't cure human nature."

"Religion can't either," he says. "My uncle went to church. He's also my father."

"You never told me that."

"I never told anyone. I didn't want to think so, but it's true. He wanted his brother's wife and he had her."

"People are people. Like you said—greedy."

"He's a policeman, against Communism. He doesn't like the SS. But he does what they say. If talking to someone doesn't get answers, he's all right with torture."

"Does that bother you?"

"It's wrong."

"If you have no ideology, how do you know what's wrong?"

He taps his chest. "My heart tells me. It's disgusting."

"My heart tells me that Fascists are disgusting. But you're not so gross."

"I'm not a Fascist." Since their horses were shot, he's changed—there is a gravity in his manner, a refusal to accept easy answers, a scorn for superficial talk. He sketches caricatures in his notebook: Gerhard in a stupor; the depot's commander in eighteenth-century ruffles; Lily walking on water, her eyes wide as one foot sinks.

She shakes her head. "I don't think your heart can tell right from wrong."

"Then what? Follow the leader? See where that gets us. No, tell me something else."

Her lips are pressed together, but her hands have their own ideas. Slow, intense. He watches with interest as she signs and spells,"You have to see for yourself, find out all the facts, weigh them, then make up your mind. Is your uncle greedy?"

"Yes, but he would give his life for me. That's love. It balances greed."

"I miss my friends. I loved them. I don't know what they'd want me to do here. They're gone, and I'm so far away from myself. Sometimes I feel like I'm sleepwalking."

"Horses would keep you awake. They bite and kick." Pinned to the wall is a drawing of a horse.

"You should be an artist. In the Soviet Union your talent would be recognized, and you'd be given every assistance so that it could be useful."

"In its service, right? Yes, the same is true in my country. But if I did this . . ." The drawing on the wall is Gerhard's nightmare, a stallion throwing a soldier off its back by grabbing his neck and biting through it. Fritz takes his pencil and adds a Hitler moustache above the soldier's nose. "It's finished." He rips the drawing down and tosses it into the fire.

"If you . . ." She doesn't finish the sentence. It always seems as if these conversations are interrupted as soon as they become interesting. The door to the smithy is opening, and a clipboard-carrying adjutant stamps snow off his feet, readying himself to count the inventory of horseshoes.

Lily buttons her coat and picks up her mailbag.

Behind the adjutant's back, Fritz signs, "A rose has thorns. They're equal to the scent."

It's a ten-minute walk along the path from the smithy to the stable. Inside, she calls out, "Mail," and pauses while her eyes adjust to the dimmer light.

Near the door, a Russian prisoner lies on the ground. Several Americans crowd around him. Half the horses are in the pasture, and while the stalls are vacant, prisoners are mucking them out, scrubbing feeders and water buckets, throwing hay, unloading oats. They organize themselves by nation and, within each nation, by region. Some of them go on with their chores, ignoring the Russian, flat on his back. Others lean on shovels, watching, curious, excited by another's trouble.

SS-Schütze Graf—the *Arbeitskommando*'s only SS man—is a new guard with three fingers missing on his right hand. He stands over the prisoner while one of the Americans tucks a rolled jacket under his head.

"I have mail for you." Lily gives the guard a letter, which he takes between the thumb and trigger finger of his crippled hand, skilfully tucking it into his pocket. "What happened here?" she asks.

"He's bleeding," Graf says.

"I see that." The rusty trail goes out the barn door, dotting the snow all the way to the pasture. There the younger guards are walking back and forth to keep warm while they watch the outside prison detail at work.

"What's your name?" she asks in Russian as she squats on her heels, shifting the bag to her lap, lifting the edges of her coat so it won't soak up blood.

"Igor Pavlovich. Horse . . ." His voice is mangled with pain, his words distorted. She can't make out anything more.

"It kicked him into barbed wire," the American explains in the camp language all the prisoners speak, a mix of pidgin German and smatterings of their own tongues.

"Dr. Fischer could sew this up," she says. A physician would be called for an injured American or British prisoner, who'd recover in an infirmary and receive his Red Cross parcels as usual. But the Soviets didn't sign the Geneva Convention. There are no doctors, parcels, or pennies for them. "Can a couple of you carry him to the surgery?"

"No," Graf says. "Not permitted."

"He's treated Russian prisoners before."

"This is camp business, Fräulein. Not the remount depot's."

"But the prisoners work for the depot. What do you say, Bruno?" she appeals to one of the other guards. He's elderly, a superannuated cavalryman under whose bleary watch the prisoners have been labouring.

"I don't know." Bruno is usually lenient, but the presence of an SS man, even a private second-class, makes him nervous. "Just finish up the mail, Rosie."

"But what happens to *him*?" she insists.

"If he can't work here, he'll go to Flossenbürg," the SS man says. He joined the SS for the extra pay. A month later, while unloading a transport, he caught his hand in a train door. "Or I could shoot him. Want to see?" He unshoulders his rifle, smiling down, expecting her to be impressed. The barn goes quiet except for the whistling of horses, a shovel clanging against a pail. The cavalryman looks away.

"You could. But there's the bother of it."

"What bother?"

"You've got the body to deal with." She stands up and balls her fists, resting them on her hips. "Do you really want to use prisoner labour for digging up frozen ground? Colonel Rudofsky"—she elevates the commander's rank a degree—"would complain about that. Nobody likes dealing with complaints. On the other hand, I could fix him up right here." Joining the flaps around the wound shouldn't be much different from fixing Fritz's old jacket, which he won't discard because it used to be his uncle's. "Then you wouldn't even have to write up a transfer report."

"Do it."

"If you say so."

"Prisoners! Back to work! *Schnell!*" Graf pushes open the barn door, looking outside while snow drifts in.

"They're short-handed in the pasture," Bruno says to Graf. "You could go back to your post. Unless you'd rather stay in the barn. I know which I'd choose—my old bones appreciate the warmth."

Graf glances at the old guard with contempt, shoulders his rifle, and leaves for the field. The prisoners return to work, carrying manure to the high pile at the side of the stables, talking among themselves. Lily divests herself of mailbag, satchel, and the scarf made of parachute silk, so she won't accidentally stain it with bloody fingers. From her satchel she withdraws matches and her sewing kit. Lamplight flashes on wooden beams, one of them honeycombed from bees long departed.

"I need more light." She kneels beside the injured man, his blood oozing under her knees. "Bring the lamp."

The American complies, and under the lamplight she pulls away the rag that Igor holds pressed to his side. The gash is just trickling now, but he's thinner than the American; he won't survive an infection. "Bruno, can I have your flask?"

The guard passes it to her. As the spirits hit the open wound, Igor gasps. Fainting is the only anaesthetic available, and she's sorry when he doesn't lose consciousness. While she lights a match to sterilize the needle, she instructs several prisoners to hold his arms and legs. She begins, and he writhes under their grip, yelps, curses, apologizes for it, but she doesn't rush as she pushes her needle in a diagonal zigzag. Sewing skin is more difficult than cloth. The needle is too large, the skin slippery. She tears a piece from her shirt to grip the edges. Beads of blood seep ahead of each stitch until she reaches the end, wipes them away, and knots the thread. In the light from the lamp, Igor's cheeks are green as he reaches for her hand to thank her.

"She has nerve, but it's wasted on helping a Russian," one of the Poles says. He's a big man, round-faced and round-nosed; he could have been Perelman the boxer's cousin but is twice lucky—first to be born a Gentile, then to end up in the genteel labour camp at Hostau.

She says in Polish, "We need to carry him to the barracks before the SS boy comes back. Help me, and I'll consider it a favour. You never know, you might need a cure for something that isn't covered by the Geneva Convention. For lice? For syphilis?" A word, like *pilot* and *engineer*, that's the same in many languages. It makes Bruno tsk.

But the Pole laughs and says in camp German, "He won't be heavy. There's not much to him anymore. Let's roll him onto a horse blanket."

She brushes the straw off her boots, looks askance at her dirty stockings, and stands up. With Bruno's permission, they depart. It isn't far to the prisoners' barracks, and they walk along a path in the snow, the three of them gripping the blanket, the injured man swinging silently in it like a sleeping baby. The other prisoners speak in bursts. The Pole's name is Bartek, he has a toothache, he was a carpenter; the American's name is John, he likes baseball, he hopes to see Yankee Stadium after the war's end. They come to the pad-locked hut where Red Cross parcels are stored and distributed. Beside it, the barrack is a long, low building like the stable, with a stove to warm it and a chimney pipe poking out. She opens the door, and John walks in backward. Every soldier has his own bunk and two blankets. She covers Igor with his and promises to look in on him. Her hands ache with pleasure at being useful and the craving to be useful again. The edge of her skirt is trimmed in blood. She's wide awake.

In January, the Red Army enters Poland, the RAF drops 2,300 tons of bombs on Berlin, Lily sneaks bread to Igor until he recovers, she learns the other prisoners' names. Instead of a rope, Gerhard offers her a medic's kit he acquired in exchange for his best shaving brush, complete with tweezers, surgical needle, and sutures. As his fiancée, she receives an allowance from him and spends it in the village, as would be expected from someone in her position. Gerhard is calmer here among the healthy animals; it's Lily's turn to scream herself awake and his to guide her back with the sound of his voice, the dropped *r* of his accent now familiar, comforting.

In the house where she lives with Gerhard and Fritz, she can sit by the window and see a barn, the tree-lined dirt road, the snowy ridge of the Bohemian Forest. The house is in Taschlowitz, on the eastern edge of the remount depot, and it belongs to a widow. Their second-floor rooms face the back: a bathroom with hot water boiler and tub, a room for Fritz, and a larger one for themselves. This is furnished with a bed and wardrobe, a small round table, a pair of armchairs, a bookcase, a glass-shaded lamp, and a radio, which Gerhard enhances by sticking a length of wire down the back panel. On the wall is a painting of a pond, sun-drenched hay bales, and rosy-cheeked youth, which could be mistaken for socialist realism if not for the emphatic breasts and the missing tractor. German women are always portrayed as slender and alluring, even when breastfeeding. Never in a coat, never holding a wrench.

To keep her thoughts steady, she's sewing a needlepoint of flowers in the dusty colours of a sweater she unravelled. Some nights she can go back to sleep by imagining the needle in her hand, the pale thread pulling in and out like a string of winter light.

Between snowstorms, the British and Americans bomb Leipzig, Vienna, Budapest. Lily picks up mail, assists at the breech birth of a foal, passes messages between prisoners and girls in the village, pulls a splinter from the butt of a shy Canadian navigator, records the blood pressure of gravid mares, sews up a prisoner's sliced thumb, marvels at the beauty of the surgical needle. The prisoners call her Rosie the Riveter, Lovely Rose, Blondie. When she finds Fritz alone, they pick up the conversation where it was last interrupted. *Are humans salvageable? Is greed stronger than love?* The Red Army advances west of the Dnieper River. Odessa is liberated. Easter comes and, in Hostau, parents hide baskets of glazed cookies and daintily painted boiled eggs delivered by the "Easter bunny."

In the evening, there's the radio. Sometimes she sings along with Gerhard. Eventually she has fewer nightmares, but when she does, he sits up with her and tells nostalgic stories. When he asks questions about her family or childhood, she turns the subject back to his. Sometimes he disappears for a night and a day. When he does, she tells people that he's come down with something and is in bed, which she's sure is no lie, and at night she thinks of Fritz, who sleeps alone in the next room. Gerhard brings back books as gifts, whatever he can scrounge that's old and unpolitical. They read about cowboys and ghosts and witches in the woods and Victorian boarding schools. He likes a happy ending and she doesn't. He's just five hundred kilometres from home; her distance is infinite.

Cherry trees bloom. Canadians land in Normandy. London is buzz-bombed by V-1 rockets. Two-year-old cold-blood horses are out in the field, being trained in single and double harness, pulling a box, then an artillery cart. Berries ripen, Vilnius and Minsk are liberated. The Soviets are moving west.

Staff can't be spared, so she's given the use of a jeep and Fritz's assistance to pick up supplies in Taus. It's the nearest town of any size, known for a Gothic bell tower in the market square, which is actually a rectangle—a broad avenue lined on both sides by three-storeyed white buildings with welcoming archways. German shopkeepers stand in the archways, clean-aproned and jovial, inviting customers inside. They serve their own people first and then, for a higher price, the sombre Czechs (who call the town Domažlice). This is a town of ten thousand, big enough for a garrison, and SS men possessing a full complement of fingers guard forced labourers from occupied lands. Some of them are repairing the road, others push wheel-barrows loaded with crushed rock. They remind Lily of *zeks*: the same vacancy, the gaunt automation. As she drives past them, she averts her eyes. At the end of the main street, feathered stratus clouds brush the church spire.

"Rain is coming. Help me roll up the roof," she signs to Fritz after she parks the jeep.

"The sky is blue, the day is beautiful and warm. So you're probably right." He's grown a moustache, unfashionably full. His shirts have become too tight across the shoulders, and Gerhard offered to pay for new ones.

They leave the jeep and walk down the street together. It's busy with foot traffic. Pedestrians come in and out of shops, hurry to their business or saunter with self-importance, but no one knows her and Fritz, none would report them, nobody has orders to give or the authority to impose them. Such freedom is unprecedented. She could turn to him, put her hands on his cheeks, pull him toward her, and kiss him if it pleased her to do so. She wonders if it would.

In the general store, she purchases shaving cream and razor blades for Gerhard (who prefers Fasan blades to military issue) and Camelia pads for herself. Disposable pads are becoming scarce enough that the shopkeeper won't sell at any price to the Czech women in town, leaving them to use rags like country women. He's a talkative man, was a quartermaster in the Great War, is fond of horses, fonder of beer and facts, such as—he puts the box on the counter—*These were invented by French nurses who used American Cellucotton bandages for their monthly.* His wife smacks his back with the heel of her hand and returns to her window cleaning. They have a daughter, who looks to be about sixteen, round-cheeked with dimples. She comes out of a storage area, wipes her hands on her apron, and glances at Fritz pleasantly.

"Do you like her?" Lily signs afterward.

"I'm sure she makes good sausages," Fritz replies.

"Exactly. A farmer's wife."

"For some farmer."

"You need a girl."

He looks at her.

He loves his country as much as she loves hers, but they both lie to live, which makes them enemies of their peoples. One could say that the enemy of her enemy is her friend. If that were the gaze of a friend. It isn't. His closeness wraps a haze around her as if her head exists outside time and all that matters here is her body. She likes his new moustache, a pair of coppery velvet strips angled from nose to the corners of his lips. Her finger wants to test the texture of it. She needs to shake herself out of this mood, but within the fiction of her life she relies on her body to keep her moving, to carry her securely from moment to moment, to remind her that something is real.

Fritz takes her elbow as they enter the jeweller's shop, and she doesn't shake him off. Her father's watch has been repaired by a grey-haired, bow-shaped man with tremulous hands and liquored breath. She pays, and they walk to the next shop.

She chatters to herself without facing him, hoping the sound of her own voice in a foreign tongue will make her rational again. Working her way through the list compiled by the veterinary staff, she loads Fritz down with packages and bags, which he periodically deposits in the jeep. When he looks at her, she looks at him and stops talking. In the men's clothing shop, the clerk measures his chest and offers him three possibilities. He takes off his old shirt and tries on each of them, waiting for her to approve or shake her head. The purchase is made. They walk on, and rain comes. In a narrow doorway she shelters in the curve of his arm and inhales the smell of him, horse and hay and something approximating wine. She wonders if kissing him would be like drinking it, which ought to shame her but instead makes her wish that raindrops could pause in their fall and the earth in its spin so they could remain together in a nation of two, this doorway their neutral territory.

Her time is running out. The Red Army is in eastern Poland. The errands are done. As the rain slows, they dash from the doorway, splashing through puddles, her shoes soon soaked through.

Taus is a fifteen-minute drive from the remount depot, just past the border between the Sudetenland and the Protectorate of Bohemia and Moravia. At the border, rain sputters like a dying engine. Their papers are inspected again, and a sad soldier with stomach trouble waves them along. They pass through the rural landscape with its low hills, pastures, and fences, so unlike the vast spaces of her homeland. They come to the medieval village of Ronsperg, a near twin to Hostau, the sky small above it and whitewashed. This village marks the halfway point; it has two cemeteries right beyond it. At the second, she stops the jeep and puts a hand on his arm, turning her head to meet his gaze. She can hear the quickening of his breathing; he must see hers in the small, rapid movements of her chest. She's been by here several times. No one ever comes, no one will disturb them.

In the abandoned shack of the groundskeeper, they sit on a mattress, facing each other. She touches his moustache. The smoothness of it. He puts his hands on her shoulders. He kisses and her lips open. She's nearly twenty-one. She doesn't want to die thinking that she's wasted any chances.

They make love in a hurry and again at leisure, satisfying her curiosity and his, graceful with their courtesies and discoveries. He strokes her hand, her arm, the softness under her arm, her ribs, her belly, her scarred leg. Even when they're done, she doesn't care about the rickety bed and the provenance of the mattress. The last time she felt as weightless, she was falling through the clouds, and she has no intention of pulling the cord. Sweat glistens and evaporates.

"What are you thinking?" he asks.

"You'd make a good pilot," she signs. "In the sky, what's most important is how well you can see."

"You've been in a plane?"

"Many times. Since high school. I started in a glider club."

"Tell me what it's like." He lies back, hands behind his head indicating that he won't interrupt, eyes on her as she sits cross-legged, uncaring of her nakedness, dripping him onto her heel.

"Everything is different," she says. "Vapour trails make loops and hoops. A moment later you find yourself in a blue emptiness— you're a swan in an endless lake. You flip and in your palace the earth is your tiled ceiling, a beautiful mural of blue and green. You and me, we're not visible. Neither is the Führer. He's as small as a speck. Does that shock you, me saying so?"

He shakes his head, he traces her belly button with his fore-finger. "Are you sad without it?" he signs. "Is the earth such a disappointment?"

"It changes the meaning of everything. I had a great purpose, to build my country and save it from our enemies. And a smaller pur-pose that mattered more, to change my family's terrible destiny. But . . ." This is the only place she can admit it, in the cemetery, impossibly naked, speaking without a sound. "So many mistakes were made. So much life wasted. Nothing makes sense to me."

"What about the power that no one can take away?"

"You remember."

"I didn't see it before. But I do now when I look at you."

"That's just sex."

"No. It's you . . . like no one else. But you have to see me, too. For the power."

"There's more to it."

"Then tell me."

"The newspaperman who talked to me about it—everyone loves his column. He's the only one who lived with soldiers and wrote about how it really was for them. He was visiting his friend, a poet, when he was in town to write a column about the anniversary of a famous air battle. That's how I met him. I was shy, but I knew the poet, and she introduced me. I told him that my grandmother used to read me his stories when I was young, but his columns were so different. I asked him how he did it, and he said that every person is multifaceted, and there are other stories in him that will be different still. Life is only happy when someone exists as a whole world. If he does, then he can discover the worlds of others, and that is what gives life meaning."

She has come to the point of the story. Her hands rest in her lap while she wonders whether to skip it. She signs, "The writer's name is Vasily Grossman."

"A Volga German?"

"A Jew. Like everyone buried here."

"You're testing me."

"Yes."

"I like what he says. If a Jew says it, then I like what a Jew says."

He's looking at her earnestly. Does that make what she's done excusable? "Let's say you didn't. Then would it be all right to throw him in the pit?"

"All life is worthy of life or none is. But if it was him or me, I'd choose me."

"What if the choice is based on lies?"

"Only a saint loves strangers enough to sacrifice himself for them."

"People sacrifice themselves all the time in war." She leans against him, and he puts his arms around her so they speak hands within hands. "The newspaperman lived in Switzerland when he was very young. I told him that neutral countries are despicable. Maybe I was wrong."

"This is right. Here, us."

"How can you say that?"

"I know about Dr. Fischer."

"You know what?"

"He doesn't sleep in his bed. He goes to someone else." Fritz's hands are emphatic, as if her engagement is all that should separate them. "Will you come to me then?"

"I will." She retrieves his underwear from the floor, finds hers entangled inside. "Before we go, I want to fix the stones. Will you help?"

"Yes." He kisses the nape of her neck and bends to pick up the rest of his clothes.

When they're dressed and exit the shack, she looks for a rainbow but sees none, only the sullen grey of an approaching downpour. It takes time to straighten the gravestones. The rain comes and it goes and, drenched, they keep at it. She pulls ivy away where it obscures names. If she comes again, she'll pull out weeds. The cemetery doesn't frighten her. Everyone buried here has had a peaceful death: cholera, pneumonia, hemorrhage, hit by lightning, run over by a frightened horse, heart failure not due to the entry of a bullet. She catches sight of names: Mejer, Mantler, Mandler, Zelig; on the stones of Katz and Altman, hands are engraved, outer fingers spread to form an inner V. At the eastern edge of the wall, dry leaves flutter in the base of a fountain. The wall is made of brick; the double gate has a six-pointed star in each iron door. She thinks about the children of the families buried here. She wonders if they're anywhere still or if the earth has swallowed them unnoted as Katz and Altman, Mejer, Mantler, Mandler, and Zelig.

She won't live long enough to make restitution—and for that, she's sorry.

It's Wednesday, July 19.

On the way back, Fritz pressures Lily to break off her engagement. She tells him it's impossible, they fight, they don't speak, they make up.

On Thursday, a bomb explodes next to Hitler. His life is saved by the nudge of a foot that pushed a briefcase out of the way behind a table leg, which shields the Führer from the full blast. There's only one bomb in the briefcase. The plan was for two. But the conspirator who plants it is injured from battle; with one hand and one eye, he only manages to prime the single charge that takes the lives of three officers and a stenographer. Hitler's trousers are singed. For this and the attempted coup, five thousand people are executed, a small surgery on the body politic, equivalent to half a day's war casualties.

Security everywhere is tightened. Personnel files of support operations have to be reviewed by the SS. The village of Hostau is under the administration of the SS in Bischofteinitz, the county seat, and as the commander of the stud farm and remount depot has a relative working there, the review is conducted quickly. When his relative arrives, he offers her his office. She spends a full day on the job, the commander's aide bringing her file after file. In the end, she writes her report. Everything is in order. She would expect no less from her nephew. If he'd been born in the Fatherland, he would have been a colonel by now. But life has a way of settling things.

Who would think a humble table leg could save the most important man in their people's history?

Pilot

RUSSIA

Three Months before Her Fall

May 1943

Where Were You,
My Honey, My Own?

When Lily and Katie came back to Rostov-on-Don after an absence of six weeks, the snow was gone and trees were in bloom. Their base had been cleaned up, the wreckage from the bombardment pushed into hills of rubble, the runways re-sanded. Their comrades cheered and embraced them. Lily felt Alexei's arms around her and expected him to pull her close, to overcome her ambivalence and her promises to herself. But he kissed her with a brisk peck and whispered, "Don't worry. Katie told me how you feel. I won't bother you anymore." She nodded, not trusting herself to speak. And louder he said, "I hope you learned your lesson. Next time, you fly with us." On his chest was a new ribbon. He'd been made a Hero of the Soviet Union. Her commander had been promoted to lieutenant colonel and given a vehicle, which he drove around in circles, showing it off.

When he stopped, the driver's side opened and Papa Nick stuck out a foot adorned with a tan boot. "Look, boys and girls! New! Aren't they great?"

Sasha bent down to study the boots more closely. Standing on the other side of the car, Alexei looked over the roof and Lily leaned on the hood. Katie stepped back to get them all in view.

"Stay still and I'll take a picture," she said. She'd brought the camera back from Moscow, the first she'd ever had, and she lifted it to her eye with affected nonchalance.

"Not yet. I want those!" Sasha threatened to pull off the boots while Alexei gazed gravely at the camera, his arms crossed and resting on the car's roof. Lily's chin was cupped in a hand, her elbow on the hood. She thought to herself, *These are my comrades. When we defeat the Fascists, Grandma Rose will come home, then Dad, and we'll all be together again.* She imagined it so hard, she smiled as if she brimmed with happiness, flight goggles still on her forehead.

Katie focused and snapped. "Very nice, Comrade Commander."

"Finally, you've got boots with no holes!" Lily said.

"Welcome back," Papa Nick said. "Take the rest of the day off, Lily. That's a strict order. We're going to party tonight."

"I don't know if it's worth it. What are we having?"

"Trust me. It's good."

Her friends insisted, teasing, until she held up her hands in capitulation and handed her flight gear to Katie.

Before evening fell, Lily walked down to the south end of the air base and picked flowers near the bank of the Don River. They poked up from the grass in a flurry of colour, and she made a bouquet though they'd wilt before she could put them in her cockpit. Wherever there was a patch of earth, iris spears were budding purple. Cherry trees were in blossom, so were lilacs. Surrendering herself to the beauty, she was lost in daydreams of a boat on a lake and someone in the boat, a memory of her father or a shadow of the future, when she was startled by her commander.

Nick said, "I've been looking for you."

"What for?"

"I have to approve the flight roster, but I was surprised to see your name on the rotation list. Do you really think you're well enough for combat? You look pale."

"My mother had a cold," she said, hiding the effort it took to keep up as they walked back. "I didn't sleep well when she snored."

"You need another day of rest. Your first time back up, you'll be nervous anyway. Don't shake your head. It's normal after you've been shot down." On lines strung between remaining vertical structures, gutted fish had been hung to dry, their scales pinkened by twilight. Gulls flapped overhead. "One more day. There's no point in arguing—I won't change my mind."

"Without me to push around, Comrade Papa, what will you do when the war is over?"

"I'm going to be a farmer." Nick's red hair was burnished to fire as he turned to look at her. "My own plot of land. Nothing big. With a horse. I always liked dark horses. A place to settle in, get used to peace. Private farms are going to be allowed for veterans. That's what I've heard."

It was a good rumour, improbable, but revolutionaries believe in improbabilities. She could picture him with a neat little farm-house. She would come with her friends, bringing gifts of bread and vodka, and he'd jump off his black horse and smile at them, straw sticking out of his hair. Maybe it was true. The picture so clear. "You could give up flying?"

"Any fish is good if it's on your hook," he said.

"All I've ever wanted to do is fly."

"I know, but . . ." He was hesitant, a hint of worry in his voice. "I received a letter. You're still officially in Air Defence."

"Aren't I needed here?"

"You are—but maybe it's best. Your injuries—"

"Won't slow me down."

"I just want to be sure, Lily."

"Don't send me away," she pleaded. "I couldn't stand it."

"Shhh, don't cry. Your comrades would kill me if I let you go. I'll telegraph Moscow and tell them I can't spare you." They were approaching the dugouts. Men were sitting outside, writing letters home in the last of the light. A couple of them were throwing dice. "After the war, you'll visit me, right?"

"I'll stay until you're sick of me." Past the dugouts and to her right, the mess tent was set up in place of the destroyed canteen. Away to the left was the airfield and their fighters waiting in rows.

"My wife will fatten you up into a proper babushka, Lily. So remember that we're expecting you. Don't take unnecessary risks. Look twice, shoot once."

"I promise, Papa."

Afterward, she'd remember that it was May 5.

The burning sun dropped below the horizon behind the mess tent. The sky was indigo, the tent an oblong shape; straight above it, the first star winked. They arrived at the long trestle table, which had been set up outside so they could feast under the stars. Nearby, an unharnessed horse was gratefully nibbling at wild grass here at the far end of the base, away from the smell of fuel and metal welding. The regimental cook and his assistant unloaded pots, tureens, and bottles from the cart. The smell of supper was more insistent than the cook's bell, and pilots hurried to the table along with their chief of staff, their political officer, and a newly assigned NKVD agent.

Like a favourite child, Lily put her flowers on the table and took a spot next to Papa Nick, unperturbed that she was ignored while he spoke with old Ivan, who had the same deep bags under his eyes and the perpetually mournful expression she remembered. Across from her, Sasha and Alexei now had matching Gold Stars. Katie settled herself beside Alexei, who put his arm around her shoulders.

He said, "Sweet Volodya, don't you want to marry a Hero of the Soviet Union?"

"If I do, it'll be someone prettier than you."

"But then there's the wedding night. The darling might be disgruntled by the missing pistol."

"There are other weapons. It's how they're used that makes all the difference."

"But who eats fish when they can have meat?"

Katie coloured.

"Shut up," Lily said.

"So you're going to abandon me to my lonely life, Lily?" he asked.

"I think so."

"Then there's nothing else to do but this." Turning away, he opened his jacket and flourished a knife, the handle ivory or bone, and before Lily could say anything sarcastic, he plunged it into his chest.

"Alexei!" The commander turned. A splotch of red was expanding, staining his shirt as he slid off the bench. She rushed around the table, her heart pounding as if she was outnumbered, out of fuel, out of ammunition.

"Kiss me," he groaned. "One last . . ."

Just as Lily leaned over him, she smelled the beet juice, and she slapped his face so hard her hand stung. Sasha burst out laughing.

"I hate you," Lily said.

"Good, wasn't it?" Alexei pulled the knife out of the potato held under his arm and withdrew the packet of beet juice. He removed his jacket and stripped off his shirt, then the undershirt beneath. "My lucky one with the cross," he said, "but it was worth it."

"Put on your jacket, my boy, and get back to your seat," Nick said. He rose to his feet and lifted his glass. "To our funny Hero of the Soviet Union, Alexei Solomatin! Drink to the bottom!" Glasses were tipped back, emptied.

"To the feast!" Sasha shouted.

Bowls were passed, soup ladled, slurping followed.

There was fish soup, of course, but the cook had also managed to obtain chewy meat and turn it into a kind of beef stroganoff with mushrooms, served on potatoes, and topped with sour cream. More bottles were opened. Everyone ate, drank, toasted their aircraft and each other, ridiculous stories were told. By the time they got to a dessert of preserved plums, they were all as ebullient as roosters at cock crow. The Ukrainians danced, all those boys without a *v* to top off their surname: Kutsenko, Borisenko, Radchenko. They outdid the Russians with their high steps until Katie leaped into the air. A couple of pilots wrestled in the grass, others were betting or egging them on. Lily stood on the table amidst the festive debris, singing, *Nightingales, nightingales, don't disturb the soldiers' sleep* . . .

And in the small hours of the starry night, a miracle: Papa Nick claimed to hear a melody through the din of their celebration, and Lily hopped down from the table. Pilots followed their commander like ducklings as he walked through the rubble of the air base to a half-collapsed building with a splintered doorway. Inside, Nick shone his flashlight on a piano that had somehow survived the bombing. A middle-aged telegraph operator with a bulbous nose and large knuckles was playing "The Blue Scarf." The flashlight went off. The pianist played by touch while, in the darkness, soldiers leaned against the piano and each other to sing their unofficial anthem: *Where are you, my honey, my own, darling scarf? Remember the joyful night you fell from her shoulders. She promised to save you* . . .

In the bombed-out clubhouse on the outskirts of a ruined city, young men and women sang until they wept for the pleasure of human love, its touch and its longing, its holiness and its profanity. The floorboards reverberated with it, the walls, the skulls of these fliers, their veins and their bowels as they crowded closer for comfort. This was Lily's family; she knew them by the smell of their unwashed skin, their breath, their covert actions hidden from Moscow but not from her or each other or Death, who breathed with them, in and out, keeping time.

At 0200 hours, just as the party was breaking up, the radio operator on duty advised Lieutenant Colonel Baranov that he was wanted at divisional HQ. When Nick arrived there, he met with the divisional commander, who informed him that Moscow had ordered

the simultaneous bombardment of enemy airfields. It was a hastily
organized mission, but the objective was to push into the Ukraine
and achieve air supremacy. That day. At dawn.

Lily slept through their takeoff. She didn't see the burning line
in the east that bordered the horizon or the waxing crescent of the
moon, a thumbnail pressing into dark cloud to make a hole for
the sun. She missed the flight to the Donetsk region, the escorted
Soviet bombers releasing their load over the German air base in
Stalino, the explosion of an ammunition depot. The ball of fire was
red and white, then rolled into a pulsing cloud of rising black smoke
while she turned over in her cot. So there was no way she could
have alerted Papa Nick when, in his sleep-deprived and hung-
over state, on the way back he turned left instead of right and lost
sight of his group. Diving through clouds, German fighters found
a solitary target. They came at it from all directions, riddling the
aircraft with ammunition. In the village below, people saw a pilot
attempting to bail, his parachute caught on the aircraft. The canopy slowly extended like a white cigar, the tip of it aflame. His
machine exploded above the ground.

The operation resulted in a single destroyed enemy bomber in
exchange for their commander's life.

There was no time to mourn. They were moving forward to
another airfield closer to the border with Ukraine. The next day at
dawn, they were in the air again.

On the second day of the mission, Lily was on the roster with Alexei
and Katie and the Ukrainians. The divisional commander ordered
them to repeat the previous day's mission exactly as it had been
done, flying the same route at the same altitude, as if the enemy
would be surprised by no surprise. The sky was the unsullied blue
of clean-washed spring, an azure sea with fine-spun vapour trails

like silvery foam. Up here, Lily had no more anxiety about Alexei or suspicions about Katie. Her passion had a clean and simple focus. For if, in her mind, her commander—her father here—and the father of her childhood merged, it only served her country all the more as her thumb rested on the trigger button.

Fighters from the Fourth Air Fleet met them at the front line. All the way to the target, they were fighting, and on the way home the Soviets scattered in pairs, unable to maintain any formation. Messers came in groups of six and four and by the dozen. Smoke greyed the universe, it gathered as thick as clouds. Lily shot down an enemy fighter and, running out of fuel, landed at the first airfield in friendly territory. Communications were out, and by the time she refuelled and returned to her own base, it was evening. Only then did she learn that they'd lost a bomber crew as well as another one of their fighter pilots—Captain Kutsenko—and that the mission had been cancelled.

After she gave her report to Ivan, who was acting commander, she begged a bowl of potato soup from the field kitchen and sat on the grass to eat. Katie dragged over an empty oil drum, and soon there was a fire burning in it. Nights were still cool, they could all use the warmth. One by one Papa Nick's children joined them around the oil drum, Ivan bringing his accordion, and they sat on the grass like kids at a Pioneers camp, the black sky shot through with stars, tents rustling in the wind.

"Was it worth it?" Lily asked of the fire.

"Hard to see how," Katie said.

"We got three enemy fighters and destroyed a German bomber," Ivan said as a dutiful superior officer should, though he bowed his head with the effort of it, knocking his chest with a fist as he coughed. "We came out on the plus side today. Lost just two."

"A fighter pilot, a bomber pilot, a gunner, and a navigator died. That's four brothers," Alexei said. "Yesterday, our commander.

Unforgivable." He stood up. He was ready to go. Ivan was on his feet too, his scrawny arm like a bundle of strung wire around Alexei's shoulders.

"The higher-ups push pins around, and we drip blood," Ivan said. "A soldier's a soldier. You can't fight it. If you think it'll make any difference, go ahead and hit me, I won't report you."

Alexei threw a punch, Ivan caught it in the shoulder, streaking the air with curses, and then they sat. Cigarettes were passed around and lit. Sasha grumbled at the scanty amount of tobacco in them.

"Someone should be shot. And they will be when the Party investigates," Alexei said. Nothing shook his faith. "Remember, you heard it from me."

"I heard that one of the pilots in our division went down near Amvrosiivka," Katie said.

"Dead?" Alexei asked.

"Observers think he parachuted successfully," Sasha said. "At least he's alive."

"Too bad for him," Lily said. "His family will pay for it."

"Does anybody have a bottle to toast Papa Nick?" Ivan muttered.

No one did. They'd moved forward in haste, and the supply trucks hadn't arrived yet.

Someone said, *He made us bathe.* And someone else, *He just got new boots.* Ivan played a sad tune on the accordion. And the air wept for the futility of their commander's optimism.

They were based near a small village just north of Rostov-on-Don. For the next two weeks there were training exercises, experienced pilots taking up newcomers for mock combat. Lily and Alexei were cordial. Sometimes he joked with her, and she tolerated the sharp edges of his tone, the extra bite in his pranks. At night she put herself to sleep with a favourite daydream: a man with Alexei's face was a poet; she succumbed to his kisses; they registered their marriage; this was their dugout, and he was curled around her back, his lips on her neck, his hand finding her hidden self.

The accident was unexpected. The official report explained the pilot's death as the casualty of a dogfight with the enemy. In fact, it happened during mock combat when Alexei demonstrated a tricky manoeuvre he'd done a hundred times. Only this time his aircraft stalled. Because the crash occurred during a training exercise, the regiment had a body to honour, which they placed in a flower-draped coffin and laid to rest in the cemetery by the old church. Villagers stood to the right, the regiment to the left, Alexei's closest friends at the foot of the coffin. The sky was grey, the earth was dun, cleared of brush and pocked by heels, hooves, tools. Their new commander, Colonel Golyshev, recently transferred from divisional HQ, gave the eulogy: *Alexei Solomatin fulfilled his oath to the letter, not sparing life itself for victory; he was a loyal member of the Party; admired and beloved* . . . The shadow of the grave marker merged with the shadows of mourners. Lily knelt on the ground, hugging the coffin as she wept for Alexei, for all the deaths she'd witnessed and those out of sight, for the torn families, the abandoned friends, the desolate.

That night she was drawn from her nightmare by Katie shaking her.

"You were moaning."

"I had a bad dream."

"You'll feel better if you talk about it. What did you dream?" Katie sat on the cot, flattening the straw.

"Alexei was calling me." Lily didn't say that he was in a crowd of soldiers and civilians. Some relatives were there, including her father and grandmother, whom her dream state confused with the dead, and now the wavery forms wouldn't leave her mind. "There was a river between us. The bank was muddy. It would have been easy to slide into the water."

Katie lifted her feet onto the cot as if it were a raft on the roiling river. "And then?"

"Alexei said, *Papa got me on his side, after all. He couldn't do without me. Lil'ka, when are you coming?*"

"What did you say?"

"*When they let me.*" In the dream she'd been standing on the river-bank, studying the faces she knew, looking for permission. "The current was strong, and I wasn't sure if I could swim across."

"That's some dream. Listen, Lily. We're all upset, but you've worked yourself up into hysteria. It was an accident. You had nothing to do with it."

"I could have given him a moment's happiness when there was time, but I didn't. I pushed him away. And now I'll never have the chance."

"Don't start blubbering again, you cried enough when we buried him."

Lily couldn't help herself even though her eyes were empty and itched as they squeezed, unable to find another drop while she stifled dry sobs in the crook of her arm. The ghosts she'd failed crowded her, pushing Alexei to the front to egg her on. Katie rubbed her back, her shoulder, until the wave ebbed.

"Done? Don't blow your nose onto the floor, I hate stepping in snot with bare feet. Here, take this."

Lily blew into the bit of rag. "He loved me . . . but I . . . He wasn't my . . . my type and so . . ."

"So you weren't attracted to him. It's a common problem." Katie got up and moved to her own cot, smacking the length of the straw pallet as she flopped down on it. "You'd better believe he didn't pickle his dick because you didn't want it. He amused himself when he could, same as me."

"Same as you?" Lily asked.

"You heard me." The bitterness in Katie's voice ripped Lily out of herself.

A dozen small things came to mind. How Katie looked away when Lily undressed, as if caught off guard. The throttled sigh on cold nights they shared a blanket. Risking a reprimand to bring Lily a potato in the guardhouse. How she'd changed regiments for Lily, though Katie would have been better off staying where she was. Saying that it was kinder to keep away from someone you can't love. *It's got to be you. He won't be able to, that's for sure. Trust me.* The only conclusion shamed Lily for her obliviousness, her self-absorption. She'd thought only of herself. How could she not have known?

She wasn't the only one to be starved of love. Her eyes welled with pity. "Katie . . ."

"I should probably tell you."

"What?"

"I've got orders. I'm going back to Moscow."

"You're not leaving!" The tent was small, just room enough for a pair of cots, and it was suddenly airless, the canvas squeezing Lily's diaphragm.

"For a month. Make speeches, boost morale, talk to reporters, the same as before. The Komsomol arranged it."

"You could ask the commander to intervene."

"I'll see my mother and sister. And I'm tired. I want a break, Lil'ka. You're not the only one whose friends have died."

"A whole month. But you'll come back?" She didn't like Katie's silence. "Say something."

"Major Kazarinova thinks I could make more of a difference in Moscow."

And what could Lily say? That she'd refused to be recruited, ask whether Katie was threatened too, risk it being reported? Statues were erected to honour the boy who had turned in his own parents. Lily said, "I've got nobody left but you."

Katie sat up, and in the dimming darkness of early morning Lily could see her head in her hands. "I've always come back so far, haven't I? Just don't."

"Don't what?"

"Whatever you're thinking."

"I'm thinking that you'll have to put on lipstick again."

Love was impossible in her country. And if death didn't take a friend, then Moscow would.

No one called Colonel Golyshev Papa. He was a military man with a military bearing who tolerated no breaches of discipline and assumed that his pilots would fly as sober as he did. The evening meal was at a set time and accompanied by an accordionist. There was a table for each squadron, every pilot with a given place, and a small table for their superiors. When he called a meeting, he expected pilots to stick to their designated dinner seats while Ivan, still deputy commander, plied chalk on the chalkboard. At the end of May it was a diagram: anti-aircraft guns, observation balloon, the front line.

A spotter balloon, a giant fish with grooved fins that loomed in full view of the airfield, was humiliating them. It was fifteen kilometres from the border and used for directing artillery against Soviet ground forces to keep them from penetrating the Ukraine. Five of their regiment's pilots had attempted to take it down, with no success. Lily proposed a plan. The problem was that the enemy saw the Soviet fighters coming, which gave them time to lower the balloon before it was in firing range. Lily intended to fly east, in the opposite direction, then circle around into enemy territory and come at the balloon from the rear. It was risky, it was dangerous. It made the new commander smile.

———

Mixture full rich. RPM max. Lily had had another bad dream and no one in her tent to wake her. Open radiators. Increase throttle to max. She'd had a letter from Katie in Moscow, which she'd read many times, trying to decipher the message between the lines. For instance, Katie had lined up at dawn to get a seat for a Walt Disney cartoon but didn't find it funny. Was this a comfort? A warning? An ambush? Lily had come to no conclusion. She was rolling down the runway: 150 k.p.h., 175 k.p.h., 200 k.p.h. The base blurred. Her nose lifted, and she was airborne. Retract gear. She felt the click in her breastbone as wheels entered the well; she swivelled her head like an owl with silk neck feathers, looking up and back and down.

Twisty peasant creeks sank into the landscape as she gained altitude, and squares of cultivated land blended into motley shades of green. She climbed higher, the river Donets a sinuous line that she followed down to its junction with the Don. Her engines had twelve cylinders, each with double lungs breathing in fuel and air, her exhalation a white stream that looped and swirled as she hastened to her target. The fingers of the delta reached for the Sea of Azov's blue basin, and she ascended to six thousand metres, heading north. She was in enemy territory, out of radio range. She climbed to seven thousand metres, nine thousand. Bombers flew up here unaccompanied, no one would expect a lone fighter hiding in the clouds. She was approaching her ceiling, pushing it to thumb her nose at mortality.

When she was close, she dived, levelled, and dived again. Gravity tried to yank her through her tail, acceleration squeezed blood from her ears. By force of will she hung on to consciousness, her filmy eyes clearing, and as she broke through the clouds the colours of the world astonished her with their brightness. Behind the invisible front line a green balloon with silver cross floated haughty and aloof. How silly it was in its reliance on the earth and the guns squatting on it, manned by soldiers who were blinded by the sun's aurora in its sapphire square. On the platform that hung from the balloon, a man peered out too late.

Everything here was clear: who she was, what she had to do. Her eyes could set anything on fire.

The first time Lily flew an aircraft and escaped into the sky, she discovered that everything she thought was movement was only the shadow of movement. On the ground, every creature scuttled in two dimensions: forward, back, right, left. But in the air she climbed and dived, she looped and rolled, manoeuvring through the entire sphere of light and cloud like the creator of space. And if two dimensions could give way to three, why stop there? What was next—time? Freedom? It was a dangerous progression.

That was why pilots had to fly in military formation—the battle tactics of flying in pairs or triads were secondary. What mattered most was that everyone had his place, and everywhere the eye could see, there was someone higher up and someone below, all watching each other. Independent thought was depleted of oxygen. Space was kept neatly organized.

Prisoner

THE CZECH LANDS

October 1944 to April 1945

White Velvet

By autumn, the former allies of the Reich are negotiating peace treaties, and refugees are on the run from the Red Army in the east—thirty-five Lipizzaners and their foals fleeing ahead of the Red Army. To make room for them, some horses have to be sold, and the chief equerry has ordered a thorough examination of the herd at Hostau as a first step for selection.

In the field, mares suckle their foals while colts dash around the paddock. Light shimmers on their white coats, and Gerhard is struck by their purity, as if it's a symbol of mythical power, which could reset the tilt of the earth, turn fall into spring, make the sun advance like the army of the Reich in an earlier time. Among these white beings, the veterinary staff are flawed, puny, mere servants useful for checking temperature and heart rate.

From here, he can see the *Schloss* and the church spire, Stable A being closest to the mansion that houses the military command post. He's been ordered here with Rose to assist, and, over his objections, he's been assigned the stallions. Shut in their stalls, they'll be restive, unhappy. "Look at these charts, sir. They've just had a complete review. I have foals in my stable," he says to his commanding officer.

"I know it's a nuisance, but we have to do it." Lieutenant Colonel Rudofsky is a cavalryman who disdains cars and never learned to drive them. Every Sunday he arrives at his mother's church in a buggy pulled by a matched pair of white Lipizzaners. He's middle-aged, unmarried, and changes his outfit several times a day. Gerhard has his suspicions, and in turn Rudofsky usually leaves him alone. "Just get it over with before the chief equerry comes charging down, and you can get back to your cold-bloods and ponies." He turns to

Rose. "Do you exercise the horses, Fräulein Allendorf?" A rider of horses is not a horse's servant.

"The small ones."

"Good," he says with the distracted air of a parent about to receive a visit from rich relatives.

"Someone has to," she teases.

"Quite right." He attends to her more closely. "But not once you're expecting."

"Is that soon, sir?"

"It should be. You'd make pretty babies for the Reich."

"Better than the chief equerry's, I hope." Some of his experiments in breeding have been lumpen.

"Rose!"

"Don't scold, Gerhard. I'm not wrong, am I?" Something's changed in her, an occasional absent-minded bliss, a humming in her movements. He almost thinks she could have a supply of something better than Pervitin. See how she smiles at Rudofsky, and he smiles back.

"Not at all, my dear. If you're not done by dinner, come and eat at my table." The commander walks away, swinging a silver-topped cane.

"I'm not going to be here at dinner," Gerhard grumbles. He hasn't felt this cranky for months, and his hand reaches into his pocket for a bottle of pills that isn't there, the last of his supply long gone.

"Are you all right?" Rose asks.

He's got used to calling her Rose as easily as Sofia, and he never asks himself if she had a name before then. Hardly ever. The less you know, the less you can fuck up.

"I'm fine," he says.

The prisoners follow them into the barn, awaiting his instructions.

"It's not your dream," she says.

"Rose, I know. Stop pestering." He points to the nearest stall. "I'll do him first. I want him outside."

Like the horses installed here, the prisoners of Stable A are high-quality, strong and healthy because of Red Cross packages. They're good sleepers who've never known the terrors of the eastern front, and they're sought after by competing industries. Surely a couple of them can manage to hold the stallion's head while he conducts the examination in open air, where he's got space to move. An American prisoner enters the stall and hooks on the lead. The stallion emerges and lifts his head, nostrils wide, sniffing for a mare in heat though it's just about the end of the season.

"Ready, sir," the prisoner says.

"Not ready. I want two lead ropes—one of you on each." He leaves the barn and waits until they're outside with ropes tautly extended from the bridle before he leans in with his stethoscope. "Pulse, thirty-two beats. Write that down, Rose. Breaths, fifteen."

"I've got it."

"Move away from the horse. I don't like you so close. Farther. Good." He listens to the abdomen. Goes to the other side. She takes notes.

He's not in the forest. He's wide awake. It's been ages since he's needed a pill. He stays away from the stallion's nose, its muscular jaw. Perhaps it isn't necessary to flip the horse's lip. The chart is perfect. The gums were recently checked. But Rose is watching him, and so he says to the prisoners, "Hold his head firmly. Steady . . . No! Shit!"

"Sorry." The American has loosened his grip on the rope. The horse jerks his head, stamps a foreleg. The prisoner falls.

Ambush! Everybody down!

He's only thought it, said nothing aloud. Though he hears the gurgle of a young man's torn throat, all he does is sigh, and Rose is at his side, her hand on his arm. She speaks in an undertone. "No blood. See?"

"It's all right, sir." The American fell on his backside. The other prisoner, a Brit, is holding on to his rope, laughing. He has a long, horsey face, and he's lucky that Gerhard doesn't knock a tooth out of it.

"I want another man," he orders. "Get me someone, now!"

The prisoners confer, the American goes into the barn and hauls out a man who's been shovelling manure. He's scrawny and unkempt, a recent arrival. He takes the rope and moves around to look the pacing horse in the eye. He speaks to the horse in Russian until the stallion is calm, and then the prisoner lowers his head in a polite bow.

"I thought we had all the Russians in Stable C. What did he say?" Gerhard asks.

"Just 'Good man, good fellow,'" Rose says.

"Not the words," the prisoner says in the broken German these men speak in the camp, and he taps his throat.

"You mean it's the tone of voice?"

"Yes. Father owned horse like this. Before Revolution."

"A landowner?" Rose asks. The prisoner nods. "Were you in a punishment unit?"

He nods. "Everyone else . . ." He imitates the sound of exploding mines.

"You could have deserted," she says.

"No." He continues in his mother tongue, and Rose translates.

"He says that he's Russian, not a Cossack, so he can't abandon the land at whose breast he suckled."

The Russian is gazing at Gerhard with the same steadiness that calmed the stallion, and Gerhard wants him, fiercely. He thinks of taking him, right now, on the ground. He has the right. Soldiers do things like that to prisoners. It doesn't mean they're homosexual, only rapists. On the ridge to the west, the trees are dark conifers. He doesn't like to walk there in the woods where light and leaves never fall. Where can he go to breathe?

"I changed my mind. These two men are enough," Gerhard says.

"I help. Good horse."

"No, these men are all I need. Go back."

Downcast, the Russian retreats into the barn, returning to dim stalls and his shovel and the smell of manure. The rest of the physical examinations are conducted without incident, and when Gerhard is done, he asks Rose to return to his office and type up the report. Before he leaves, he finds Lieutenant Colonel Rudofsky and gets permission to take a jeep.

When he goes home to change his clothes, he tells Rose that he's got business in the regional capital. She packs his bag, and he throws it into the back of the jeep. There's a bar he knows, where jazz is still played. He'll get ripped. He'll pick up a friend for the night.

Sitting at the window, a book in her hand, Lily listens to Gerhard's footsteps on the stairs, then the jeep rev up and take off down the drive. The book is *The Scarlet Pimpernel*, a story about good aristocrats and bad revolutionaries, and it's making her laugh. Today she met a landowner. She's never met one before, not knowingly. She tries to imagine him hiding in the cart driven by the Scarlet Pimpernel, but in her mind he only appears as a prisoner who loves his country the way a woman loves the husband who tries to kill her when he's drunk.

She puts the book down and opens another that she bought when she picked up supplies in Taus: *Introduction to Philosophy*. The first page makes her head swim. The first paragraph has too many new ideas. And she's restless, listening to the sounds of the house. A full day of activity is never enough—the cutting and suturing and

blood is too brief; the note taking, filing, and typing require insufficient exertion. Her breath is quick, her pelvis is the centre of her
being, and when she's sure that her landlady has gone to sleep, she
leaves her book and tiptoes down the hall to Fritz's room.

In his narrow bed, he lies on his back. She strips and sits, a leg
on either side. Bends to him as he grips her. They kill each other
with lovemaking, they kiss and bite and shove and roll, knocking
against the wall. She can't signal with her voice, but she does with
her hands raking his back, and in his breathing she hears desire rising with hers. He pants, she gasps, they fall into each other. They
sleep and wake, calmer. Calm. He lights a candle.

And in the languid afterward, they untwine. Now she notices the
half moon shining through the window, the lump of his clothes on
a chair, and the rectangle of the needlepoint flamingo she stitched,
which he framed and hung beside the door. Forgetting the day
and the foreign terrain, they speak by candlelight, their hands
shaping thought on the wall where Fritz has pinned his drawings
like a backdrop.

"How do you know what's true?" she asks.

He kisses her. He pulls her on top of him again.

"I want to talk."

He signs, "Why is truth important?"

"People should know what they're dying for."

"They should know what they're living for."

"I thought I knew, but I didn't."

"I do," he says. "I love you."

"Then prove it."

"How?"

"Tell me something no one else knows."

"Good or bad?"

"Either."

"My best friend in school was a boy named Kurt."

"Other people must know that!" The exclamation mark is in the speed of her hands, the force of her fingers.

"Be patient and let me finish. Kurt was a year older but in the same class. He taught me to sign, he taught all the new boys. He was big, he knew things, and he protected me. I did his homework for him."

"Did he make you?"

"No, I wanted to help him. He wasn't stupid. He'd been in a different school and he wasn't used to teachers who hit your hands with a ruler. He had the best laugh. His eyes went wide then small, and you could see the back of his throat, then he'd slap his knees, and he was so funny, you couldn't help laughing with him, even when you missed home. He had the biggest nose I ever saw. He was Aryan, but that didn't stop the school from sending him away for being stupid, deaf, and ugly on top of it. Before he left, he gave me his lucky coin that was run over by a train. I still have it. I carry it with me all the time. I don't think he's alive. So there, you have both."

"He sounds like a good friend," she says.

"He was. Tell me about yours."

"How to describe them? Let me think." She can't say that they're air force pilots—not even love should reveal that much. So she makes a shadow duck and a dog and a bunny hop across a sketch of the Bohemian Forest to give herself time. "Katie was my best friend. She taught me to dance the tango. It was a comical sight because of the difference in our height, and I thought she'd be clumsy, she was such a boy, but she was graceful and I was the one stepping on her feet. Every time I did it, she hit me in the shoulder and I got black and blue, but I learned the tango. Can you dance?"

"I could if someone would teach me."

"I will when we have time. Katie was always worrying about her mother and her sister. She got news that they died in a bombing, and she swore that if it wasn't true, she'd be sober the rest of her life. It turned out that they'd survived, and to celebrate she drank so much that she was drunk for three days. She said it was all right because she was an atheist, but after she sobered up, she didn't have her daily shot of vodka until she got another letter from them. She drank with Alexei." Lily's hands are slow and heavy. "He was a loyal friend."

"Was he good-looking?" Fritz's face sours with the asking. Eyebrows pull inward, thickened by the flicker of candlelight.

"Don't be jealous. He wasn't my type. I wanted a boy who'd write love poems for me."

"I'll write one for you." He pokes a thumb at his chest.

"No need, it was childish." She grimaces. "Alexei was always scaring me with his jokes. But he made me feel that I belonged. He had the smelliest farts, and when he cut one, he'd look around as if his own backside had surprised him. And what's awful? I miss the smell."

"Couldn't have been as stinky as Kurt's."

"I had a friend with a big nose like his too. Sasha—he loved kites."

"I used to wrestle with Kurt for the sweets he got from home."

"We called the leader of our group Papa. He'd been a black-smith, and I think of him when I see you hammering a horseshoe. He wanted a black horse so he could name it Midnight."

They make love again; she exerts herself; the sweat washes away memory. The narrow bed is in a dormer just big enough for it. They talk with their hands, saying more than they intend because no one can overhear them. *Katie was my sister. She'd rather have been someone's brother, but that's not what nature gave her. I think she was an informant. If there was a world without informants, I could have a child in it, and if I did, I would name her Katie.*

The candle goes out, the sun rises, and Lily has to get dressed for the day.

———

The formation of the Volkssturm is announced. Every German male between the ages of sixteen and sixty who isn't already serving in a military unit is supposed to report to his regional Party leader to join the National Militia. Boys and elderly men are called up, invalids are miraculously pronounced cured. They're given no uniforms, but they have arm bands and weapons, which aren't all that rusty and fire from time to time, and it's expected that any lack in equipment will be compensated for by enthusiasm. There are rumours of a secret weapon in development, something much bigger than the V-1 and V-2 rockets, which will bring German victory at the eleventh hour. Some people believe it. None of them are sober. The world that made them is ailing and, in anticipation of its demise, men and women get drunk and have affairs and tell jokes like, *Why is the Volkssturm Germany's most valuable resource? Because its conscripts have silver in their hair, gold in their mouth, and lead in their bones.*

Snow falls, quieting the earth. It covers graves and ash and the generations of soldiers turning into earth. It covers fields and paddocks, it covers the roofs of barracks and stables, piling drifts against the windward side of buildings. Inside the smithy, Lily inserts a loud-tone needle—which increases volume—into the arm of a gramophone. She opens the doors of the box in which the gramophone is set so that the sound will emerge more fully. She cranks the handle, turns the switch, lowers the needle.

"Can you feel it?" she asks Fritz.

"Yes."

"Hold out your arms . . . No!" She smacks his shoulder. "Like this," she says, correcting his posture.

They step to the music. She moves back, he moves forward, avoiding her feet this time. Legs swing out, beside and between. He turns her around him.

"Do you love me?" he asks aloud.

"Yes," she says.

He lets go of her to sign, "Then tell me."

"First we dance."

She puts his hand on her waist, takes his other hand in hers. They dip.

On Christmas Eve, in the ballroom of a mansion, the eyes of Trauttmansdorff counts and countesses, bejewelled generations of them, wink in their portraits as if entertained by the young men and women mingling around the tree. There are four doors to the ballroom because Germans are fond of doors, thick and oak and closed. Men enter from the left after their smoke and port in the lounge. The women—after removing coats, reapplying lipstick, checking stockings, and swigging from their flasks—use the rear door behind the queenly fir tree, which is well over two metres tall and adorned with garlands, tinsel, ornaments. Crystal chandeliers refract colour into oblong rainbows like swashes of satin high on the wall, as frivolous as last year or the year before that.

The music is loud, the record player hooked into the public address system. On the dance floor, young women in parrot colours twirl. Men kick up legs, tap feet, dip their partners, or bend backs to roll women over them. Fingers snap and shoulders roll, and shouts of *Watch this* and laughter bounce off the portraits of counts and countesses who never had such drunken fun. War, war, who cares?

Lily wears a dress she bought from the landlady and made over. It's blue, it sparkles, someone compliments her, and she acts as if she belongs, dancing with Gerhard, their steps correct and expressionless. As agreed, Fritz partners every woman but her, from the spinster who chaperones the young women to the most beautiful of them, who was the model in a soda ad.

Every time he turns, Fritz glances her way.

Lieutenant Colonel Rudofsky claps his hands and calls for attention. *My dears, have you written your letter to the Christkind?* he jokes. Such a jolly lieutenant colonel, a Bohemian German presiding over his party of young people. At the age of forty-seven, he's as dapper as such an old man can be. He wears a tailcoat and cravat, last decade's fashion, but he's dignified. On special occasions he recites poetry from his mother's two published books, and it's tolerable with wine and chocolate.

The French POWs, who clean up very well, bring in chilled and glistening goblets while Rudofsky proclaims: *From the forest on the mountain crest it blows . . .*

He always begins with this, the most rousing of his mother's patriotic poems, but he doesn't even get to the verse about sprouting German hope when the oak door on the right opens. Light flashes on metal gorgets and shiny boots and helmets worn as if the ballroom ceiling might crack at any moment above the six *SS-Feldgendarmerie* led by a cap-wearing captain. Fritz slides away from his dance partner, makes his way to Lily's side.

"Heil Hitler!"

"Heil Hitler," Lieutenant Colonel Rudofsky says. "Merry Christmas."

"I'm sorry to interrupt your festivities." The captain presents his credentials. "I have a list of names," he said. "Men who didn't report to the Volkssturm for duty."

"There must be a mistake," Lieutenant Colonel Rudofsky said. "Everyone here is already engaged in vital war work."

"I see. Then they're all enlisted men."

"Not all. But they're serving under me."

"If they're not registered to the army, they're ours. I have to pick up Paul Berger."

A German boy, slow of mind and movement, who assists the Polish cook. "He's only fifteen," Rudofsky says.

"You're wrong about that, Lieutenant Colonel. He's on my list. Therefore, he's sixteen or older. Where is he?"

"In the kitchen."

The captain orders a pair of his men to bring the boy. "Also Bruno Ebenstreit. His location, please."

Fritz is watching the conversation trying to figure out what's going on by reading lips while Lily frantically plans how to save him. If they can just slip away, she'll hitch the horse to the sleigh, hide him under the blanket until they reach home, sneak him up into the attic. The end can't be far away. He'll come out of the attic. He'll stand in the sun. She'll kiss his ear and sound will enter it again.

"That old man is one of my guards," Rudofsky says. "How will we deal with our prisoners if we're short-handed?"

"Any delay or refusal to join the Volkssturm is desertion. Anyone who assists is an accomplice and subject to the same retribution. Are any of your men concealing his whereabouts?"

"Nothing of the sort. We're going to midnight Mass in half an hour."

Fritz takes out his notebook and writes, *Why are they here?*

She signs back because it's quicker and what difference will it make if anyone sees? "They're taking people away."

"Who?"

She spells out the names and also "Volkssturm." She says, "I'm afraid for you."

He shakes his head, observing the room and every movement in it. A space has cleared around the lieutenant colonel and the captain and their downward-pointing brows. The remaining military police stand a respectful distance from their leader. The veterinary staff and volunteers have slunk toward the walls, separating from their earlier dance partners. Dr. Kroll and Dr. Lessing, the veterinarians in charge of the important horses, confer near an exit, their faces worried. Mrs. Lessing looks toward her husband. Only Dr. Fischer moves purposefully toward the arguing commanders.

"Bruno's in his room on the second floor, asleep. He goes to bed early. He's an elderly man, I told you," Rudofsky says.

The captain instructs a second pair of military police to let the old man dress and then bring him to the truck in back of the *Schloss*. "Also Friedrich Fischer."

Gerhard salutes. "I can speak for him. That's my brother. He's exempt from military service. I have his documents, and I can bring them tomorrow or tonight. If you'll just allow me to fetch them."

"That won't be necessary. There are no exemptions, *Stabs-veterinär*. Not anymore."

Lily pushes her way past Gerhard, who looks helplessly at Fritz.

"You don't understand. He's deaf," she says, her voice too loud, the partygoers turned to stone and echoing every sound.

"Are you talking to me, Fräulein?" the captain says.

She stands right below his chin. There's a nick on it where he shaved this morning. "He can't hear orders. What good would he do your army?" Her hand is on the SS man's arm. He looks down at it, half-smiling in surprise, and he isn't rough as he removes it, no more than if he waved a fly from his picnic lunch. If her knuckles are uncomfortably squeezed, it's the fault of their delicate structure.

She doesn't hear his response, which isn't addressed to her but to Rudofsky, because the fourth door to the ballroom opens, and the noise of feet and squalling drown out his voice as the returning Feldgendarmerie drag the wailing kitchen boy, his eyes wide and white, toward their captain. It seems there's some mix-up. Another fellow with the same name is just up the hill, a cleaner for the observation unit there.

She runs back to Fritz. He cups her face in his hands. He bends his head. Like the departing soldier in a song or a movie, he kisses her. His moustache tickles. Her body presses against his, willing his arms to undo the world, her heart to leave off its interminable beating of time. Then he unravels himself. He goes toward the military police, steadfastly, without hurry and without pause. He stands by the boy, who's going to be taken anyway, and the boy quiets next to his quiet presence. A quartet of Feldgendarmerie flank them. Fritz turns a last time to smile at her and sign, "I can't hear them tell me what to think."

On the windowsills of the village, children have placed letters to the *Christkindl*, not dusted with sugar in the traditional manner but in full expectation of a cookie, an apple, a sweater knit from the yarn of an older one, a repainted sled, a carved doll or miniature cart, maybe even with a tiny wooden horse brought by the winged and golden-haired gift giver. While they sleep, their parents put presents under the tree, and, saving candles for tomorrow, they sit up in stiff-backed chairs, talking about what to do if the secret weapon doesn't arrive and the Russians do.

It's a cloudless night, the quarter moon low in the million-pointed sky. Gerhard holds the reins loosely as they leave the main road, their sleigh pulled by a brown gelding who's due to leave for the front on the next train. Snow drifts in the wind, it laces her vision with filigreed stars, but the blanket that keeps her warm smells of horses and Fritz. Under the blanket her body is dismembered.

"He'll die," Lily says.

"You never know," Gerhard says. They'd both applied themselves to schnapps before leaving the *Schloss*. "Sometimes it's the weakest who survive."

"He's not weak."

"True. That might be his undoing."

"Did you love him too?" she asks.

"I loved someone like him."

"Did he love you back?"

"I think he did. But he was afraid. And then he died in the forest. I led the attack."

"You?"

"I was the senior officer. Everyone who knew what they were doing had already died." Gerhard sings sadly in a language she doesn't recognize.

"What's that?"

"A folk song our maid used to sing."

"It's a bit like Polish."

"Sorbian," Gerhard says.

"What's that?"

"An ethnic group in my home province."

"Better sing something German or the chained dogs will come running over the snow for you."

"Our town of Cottbus has always had a Sorbian minority. They say it's a Germanic tribe."

"Don't count on minorities." The black mirror of night reflects nothing. Not a ghost speaks in the wind, no one with a cocky smile, nobody she's loved, none she's wanted or who wanted her. "My first boyfriend was Polish."

"Mine too," Gerhard says.

"*My* Polish boyfriend cheated on me."

"*I* cheated on mine."

"My boyfriend went to Siberia with the deportation of Poles."

"Mine to Auschwitz." Hills roll and valleys undulate and in them stubby hamlets blow smoke from the chimneys of farmhouses. "Are there crematoria in Siberia?"

"Just ice."

"Smoke is more final."

"So is a firing squad." She sticks out her tongue, wondering if she can re-drink her alcoholic breath, but all she tastes is snow. "How did you meet him?"

"Visiting cousins in Brody."

"I'm surprised you had cousins in Poland."

"No, in Germany. It's a village not far from the border and maybe forty-five kilometres from my hometown. My grandmother was born there."

"My grandmother was born in the other Brody. The one that was Austro-Hungarian, then Polish, then Soviet, then German. But probably not much longer."

"You aren't really a nurse," Gerhard says.

"I am now."

"What were you?"

"You'll laugh."

"I won't."

"You'll give me up."

"Too late for that."

"People say anything when they're interrogated."

"Then your name. Someone should know it."

"All right. It's Lily."

"Like Lili Marleen."

Mimicking the slow, smoky voice of the radio singer, he does all five verses, and he's plastered, so it's almost certain that he doesn't hear her say, *Like Lily Litvak*.

And who is that?

The world consists of this sleigh, the wool blanket, the wind's snort, snow in her hair, the guardianship of trees between which they slide across white velvet in a poem devoid of sides and skin.

Like a Lily

There's a letter from Fritz with sketches of an old man and a boy in his unit, and one of a water lily, which she pins to the wall in his room. After that, no letters are delivered and no telegram sent. Lily doesn't know whether he's alive or dead or captured. She's working long hours. More refugees have to be accommodated—two hundred Cossack and mountain horses thinned by their march. People come through, fleeing from the east with stories of atrocities and rape by Soviet soldiers, and cross the border into Germany, hoping to be conquered by Americans.

Hostau is a sliver of hungry peace between the Red Army in the east and its allies to the west. Civilians subsist on a dwindling supply of flour, sausage, and potatoes, tempted by the remount depot's six hundred tons of meat on the hoof. A couple of horses are stolen, and after a boy is caught sneaking into the barn with a musket (ancient but operational), all veterinary staff, including Lily, are ordered to carry arms. Guards are placed around the perimeter. Prisoners work when they feel like it. The April sun melts snow that runs in rivulets and freezes overnight.

"After it's over, I'm going home to Cottbus," Gerhard says. He's alone with Lily in the surgery. An anaesthetized yearling lies on the scrubbed floor. "I want to set up practice there."

"Good." She cleans the scrotal area with water and iodine and doesn't mention that the Soviets will stick him in a POW camp from which he may never emerge.

He injects the testicles to numb them. "And you?"

"I haven't thought about it." She's thought of nothing else—it all ends with the same conclusion. Interrogation. After she's tossed on the heap, her family will be called in. At the very least, her mother will lose her job, her brother will be kicked out of school, both of them thrown onto the street. Or they might get hard labour. The thought leaves her panic-stricken.

"Scalpel." He slices the scrotum and pops out a testicle; she wipes away blood. He stitches. "My home will always be open to you."

"As your fiancée?" In her pocket she has a Dreyse pistol, First World War issue, which has been rereleased for the Volkssturm. She hasn't figured out what to do with it. Arrest a rabbit and make stew out of it?

He glances up, his eyes her father's blue. "My sister in arms."

She tries to picture it, not being alone in the world, but all she can envision is her mother, a convict, face down in the mud. "Could *you* live among your former enemies for the rest of your life?" she asks him.

"We've had the same life, you and me. We know who each other is. That's something rare even in peacetime."

"It's a nice thought." What's waiting for her is the special branch of the NKVD, the department of the secret police called SMERSH— the acronym stands for "death to spies." They screen all liberated citizens. A special agent will conduct the questioning. She wonders if it's true that someone who's shot is blindfolded first, or if that's only done in the movies. "Will you get another dog?" she asks.

"Yes, but I won't call him Adolf," he says. "Maybe Joseph, after your man . . . Do you smell smoke? Shit." He wipes his hands and rises to his feet. "Someone's trying to burn us out again. I'll be right back. I still have to do the other one."

Picking up a horse blanket as he runs, he leaves the surgery door ajar. Smoke is rising from a straw bale, and he pounds it with the blanket.

———

That afternoon a thousand women, half of them Jewish, march out of Helmbrechts, a women's sub-camp of Flossenbürg. Escorted by the camp commander and some four dozen SS guards, the inmates walk southeast, away from Allied forces closing in from the west. Horse-drawn wagons carry the dead and the sick. When a wagon is full, anyone still breathing is shot and the whole mess tossed into a mass grave. Then it's ready to fill again. After days of walking, the commander receives orders to let the women go, but he only allows the Gentiles to leave. The remaining prisoners, a hundred or so, stop for the night in a village north of Hostau, drenched from a downpour. Among them is Gizela, a music professor from Kraków, and Bronia, a music student from Łódź, who secretly share a raw egg they've found. The next day, they walk in the direction of Hostau.

Fifteen kilometres away, rain drums on the roof while Lily sits on the bed, arms around her knees, aimlessly staring at the happy painting on the wall. The blond, chesty mother; the golden hay; a sparkling pond. The radio announces that the Führer is out front in the main fighting line in Berlin. Growling with frustration, Gerhard fiddles with the wire on his radio, trying to tune in foreign news. He moves the wire, the radio spits static. And out of the blue, from the painted pond, an idea blooms like a lily that's been growing imperceptibly in the muck and suddenly flowers on the water's surface. Graceful. Perfect. Holy.

She pictures a body found in the Jewish cemetery at Ronsperg. In the pocket are German identity papers and a note confessing remorse, guilt, atonement. She could throw in a deported Jewish lover for good measure. *I have no one left, not mother or husband, and no one to miss me. In my death, I atone for the ruthlessness of my people and my own inaction.* Who's going to bother to investigate one more corpse? The barrel of the Dreyse is shorter than a Russian pistol, its effective firing range half as far. But held under her chin or inside her mouth, it will do what is needed. No one will dissuade her this time. She'll remain missing in action. Her mother won't get a pension, but at least she and Yuri will be safe. Elated, Lily jumps up from the bed, throws her arms around Gerhard, and kisses him on the cheek with a loud smack.

"What's that for?" he asks, rubbing his cheek.

"For being a friend. To me and Fritz. I want to thank you for that."

"Great. Then can you hold this end of the wire while I try to get the other end higher?"

By the next morning, she's lost her nerve. The sky has cleared. The air smells of spring and trees are budding. The midday meal is just fresh bread and butter, but how good it is. Afterward, she goes into the village to pick up mail, not in a jeep because of the scarcity of fuel but in a horse-drawn cart, and when she returns with it, the guards thank her as usual. The American and British prisoners are playing football while they wait for liberation; they don't call out to her, not Rosie the Riveter nor Lovely Rose, as if they don't see her, as if they've already left her behind as she left her friends.

Igor is forking hay, but he stops and waves.

"Why are you working when the others aren't?" she asks.

"I'll be on a train to one of our labour camps soon enough. In the meantime, why should the horses suffer?"

"A pessimist," she says.

"A Russian." He lifts the pitchfork, heavy with hay, tosses it. "You're too pretty. Like a girl on the cover of a magazine." He stops again, leans on the pitchfork, looks at her with the piercing glance of someone who's recognized her but never let on. "You'd better make yourself look very sick before our forces get here."

The warning spurs her into action. She flicks the reins. The horse takes her out of the yard and along the dirt lane that winds down to a country road. If she had the jeep, she could be at the cemetery in a few minutes, but a horse at walking speed is hardly faster than she'd be on her own feet, and she has to stiffen her resolve by thinking of her mother and brother living peacefully. She imagines them growing older, a wife for her brother, a baby named after her, stories about the auntie in the sky, newspaper clippings in a scrapbook that won't have to be burned.

Pilot

RUSSIA & UKRAINE
Two Months before Her Fall

June to August 1, 1943

Something Slid Back

The Brooklyn Daily Eagle
Sunday, June 6, 1943
LADY BAGS A BALLOON
Junior Lt. Lily Litviak flying her Russian plane against the Nazis, marked up a big personal lady-victory the other day on the eastern Ukrainian front when she zoomed in upon a German observation balloon, popped it for fair, so that it would never direct Germany artillery fire ever again. Other pilots, believe it or not (all men) had zoomed in, too, and each time been driven off by Uncle Adolf's fighter planes. Score one for milady at war.

Lily had a new ribbon: the Order of the Red Banner. Her regiment occupied temporary air bases, setting up tents in fields near the border with Ukraine. Personnel came and went. Pilots killed in battle or accidents were replaced by others, whose names Lily barely learned before they were gone too. Sometimes there was a grave and more often none, and the flowers in her cockpit were for them. In mid-June, Lily scrambled to intercept a formation of tactical reconnaissance aircraft protected by four Messers and was frustrated because she got no kills. She needed to shoot something and recover her purpose. Unorthodox thoughts were plaguing her.

At the end of the month, Katie kept her word and returned from Moscow, but she was changed—taciturn, aloof from the young replacement pilots, uninterested in drinking with them or trading jokes. Katie and Lily were assigned to different squadrons, and they only saw each other when they got up at dawn, at hasty meals, and after sunset, when they fell into their cots exhausted. The days were long. The weather was hot and dry and smelled electric; the commander warned them that there was lightning to the north.

To enter the Ukraine, Soviet forces had to break the German Mius Line, a series of impenetrable defences running south from the vicinity of Stalino in the Donetsk region along the Mius River, which wended its way like thread back and forth over the edges of the Ukraine and Russia. A massive attack was planned for mid-July, the 8th Air Army to support Soviet ground troops, who were ordered to throw themselves against the Mius Line at any cost. Lily sweated under her helmet as if she was feverish, flying into the Ukraine and coming home to her tent to sleep and dream about the river where the dead awaited her.

Friday, July 16. Evening.

The nearly full moon was in the east, nested in a hollow of cloud, trimming the edge with light. Lily was at three thousand metres. Yellow flowers in the cockpit. Oily flames shimmered between paler puffs of ack-ack fire. Weeds of brown smoke bloomed in wavering columns. Their flight of six was arrayed against thirty Ju 88 bombers escorted by eight German fighters coming from Donetsk, where the Fourth Air Fleet had shot down Papa Nick.

When the bombers separated into groups, Lily took on the last one at the far left of the array, her preferred side, using her favourite tactic, coming in head-on. One second, two seconds, three. The line of planes receded, a single bomber filled her gunsight, and she sprayed him with ammunition. The surface of his left wing glittered and burst and for a moment her tension broke, she was in harmony with herself, her country, the lost comrades she avenged. With a steep slide, the bomber broke off from the formation, and she followed with cannon fire until it exploded, the wave catching her aircraft and pushing her sideways. She compensated, regained control, craving release again. And where was her new wingman, what's his name? She looked all around, but he was gone, and she couldn't search for him in the melee of propellers and wings, tracers and fluttering flames because a pair of Messers were banking toward her. She turned within their orbit, and the lead pilot must have been falling asleep. Wobbling right into her fire, he chopped his wings in a steep dive that turned into a fatal spin of greasy smoke. His wingman joined another pair to form a triad—now it was her turn to be shot on the left side, in the radiator, through the fuel lines, up and down her fuselage. A fragment scraped her leg; the pain surprised her. Such a small loss, this scrap of skin and blood, and she'd thought herself immune to any more hurt.

She wasn't too far from base, she just had to follow her map and get down without losing pieces of her winged body, and she called into the radio, "White 23 heading home." She didn't dare roll or even dive steeply, but gently nosed through the swirl of vapour trails and smoke. She landed her plane without fainting, belly scraping the earth. Colonel Golyshev wanted her to go to the field hospital, but she knew where that led, and she wasn't returning to Moscow with its sly conversations. She got a medic to patch her up. He administered the universal anaesthetic, vodka, and insisted that she eat. The two kills today made her an ace in accordance with Soviet standards, a double ace with one to spare by American and British. A Gold Star should be forthcoming.

The thought of it wasn't as pleasurable as she'd expected, not among strangers. She hardly knew the pilots congratulating her in the mess tent, interchangeable bodies that supplied aircraft with hands and feet and eyes. In a daze, she thanked them numbly; she was half a ghost herself. Maybe it had happened in the cloud, her inner self taking the opposite direction, climbing to look for missing faces while she descended. Now it was beyond the earth's atmosphere and she was earthbound, dutiful, correct, wingless. The sun had set, the start of her grandmother's Sabbath. She returned the tray with her half-eaten meal and went back to her quarters.

The canvas of their tent created a heat dome, and Lily was boiling on top of her straw pallet.

"Are you awake?" Katie asked.

"Yes." Lily lay with her arms and legs spread, wondering whether mosquitoes would keep her up if she lay outside in the field near her aircraft like the mechanics did.

"How's your leg, Ace?"

"Attached." The tent was small, there was barely room between their cots to walk sideways.

"Need anything?" Katie shifted in hers. "Water?"

"I'm fine, thanks." The rustling and squeaking sounded like mice, which reminded Lily of the infested gym near the banks of the frozen Volga River, where she'd slid with other girls before anyone died.

"Why don't you talk to me like you used to?" Katie said.

"It's not me. You're the one who doesn't talk anymore."

"Since when?"

"Since you went to Moscow."

"You're so polite, it's spooky. Like I'm sharing a tent with a suck-up."

"After you left, I committed myself to improvement, that's all. Isn't this better than being a brat?"

"I liked the brat. From the first time I met her on the platform. Enough to go to Moscow for her."

"I have no idea what you're going on about."

"They wanted a girl. You think I like being a girl? I had to go to a beauty salon."

"You could have turned it down. I wouldn't have gone," Lily said.

"You only had a choice because I volunteered. Our commander got the letter, and—"

"You mean Nick? Our Papa?" Lily sat up, forgetting her leg, and winced. "When?"

"The day we had the party for Alexei. It was from Kazarinova the elder."

"He didn't tell me she wrote."

"Because you're a brat and he was afraid you'd do something stupid and get yourself in some kind of trouble he couldn't get you out of. So I offered to write to the younger Kazarinova and ask if I could go to Moscow instead. She likes me better. Because she has good judgment."

"You said you wanted to see your mother and sister."

"Of course. I miss them again, already."

"You said you wanted a break."

"A break is a bonus. Better than rubles. So you don't have to be nice anymore. Go back to being a brat. It comes more naturally to you."

"If you're sure."

"Uh-huh."

"Then I've got a question."

"Go ahead."

"Are you working for them?"

A long silence. There could only be silence or an answer that was inconclusive. *Yes* was inadmissible, making *no* almost certainly a lie. "Who's them?" Katie asked.

"Don't play with me. You know what I mean." Lily's voice was urgent with pain and heat and a longing for honesty between friends, and Katie replied with the same intensity.

"I have a sister. They had something on her, and I said I'd co-operate. What would you do?"

"They let her go?" Lily asked.

"Yes."

Lily thought of her father in a camp somewhere. There hadn't been a single letter from him. But there wouldn't be, because he'd been sentenced without the right to correspond. "I would do the same. But Katie, isn't it . . . lonely?"

"Very." On earth, as in the air, it was easier to take down a solitary target.

"I want to tell you something."

"Are you sure?"

"It's nothing you have to repeat." Searchlights brushed the sky, and the tent's darkness greyed. "I broke it off with Alexei because there wasn't anything more to him than what you could see on the surface. He was an all-right kisser. Pretty good, actually. But it wasn't enough. I'm that fussy. So, you see, I'll be lonely for life."

"Maybe not. Life is long if you don't die." Katie reached across the narrow space between their cots. She gently patted Lily's cheek. "And anyway, you told me you weren't planning to marry."

"Who said anything about marriage?"

"Ha! You got me."

"Remember arriving at the wrong airfield?"

"His burnt trousers." There was a solicitousness in their reminiscing, an unspoken agreement to avoid any calamitous truths. They remembered lightning during the dance at the community hall. Buying a new record when "Rio Rita" wore out. The piano in the gym. Having nothing left to eat on the train from Moscow but cabbages. They remembered back and back, lightly skipping over the serious, the tragic, the appalling and confusing, to the beginning in a ballroom with numbers marked in chalk. Standing on the platform of the train station. Huddling under a greatcoat, arms around each other. They yawned. Their voices got fainter. The tent flapped in the wind. Maybe the heat was breaking.

"Tell me about your grandmother," Katie said.

As long as their country was at war with itself, tearing at its own skin, shredding it with mistrust, sharing these old stories was a kind of small rebellion, a way for friends to be close, soothing each other with the interplay of their voices back and forth in the night. "What do you want to know?" Lily asked.

"What the Vila did. Your babushka was hiding in the woods . . ." Katie prompted.

"It was a night like this. The moon was full, and she was worried that the Tsar's soldiers would use the additional light to scour the woods. My father was ten. He fell asleep while she guarded him. She sat with her back against a tree, holding an axe. Behind her she heard a voice, and she stood up so quickly, she got dizzy. It was a woman's voice, and it said, *Don't give a fuck what people say, just make your luck and make them pay.*"

"Not very ladylike."

"No."

"I thought Vilas were all girlie and obsessed with gold and jewels and any pretty man that looks their way."

"When they're alive, yes, but when they're dead, they recover from it. My grandma looked all around her but didn't see anyone. That was when she realized it was a spirit, and she was worried about what kind of spirit it was. What if it was someone who didn't like Jews?"

"There are plenty of those."

"Or someone friendly to the Tsar. It was hard enough hiding from soldiers without them having ghosts on their side too."

"So what did she do?"

"My grandmother was a pretty good liar when she needed to be, so she considered a few possibilities, but she wasn't sure how much spirits know."

"If they're like the NKVD, they know more than you want."

"So she did what she taught me—tell the truth . . . mostly. She said, *This is my child. I'm scared for his life more than mine. I have a weapon, but how much good is an axe against guns? Soldiers are looking for us because my husband was a fool.* She said it in three languages: Russian, Ukrainian, and then in Polish. That made the spirit appear, and from the white dress and the blue robe she saw it was a Vila."

"What did the Vila say?"

"Nothing. She started to sing without words, and the wind picked up everywhere except for a metre around my grandmother and my father. Somehow he stayed asleep though there was thunder and lightning and trees bending halfway to the ground. The storm drove the soldiers out of the woods except for one of them. He was a young man, very handsome, and the Vila kept him there for her pleasure."

"What happened to him?"

"I don't know. The storm died down, and while the Vila was dancing with the young soldier, my grandmother woke my father and snuck out of the woods. They walked along country roads to Berdichev, where they had relatives, and they stayed there until the furor died down. That's the story, anyway."

"Quick thinker, your babushka. She'd have made a good pilot."

"No, she liked her feet on the ground. But she got me the papers for my solo anyway." Tomorrow, Lily would live in the sky. Before she fell—which she would, that day or another, because the sky was a temporary abode and the earth reclaimed everyone as its own—she had one more question. "Katie, did you really see Koschei the Deathless?"

"I did. He was in a uniform. Otherwise he looked exactly like our neighbour."

"Where?"

"The barn. I was hiding in the hay." Katie's voice was slow and drowsy. "He shot the cow my uncle didn't want to give up to the collective farm. Then my uncle."

"I'm sorry, Volodya."

There was no answer; her friend's breathing was slow and even.

Lily rolled onto her side. The tent was silent. If she spoke, there was no one awake to report her, not even a ghost. "I love you," she said, for all the times she hadn't. As Lily drifted into sleep, something slid back from the stars along a slender thread and heard a soft voice in the tent.

"I love you, too, Lil'ka."

Saturday.

The counteroffensive began; the full moon would allow Soviet troops to press toward the Ukraine through the night. That was the plan. First there was an artillery barrage. But then, after just a few kilometres, the advance bogged down. Enemy artillery and air attacks were still too strong. German dive-bombers came in waves, in each group eighteen or thirty-six bombers. The Soviet forces managed to get as far as a small village, slightly expanding their bridgehead on the far bank of the Mius River. The enemy pulled up reserves. In the darkness, Soviet wounded were taken across the river by ferry and then trucked to the rear. The village was bombed over and over by carousels of bombers. Soon it was retaken by the Germans.

Monday.

On the right bank of the Mius River, the Soviet beachhead was about ten by ten kilometres. The 5th Shock Army had been called to join up with the 18th and the 2nd Guards Armies. They were to move toward the Krynka River, supported by ground attack planes and Yak fighters. Against them was their familiar foe—the Fourth Air Fleet. The maps in command headquarters, German and Russian, were neatly pinned, flags were inserted. A dotted line represented a tank brigade on the way.

The sky roared; it burned.

Above a village about fifteen minutes north of Amvrosiivka, six Messers engaged a pair of Yakkis. The wingman's machine was damaged, and the leader ordered him home, taking on the enemy herself, giving him the seconds he needed to get away. Her aircraft smoked as it descended, swerving incoherently before it nosedived into a hill. A medic from the field hospital of the 2nd Guards Army was the first to the site. Over the roar of shells and aircraft, she shouted at her staff for assistance. The pilot lay near the plane. The parachute was soaked in blood.

To: Alexandra Yakovlevna,

Battle greetings from the Air Force family of pilots and technicians who share your sorrow.

On July 19th, we lost our beloved pilot, Guard Lieutenant Katherine Budanova. Your daughter, Katie, our friend and fellow soldier, was killed in the fight for our Soviet Motherland. Hers was the death of a heroine of our people.

We thank you for nurturing your daughter and raising her to be a fearless fighter.

We will long remember the fearlessness in battle Katie showed during the most difficult days of our country in the city of Stalingrad. When the Nazi vultures hovered in black clouds, she flew to the alarm and engaged them. She did not flinch, not even when met in great numbers, but returned to the fray until the ground was littered with their destruction.

You brought up Katie, you her mother, and therefore we regard you as dearly as our own mothers. The cause for which she struggled, we

*will carry to the end, and the red banner will once again soar across
our land.*

*Her death cannot leave anyone indifferent. Those who knew her will
never forget her bright image. She was a great friend, a great fighter, a true
daughter of the country, which she defended to the death, to the last breath.*

*To the depths of her being, she hated the power of the enemy and was
entirely committed to his speedy defeat. Here, at the front, she was a
formidable air warrior, brave, cunning, and ruthless to the vile enemy,
whom she sought and destroyed. Over Stalingrad and Rostov, she had
already shot down six German aircraft when death interrupted her brilliant
trajectory. She died as a hero dies, at her post.*

*The government awarded her medals, but the people reward her with
the immortality of memory. Songs will be sung about her. And for her cruel
death, we promise revenge on the accursed enemy.*

*Revenge, revenge against the merciless enemy will be our monument to
Katherine Budanova, who fought furiously and gloriously for the happiness
of our country. We swear to you that our Guards division will avenge
Katie's young life.*

Signed,
*Zapryagev, Eryukin, Vikhorev, Sherbin, Sidnev, Doronenko, Golyshev,
Shestakov, Verkhovets, Korolev, Tron'ko, Litvyak, Linovizky, Filippov,
Belikov, Boyko, Kraynov, Zuev.*

Above All, I've Always Loved

28 July 1943

*Dearest Mama, I'm entirely absorbed in the fighting life. It's hard to snatch
a moment to write and let you know that I'm alive and well, that above
all I've always loved my homeland and you, my dear. What I want
with all my heart is a land without enemies, to live happy again,
a quiet life. When I come back to you and we're sitting face to face,
Mama, I'll tell you everything I've gone through. Right now, I'm
in the cockpit and about to scramble, so an adjutant is writing this and
will mail it for me. I might be far away, but still I send you kisses . . .*

Your Lil'ka

After Katie died, Lily stopped winding her father's watch so that
time could stop and every day repeat itself: flying into thick clouds,
a country of clouds with hills and canyons and misty hollows, the
habitat of ghosts who spoke to Lily, offered advice, sang with her.
As long as Lily stayed aloft, she could hear them, and when she
came down, she wanted only to go up again.

One evening, no different from any other, Lily was pulled away
from her meal. No explanation was given, only that she was needed
in the dugout, formerly HQ, which had been given over to SMERSH.
Special Lieutenant Perushev was sitting behind a desk. A soldier
stood guard. A stenographer in uniform, wearing the insignia
of the NKVD, recorded proceedings while a haggard man in a
muddy pilot's uniform swayed on his feet. He had a burn on his left
cheek. She didn't recognize him. What did they want from her?

"Lost your way, brother?" she said.

He struggled to meet her gaze, his eyes bleary. "Seems so."

"Have a seat, Lieutenant Litvyak," the Special said. "And you too, Prisoner."

There were two wooden chairs, and the pilot dropped into one of them with a grunt. Lily took the other, then leaped to her feet, thinking how thirsty he must be from enduring fire and questions. "Can I give him tea, Comrade Lieutenant?" she asked.

"Yes, do. That's a good idea."

Sergeant Alenin, the stenographer, was busy with pen and notebook at a small table beside the SMERSH officer's. As she wrote, she murmured to herself, *Good idea*, as if repetition helped her get to the end of the sentence.

Lily made her way around the table to the back of the dugout where the map used to hang above the signaller's communication equipment. Now there was a large and ornate samovar on the stand. With her back to the Special, she made the tea, sneaking a lump of sugar into it.

"Blow on this," she said as she put the glass in the prisoner's hands. "You don't need to burn your tongue too."

"Thanks."

While he slurped tea, she returned to her seat and waited for instructions. Special Lieutenant Perushev sat; the stenographer sat, her pen poised, notebook open. No one spoke, and at last she said, "My name is Lily Litvyak. I'm a fighter pilot."

"I've heard of you," the prisoner said, his voice croaky. "I fly ground attack planes. Flew."

"What happened?"

"Machine gun jammed, engine blew out, so I had to bail. I hid during the day. Once, in a hole, the Germans walked right over. I travelled at night. Went down west of Stepanovka. Focke-Wulfs got through our escort. They killed my gunner."

"Did you know him long?"

"Since the beginning."

"I've lost my friends too," she said. "The ones from the beginning. Now I don't try to make friends."

"I just want to get back to my unit. Can I, Comrade Lieutenant?"

Perushev's arms were crossed. He'd had rickets as a child, and his legs were bowed, but behind a table he was as strong as any pilot. His voice was quiet as he said, "First we have to check you."

"I've already told you—"

Lily jumped as Perushev shouted, "Get to your feet, German dog! What is this?" He took a piece of bread previously hidden under a newspaper and held it out on the flat of his hand.

"Bread," the prisoner said.

"Does this look like Russian bread, you son of a whore?"

"I stole it."

"You took German bread."

While the pilot stammered that he'd been fainting with hunger, he'd needed to eat, he'd been lucky to find it, Lily wondered whether the crime was that it had been made by German hands or that it was better than Russian bread.

"Am I to believe it just fell from the sky? No! Someone gave you this bread." Perushev pounded the table with every word. "You're a spy. You don't deserve that uniform. You don't deserve the air you breathe. What's your assignment, asshole? Who do you report to? Who's your contact on this side?!"

"Nothing. No one. I just want to get back to my unit."

Lily glanced up at the pilot with sympathy and down at her father's watch, winding it so she could follow the second hand around and around. The same questions were posed, sometimes quietly, sometimes yelled. The same answers were stuttered. The stenographer's pen scratched, her murmur echoed. The prisoner asked to go outside to relieve himself. Perushev bellowed, "Piss yourself, you son of a bitch," and the man did, urine pouring down his leg.

"Lock him up in the latrine until he dries out," Perushev said to the guard.

Now Lily was allowed to go, accompanied by Sergeant Alenin, who'd been assigned to her tent. An NKVD sergeant was a cut above an army lieutenant. Naturally, the sergeant had felt entitled to appropriate all the underwear Lily had received from home, leaving her to wear men's army issue. But in the darkness, Sergeant Alenin was just another impersonal shape, like the stars obscured by clouds above.

"Aren't you going back to finish supper?" Sergeant Alenin asked.

The mess tent was still rowdy with pilots. They'd surround Lily, clamouring, curious and trying not to imagine themselves in the prisoner's position, wanting to know who he was and what had happened. Could that be the reason she was made to witness the interrogation—so that she could tell the other pilots and frighten them?

"I need sleep," Lily said.

"Me too." Sergeant Alenin put her arm through Lily's and held her close as they followed the dirt road past the large canvas shadow, toward its smaller brothers. "I can't stand collaborators."

"Me neither. But he isn't a collaborator."

"So he fooled you? Not me. What a stinker. Pew! He smelled like a man sentenced to hard labour with no right of correspondence."

"I don't understand."

"You know, Lily. Dead. It means someone's been executed. That's why they can't write home."

A smoky wind was blowing the residue of air battle into her lungs, making her breathless, so she forced the words out. "But why report it as a sentence for hard labour?"

"People would panic if they knew how many spies we have to eliminate. Sorry, I didn't mean to show off." Sergeant Alenin squeezed her arm. "There isn't another girl here that I can talk to."

Lily froze. In the hot summer night, she was ice. But Sergeant Alenin was pulling her along as easily as sliding wood along a frozen river.

"I'm so comfortable with you, Lily, I can share everything. And you should feel the same way about me."

Inside the tent, they stripped out of their uniforms in the dark. Sergeant Alenin lay down on Katie's cot, occupying the hollow where Lily's friend had pressed skin and breath into the straw pallet. And then Sergeant Alenin stalked the night with her whispers. *Do you know, Lily, that in every village we recover there are collaborators? Everyone is checked. Even a babushka can be a spy. They asked me to shoot a German major and I could have cut him up, I hated him so much for killing our people. But worse than him, I hate our own people who are traitors, don't you, Lily?*

How long could it be until Lily slapped the woman across the face for using her name like a profanity?

When the sergeant finally succumbed to tiredness, Lily took her blanket outside and away from living beings. There was no wind down here in the hollow at the edge of the base, but it was busy high in the sky. She counted the days—twelve since Katie had died. Sitting on her rolled-up blanket, arms around her knees, Lily watched clouds scud over the moon, and she recited to it the exiled poet's truth:

> *The sky is a dead canvas*
> *Your world sallow and strange*
> *I accept—its emptiness.*

On August 1, at 4,500 metres above the village of Dmitrievka in the Donetsk region, the outside temperature was below freezing, but the cockpit was heated, and a chorus of ghosts was singing in the sky.

It was Lily's fourth flight of the morning, three weeks before her paper birthday. She still had ammunition, and a Messer was in her crosshairs. Her thumb on the trigger button, she gave him a good burst, and bullets danced across the sky like ballet swans. In a moment he was falling wing over wing, while adrenalin massaged her numb and empty heart.

The singing grew louder; it drowned out the engine as she hummed along. Six hundred metres to starboard and five hundred above, the Junkers formation was separating into three groups. Through a haze of exhaustion, she gauged her angle of attack. *Do I need oxygen?* she asked, and was it Alexei who said yes or Papa Nick? Reaching for the mask, she climbed while searching for a hole in their defensive position.

Her hand jerked away from the oxygen mask as her machine was jolted.

She was under attack by a pair of Messers, or maybe four crowned by the sun's blaze. Her eyes were gritty, her count uncertain. Exploding shells deafened her, fragments burst from her instrument panel. Her wings wobbled and she staggered back into the clouds, struggling for control as she spun in a figure eight, the sign of infinity.

"8-23, 8-23. Hit but viable," she called to her wingman over the crackling radio. "If I can come . . ." Sparks and a pop and her radio smelled of burnt wire. She flipped the dial, but there was no hum, no static, only the silence of dead air.

Above her the clouds were a grey mat of altostratus, below her the cotton batting of cumulonimbus. What heading? Her instruments had no advice, stuck in the broken glass of the panel, and she flew by instinct, listening to voices like propeller blades whisking the wind. *Go west, go west.*

Two minutes into the clouds, she opened throttle, putting power to her engine so she could break through and get a visual reading.

By her estimates she was at 3,500 metres, fifteen or twenty kilometres west of her previous position. Her nose broke through the
clouds, her engine shaking as she forced it to the edge of its limits.
The battle had dispersed, her comrades somewhere east, the sky
not quite empty.

A butcher bird had found her out. His nose was painted with
a Cupid's heart under the cockpit.

Tracers shot across the blue, veining it with stringy smoke.
Shrapnel rattled and banged her metal frame with the hot smell of
powder. She had to drop into cloud cover, where she could hide, but
her aircraft was lifting in a hypnotic rise. The stick was loose in her
hand, it had no traction, no resistance, flipping forward to the instrument panel with no engagement. Her feet pumped back and forth on
the pedals as if she could make them connect to the rudder with per-
sistence and effort, but the cables were gone here too. She had no say
over yaw, none over angle. Her shoulder was hit, her right hand had
no strength, and her enemy was climbing for another dive to finish
her off.

Smoke might shield her from sight. Her machine's momentum
could carry it forward for another minute or two, misdirecting
searchers if she was lucky. And if not, there was a dream river to
cross, with friends on the other side.

She opened the cockpit, preparing to bail. Wind rushed in. It
fanned the pretty flames, it lifted and pulled taffy metal. She
unbuckled herself, grasped the frame with her left hand, and
screamed as heat seared the skin. She stepped out, she fell.
Unconscious, she slid along the wing as her grandmother pulled
her down into the clouds.

It was her fourth flight of the day on the first of August, and she was
having a chat with her grandmother. They were sitting on a puffy

cloud, which didn't feel at all damp. She looked down at her wounded aircraft as it spiralled west, spouting sickly smoke.

You fly like you want to die, her grandmother said.

My friends are waiting for me.

There are other friends waiting to know you.

Lily changed the subject. *I got my fourteenth solo today. More than enough for a Gold Star.*

No medal is shiny enough to bring back the dead. What were you thinking?

That I could go deeper into enemy territory and then come back around. Like with the balloon.

My girl, my girl. What am I going to do with you? Once you're on the ground, that's it, Bubbeleh. You're on your own.

Then talk to me now. What should I do, Grandma?

Tell the rest of the story.

That's not the advice I'm looking for! I want to get home.

Sometimes that's all we can do, my dearest.

When Lily didn't return to base, her regimental commander submitted a certificate recommending her for the title Hero of the Soviet Union. But before the end of August, Vladimir Lavrinenkov was shot down west of the Mius River and was first transported to Stalino (Donetsk) and from there flown to the aviators' prison camp in Dneprodzerzhinsk, or Kamenskoje as the Germans called it. Twelve days later he jumped off a train and made his way across the Ukraine to his regiment, which he reached in October. Under strenuous questioning by SMERSH, he admitted that he'd seen Lily Litvyak in a POW camp. As a result, the certificate sent to HQ by Lily's commander was rejected. Prisoners were not heroes.

Prisoner

THE CZECH LANDS

April to May 1945

Among the Living

The cemetery gates are in sight when she hears the roar of a vehicle. It speeds past, shiny and black and hard-roofed, nearly sheering her off the road. As the wheels of the cart rock, she pulls back on the reins, then jumps down to calm the young horse. By the time his nostrils stop flaring and his head is steady, she can see the straggling line of walkers with shaven heads and scraped bones shambling under a damp sky patched with cloud.

The women—she can tell they're women by the sound of their voices—stay vertical without muscle, without flesh, the stars sewn onto rags pulling them toward the sky while their fluids bubble and drain. They stain the air with their smell. Every ten metres, inured to a stench stronger than the battlefield, a guard marches along-side. From time to time a military truck passes, splashing through puddles left from last night's rain. The line moves forward in its jagged pace.

Directly across from Lily, one of the walkers suddenly bends down. She's found something grey, stone-like, maybe a rotting potato fallen from a peasant's wagon, and she scoops it up. Her face tightens as she bites into it, exerting her jaw. Another step granted, another moment of life.

The bullet hits her in the knee, and she topples.

Lily didn't see the guard aim, her gaze was fixed on the walkers, but now she turns her head toward him and his rifle, still raised. The sun breaks through a cloud. The puddles in the road refract oily rainbows.

"Gizi!" A prisoner stops and leans into the fallen woman, trying to help her up.

"Bronia, leave me," she says in Polish.

"It's only your leg." The guard is approaching, and she frantically pulls on her friend's arms. "Come, Gizi, come on."

Another shot rings out, and Bronia falls, blood washing her
chest.

The SS guard who shot her is neither young nor old. Maybe
thirty or so. Big ears. Clean-shaven. Wearing a long coat, belted.
Trouser cuffs neatly rolled. Boots scuffed from the road. He orders
several of the prisoners to carry the two women, one dead and the
other unable to walk, as good as dead, and deposit them in a wagon,
which is pulled by a pair of shaggy horses with wide hooves.

"Civilian! Stay at the side of the road," he commands Lily.

"Yes, sir." She stands straight, holding the reins taut, every
muscle stiff with rage. The wagon passes her. A military vehicle
drives by. Another wagon pulled by horses.

The prisoners walk. They cling to life beyond all possibility.
And here she is, intending to throw hers away. Because of what? A
piece of paper. An order that makes it an offence to live and a crime
to be the relative of someone who lives. How far is that from the
orders that put those women on this road? Orders that are upheld
by people who think they love their country but love the look of fear
in another person's eyes so much more.

She remembers the thrill of small power when the peasants in
a snow-covered dugout regarded her so.

The female guards look like no one in particular. They wear
jackets and matching skirts, either A-line or with an inverted pleat,
stockings and socks rolled over sturdy shoes, like the leaders of a
troop of hiking girls. That she has anything in common with them
is enough to make her want to heave into the ditch, and only the
realization of the attention it would attract keeps her lunch from
lurching out.

No wonder the SS are walking victims to their death; their
existence is a complication that unhinges all doctrines.

When the end of the line passes her cart, Lily climbs into it, flicks the reins, and follows at a short distance. She has twenty minutes to think. Then the strafing begins.

Below the Allied aircraft are squares of green, obviously fields in spring, bisected by a long white line. That's the road. On the road, tiny, dark oblongs scuttle like cockroaches. Military vehicles. Behind the vehicles, a dotted line of advancing specks. A marching convoy. On the other side of the road, woods. In the air and moving at ten times the speed of the SS commander's car, the fighter pilots dive and level, pummelling the earth, avenging every comrade's death.

She knows how they feel.

From the air, how can they tell that this isn't a line of soldiers?

What else might someone miss from the vantage point of an eagle?

Guards lie in the ditch, rifles extended, pointing at their prisoners. The women sprawl flat on the ground, hands scrabbling, digging deeper into the road while Lily crouches under her cart.

No screams can be heard above the din of engines and machine-gun fire. Not the prisoners', not the horses'. Nor the scream of a guard who kneels for a moment as if in prayer before she falls. Fighters climb to come around again.

What if this is the last pass and she doesn't act? The moment will be gone. She'll have to live with its absence, wondering always what she could have done with a pistol and a horse blanket.

Lily scuttles out from under the cart and crawls toward the damp ditch, then crabs along it, using muddy elbows to propel herself. Her skirt bunches up. Small rocks dig into her thighs.

The guard who shot Bronia peers through his rifle sight as he shouts, "Swine! Any bitch that moves, I'll shoot ten in your place." He turns his head. "You! What?"

"Want a drink? I've got a flask."

"I'd rather a blow job."

"I'm not that much of a patriot. Don't you have a hundred Jewesses for that?"

"Ha! All right. Give over the flask."

He keeps a hand on his rifle, the stock against cheek and shoulder, while he reaches out with the other. She creeps closer, near enough to know that, even after days of marching, his stink is better than his prisoners'. If, out of the corner of his eye, he sees her reach into her pocket, it only makes him anticipate the approach of a burning, blurring drink. The Dreyse pistol fits neatly into her hand, a dark shape in his peripheral vision, not unlike the neck of a small bottle until it swiftly presses into the back of his neck.

"What are you doing?"

"Don't move or I'll shoot."

"What the devil? Not a partisan! Not here!"

She hopes he won't beg. She doesn't want to feel the pleasure of it. All she needs is a minute until the din of engines and guns covers every other sound. The guard says, *No* and *Please*, and his gasp might be a sob, but maybe not. The Americans are overhead, casting noisy shadows, the white stars in their blue circles tipped toward the road. Dust and debris and blood spurt. The Dreyse pistol is outdated, but the firing mechanism doesn't fail. She removes her blue scarf and spits on it. She wipes his blood off her skin.

When the American fighters wing away, the guards wait to see if they're coming back before they check the wounded among them. While they're busy, a few prisoners in the middle of the line run into the woods, but they can't move quickly on their spindly legs. They're soon caught and corralled among the trees. In the meantime, farther back, women cut into the carcasses of dead horses. They reach into the warmth with their thin, cold hands, wrenching meat, searching for the liver. The horses hitched to one of the death wagons still live, as does the gelding attached to Lily's cart. He reared, but the harness held and the cart is still upright.

She darts down the ditch to the end of the line, and there she comes onto the road and puts a hand on a prisoner. There's no thought as to whom, there are no spirits here to guide her, no grandmother's voice, no singing cloud. Only her hand, her human fingers, as knuckled and selfish as anyone's, press an unknown elbow as she murmurs in a mix of German and Polish, "Come with me, lady."

The prisoner doesn't look over her shoulder as she goes with Lily, not even when another woman laments, "Julia, what are you doing?"

They have to be quick. The woman is too weak to climb in, but it's easy to give her a boost as Julia is no heavier than a ten-year-old, and as she lies under the horse blanket, her frame is as flat as empty mailbags. Lily clicks her tongue at the gelding and turns the cart around. From time to time, as the horse trots toward the remount depot, she glances back at the still blanket, wondering if anything with so little life in it can breathe under the heavy wool.

When she arrives in the hamlet of Taschlowitz, she drives over the bridge and turns into the remount depot from the back, hoping to run into Igor away from the other prisoners. She finds him standing at the pasture fence, watching an early foal nudge his mother. The mare is kneeling on the grass, the foal rears and gets his skinny legs over his mother's neck. He stands over her the way she usually stands over him. Then he hitches himself around to face her, touching his head to hers. She rises to her feet, and he comes in to suckle. Behind them are bushes with sprouting leaves to chew when he's weaned.

"Igor, can you do something for me?" she asks in her mother tongue.

"Whatever you need," he says.

She glances at her father's watch. It's just after four. Gerhard ought to be in the dispensary. "Tell Dr. Fischer that I have a surprise package, and I need his help to get it home."

Igor comes over to the cart. She doesn't stop him but keeps a hand on her pistol.

He lifts a corner of the blanket. His face pales.

"Death just blinked at me," he says.

The end is coming, but it zigs and zags. German tanks pass through Hostau. Americans come through the Bohemian Forest. They leave thirty soldiers to guard the valuable thoroughbreds in Hostau, but their group is too small to occupy the entire depot. On the far edge of it, Stable C with its unremarkable horses and unremarkable horse doctor is no man's land. Just to the east, in the county seat, an SS captain leads the defence. Roads already rough and narrow for military vehicles are made impassable by logs thrown onto them by zealous Hitler Youth and their teachers at Nazi military schools. A troop of them ambushes and wipes out a platoon of American cavalry. The Red Army is in Bohemia. The end is coming, casualties accelerate—death is an addiction with a long supply chain.

On the second floor of the widow's house, where the window overlooks the stream and a bridge, Lily is kneeling beside the bathtub. Water flows over her guest's knobby knees. Julia comes from Katowice, a city near the border between Poland and the Czech lands. The sound of birds cheers her up; the radio annoys her; she asks blunt questions; she's frightened by barking dogs, leather, and sparks.

"You're my hero," Julia says.

"I always wanted to be one."

"Too bad I'm such an ugly princess."

"Maybe I'll give up on being a hero," Lily says. "It doesn't seem to be worth it."

Julia laughs. At least, Lily thinks it's laughter. The woman's lips turn up, the mouth opens, her chest moves, and there is a coughing, weepy, braying sound. She's having her second lice treatment, short hair soaked with kerosene while she sits in the tub. Her teeth are yellowed and cracked, her breasts nippled flaps of skin. "Do I still smell?" she asks.

Lily is washing her back as gently as she once washed an imprisoned pilot. "It's the sores. They'll heal."

"The smell doesn't bother you?"

"It's already much better. No worse than a battlefield now."

"I don't know how you can stand to touch me with bare hands."

"You saved my life," Lily says.

"You don't need to make fun of me."

"I'm not. I was going to kill myself."

"You? And you had bread?" She moves away as if Lily's touch is abhorrent.

"It's not as bad as it sounds."

The first day, Julia was offered all the food in the house, but all she'd have was a potato. Her eyes wrinkled as if she'd cry with the refusal, but her body lacked any fluid to spare for tears. While she was walking, people in Czech villages sometimes threw food. Anyone who managed to grab more than a morsel died in agony, unable to digest it.

"It wasn't for myself," Lily says, "but for my mother and brother."

"You're lucky." Julia bends her back, lets Lily rinse it. "I'd die too, if it would bring my family back to life."

Gerhard's staff has deserted, and the prisoners of war are living in the village, a lawless free-for-all protected by no one and under no one's control. He looks after the few remaining horses on his own, and when Lily brings him the rooster, he wrings its neck with adequate skill. She plucks it, eviscerates it, and boils it up under the scowling gaze of the landlady, who's been told that a refugee abused by Red Army soldiers is occupying Fritz's room. When the soup is ready, Lily brings it up. The wall at the foot of Fritz's bed is still plastered with sketches drawn on paper torn from a notebook: the Bohemian Forest, a cemetery, Lily in a rain of flowers, Lily walking on water, a water lily. Julia sits up to eat, but her hands are shaky, she doesn't want to lose a drop. Lily spoons soup into her bird mouth, and they talk while Julia rests between sips.

"I want something to read," Julia says.

"You need sleep."

"I need to catch up. I was in grade ten when the war started."

"I could read to you." Lily hopes her surprise doesn't show. She thought her guest was at least thirty-five. "*Introduction to Philosophy* or *The Scarlet Pimpernel*?"

"Philosophy."

"Then we'll both be happy. It'll put you to sleep." She dips the spoon, scoops up a bit of stringy meat.

"This tastes like a Jewish soup," Julia says.

"It's my grandmother's recipe. She died in the Zhytomyr ghetto."

"I was in Auschwitz, but workers were needed in factories, and here I am. How did you survive?"

"On false papers."

"I didn't think you were a Rose Allendorf." Julia has another sip. "Your mother and brother?"

"Safe. Until I'm checked by the NKVD and charged as a collaborator. For that, I'm supposed to be shot, and they'll be punished."

"So you helped me out of guilt? It won't atone for a thing. What did you do?" Julia's tone is harsh, she glares, she waits to pass judgment, and she has the right, this woman who is alive by the miracle of chance.

"I nursed horses and prisoners of war," Lily says.

"And?"

"And I lived."

"Why would you upset me? That isn't collaboration." Julia nods as if it's settled. She opens her mouth for soup.

Lily hears the creak of a floorboard. She turns to see Gerhard in the doorway, listening to everything.

"Do you think my bones are pretty, Dr. Fischer?" Julia asks.

"The world will hate us when they see what we've done," he says. "I'm taking the radio out to the barn so it won't bother you."

Gerhard tries to surrender. He rides to Stable A and asks only to bring his fiancée and her sick relative with him, but the American captain isn't accepting any more German prisoners of war. He doesn't have the manpower to handle those he already has, and he sends Gerhard back to Taschlowitz. In the room he shares with Lily, he sits and hangs his head, ashamed that he can't save her from the NKVD as she saved him from the Gestapo.

Lily is sewing, making over a dress she found in a trunk in the attic. It's for Julia, something pretty that a young woman would wear. While Lily sews, she glances out the window, her eyes on the road between the barn and the forest. Anything might come down that road, their fate decided by the marking on a random vehicle: white star, red star, swastika. But all she sees is a portly man on foot, a shotgun over his shoulder, the kind a farmer would use to shoot animals after his chickens.

"Gerhard," she says. "Someone's coming."

He picks up his binoculars to better see what she's spied with her naked eye. "It's the postmaster," he says. "I'll get the girl."

The entrance to the attic is in the hallway. Lily pulls on the cord, a ladder unfolds. Gerhard has their guest in his arms. While he climbs up, Lily descends to the kitchen, where she flashes her pistol and warns the landlady to say nothing. The postmaster, who's in a patchwork of uniform pieces, wearing an arm band with a roughly sewn swastika, waddles to the back door under the clean sky of early May.

"Hello!" Lily greets him with a smile, smoothing her dress to give the impression that she's making herself presentable. "A personal mail delivery?"

"I'm here to inspect the house, Fräulein." The postmaster puffs his chest. A shotgun meant for a weasel can still kill a man.

"Come in, please. What do you want to see?"

"Everything. My commander sent me to check whether it's a suitable staging area for a counteroffensive."

"What an honour," Lily says as she leads him in. Behind his back she shows her pistol to the widow, who closes her mouth and returns to scrubbing her stove.

The postmaster knocks on walls to assess their solidity. He feels the thickness of the curtains in the widow's parlour. He stands before every window, lifts the sash, and aims his shotgun through the opening. When he's satisfied, he climbs the stairs to examine the upper floor. "Where's your fiancé?" he asks.

"With his horses," she says.

"We'll need them for transportation, and for meat if there's a siege." His pupils are dilated. His superior must have his own supply of Pervitin. "Dr. Fischer served at the front. He'll be a good man—I'll make him a captain."

"Then you must be a . . ."

"You can address me as Colonel . . . What's that sound?" He looks up.

"Just rats, Herr Colonel. It's a bad spring for rats, and we've run out of traps."

With one hand, he holds the shotgun against his shoulder, leaving him free to admonish Lily by shaking the index finger of the other. His chin wobbles, but he has a shotgun, and she hears a shuffle overhead. "We can't consider the Reich purified as long as vermin still plague us. It's intolerable. Dr. Fischer should have taken care of this."

"You're right, and I'm very sorry. When he returns from exercising the horses, I'll let him know that you were here and what you said."

"A doctor doesn't need traps, he should have poison. Arsenic. Tell him to clear the house. Tell him that we'll come first thing in the morning. The house will suit us nicely."

"I'll have food ready, whatever I can find, and make up beds. How many can we expect?"

"Ten men. Heil Hitler!"

"Heil Hitler," she says, considering it imprudent to bring up the Führer's recent suicide.

As soon as the postmaster is gone, she knocks on the ceiling with a broom handle and Gerhard brings Julia down from the attic. Her cheeks are red, her forehead hot. After Julia's settled back in her bed, Lily gets a rag and soaks it in cold water, then lays it across her forehead.

They need to eat before they leave this house, and when Lily goes down to the kitchen to scrounge something, she finds the landlady still there. Excited, she squawks about the return of the Führer and the secret weapon and how they'll pay for stealing her rooster, and don't think she's fooled by the story of the refugee; when the SS men come, they'll take care of the dirty Jew under her roof, which she didn't mention only because Lily is a harlot with a pistol. Lily boils potatoes and brings them up in a bowl.

After they eat, Gerhard packs up a few belongings, the practical and the treasured. Lily unstitches the lining of her coat and his, inserts money and small sellable items. They debate their direction and what to risk: the gangs in Hostau or the fighting south and north of it. All they can agree on is that east is out of the question, the Red Army dangerous for them both. While they argue, Julia's fever is mounting. She tosses and turns, the wet rag on her forehead falling to the pillow. After the half moon rises, Gerhard hitches the horse then comes in to carry her down. They can hear the landlady snoring like a saw.

When they're in the yard, Lily says, "The attic was too much of a strain. She needs a doctor."

"The doctor in Hostau is a Nazi." Gerhard lays the girl on a nest of blankets in the cart.

"Then we should go south." Lily covers her with a feather quilt.

"Toward shelling?"

"Toward Taus. And Czech doctors."

"We have to go somewhere." He climbs onto the seat, she slides in beside him. "Let it be there."

Avoiding roads traversable by motorized vehicles, they take a winding route along tracks through the woods and between fields, moving slowly in the light thrown by a kerosene lamp. Even on these narrow paths, the Hitler Youth have thrown logs, and detours slow them down further. Sometimes Lily isn't sure where they're going, and when Gerhard climbs out of the cart and holds up his lamp to see if he can identify where they are, he discovers they've ended up in a spot they've already passed through. Artillery fire sounds like a distant storm, tendrils of smoke infiltrate the sweetness of spring air. The sky is becoming pale. She tries to remember everything, her friends, her family, the way dark shapes are transformed into colour with the rising sun, the smell of these horses, of a camel. A friend's frightening joke. She was holding flowers in her hands that day. Cherry trees were in bloom. Cherry trees are in bloom.

"My grandmother used to tell me a story," she says. "It was long, and sometimes parts of it changed. When my father was ten, she took her kids and went to live with relatives, but she needed money. So she pretended to be a Russian nanny and got a job with a Mrs. Grossman. The baby's name was Joseph, but my grandmother called him Vasya, short for Vasily, a good Russian name, and it stuck. When he grew up, he became a writer, and in a story about his hometown he mentioned my great-uncle, who was a grocer. I don't know if it's true, but of everyone in the story, only the writer is still alive."

"It doesn't have to end the way you think," Gerhard says.

"What do you mean?"

"You're not Rose Allendorf."

"Obviously."

"You're fluent in how many languages?"

"Enough."

"When I went to Stable A, I was so focused on moving us there, I didn't pay attention to what Dr. Lessing told me. But there might be a way out."

"You're dreaming."

"No, listen. Millions of people are displaced. There's an agreement to sort them out and send them back to their original place of residence. But it isn't straightforward. Borders are being redrawn. The Polish territory that Russia took under the pact, it's going to the Ukraine for Ukrainians."

An old song, she thinks. Germany for Germans. The Workers' State for workers. When will it end?

"What's that got to do with me?" she asks.

"Poles and . . ." He hesitates, then pushes forward. ". . . and Jews—they aren't returning to that part of the Soviet Union. I've been thinking . . . If you were one of them, from eastern Poland . . .

You said your grandmother was born in Brody. Isn't that some-where east?"

"Yes, it's in the part of Poland that was annexed by the Soviets."

"If she was alive, she couldn't go home."

The sky is becoming pale. They've ended up south of the town, and, looking through his binoculars, Gerhard sees only fields tram-melled by the movement of tanks. The shelling has stopped; she wonders which side won.

She thinks of Papa Nick. It was May 5; it is again.

"A while ago, you asked me what I want to do," Lily says. "I've been thinking about it."

"And?"

"I want to grow flowers," she says. "In a place without heroes or enemies of the people."

The Czech flag flies above the town, and on a signpost the German name, Taus, is crossed out, Domažlice painted above it. Over the stone archway of the lower gate, a banner in near English pro-claims, WELCOME OUR DELIVERES.

From the bell tower to the medieval gate, white-starred military vehicles proceed down the avenue. Behind the Americans, a group of partisans march. They wear arm bands and carry rifles. Among them a woman waves the red-and-white national flag.

An impromptu band in the cheering crowd plays the Czech anthem on trumpet, tuba, and bugle. Children hold quickly painted American flags. Women—some of them in coats and kerchiefs, others still in striped camp garb—are hugging soldiers. The wind carries ash and the tart smell of artillery fire, the spring sun glazes the pallid faces of winter.

At the entrance to the market square, a soldier stands sentry, chewing gum and watching the festivities. He's tall, all-American, cleft-chinned like a movie hero, Clark Gable or Cary Grant, or like a pilot of the elite 9th Guards. On the sleeve of his uniform he wears the patch of the 2nd Infantry Division: a star and, in its centre, a hawk-nosed profile in a war bonnet.

Halting the horses at the sentry post, Gerhard gives the reins to Lily and raises his hands, holding aloft the white handkerchief he's brought for this purpose. "I surrender," he says.

The handsome soldier snaps his gum. "Another one. Where will we put them all?"

Gerhard relinquishes the pistols. A corporal is called over to pat them down while the first soldier checks the cart for hidden weapons.

"What's your position and rank, Nazi?" He speaks in a language related to German and therefore sufficiently comprehensible to Gerhard.

He answers, "I'm Dr. Fischer, a staff veterinarian. Not a member of the Nazi Party."

"That's what they all tell me," the soldier says in Yiddish. "You'll have to wait your turn in the barracks. We've got a lot of prisoners to sort through. Who's that?" He points at Lily. "Your slut?"

"You bad boy!" she shouts back in the same tongue. "Didn't your grandmother teach you anything? How dare you! This man saved my life. He hid me for nearly two years. And are you blind? I have a sick girl lying here. A Jewish girl from the camps. Did she survive for you to kill her? She needs medical treatment. Immediately!"

"Why didn't you say so before?" The soldier sticks out his hand to shake hers, which he holds tight and won't leave off shaking, telling her that he liberated a sub-camp of Buchenwald and will personally escort them to the hospital. "I'm Captain Epstein. Samuel Epstein. Call me Sam." He scribbles a note and hands it to a corporal waiting to escort Gerhard. "You have to be processed, but you won't get handed to the Reds."

———

At the makeshift hospital, Lily refuses to leave Julia's side. For a week she assists the overworked nursing staff. Captain Epstein comes to visit, looking past her at Julia, whose fever comes down, her cheeks filling out, eyes brightening at the sight of her soldier friend. His company is moving out, but he promises to come back when he has furlough and advises Lily to get her papers at the registration office while it's still under military command. She kisses Julia on the cheek. They say goodbye.

The walls are starkly bare, nail holes and pale squares indicating the fresh and hasty removal of Nazi paraphernalia. There's an American flag in the corner, but no portrait of their president takes the place of Hitler's, which Lily finds puzzling. Aside from this, the waiting room has the familiar atmosphere of any bureaucratic office. At a desk, a bored subordinate ignores the people standing in front of him, checks a list, answers a black telephone, eventually and only after repetitive ringing. The few chairs are occupied by people in good coats, who smell as sweaty as the rest of them. Everyone else stands, tense and waiting, listening for their name, which will be long in coming. Lily has time, she hopes enough, to think over the problem of identifying herself in a weary and hate-wrenched world.

She'll have to lie about her name and her past for the rest of her life, but she's had practice. And the more she thinks, the longer the list of what she wants grows: to eat fresh bread and butter, to grow geraniums for the spicy scent, to make herself a dress with a wide skirt that will lift and swirl when she dances, to recite aloud the words of banned poets, to be kissed among the living.

When she's finally called, an assistant leads her to an interior office with no windows. A tired-looking man in uniform deposits a file in the cabinet as he tells her to take a seat. On his desk is another black telephone, a stack of files, a full ashtray, and a typewriter. He turns toward it, slides carbon sheets between layers of paper, straightens the edges, and passes the bundle through the roller of his typewriter. He has the look of a schoolteacher with a pencil stick nose and ruler mouth.

"Czech or German?"

"I speak German."

"Name?"

"Rose Litvak."

The keys clack as he types in a two-finger staccato. "Papers."

She hands them over. "They're false. It's not my real name."

"We'll see. Nationality?"

"Mixed."

"Can you be more specific?"

"Father Jewish. My mother was Russian. I nursed the POWs in Hostau. I've been helping out at the hospital here."

"All Soviet citizens are to be repatriated, Miss Litvak. Is that correct—it's Miss . . . not Mrs.? Right, then. When the Soviet zone is secured, we'll arrange transport." Through the adjoining wall she can hear someone crying in the next office.

She doesn't argue, she doesn't plead. To do so with a bureaucrat is to excite suspicion. She has a plan, she has a story. "When would that be, sir?"

"You'll be informed." He looks down at the German identity papers. "According to this, your birthplace was Engels."

"As I said, the papers are false. If I could get my birth certificate, it would indicate Brody." The typewriter click-clacks. "I mean the Polish town named after the castle, not the German village, but I don't have any family left there." She doesn't let any tears fall, and the rims of her eyes redden with effort. "Or maybe it's got a new, Ukrainian name?"

"I wouldn't know." He looks up from the typewriter. His eyes are a mix of green and brown. The American prisoners called this colour *hazel*.

"Then where would you say I'm from?"

"The demarcation lines are a bit complicated." He opens a desk drawer and withdraws a binder. After studying several pages, he steeples his fingers and gazes at her. Americans aren't so different from her countrymen; among them, too, the whim of a bureaucrat means life or death. "Jewish father?"

"Yes."

On the form, under Place of Birth, he types, *Poland (Refugee).* "I can take down your story and refer you to UNRRA. You'll need their approval to qualify as a refugee. How did you get to Domažlice?"

This is what she's been waiting for. It'll be as true as any story her grandmother told.

Friend

RUSSIA &
SWITZERLAND

May 5, 1990

Gold Star

President Mikhail Gorbachev awards the title, Hero of the Soviet Union, to a number of deceased soldiers who were disgraced for survival and other political crimes. The Gold Stars and certificates are presented to relatives. Among them is Lily's brother—Yuri Kunavin. Having changed his name during Stalin's anti-Semitic campaigns, he's grown old and respectable. He's on the shortish side, double-chinned, impressively eyebrowed, fond of his camera.

A body had to be found and it was, selected from a mass grave with many bones to choose from, so that the service record could be changed from Missing in Action to Killed in Action. The Award Certificate for Lydia Vladimirovna Litvyak was compiled and signed by the Chairman of the Presidium of the Council of War Veterans of the 8th Air Army, Lieutenant General of Aviation Boris Eremin, who'd refused Lily's transfer to his regiment. The certificate was also signed by Inna Pasportnikovo, who served as Lily's mechanic for a time. It was stamped with two seals: the Council of War Veterans and the Central Order of the Red Star, Ministry of Defence of the Soviet Union, a nation about to dissolve.

In front of a small and elderly audience, Yuri accepts the Gold Star on his sister's behalf from the friendly hand of the last leader of the Soviet Union. Yuri is nervous, but the statesman's grip is firm. They both turn toward the official photographer, as sober and dignified as the occasion suggests.

Beckoning

The airstrip is in a Swiss valley with low green hills immediately around it and mountains in the distance. She stands to the side of the hangar, waiting for the pilot to complete his check. According to her passport, she's nearly sixty-eight. Her hair is white, courtesy of nature not peroxide, her eyes are grey. She's shorter than she used to be, and a little stouter too. Inside the collar of her jumpsuit, protecting her neck from the scratchy fabric, is a silk scarf, a birthday present, the nicest scarf in her collection. She's wearing goggles and a sports helmet borrowed from her middle-aged middle child.

Her friend is seventy-five, as lean as ever, his eyes a more watery blue. After the Berlin Wall came down, she located him still living in his hometown in East Germany, which, until recently, was under Communist rule. She was nervous sending him the letter, wondering if he would remember her real name from that night in the sleigh, and, if he did, whether he'd tell someone.

It's still an unshakable habit, casting about for repercussions.

He says, "You're telling me that you flew your first solo when you were fourteen or fifteen."

"I thought I owned the sky," she says.

"I figured that you understood combat too well to be a civilian, but it never occurred to me that you could be a pilot."

She smiles. She still can't believe he's here. She's never been able to find out what happened to Fritz.

"Is something funny?"

"Well, yes. After the war we switched places. Me in the West. You behind the Iron Curtain."

"Not anymore," he says. Capitalist West Germany and Communist East Germany are negotiating reunification. He believes the

364

Cold War is over. "Remember what we talked about last night. No more fear. I'm finished with that." He has a son from a short-lived marriage. He's had a partner for thirty years. A few months ago he came out to his son after bringing home a piece of concrete from the Wall. He's always wanted to try skydiving.

"And if I've changed my mind?"

"About what?"

She doesn't want to seem old. She thought she could do this. "It can't be good for someone's heart."

"You're not telling me you're scared?" He laughs. "You?"

She puts her hands on her hips. Inside her head she's still the person she always was. "Do you think I'm immune?"

"You fought in Stalingrad! And you're afraid of a little jump?"

"When you fly, you're inside a ton of metal. You steer it. You're not debris flung around by the wind. The best thing about a parachute is cutting it up for the silk. Jumping into the air? With nothing but a bit of cloth and string to hang on to?"

"Surely it was part of your training."

"Major Kazarinova was hard on me about everything except jumping, because she was afraid of it herself."

"But you've done it before. You told me so last night. You had to bail out of your fighter. It was euphoric. You'll love it. That's what you said."

"I was unconscious! The last thing I remember is the pain in my hand. I burned it trying to steady myself, and I decided not to jump but to try to land like every other time I had a badly damaged aircraft. I came to below the clouds, out of my mind. I sweat when I dream about it."

"Then all the more reason to do it with your eyes open."

"I'm not sure if I can."

"It's your liberation day."

"My forty-fifth."

"What I'm saying. Our last years are a gift not to be wasted."
He puts his arm through hers. He walks her toward fear, and she
lets him because her husband, who's a paragon of prudence, was
willing to splurge on the tickets, and he'll be expecting a full report.

The single-engine aircraft is a Cessna six-seater. With half the
speed of her Yakki, it takes twenty minutes to reach their position at
3,500 metres. She has time to think of human frailty, her quiet life
in this neutral country, her sewing room where she left her reading
glasses on a book, her husband's hiking boots, which need re-soling,
the window boxes with blooming geraniums, and the nature of
hate, which floats like the imperceptible spore of microbes until it
alights on fertile soil.

The pilot announces that they're in position. The jump orga-
nizer, who has the tone and bearing of a tour bus conductor, opens
a door wide enough for it to be the entrance to a bomb bay. A
swoosh of air. Her scarf flutters, and she tucks it in. The trainer
rises, a hand on her shoulder, and she crab-walks forward with him
attached like a shell. At the exit, they stop. Her friend is shouting,
Right behind you! The trainer has her sit with her legs dangling out of
the aircraft, then puts his hand on her forehead and leans her head
back against his shoulder.

"Ready?"

"And if I'm not?"

He bends forward and slides them away from anything solid.

Wind rushes in her ears. Her heart beats madly, it's the rattle of
her U-2, it's the clickety-clack of her sewing machine. She spreads
arms and legs, as she's been instructed, to slow the terminal velocity
of free fall. Time suspends; the sky is polished sapphire, and she's
skimming across it.

Below her is a castle of cumulus, and as they enter it, the trainer
pulls the cord. A canopy opens. They drift through white puffs; quiet
encloses her.

Uncoiling from its bed of meat, her soul slips through the open mouth. There are friends and relatives to greet in the towering clouds. Katie and Alexei; Papa Nick and Fritz; her soul cries out to every Vladimir and Vasily, to Elena and Julia—pierced with the need to feel them near, to recall their names, to speak them recklessly with the abandon of affection and reverence. And in so saying, the soul slips back into the old body with its roughened skin and slow-pulsing veins, life still living itself.

There is this. Stories grow wild like plants through a crack in the cement or on the forest floor. Seeds pass from person to person, and from them new stories grow. Let them be antimicrobial; let them be of friendship beyond reason.

She sees the earth below, its etched lines, its curvaceous shapes, its beckoning.

Author's Note

The characters in the "Pilot" sections are historical figures, with several exceptions. Elena Grinberg is a composite of several real people whose accounts of life and death under Nazi occupation were collected in *The Black Book*, edited by Vasily Grossman and Ilya Ehrenburg. Sergeant Alenin's character is based on an interview with a female (former) NKVD agent. The prisoner whose interrogation she records is also fictional, drawn from the memoirs of captured pilots. Lily's grandmothers—who obviously did exist!—are fully imagined, as nothing is known about them. I dug for information on the historical characters and found it inconsistent, sometimes demonstrably incorrect, and full of holes. I used what there was, searched for the truth between the lines, and relied on fiction to tell it.

All the air battles are historically accurate, with one modification. The pilot saved by Lily at Stalingrad was Raisa Belyaeva, not Katie Budanova. Raisa and another female pilot, Maria Kuznetsova, fought alongside Lily for a short time at Stalingrad before returning to the 586th women's Fighter Air Regiment. To keep the narrative flow, I made the difficult choice not to include them.

No one knows what happened to Lily after she was shot down on August 1, 1943. There were conflicting rumours during and after the war, and the few experts on the history of the air women are equally divided. A body was located decades after the war and said to be hers, which allowed her status to be changed from Missing in Action to Killed in Action, a prerequisite to her receiving the gold medal she deserved. Yet one of the female mechanics who knew Lily claimed to have seen her during a TV interview in the early 2000s in which an elderly woman who was living in Switzerland described herself as a Soviet fighter pilot. Given the small number of female fighter pilots and Lily's distinctively small stature, it would be easy to recognize her. The more interesting story, for me as a novelist, is that she survived, and I imagined how that could have happened and what that would have meant for Lily.

Of necessity, then, the characters and situations in the "Prisoner" sections are fictional, except for Lieutenant Colonel Rudofsky, who was the commander of the Hostau stud farm and remount depot. However, the settings, the types of characters, and their experiences are factual. The actions against Jews in Zhytomyr come from a soldier's account of it. The comments at the train station were made by German POWs in conversation with each other, unaware that it was being recorded.

I used English, Russian, and German sources—books, online memoirs, photographs, digitized war footage, and other films. Without Google Translate, I would have been helpless. Though its "English" is practically another language, with patience and insatiable curiosity I learned how to decipher it. When in doubt, I consulted bilingual friends.

There was much more fascinating material than could be included in a novel, and I'll post the most interesting aspects of it online. The link and other information can be found on my website: http://liliannattel.com.

Working on this novel kept me going during the illness and passing of my sister-in-law, Julia Greenbaum, truly my sister, a remarkable woman who appreciated the humour in every situation, however difficult. I named the character Julia after her as a tribute to my Julia's strength and life force. I miss her terribly and always will.

The story has had a long germination. I first read about Lily fifteen years ago. The Second World War is an emotionally demanding and complex subject, but the women who flew for freedom wouldn't let me go, and Lily—whose historical record is slim, contradictory, and yet indelible—required the imaginative exploration that only fiction can provide. The fact that I'm similarly height challenged, and that my childhood name was Lily too, made her irresistible.

Acknowledgements

This work came into being because of dedicated people who love books, and now I get to express my thanks and gratitude for: the financial support and encouragement provided by the Canada Council for the Arts, The Ontario Arts Council, and the Toronto Arts Council; the sagacity of my agent, Dean Cooke, as well as the talents of Paige Sisley, Ron Eckel, Suzanne Brandreth, Rachel Letofsky, and the rest of the team at CookeMcDermid; the keen eye of my editor, Anne Collins, along with the attentions of John Sweet, Sarah Jackson, Andrew Roberts and the enthusiastic staff at Random House Canada; the willing aid of my translators, led by the indefatigable Eva Bednar—Agnieszka Borkowska, Mariusz Drewniak, Agnieszka Kaczmarek, Oleg Kiełpińskilist, Andrzej Mierzejewski, Anna Piątkowska, Olga Zdanowska—as well as Edgar Ilyasov; the insight of my first readers—Victoria Best, Beth Kephart, Marilyn Lerner. As always, I am deeply grateful for my family—Allan, Hadara and Meira. And a final shout-out to the memoirists and historians, professional and amateur, who made their research available online—thank you. May we all bring light into the world and remember there are peaches.

A NOTE ABOUT THE TYPE

The text of *Girl at the Edge of Sky* has been set in Baskerville MT, a British Monotype Corporation copy of the serif typeface first designed in 1754 by John Baskerville (1706–75). Baskerville's typeface is classified as transitional, as it was intended to refine the "old-style" typefaces of the period and was part of a larger project to create books of the greatest possible quality. It is characterized by crisp edges, sharp, tapered serifs, high contrast between thick and thin strokes, and consistency in both shape and form.